SEEDS OF DESTRUCTION

GARY MILLER PROULX

abbott press

Abbott Press books may be ordered through booksellers or by contacting:

Abbott Press
1663 Liberty Drive
Bloomington, IN 47403
www.abbottpress.com
Phone: 1 (866) 697-5310

Because of the dynamic nature of the Internet, any web addresses or links contained in this book may have changed since publication and may no longer be valid. The views expressed in this work are solely those of the author and do not necessarily reflect the views of the publisher, and the publisher hereby disclaims any responsibility for them.

Any people depicted in stock imagery provided by Thinkstock are models, and such images are being used for illustrative purposes only.
Certain stock imagery © Thinkstock.

ISBN: 978-1-4582-1870-4 (sc)
ISBN: 978-1-4582-1871-1 (hc)
ISBN: 978-1-4582-1872-8 (e)

Library of Congress Control Number: 2015903252

Print information available on the last page.

Abbott Press rev. date: 4/8/2015

CONTENTS

acknowledgements

My wife, Sarah, who is the love of my life and my staunchest supporter of my writing. Also to everyone who has helped me not only to survive but also to fully recover from my accident about a year ago so that I could complete this book and continue caring for and treating my cancer patients. And to all those who have given me support and encouragement through the writing process including family, friends, patients.

Dedications

To my mother who lived an angelic life and loved and lived life to the fullest, raising a family and writing poetry despite her being legally blind.

A portion of the proceeds from the sale of this book and the other two to follow it, in the trilogy, will be used to help charities including the victims of the Boston bombings.

CHAPTER 1: PLANTING SEEDS

POISON HIM? CUT HIM? OR BURN HIM?

Everyone eventually agreed to burn him.

Dr. Jacob Miller and his medical team stood over the patient lying naked on the operating room table. They were dressed in lead-lined gear from head to toe to protect themselves from radiation exposure, which made them look more like a police SWAT team than doctors and nurses. Only a hint of blue scrubs sticking out beyond their vests and thyroid shields gave away their identity.

Behind Dr. Miller sat Buzz, his dosimetrist, peering at his laptop in front of him. His job was to design the radiation treatment plan per Dr. Miller's specifications and prepare the radioactive seeds for each needle planned for the patient's surgery. Miller turned around to take the trocar with its needle filled with radioactive seeds.

"Buzz, hand me the next one."

Done incorrectly, radiation implants could kill the patient. But in the skillful hands of Dr. Miller, a world-renowned radiation surgeon, he had at least a chance for a cure. Patients came from around the world for treatment by Dr. Miller, whose reputation included his being a miracle worker.

Prior to inserting each seed-filled needle with the trocar into the patient, Miller stared at the prostate target on the ultrasound projection on the monitor, hanging just above the patient's abdomen. It was like the prostate was the enemy he studied before he was about to attack. "These are the last seeds, Buzz. What do you think?"

Buzz reviewed his laptop screen and compared it to the overhead monitor. While waiting for Buzz's reply, Dr. Miller looked around the operating room. Only the sounds of the respirator attached to the patient could be heard, with its rhythmically pulsing diaphragm pushing vital oxygen into the lungs on its way down and removing carbon dioxide and other waste products on its way up. The patient, sedated and intubated, was not aware of the ongoing violations of his body.

The operating room was cold and dark, except in the center where the overhead lights provided illumination and heat. Standing in the center of it all, his thoughts drifting, Miller pictured the operating room as his Carnegie Hall, where he conducted the music of 'destroying cancer to create life'. He led his staff of musicians through the symphony, each working independently throughout the procedure, but in the end, collectively to create the 'sound of life'.

"About the needle placement," Buzz said. He peered into the laptop screen to view the patient's three-dimensional plan showing where each seed was to be placed within the prostate to within millimeter accuracy. He then stared at the ultrasound projection above the patient. "The location looks spot on to the plan we have here up on the computer."

As he had done twenty-four times on the patient over the previous hour, Dr. Miller held up the trocar, the steel, hollowed-out needle that held the plastic needle inside it, loaded with radiation in the form of "seeds," each the size of a grain of rice. Big and thick, heavy, lead-lined gloves enveloped his hands, and he leaned over the patient's pelvis and placed the trocar over the entry point marked on the patient's perineal skin. As with each of the needles placed before, he took in a slow, deep breath that pulled his face mask inward, and with both hands, he stabbed the skin to feel the needle tear through the epidermis, then into the thick gluteal muscles and connective tissue below it to reach inside the prostate, which was ground zero for the attack on the cancer. It felt like stabbing with an ice pick into a tightly fitted, leather-covered chair. Blood oozed out of the puncture wounds around each needle. The patient's monitors immediately showed stress with a jump in his blood pressure and an increase in his heart and respiration rate.

To Miller's immediate right stood Bridget, his recently hired physician assistant. Dr. Miller felt like a giant next to her with his six-foot-two, wide-shouldered frame and her five-foot-three, petite frame. It was her first case in the operating room with him, and he had planned only to instruct her on the procedure, so she would be an observer only and not directly involved. He looked over to see her riveted in her spot, leaning forward, her arms folded across her chest, watching intently everything going on with the procedure, like a sponge absorbing every drop of information. "Bridget, see how clearly the radiation seeds on the ultrasound images are?"

She nodded. "Yes, I see them."

"It shows just about another centimeter, according to the plan, before dropping these seeds into the prostate. This last one is a bit tricky because it's close to his urethra. And even more dangerous, it's close to that blood vessel behind it . "Miller pointed to the ultrasound projection in front of them. "See it?"

Bridget studied the ultrasound image on the projector in front of her and nodded again with her eyes wide open. "Yes, I see them. Each twinkling, like stars in the sky."

"I have to be careful not to stick that vessel," said Miller.

"Dr. Miller, what would happen if you did hit it with the needle? The blood vessel, that is?" asked Bridget.

"Don't even think that. Because it's an artery, it could be a real bleeder, requiring surgery to close it. Even worse, if just one of these seeds gets into the bloodstream, it could travel to his heart, or to his lungs, or even worse, to his brain, causing him injury—even killing him."

She nodded nervously, and above her mask covering her nose, her eyes again opened wide.

Miller turned to Buzz behind him. "Buzz, are you positive that the needle location conforms to the plan we designed?"

He looked at the screen on his laptop, then back to the projector over the patient. "Looks spot on to the plan. Why? Something wrong, Doc?"

Miller squinted and looked more closely to the screen in front of him. "I'm not sure. It looks uncomfortably close to that vessel running behind the prostate, but it must be the two-dimensional view we're seeing on the screen, making it look closer than it actually is."

He took a deep breath, then readied the needle and pushed it in a full centimeter. He looked up to the ultrasound projection, which showed the tip of the needle exactly where the seeds were to be dropped.

He exhaled a deep breath, pushed the needle inward the last few millimeters, and the seeds exited the needle.

"That's it," said Miller, and pulled the empty needle out. Everything looked good on the screen, but then seconds later, blood shot out of the body where the needle had been, like a racehorse jumping out of the starting gate, coming straight at Miller, splattering his face shield.

Miller jumped backwards, quickly put his hand over his face shield to block the blood, and twisted around. "Damn! I can't see anything."

The blood was velvet-red and pulsing to the rhythm of the patient's heartbeat, which told everyone that an artery had just been pierced. Miller then turned back around to the patient and placed one hand over the bloodstream, applying pressure on the hole the trocar created in the perineum.

The life support system showed the patient's blood pressure first increasing and then rapidly dropping. The trauma of cutting through the artery had shocked the patient's vascular supply.

The anesthesiologist popped his head above the screen at the head of the operating table with his raised eyebrows and wide-open eyes. "Miller! Stop the bleeding!"

Miller looked over at Bridget and wiped the blood off his mask. "Quick, Bridget, take over and press on this bleeder."

Bridget's eyes widened. "Me? Are you sure?"

Miller nodded. "Yes, I'm sure."

She stepped forward with slow, timid, baby steps, and pressed her hand over the shooting stream of blood, then looked over at Dr. Miller.

"Perfect, " said Miller. He then twisted the ultrasound probe placed within the rectum to visualize the prostate area better. "Keep pressing while I check the vessel." Miller then scanned up the vessel. "Buzz, hand me the Geiger counter." Miller turned, grabbed it quickly, and turned back to lean down onto the patients exposed pelvic area. He scanned it to make sure no radiation was detected outside of the prostate target. Where the Geiger counter clicks became louder, he moved the ultrasound probe over to the spot to focus in on it. He moved the Geiger counter a half centimeter at a time so as to not miss any of the half-center-length radiation seeds. His own heart kicked his chest from within, and his mask continually fogged up and down mirroring his respiration rate and intensity. The on and off hissing of the ventilator echoed in his head, and the bright, hot overhead lights cooked his outsides, while his adrenal surge baked his insides. If not for the coldness of the operating room sucking heat from his body, he would surely have overheated and collapsed.

"Dr. Miller, what are you looking for?" asked Bridget gingerly.

"The radioactive seed." He pointed to the bright signal given off from the seed within the blood vessel on the ultrasound projection. "There. See it? We have to get that out. And pronto." He extended his right arm out and lowered his hand to the circulating nurse who stood patiently behind him and to his right. "Hand me the fiber optic scope with the clamp attachment." Miller then passed the scope through the hole in the perineum left by the trocar, extended the tiny forceps attached to it over the vessel, and clamped it just above the seed. Miller then worked quickly to enter the clamped vessel with the other attached forceps to retrieve the radioactive seed. He slowly worked the scope into the vessel, being careful not to stretch it too much, which could tear it.

"Patient is stressed." The anxious voice of the anesthesiologist sounded from behind the curtain that draped the patient's head and upper thorax. "Don't want to give him any more meds with his bad heart, but I have no choice. His heart is too weak to compensate for the drop in blood pressure on its own."

Miller looked up at the head of the table. "I understand," said Miller, as he began to rub his right arm like he had a bad itch that could not wait to be scratched. "Do whatever you need to keep him stable while I work to get this seed out."

"Okay then. Giving more anesthetic." He then injected more pressure medication and more anesthetic for pain control into the patient's vein, as it was obvious from the vital sign readings that the patient felt the deep trauma from inserting the scope first into his soft tissues and then into his blood vessel.

Miller's mind raced in several directions without his hands missing a beat to retrieve the lost seed. He never once took his sights off the patient and ultrasound image in front of him, and yet he was somehow able to picture the operating room around him simultaneously, while his thoughts began to drift in and out from his immediate surroundings and circumstances. *When I look around me, I see a fortress of walls protecting my kingdom, inside of which I control everything, but not for evil purposes. Only for good. I save lives here. I cure people of the enemy within them, the cancer. I stand high above all others, looking down on those that I am to save today, and, from above, the overhead lights shine only on me as I direct my orchestra.*

Miller slowly worked the optic scope up the vessel, being careful not to touch the inner lining along the way, deeper and deeper until the shiny seed came into view. "There it is!" he said. He moved the tiny forceps attached to the scope forward to grab the seed. "Just a few more millimeters." The video camera on the scope showed the forceps opening ever so slowly around the seed, like the jaw of a great white shark about to swallow its prey. Miller held his breath and closed the forceps down on the seed. "There. Got it." He looked at the ultrasound, which showed the forceps grasping the seed and slowly being pulled out of the vessel. Everything on the screen looked like it was occurring underwater, with any movement of the scope creating little ripples of sound waves. "Okay, Bridget, take the forceps off the vessel to let the blood flow before he gets ischemic. Just … another … centimeter to go," said Miller.

Bridget did as he said. And just as she did, the seed slipped out of the other forceps, shot a centimeter downstream, and began swimming away again within the vessel.

"Damn!" shouted Miller. "Bridget, quick, clamp the vessel above the seed again. Hurry! Before it gets to where the vessel branches above."

Sweat bubbled off Bridget's brow. She grabbed the clamp from the nurse, but as she opened it, using only her forefinger and thumb, gravity pulled down on it, and it slipped out of her hand and fell to the floor. Bridget's head snapped back and over to look at Dr. Miller with horror on her face.

Dr. Miller looked sternly at her, and fog built up on his mask from his rapid breathing. "Nurse, give her a new one," he said.

Bridget took the new clamp, placed it inside the hole, pushed it to the vessel, and quickly reached above where Dr. Miller had the scope in the vessel. "Where do I clamp it now?"

"Bridget, look at the ultrasound monitor," said Miller. "Now, I will slide the ultrasound forward so you can see the branch point. There! See the seed just below the branch point?"

She nodded nervously. "Yes! I see it."

"Good, now clamp it just before where it divides."

The ultrasound showed the seed migrating upward, wiggling along as the current from the blood flow pushed on it, causing it to bump into the sides of the vessel wall and spin out of control when caught in areas of turbulence. It was like watching an object tossing and turning while being dragged helplessly through white-water rapids.

Bridget struggled to keep her forceps steady with her body appearing tense as she adjusted her position over the body. "Here?" she said, placing the forceps over the exposed vessel just below the branch point, where it formed the shape of the letter Y.

"Yes, there. Steady. Steady. Now! Quickly! It's just a few centimeters away."

Bridget grabbed the vessel just below the division and squeezed it shut, just as the seed reached the beginning of the division. The ultrasound showed that the seed again had been stopped just before the branch point.

"Thank God," said Miller. "Good job, Bridget. If that had gotten away, we may have had to open up his chest where the seed was likely to travel."

Miller grabbed the forceps, pulled the seed out of the vessel, then through the soft tissues of muscle and fat, and turned to give it to Buzz behind him. "Put that bad boy away," said Miller.

"Yes, sir." Buzz placed the seed into the lead radiation seed container (aka, the Pig) next to him. "Now you stay in there and behave." He shook his forefinger at the lead pig. "You have been a naughty boy, Mr Seed," said Buzz.

From behind the curtain, again came the anxious voice of the anesthesiologist. "Come on. Come on, everyone. Let's hurry it up. Another sixty seconds, and we may have a code on our hands. His heart rate is now tachycardic with occasional atrial fibrillations."

"Bridget, I need you to move the clamp back down to just before the tear in the vessel and then step away so I can stitch this sucker up," said Dr. Miller.

Bridget stared at Dr. Miller like she had just been told to jump off the Empire State Building.

Miller lowered his head and gave a penetrating look. "Got it?"

Bridget looked directly into Miller's eyes. "Yes. I got it." With beads of sweat coming down her temples, she slowly let go of the clamp. Immediately, blood shot back out of the trocar-needle hole in the perineum, but for only the few seconds it took for her to clamp above the tear in the vessel.

"Good job," said Miller. "Now, Carol, hand me that suture."

Carol, one of the scrub nurses, slapped it into his outstretched hand.

"Ow! Damn! It stuck me," said Miller. He transferred the suture to the other hand and and shook the one just stuck as if to send the pain away.

The nurse put her hand up to her mouth. "Oh, my—I am so sorry, Dr. Miller. Do you want to re-glove?"

He looked closely at it under the light. "No time for that. Just glove over it." Within seconds, he had a new sterile glove over the old one to cover the hole in it. Immediately, he brought a new needle and thread into the hole with the scope and began to suture the tear in the vessel using the scope with forceps.

"Thirty seconds. I'm not kidding. This guy is not tolerating this," said the anesthesiologist.

Miller worked quickly, placing three stitches as fast as anyone in the operating room had ever seen.

In an even higher octave this time, "Ten seconds," said the anesthesiologist.

Miller did not look up from where his hands worked furiously. "Not to worry … got everything under … control. There. Stopped!" said Miller as the pulsing jet stream of blood became only a slight trickle, like that of a garden hose being shut off from full force to a slow trickle before it emptied itself out.

"Phew, two seconds to spare," said the anesthesiologist, now in his normal baritone voice, poking his head out above the drapes. "Heart rate and pressure stabilizing. You know, Miller, you put a scare, something fierce, in me. For a few seconds there, I thought we might lose him."

Miller quietly sucked in a deep breath, like he had just surfaced from being underwater longer than he should have. "Sorry about that. The patient is doing fine now, so let's all take a deep breath and get the patient to recovery." Miller glanced around at his team and saw nods all around. "Great job, everyone. It was a bit more than we expected. But thanks to all of you, the patient will do well. Let's get a quick X-ray for prostate-seed placement check and cystoscopy for bladder check and then get the patient cleaned up and to recovery. I'll meet him there after I talk with his wife."

Buzz approached Miller, put his arm on his shoulder, and wiped the sweat off his brow with his other forearm. "Doc, you never stop amazing me. And I don't mean just your skill at placing the radiation seeds. If you could only stay so calm when I'm late for a case as you do with getting bleeding controlled."

"Thanks, Buzz, but I'm lucky to have a great team with me." Dr. Miller turned to Bridget, who was helping the nurses prepare the patient for the recovery room. "Bridget, you did terrific. I mean it."

Bridget rubbed her gloved hands together and raised her eyebrows. "Really? You're not just saying that to make me feel good?"

"No. I would never do that. This is serious business. We deal with life and death, so I would never sugarcoat things. That wouldn't help you, me, or our patients."

Bridget sighed while rolling her shoulders. "Dr. Miller, I can't tell you how nervous I was in there."

Miller chuckled. "Yes, I know. I could tell. And that's a normal response. I would have been worried if you hadn't been nervous. Someone who's too cocky is likely too dangerous. A healthy degree of nervousness keeps you on your toes." Miller moved over to her and put his arm around her. "So, I will say it again, for your first time in the operating room, you did pretty damn good."

Bridget moved her eyes over and up to look at him, smiled, and said, "Thank you, Dr. Miller. That means a lot to me."

"When we have more time, perhaps later today, I'd like to go over today's case with you to help you better understand it and prepare you for your next case with me. I just want you to know that what you just went through is something you have to go through. I didn't leave you hanging there to torture you. It's the only way you'll learn to think on your feet under stress." He looked at his watch. "Right now, I need to talk with my patient and his family." He turned to walk away.

"Dr. Miller?"

He stopped and looked back. "Yes, Bridget?"

"May I go with you to see the patient?"

He hesitated and stared at her for a moment, then nodded. "Of course. Glad you asked."

They left the operating room, removed their sterile protective paper coverings and the radiation shielding, and walked down the hall to the patients' waiting room. As soon as they entered it, Henry's wife and family stood up with anxious looks on their faces.

She stepped forward. "Dr. Miller, how is my husband doing? Did everything go all right? We heard from one of the nurses that there were a few problems," she said, all in one breath.

Miller walked right up to her. "Your husband is doing fine. We had a few challenges, but everything came out well. He'll be in the recovery room for a few hours before we have him go to the floor overnight for observations."

She looked up at Dr. Miller. "I want to thank you for what you did for us."

Miller put a hand onto her shoulder and smiled. "There is no need. This is what I do. I'm glad I could help."

"Dr. Miller, I'm not talking only about your treating my husband for his cancer."

Miller removed his hand from her shoulder and leaned back while placing his hands on his hips. "I'm sorry, but I'm not following you. What do you mean then?"

"I'm talking about your paying his—our—medical bills."

He looked down and askance at her. "Who told you that?"

"When I went down to talk with the billing people at the hospital because he was laid off from his job and lost our insurance, the lady said we didn't need to worry about the bills. I didn't believe her, and I guess I started to make a scene, so she broke down to shut me up and told me you had paid them after you found out he lost his insurance." She began to cry and stepped forward to hug him. She was such a diminutive woman that when she hugged Dr. Miller, her head barely reached his chest.

Miller hesitated but then bent over to hug back. "They weren't supposed to tell you that."

"You're a caring and generous man. God bless you," she said, with tears rolling down her face.

Dr. Miller looked over at Bridget, who had been watching them the whole time. Miller smiled and raised his eyebrows with a "what can I say" look on his face.

Dr. Miller looked down again at Henry's wife, and she looked straight up at him. "I have to get back to check on your husband and write orders for him. The nurses will let you know when he'll be transferred to the floor so you can visit him."

She went back to hugging him, only this time tighter. "Bless you, Doctor. Bless you."

"I'll be back to see you and your family after he goes to the floor in a few hours. I promise."

She then let go of her hug, wiped her tears away, and looked up to Dr. Miller as he walked away. "Bless you. God bless you, Doctor."

On the way out, he passed Bridget, standing in the doorway. "Come on back to the operating room with me, and I'll show how to write the orders for the patients."

They walked down the hallway leading back to the operating room. "Dr. Miller, that was a very generous and wonderful thing you did for that family," said Bridget.

"It's no big deal. I like helping those that need it, but thank you for saying so."

When they got back to the operating room, only Buzz and a maintenance person cleaning the floor were there. "Oh, Buzz, I'm glad you're still here."

"Hey, Doc. This case was a bit more challenging, so I wanted to take a bit more time checking the room for any stray radiation. Just to be sure," replied Buzz.

"Good idea. Listen, I want to meet with you and Ahzid later today in my office."

"Sure, no problem. Can you tell me what it's about?"

"Buzz, I think you know."

Buzz raised his eyebrows with a slight tilt of his head. "Let me guess, the patients who died unexpectedly? Am I right?"

"Exactly."

"Okay. I'll let Ahzid know when I go back downstairs to put the pig with the extra seeds away."

Dr. Miller and Bridget sat down at the paperwork area, and he proceeded to show her how to fill out the postoperative orders. "Any questions?" he said after they finished.

"No. That seemed pretty straightforward."

"Good, I'll go back to—"

The OR phone's loud ringing startled them.

One of the scrub nurses who had come back to get the post-op orders from Dr. Miller answered it. "OR 9," she said. "Dr. Miller? Yes, he's still here." She turned with the phone extended out toward Dr. Miller. "Dr. Miller, it's for you."

"Who is it? Can I call them back?"

"Dr. Miller is busy right this minute. Can he can call you back?" She listened intently and looked surprised. "Okay. Hold on. I'll tell him." She looked over to Dr. Miller. "It's Dr. Whittimore from the Radiology Department. He says that unless you have your hands inside someone's abdomen trying to stop their bleeding, it's important and I had to interrupt you."

Miller stood, walked over to the nurse, and looked at her with a half smile. "He's just a bit late on that," he said. He took the phone out of her hand. "Hello, Miller here. Now what's so urgent that you scared the nurse half to death?" He listened and then said, "Oh, I see. You want to go over the test results on my patients … and?" Miller paused. The silence permeated the OR. Miller felt the force of gravity pull down on him. His jaw opened, and his shoulders sagged. A burning again in his right forearm caused him to rub it.

"No. Not another patient?" he said as he shook his head.

CHAPTER 2: THE GAUNTLET

BRIDGET SAT IN THE CORNER OF THE OPERATING ROOM AND waited quietly for Dr. Miller to finish talking with Buzz. She felt closer to him after experiencing the intensity of the implant case they had just gone through together. She wondered if this is what soldiers feel when they go through battle together and survive. Up until that moment, she had looked at him only has her direct supervisor. Nothing beyond cerebral interactions.

"Good looking, isn't he?" whispered one of the OR nurses from behind in Bridget's ear.

Bridget turned quickly to her. "What? Who?"

"Oh. Come on now. I saw you gawking at Dr. Miller over there."

"I … I was just thinking about all that happened during the case. That's all." Bridget picked up the notepad on her lap that she had taken notes on and began looking through it.

The nurse gave her a questioning look, raising her eyebrows. "Listen, honey. It's okay. Not to worry, you're not alone. All of us nurses—even some of the male ones, if you know what I mean—have found ourselves daydreaming about him. He's premium eye candy. Single, smart, blue bedroom eyes—and that body." She walked away chuckling.

After the nurse walked away, Bridget felt a warmth come over her. *My face must be beet red. Was I that obvious? This relationship has to be kept strictly professional.* She sat a few more minutes until after the warm feeling went away and then walked over to Dr. Miller who was still talking with Buzz.

"Excuse me, Dr. Miller," said Bridget.

Dr. Miller looked over at her, raised his index finger to her to hold on, and turned back to Buzz. "So, I'll meet you and Ahzid in my office in about an hour."

"Sounds good," said Buzz. Buzz held up his hand in front of Bridget to high-five her. "And by the way, Bridget, nice job today in the OR."

"Thanks, Buzz," she said with a smile ear to ear and slapped his palm with hers.

Dr. Miller nodded to her. "Yes, Bridget. I agree. Like I said before, nice job."

"Thank you, both," said Bridget. "Sorry if I interrupted you and Buzz, Dr. Miller, but if you don't mind my asking, is everything all right?

"What do you mean? I don't understand," said Miller.

"Well, I gotta go," interjected Buzz. And he sauntered out of the operating room.

"See you," they both responded.

"What I mean, Dr. Miller, is that you sounded a bit upset on the phone a moment ago."

"Bridget, unfortunately, it's rarely good news when the radiologist wants to show you a patient's films in person rather than discuss them over the phone. So, I've got to get down to the Radiology Department to meet with him now."

"Mind if I tag along?" she asked.

"No. Not at all. You should see these follow-up scans I have on my patients anyway since you'll likely be involved with the care of some of them."

As Bridget walked alongside Dr. Miller, she noticed not only that he didn't speak a word to her but also that his initial fast pace slowed the closer they got to the Radiology Department. And when they finally got there, Dr. Miller stood in front of the closed door with the sign that said X-Ray Reading Room. He held up his right arm with his fist a few inches away, paused for a few seconds, then knocked. From the other side of the door, a voice shouted to come in. He opened the door wide to show Whitimore, the silver-haired radiologist, sitting in almost complete darkness and staring at the films that hung before him on the four rows of X-ray viewing boxes. Each row had several films. The light emanating from each of the view boxes showed patients' images of bone scans and CT scans. And below them, the silhouette of Whitimore's face and body, with the light glimmering off his hair.

Miller stepped inside first, with Bridget close behind him. He stopped short as the images on the view boxes came into their view, causing Bridget to run into him. She walked around him and saw his eyes widen, then close, then open again, as if to shut out the sight of them. His shoulders drooped; he sighed and stepped closer to the view boxes. "So ... Whit. I can assume these are the films on my patients you called me about."

Up until that point, Dr. Whitimore had not moved. He just kept staring at the films on the view boxes and talking into his microphone to dictate his findings. Hearing Dr. Miller's voice, he stopped talking and swiveled around in his thick cushioned chair to face Miller. Whitimore slapped his thigh. "Ahhh. Miller. Glad you could make it. Yes, indeed, these are the films I called you about."

"I thought so." Miller gestured with his hand to Bridget to come closer to him. "Carl, this is Bridget, my new physician assistant."

Dr. Whitimore remained seated but extended his hand to her. "Pleasure to meet you, Bridget."

She extended her hand to shake his. "Nice to meet you as well, Dr. Whitimore."

Dr. Miller moved closer to the films to scan the images on the view boxes. He turned to Bridget and waved her closer. "Come on over here."

Whitimore turned his attention back to the films. "As you both can see, the bone scans show widespread involvement of both the axial and appendage regions."

Bridget looked down to Dr. Whitimore. "I beg your pardon. I'm familiar with these diagnostic tests in general but am rather new in knowing their use for oncology patients."

"So sorry, Bridget. Let me explain a bit then for you." He stood and pointed to the areas on the bone scan images showing skeletons with very bright white spots dotting just about every bone. "These bright spots show uptake of the radioisotope we inject into the patient before taking the X-ray images. The areas of the bone that have active areas of cancer will take up the tracer and give off radiation that in turn make those areas look bright."

Bridget nodded. "Thank you for that explanation."

Dr. Miller turned away from the images. "Whit, are you seeing this on all of the patients I recently sent as a group to you for follow-up testing?"

"Unfortunately, yes. And the CTs are showing extensive spread to the lymph nodes as well." He pointed to the films in the upper two rows above the bone scans. "You see how both the pelvic and abdominal nodes are bigger than normal? Most are larger than two centimeters, which is extraordinary. The normal lymph nodes should be no bigger than 1 cm on the greatest axis; these here as measured are ranging from 2.0 cm to as big as 3.5 cm. Clearly abnormally large, and given the diagnosis of prostate cancer and the findings of the bone scan, most likely represent spread of the cancer."

Bridget nodded.

Dr. Miller turned to Bridget. "Bridget, we don't put the patient through biopsies in this situation to prove the cancer has metastasized because it is so consistent with how prostate cancer spreads; however, in these cases, I am going to recommend it to the patients because these findings are so far from what the expectations were."

"What do you mean by expectations?" she asked.

At first, he looked down in thought for a few seconds. Then he raised his head. "Bridget, if there ever is such a thing in cancer as a cure, these patients were expected to achieve that."

Bridget put her hand over her mouth. "Oh, no. Really? That's awful. What do you think happened?"

"Right now, I'm not sure. But trust me, I'm sure as hell going to do everything I can to find out—starting with my meeting with Buzz and Ahzid today. I don't believe you've met Ahzid yet."

"I've heard you and others speak of him but haven't met him yet. What does he do?"

"He's my physicist—the person who keeps all the radiation sources and machines in proper working order to treat patients."

"Do you want me to come with you to the meeting in your office, Dr. Miller?"

Miller looked at her for a moment, like he was sizing her up. "Yes, I'm glad you asked. You're now part of the team; you should be a part of this."

After they left the radiology suite, Bridget walked with Dr. Miller to his office and stood in the back, watching him as he spoke to Buzz and Ahzid, who were already seated near the front when they arrived.

Dr. Miller stood in front of his desk, looking out to them. "Guys and—excuse me—ladies," said Miller. "Bridget, please come up and take a seat. Buzz, you know Bridget." Buzz nodded with a smile. "Ahzid, this is my new assistant. Bridget, meet Ahzid, my medical physicist." Ahzid turned to look her up and down. He ignored her gesture to shake and turned back around to face Dr. Miller. Bridget looked at her hand, shrugged her shoulders at being snubbed by Ahzid, and sat down behind him.

"Bridget finished first in her physician assistant training class and since then has worked in the hospital emergency room for over a year now. She decided she wanted a change, and we are lucky to have Bridget join our team," said Dr. Miller. He turned to the drawings on the boards along the walls behind his desk, then back again to face the group. "I've asked you here because we have a problem. A very serious problem. These diagrams represent the patients we have recently treated with radiation implants and how they've done with treatment." He moved closer to the group and looked directly down at Buzz, Ahzid, and Bridget. "Folks, our patients are dying."

Ahzid rolled his eyes and looked away. "Patients die all the time," he blurted out.

Dr. Miller looked at Ahzid. "True, Ahzid. But these patients were not expected to die from their cancer. In fact, they were expected to be cured."

Ahzid did not say anything else and looked away from Miller.

Dr. Miller discussed his concerns about each patient's situation. Bridget noticed that Dr. Miller would rub his right forearm every time Ahzid would disagree with him, and throughout the hour-long meeting, Ahzid became quite fidgety, constantly crossing his legs from one to the other. But she resolved that she didn't know him well enough to know if that was his baseline or because this meeting upset him.

Buzz, on the other hand, remained cool throughout the meeting. He had a relaxed air about him but was obviously still concerned. He listened to Dr. Miller, chewing his gum slowly and quietly, sitting with one arm resting on the chair next to his.

Dr. Miller continued his discussion. "I have painstakingly put together these charts on each of the patients who has unexpectedly been diagnosed with recurrent and/or progressive cancer after we treated them with a radioactive implant." Dr. Miller pointed to the diagrams on the wall behind him. "As you can see by the flow charts and Venn diagrams up here, I have looked at each of these patients, from beginning of diagnosis to end of treatment, and any follow-up visits, to assess for anything that might indicate something was missed or not done correctly. In each case, I have not found anything grossly missing or done wrong."

Ahzid, who had been sitting with his head focused downward, suddenly unfolded his tightly crossed arms, extended them outward and upward like he was praying, and looked up at Dr. Miller. "This is all a waste of my time. Patients die from many things."

Dr. Miller turned around. "I already said that I understand that, Ahzid, but—"

Ahzid stood up. "Could be simply that the cancer was resistant to treatment."

"Yes, that's true, but keep in mind these patients statistically were not likely going to develop resistance, and it's almost impossible to have this number fail in such a short amount of time. Up until these patients, who were treated over the past year or so, we have never had a patient fail their implant treatment. Ahzid, you and I have known each other a long time, and we have always tried to look at problems as a challenge that we could solve if we put our efforts into it. It does not seem like the Ahzid I know to give up so easily. Now, do either of you have any other thoughts about how this could have happened?"

No one said a word. Buzz had a blank look on his face while Ahzid sat back down and kept looking down with his arms again tightly folded together across his chest.

"Buzz?" asked Miller.

Buzz shook his head. "No. I can't really think of any right now."

"Ahzid? Any other thoughts at this time?"

After several seconds of no response, Ahzid snapped his head up to look straight at Miller and opened up his arms widely again. "I don't think we did anything wrong. Maybe you should look at yourself instead of looking to blame others."

Buzz turned to face Ahzid, seated to the left of him. "Ahzid, I don't think Dr. Miller is trying to say we did anything wrong. I think he's just trying to look at everything to see if we can find anything that could help understand why things have gone wrong with these patients." He looked over at Dr. Miller. "Am I correct in saying that, doc?"

"Yes, that's exactly right, Buzz. I just want to examine everything about each case. I am not here to blame anyone. But at the same time, we all have to keep an open mind and be willing to consider that one or more of us may have done something wrong." Dr. Miller began to walk from poster board to poster board hung from the front wall, pointing to each one. "You see here that I have each patient's information from diagnosis to workup to treatment and subsequent follow-up. All tests are listed, and details of each step are noted alongside them. I have personally reviewed each patient's chart to look at the details of each step with particular attention to the radiation implant procedure itself."

Obviously more agitated, Ahzid began to cross his legs more frequently, right over left, left over right, each time readjusting himself in his seat as if something were biting him from underneath it. "Maybe you did something wrong, but not me. I cannot sit here and listen to this anymore. I have too much work to complete. I'm leaving," said Ahzid. He stood up, turned, and walked out.

Dr. Miller and Buzz looked at each other in surprise.

"I don't see why Ahzid takes this so personally. Nobody's saying he did anything wrong," said Miller.

"Ah, don't worry about him," said Buzz. "He always reacts to things dramatically. He'll be all right."

"I hope so. Maybe I should talk to him. We always used to be able to talk things out, even if we disagreed."

"Let him calm down. Not to worry. I'll check in on him before I go."

Dr. Miller sat on his desk. "Thanks, Buzz. I appreciate that."

"Doc, do you think the patients could have been misdiagnosed? Or maybe they had more aggressive cancer than picked up on the initial biopsies?"

"Great question. I can see you've learned a few things since working with me all these years. And one that I thought of as well, but as I pointed out, I reviewed all of those tests, even going so far as to review each patient's biopsy myself with the pathologists, and I sent the slides out for second opinions. None, not a one, were misdiagnosed or under diagnosed. Now, could something have been missed that wasn't biopsied? Yes, but again, this is statistically unlikely given the number and locations of the biopsies taken."

Buzz began to yawn and stood up to stretch. "If it's okay with you, I think my brain has reached its max capacity on this, and I should also go finish up some work before I head home."

"Sure. Have a good night, Buzz."

"You too. See ya tomorrow. And I'll peak in on Ahzid, if he's still in the department, to see how he's doing."

After Buzz left, Miller sat staring at the flow charts and Venn diagrams, his eyes following each line to each branch point, then off to another line. Bridget had stayed and slowly approached him. But as she crept closer, he quickly turned his head toward her. "Bridget, I didn't know you were still here. I must have gone over these a thousand—no, ten thousand times in my head." He slammed his fist onto the desk. "I can't find anything done by us that was done wrong." Miller then looked back at the drawing boards, as if he were waiting for them to explain something that he could not see.

Bridget had watched the whole time, not saying a word. Having seen him in the operating room handle himself to save the patient and afterword his compassion and generosity with his patients, she knew without a doubt that she had made the right decision to work with him. She saw even more of his concern for his patients and the pain he suffered now with talking about the loss of his patients. *This is a strong and confident man but also a sensitive, deeply caring man.*

"Dr. Miller, obviously there's a lot I don't know about these cases, and I have a lot to learn about their treatments … but maybe it would help to look at things that aren't similar among the cases, rather than similar things?"

Miller looked up at Bridget, who had moved closer to him, now standing only a few feet away from him next to his desk. He raised his eyebrows. "Hmmmm. Things that are not similar. Like?"

"Well, it seems to me that all the focus is on what's common about who and what is involved with each case who died unexpectedly."

Miller paused. He looked back at the board and then at her. "Well, yes. That would be logical to find out what could have gone wrong since only those present could affect the case."

"Yes, but what if you looked at a similar cohort of cases that were done during the same period but with successful outcomes, to see what might be different from those that failed?"

Miller put a hand under his chin. "Now why would that help?"

"Well, by looking at only the cases that failed, for things that could be different among them, the assumption is that nothing could go wrong if everything is constant."

"Yes ... that would be logical."

"Logical, yes. But only if the underlying assumption is that everything that occurred was done correctly and that everything and everyone involved was working toward the same outcome."

Miller shook his head. "I'm sorry, Bridget, but now I'm not following you."

"All I'm saying is that if you look at the cases that came out as expected—cured, that is—during the same time period as those that did not, maybe there would be something different, something that was not there during the case, that may be more important than what or who was there during it."

Miller stood up, moved closer to her, and held her hand with his. "Bridget, thank you for your input and thoughts. I will have to think on what you're saying." They now stood within inches of each other and kept smiling at each other.

A knock on his office door interrupted them. Miller cleared his throat. "Come in."

Mary, Dr. Miller's department secretary, opened the door and poked her head inside. Dr. Miller and Bridget jumped apart when they saw her, breaking the hand grip they had with each other.

Mary stepped into the room. "I'm sorry to interrupt, Dr. Miller. But I have a message for you before I leave to go home."

"Yes, yes, of course. What is it, Mary?"

She handed him a memo she had written. "The CEO, Mr Dinkus, called. He would like to see you up in his office tomorrow."

Dr. Miller reached out to take the memo from her. "Thank you, Mary."

"You're welcome. Bye, Bridget," she said with a slanted look and a smirk as she left the room.

"Did I say or do something wrong?" asked Bridget.

"Mary's just a little overprotective of me. That's all. Never mind her. I wonder what that pompous ass wants to meet about now."

Bridget smiled. "You don't sound too excited to meet with him."

"We better wrap this up, Bridget. It's getting late. Let me walk you out." Dr. Miller and Bridget left his office and continued their conversation, walking down the hallway to exit the building.

"Bridget, meeting with this CEO can mean only one thing: headache or heartache or both."

They both chuckled.

"Dr. Miller," his secretary shouted as she ran down the hallway to catch him.

They stopped and turned around. "Yes, Mary. What's got you so twisted?" asked Dr. Miller.

"I took one last call for you before I left and forgot to mention it. I thought you'd want to know."

Miller looked at Bridget. "Now what?" Then he looked back at Mary.

"Dr. Miller, it's about your prostate patient George, and I'm sorry to say it's not good news."

CHAPTER 3: A SURPRISE VISITOR

AFTER MILLER ESCORTED BRIDGET OUT OF THE DEPARTMENT, he went back to his office and flopped back into his leather desk chair. He picked up a ball of Play-Dough sitting on his desk, began squeezing it, and thought about his patient George and what his secretary had just told him. His tests showed his cancer had not only not been eradicated but also had spread to other sites in his body. After a few minutes, he swiveled around and stared at the flow charts lining the walls of his office. Over and over again, he ran each case through his head. He drew connecting lines again to each case, searching for anything that might reveal a link that connected to the patients' deaths. *What is common about the cases that died yet uncommon with the others of similar diagnosis, prognosis, and treated during the same time frame, but were cured? Not isotope types, not radiation dose, and not the technique of implant or specific type of implant ... Damn it, there has to be something here.*

In disgust, he threw the ball of Play-Dough he had been squeezing at the charts on the wall. It stuck to the area on the board where a Venn diagram had been made earlier, mostly ignored. It landed on the "staffing" part of the overlap between the patients who died and those still alive. Within the circle labeled 'Dosimetry'. Miller suddenly noted something that neither he nor anybody else had noticed before. He opened his eyes so wide that they looked like they were about to pop out of his head. He quickly stood up, snapped the chair backwards with the thrust of his legs, and walked with a purpose, like marching, toward the Venn diagram.

He removed the Play-Dough, and underneath was a name he knew well. The name that seemed to suddenly connect all the dots of the patients who had died. *Ahzid!*

Ahzid is the only name that is associated with all cases that have died unexpectedly. But how could each patient have been affected by him? He scratched his head, slowly walked back toward the chair, and sat for a minute. With all his thinking, his brain felt strained to the limit. Then his eyes widened again, and he hit the desk with his fist. *Of course. Why did we not think of this earlier. The staff!* Dr. Miller realized that in all his research, he had ignored the people involved with the cases and had focused on the technology.

Why would we have thought anything about who was involved? They were all to be trusted. There was no reason to think otherwise—or perhaps there was? But I've known him for years, and we've gone through so much together.

Dr. Miller realized that it was not enough to find the connection on paper with Ahzid; he had to figure out why and how it made a difference. He had to confront Ahzid today, and in Ahzid's office before the case they were doing together in the OR later that day. It was the only way to begin to figure out what was it about having Ahzid do the dosimetry and seed implants that made such a difference in the outcome, as opposed to Buzz.

Ahzid was a creature of habit, and on days when he was the person responsible for the radioactive seeds as Dr. Miller's assistant in the operating room, he would arrive to his office at 5:00 a.m. sharp with a large cup of coffee. The first case of the day could be as early at seven o'clock on the schedule, but most of the time, they were late and would not begin until seven thirty or eight. Ahzid would read the paper and sip his coffee for about thirty minutes, then change into his OR scrubs, and, lastly, recheck the plan that he had made the week earlier with Dr. Miller and the radiation seeds that he loaded the day prior into the needles to be used for that day's cases.

And this day was no different, except for Dr. Miller being an unexpected and uninvited guest. Ahzid walked into his office precisely at 5:00 a.m. with the coffee in his left hand, the paper tucked under his left arm, and his big, worn-out briefcase in his right. He sat down in his desk chair, placed his briefcase by his side on the floor, and then after taking a gulp of his coffee, he put the cup and paper onto the desk. He heard a voice come from behind him to his left.

"Morning, Ahzid."

Ahzid turned around quickly to see Dr. Miller standing, looking at the pictures and artifacts in his office. He began choking on the coffee. Dr. Miller darted over to him, put one hand on the middle of Ahzid's back and the other on his shoulder. "Are you all right? Sorry, Ahzid. I didn't mean to startle you."

He coughed a bit more and then took in a big breath. "Jake! I almost had a heart attack. What are you doing here in my office? And this early?"

Miller ignored his questions. "Are you sure you're okay? Can I get you some water?"

"I'll be fine." He glared up at Dr. Miller, who stood over him.

"Everything okay with the seeds and plan for this morning's case? Our patient is a nice guy, and I would hate to have any problems occur."

Ahmed frowned slightly. "Everything is fine. I needed to double check a few things on the seed case for today, as I always do. Why do you ask?"

"Relax, Ahzid. It's just a rhetorical question. You seem nervous. Are you sure everything is okay?"

"No problems. No problems." With that, Ahzid looked down at the paperwork on his desk to continue working on the seed implant preparation for the day. After several seconds, Ahzid looked up at Dr. Miller, who was still standing there watching him.

"Is there something else? As you know, I do need to get things ready for the case in less than hour."

"Well, I'm a bit surprised not to see any photos in your office of us together. We've known each other since we were kids together in the orphanage. And after all, we were both abandoned by our families, perhaps not by their choice, but nonetheless we ended up in a place that we didn't belong, a place that we didn't deserve. It's had everlasting effects on us both. Remember, we have much in common."

Ahzid rolled his eyes. "Yes, yes. I know all of that."

"But the main reason I wanted to see you is that I wanted to talk with you about the patients we recently implanted—the ones who have recurred, progressed, and even died from their cancer, to be more specific."

"I know that it's been hard on you—and on everyone—to be losing patients so unexpectedly."

"Exactly. 'Unexpectedly' is the key word," said Miller, giving a long look at Ahzid.

"Well, I believe I made my thoughts clear when we met in your office to discuss this."

"Yes, you certainly did. But I've got to tell you that I've been here all night working on those charts, not being able to stop thinking of, as you say, the unexpected nature of our patients dying … and …."

Ahzid, who had been fiddling with something in his desk drawer, stopped and looked up at Miller. "And what?"

"And I couldn't help but notice something common to all our implant patients that have died over the past year … unexpectedly that is. I can't believe I didn't notice it before."

Ahzid kept fiddling with objects in his drawer. "Jake, I really have to finish my work for the first case today."

"I know. I have to be there as well." Miller sauntered around the office with his hands clasped behind his back, looking at the pictures and artifacts on the shelves along the wall. "You know, Ahzid, I don't know how you get any work done in here with only one window in the office, high on the back wall and covered up like it is. It's so dark and cold in here; personally, and no disrespect intended, I always like a well-lit area."

Ahzid went back to fiddling with papers on his desk. " I happen to like it this way … so?"

"And it's one thing—although I think it's still strange—not to have pictures of us growing up together in the orphanage or our years after, getting together when going through college, but quite another not to have pictures of your wife or kids, only of yourself and others dressed in Arabic attire. And the background in all of them look as though they were taken overseas, in the Middle East somewhere." Miller walked over to the corner of the room and reached to the back of one of the shelves. *This is an interesting picture, hidden in the back of the shelf with other pictures and objects obscuring most it.* Ahzid was standing with several other men in what looked like a desert area but surrounded by hills and mountains. What had caught Miller's eye was what Ahzid was holding. It looked like a sword. "Ahzid, this picture of you, the sword in it looks just like the sword that you have over there on the wall behind your desk." He walked over to it. He looked back and forth at the picture and the sword inside the glass case on his wall. "Is it the same? Or one that's just like it?"

Clearly annoyed, exhaling with a sigh, Ahzid stood up, approached Miller, and grabbed the picture from him. "Jacob, if we could stop analyzing my photos and get back to the earlier point you were about to tell me."

"I'm sorry. My point?" Miller said with a questioning frown and a tilt of his head.

"Yes, the 'common thing' you found when studying those charts on the patients."

"Oh that! Of course. I guess I'm just so tired from being up all night and wound up over our patients' dying that I forgot."

"Jake, please tell me what that common thing is. You've raised my curiosity." Ahzid sat back down and placed the picture of him with the sword on his desk.

Miller moved over to the front of Ahzid's desk. Ahzid looked up at him, and they locked eyes for an uncomfortable several seconds. Beads of sweat bubbled to the surface of Ahzid's forehead. Miller bent over and leaned forward, inches from Ahzid's face. "You!" said Dr. Miller. Heavy silence permeated the room. Ahzid's Adam's apple moved up and down, showing him gulping a load of thickened saliva forming in the back of his throat. His eyes began to move right to left in his deep-set eye sockets with his bushy eyebrows hanging over them, like he was looking for a way out of the room.

Ahzid got up and began to walk away from him, but after a few steps, he stopped and turned around. "I don't know what, if anything, you're implying, But I don't have the time to listen to this nonsense. I need to finish preparing for today's implant cases, which begin in less than thirty minutes in case you haven't noticed."

"Ahzid, it turns out that in every case that you were not responsible for loading the seeds and helping me in the OR, but Buzz was, the cases came out as expected—successfully cured! Only your cases were the ones that failed ... Now don't you find that at all curious? I sure as hell do." Miller stared at Ahzid, who did not show any response. "Did you hear me, Ahzid? Is there something you're not telling me?"

Ahzid put his fist under his chin, pressed his lips together hard, and sat back down in his desk chair and began fidgeting with the pencil and paper on the desk. "We have this case coming up. I need the time to finish preparing for it. Jake, let's agree to talk about this after the case."

Dr. Miller folded his arms, sat on the desk, and crossed his legs. "How do I know I can trust you, Ahzid? I just told you that you seem to be the only variable difference between the cases."

"You know you can trust me. We go way back."

Miller stood, moved in front of Ahzid, and extended his hand to him to shake. "I know we go way back, and that's why I have a hard time believing what the charts seem to show. You give me your word that you have nothing to do with the deaths of our implant patients?"

Ahzid stood and extended his hand back to him. "You have my word on that." They shook hands for several seconds.

"Okay then, but I want to talk more with you at the end of today's cases, so don't go anywhere."

"Not planning to. Where would I go?"

Miller nodded. *That's what I'm going to figure out.* "Okay, meet you shortly in the operating room for our case. I have to go meet with our CEO now in his office." Dr. Miller then left.

CHAPTER 4: AHZID'S ESCAPE

THE MOMENT DR. MILLER LEFT, AHZID BEGAN TO QUIVER, AND his legs and hands could not stop shaking. He quickly looked out into the hallway, closed the door, and sat down. He tried holding his legs down, but he could not stop them from shaking. A cold sweat ran through his body like he had just been pulled from icy waters.

He picked up the phone on his desk and called. "Hello, Mohammed. This is Ahzid."

A cough came over the speaker piece, blasting Ahzid's ear. "What are you doing calling me on this phone? Where are you?"

Ahzid began to pace back and forth in front of his desk. "Mohammed, he's onto us. It's only a matter of time before he figures things out."

"Calm down, Ahzid. What are you talking about? Who's onto us?"

"Miller! He knows about everything. I just talked to him in my office."

"He knows nothing. What are you talking about?"

"He just told me that he knows that I'm involved with the implant patients dying."

"Did he say that?"

Ahzid sat down on his desk. "Not exactly, but that's what he meant."

"Ahzid, did he say why he thinks that?"

"Well. Kind of. Something about how I'm connected on his charts and diagrams that he made with all the patients dying, but—"

"If he didn't say he knows for sure and exactly how, then he knows nothing. He is grasping at straws."

He stood up again and began chewing at his nails. "I don't care. I have to get out of here. I cannot do the cases today with him."

"Then what about the sources, Ahzid?"

"Everything is taken care of for today's cases."

"What about the others?"

Ahzid started to pace again, still chewing at his fingernails. "I will have to come back for the others."

"Okay. Okay. Just come to the farm. You'll be safe here."

"What about my family?"

"Pick them up and bring them here too."

"I'm scared, Mohammed. For the first time with all this. It's like the reality of it all finally hit me or something."

"You'll be fine. I don't think he knows much, as smart as he is, but I agree that it may be time to move to the next phase of the plan. Just take everything with you. Everything else stays the same, according to plan."

"Yes, all right. I'll do that. I'm getting out of here now." He hung up the phone and quickly began grabbing things out of his desk and dropping things at the same time. He could barely hold on to the things he grabbed as he was still shaking so badly. He stuffed everything into his briefcase. Papers were literally hanging out of it. He then removed the sword off the wall, taking it out of its glass case, walked briskly to the isotope room, and stuffed the sword into one of the radioactive containers called Pigs. He gave a cursory look around the office and darted out, all the while looking both ahead of him and behind him down the hallway, heading toward the exit door in the back of the department leading to the parking lot. He opened the door with a thrust of the door rail. "Ahhhhhhh!" screamed Ahzid, and he dropped his briefcase. Papers stuffed into the open briefcase flew out and all over the ground outside. While bending down to pick them up, he looked up and, standing just outside on the other side of the door, saw Buzz, who was just coming in to work. "Buzz, you scared me almost to death."

"Sorry, man. Didn't mean to spook you, Ahzid."

Ahzid continued picking up the papers. "Oh ... no. You just surprised me a little. I didn't expect you here so early, Buzz."

"I didn't expect you to be leaving this early since I knew you were doing the early implant cases with Dr. Miller, but I got worried about him when I wasn't able to reach him last night or this morning on the phone. I was hoping I would see him in here this morning. Have you seen him?"

Ahzid stood up, sweating profusely. He took his handkerchief from his coat pocket and began wiping his forehead and face. "No—I mean, yes, I just saw him. Is there a particular problem or concern?"

"I'm not sure, but you know how he is about things. Lately he just seems so upset and obsessed with the implant patients that have died. I think he's blaming himself. It's not like him not to answer his phone or return messages, so I got worried and thought I would catch him before the first case today."

"Oh." Ahzid put his handkerchief back in his pocket. "I understand."

Buzz looked concerned. "Ahzid, are you shaking—and sweating? Everything okay with you?"

"Well, I, ahhhhh—"

"And where are you off to in such a hurry? Don't you have the morning cases with Doc?"

Ahzid started to move from side to side in place. "I ah, ah … can't stay. Have to go. Urgent. Family emergency." He grabbed his briefcase off the ground and began to walk away hurriedly.

"What? Ahzid? What's going on? You're coming back, right?"

He looked askance. "Not sure if I can. Will try. Will let you know."

"Damn, hope everything is okay. Good thing I came in early, so I can cover if you can't make it back for the cases," shouted Buzz.

"Yes, yes. Good thing. Thank you. The sources in the yellow pig are all ready for the case. Got to go now. Will call you," replied Ahzid while still walking to his car.

Buzz kept watching him as Ahzid kept looking back and forth while walking away. "Never seen you so frazzled. I guess I'd better get to the OR. It's nearly time for the first case!"

Ahzid stopped and looked one last time back at Buzz before getting into his car, and this time he saw Buzz picking up some papers from the ground. In his hurried state, he had forgotten to check all around him on the ground. *I hope one of them was not the copy of the Mona Lisa.* He shook his head. *It won't matter; others would not know what to make of the lines and numbers drawn over it or the specific dates and times on it.* He then got into his car and sped off.

CHAPTER 5: PENTHOUSE PURGATORY

JAKE COULD NOT PUT THE ENCOUNTER HE JUST HAD WITH Ahzid out of his mind as he rode the hospital elevator the five flights up to the "penthouse." The hospital doctors called it that because it was the top floor of the hospital and had the plushest offices with expensive mahogany furniture and the best views of the city. *Can I trust Ahzid for today's case? He seemed so matter of fact about my accusing him of being involved with the deaths of our patients. I would have been outraged if someone had accused me. At least defend myself—that is, if I were innocent.*

As the number five lit up, the door opened, and a switch went off in Miller's brain. He instantly began thinking of why he was up on the fifth floor. *What does that pompous asshole, Dinkus, want to see me for anyway? It is so obscene here with all the plush furniture, carpeting, and mahogany walls. But it all fits. To Dinkus, everything is all about making money, not caring for patients.*

Miller stepped out of the elevator and walked up to the CEO's secretary at the far end of the floor. "I'm here to see Mr. Dinkus for our seven o'clock meeting."

"Yes, Dr. Miller. He's expecting you. You can go right in."

"Thank you." When Miller walked into the CEO's office, his first impression was its size. It had to be four times the size of his office. There across the room sat CEO Dinkus at a desk twice the size of a normal office desk, which made the small man look even smaller. Only a few papers, a phone, and a PC were on the desk.

Dinkus was on the phone and looked up for only a second to give a quick hand wave for him to come forward. Miller approached the desk and stood there waiting. He looked around the office and noticed all the "stuff" hanging on the walls and filling the shelves. Everything from big game animals to pictures of him standing with businessmen. One picture on a bookshelf directly behind Dinkus caught his attention. This one stood out because it had him in an army officer's uniform standing next to another man, also in uniform.

"I totally understand, and we are all in agreement, as we discussed earlier. I have to go now. I have Dr. Miller standing here, now right, in front of me." He hung up the phone. "Sorry about that," he said as he looked up to Miller. "I noticed you admiring my trophies and pictures."

"Admiring? Oh, the things on the wall? Ah … yeah."

Dinkus stood, walked over to one of the pictures hanging, and chuckled. "Not easy to bring down one of those bull elephants, you know." He pointed to the photo of him having his foot on the downed elephant with the rifle in his hands.

"No doubt," said Miller. "The one with you in uniform did catch my eye."

Dinkus looked for the picture that Miller referred to. "What? Uniform? Oh. Yes. I am very proud of that." He went over and picked it up off the shelf, held it, and admired it for a moment. "That was my good friend and classmate with me after graduating from West Point. He and I remain the best of friends. We served in the first Desert Storm together. He's now a big general over there." He looked at Dr. Miller. "Bet you didn't think of me as a West Pointer, did you?"

"Well, I …"

"I know. I know. A lot of people find it hard to believe that someone as talented as I am with business and such would ever have been involved with the military. But it has taught me some very good lessons, and given me connections too. For example, did you know that I went on to Wall Street before coming here as the CEO?"

Miller stood there with his hands clasped behind his back. *Does this idiot ever stop talking about himself?*

"You're shocked. I can see it in your face. Don't worry. You don't have to answer. I know what you're thinking." Dinkus then sat back at his desk. "But I didn't have you come here today to talk about me. Please sit down."

Miller sat in one of the chairs in front of his desk. The chair was so low that he had to look up at Dinkus. "I couldn't help but hear your phone conversation. Something about me, you were discussing?"

"Yes, as a matter of fact, it was about you. I suspect you don't know exactly why I have asked to talk to you."

"No, not really. You suspect right."

"How long have you been with us, Miller?"

"Several years now. Not sure of the exact—"

Dinkus sat forward at his desk and rested his arms on it in front of him. "Miller, I'll be straight with you."

Miller fought not to laugh. *Yeah, right. This guy wouldn't know straight if a wooden ruler hit him in the face.*

"Dr. Miller, we have a problem here, a big problem."

Miller furrowed his eyebrows and looked at him askance. "Really. And what might that be?"

"Your patients."

"My patients? What about them?"

"Well … they seem to be dying—when they should not be." Dinkus sat back in his chair and began twirling his thumbs. "If you know what I mean."

Miller straightened up in his chair. "Yes, I am well aware of—"

"People are concerned—important people. I'm concerned."

"I understand, but—"

"Did you see the paper this morning?" He poked the paper on his desk.

Miller looked down at the paper and began to reach for it. "No, I didn't get a chance."

Dinkus pulled the paper off the desk and into his lap. He sat back again in his chair and began to swivel right, then left, a few inches each way, like he was trying to burn off his nervous energy. "Well, somehow they have gotten wind of the unexpected deaths of your patients and know all about our investigation."

Miller gave him a questioning look. "Investigation? I wasn't aware of any investigation."

"Don't get me wrong. I'm not blaming you directly. Your career here has been impeccable—up until now, that is."

"What do you mean up until—"

"I'm sure you can appreciate the situation here. We have to think of the hospital … and our patients of course."

Miller leaned forward and hit the desk with his fist. "What the hell are you talking about, Dinkus? Speak directly to me, not in riddles."

The fist hitting the desk startled Dinkus. He took the hanky out of his pocket and began to dab his forehead. "All right then. I'll just say it. You're suspended as of right now."

"But—"

"You will have to cancel all your clinical duties immediately."

Miller shot up and put his hands on his hips. "I can't just cancel my patients."

"You can reschedule them after our investigation shows that you're competent—which I have every confidence they will."

"But, I have an OR case this morning."

"Not now, you don't."

Miller leaned forward with fire in his eyes and pounded the desk again, but this time so hard that it knocked over the one picture on his desk. He reached over the table, grabbed Dinkus by the collar, and pulled him out of his chair and onto the desk. "Are trying to destroy my career and our hospital program? This is my job. Patients depend on me. You can't stop me from treating my patients without at least a medical committee review!"

Dinkus, with his eyes wide open, said, "Ah, ah, I can do whatever I want." Miller let go of him, and he crawled back into his chair and pushed his chair with him in it away from his desk--and from Miller.

Miller stood straight. "You are truly a very small man, Dinkus, not only on the outside but also from the inside."

Dinkus cleared his throat with a dry cough and adjusted his collar and tie. "Miller, I am going to recommend to the board that you be fired immediately, and if you don't leave now, I will have security escort you out."

"I'll leave, but this isn't over." He kicked his chair out of his way, gave a nasty last look at Dinkus, and marched to the door, slamming it on his way out. He went straight to the OR to change into scrubs for his first case that morning, a radioactive seed implant on a patient with prostate cancer. *Screw that asshole. He can't stop me for taking care of my patients. Just let him try.*

When Miller got to the operating room floor, it looked like a combination of a busy train station and a casino. People hustling every which way. Patients lined up in the preoperative holding areas, each getting prepped for whatever surgical procedure they were to have. Nurses, anesthetists, doctors, all doing their preparatory work for the first patient on their schedule. And no windows to the outside world, only bright lights everywhere, giving it the feeling of always being daytime. And no clocks to be found to reveal whatever the hour was. Bells going off and on from the monitoring equipment of the patients, like the sound of slot machines going off suddenly to announce a winner. Only no one was giving or getting money here.

Tension was created by the nervous energy of the staff and the patients, with things like attempting to insert an intravenous line into an arm vein or place a Foley catheter into someone's bladder. Medicine showed itself to be as much a business as it was anything else, with the obvious pressure to keep things moving in the operating room so each case was on time; time was money, and each case was run like the trains at the station to get them in and out on time.

Mr. Smith, the first case for Miller, lay in Bay 6, just outside OR 9, the OR suite dedicated for all the radiation procedures. It had all the necessary equipment for securing, placing, and monitoring radiation.

Miller approached Bay 6 and saw the nurse beginning to remove an IV.

"Jane, you can just leave that IV right where it is."

She looked up at him. "Dr. Miller! Someone called and said—I, I was just told, not a minute ago, that you were not coming and that your cases for today were cancelled."

Miller put his arm around her and whispered to her, "Does it look like I'm not coming?"

Jane looked around to see if anybody else was near them. "Well, I guess—"

"Good. Now that's settled. Let's get Mr. Smith here in the OR for his implant." He turned to his patient, who had been watching the exchange between Dr. Miller and the nurse.

Miller bent over to speak with his patient. "Bill, my friend, how are you doing this morning?"

"To be honest, I've been better."

"Sorry for all this commotion. There was just a misunderstanding with the scheduling."

"Tell me honestly, Doc. Is this really gonna work? I hate to ask, but I gotta tell ya, a few of my buddies in the coffee shop have been talking about the patients in the paper that have died with this treatment ... and, well, maybe this isn't such a good idea."

Dr. Miller gloved his hand over his patient's hand, sat down on the edge of the bed, and looked at him straight in the eyes. "Bill, I will be honest with you too. We never really know for sure, as we talked about before, but we know that doing this procedure gives us the best chance of curing you of your cancer." Bill looked down to collect his thoughts. Then he looked up at Dr. Miller and smiled. "Well, you know I have the most faith in you ... so ... let's do it."

Miller slapped Bill's leg and stood up. "That's the attitude I love about you, Bill."

The nurse who had been waiting patiently to bring him into the OR was given approval when Miller nodded his head for her to take him into the OR. Miller followed behind her into the OR while reviewing Bill's chart. His wooden clogs made two loud clicks when he stopped dead in his tracks, and his mouth hung open after seeing Buzz sitting at the table with the laptop computer set up with all the radioisotopes and implant equipment. "Buzz? What are you doing here? I thought Ahzid was doing the case with me."

"Oh man. I thought so too until I ran into him running out of the building earlier. He mumbled something about a family emergency."

"Emergency? I talked with him this morning in his office, and he didn't say anything about any family emergency."

Buzz shrugged his shoulders. "Maybe it happened after he saw you. Good thing I decided to come in earlier than usual. He had prepared everything for the case, so I just brought everything up, figuring you would need me to do it with you." Buzz sat back down and thought for a moment. "Oh, yeah. Another odd thing he said."

Dr. Miller moved closer to Buzz. "What? What else did he say?"

"It was very strange, but must be because he was so frazzled with his family thing and all."

Miller got into his face. "Buzz! What did he say?"

"He said he prepared everything and put the sources for today's cases in the pig with the yellow label."

"Okay … and?"

"Well that doesn't make any sense, as we always put the dummy sources in the yellow-labeled pig.'"

"I guess his being confused doesn't surprise me after our little talk this morning," said Miller.

"Talk? Did you guys fight or something?"

"No, nothing physical. We fought with words. After looking over all the charts that I had shown you guys, and thanks to Bridget's pointing out to me not to look for things unique only to the patients dying, I realized that only one pattern connected all the patients dying unexpectedly."

"A pattern?"

"Yes, Buzz, a pattern, or perhaps better to say, a link to the patients that died."

Buzz looked a bit confused. "I'm sorry. I don't totally understand— but I'm sure as hell trying."

"Buzz, a pattern is something that repeats like in science or mathematics."

"I know you're a math wiz, Doc, but—"

Miller looked around the OR and saw that everyone was waiting for him to begin the case. "Buzz, we can talk more about this after this case."

"Sure. No problem."

Miller turned around and stepped up on the stool and looked over at his patient, now all prepared for his procedure. He took the first implant needle from Buzz behind him, now loaded with the radioactive seeds, held it up, and stared at it. The chart he had been reviewing almost all night flashed into his head. He remembered the only common denominator for all the patients treated with the implanted radioactive seeds whom he expected to be cured but weren't was the physicist Ahzid. The same physicist who was now suddenly missing in action.

Miller looked up at the overhead lighting; it was bright as always, making him squint. His mind began to race with pictures of Ahzid acting nervous that morning, and the picture of Ahzid holding the sword. He heard the sound of the respirator pulsing rhythmically in the background. Sweat dripped off his brow, and he felt a sudden chill all over his body. The sweat soaked through his scrubs as his adrenal glands poured out catecholamines.

He composed himself enough to slowly place the first needle into its designated location in the template over the patient's perineum, slide it forward just enough to tent the skin, then stopped. Without looking up, he said, "Buzz, what did you say a few minutes earlier about Ahzid's saying he put the radioactive needles in the yellow container and not the usual red one we use to indicate radiation is inside?"

"I said that I thought he misspoke since that's the one we use to indicate the needles are empty or contain dummy sources."

Miller looked behind at Buzz. "Dummy sources." Miller nodded. "Yeah, that's it."

"What? What's it?" said Buzz.

Miller pulled the needle back out and handed it to Buzz. "Buzz, quick, take the needle back and get the Geiger counter out."

Buzz sat up and looked askance. "What? Why?"

Miller clenched his fist in frustration. "Buzz, just do what I say—now!

Buzz grabbed the needle from Dr. Miller and reached underneath his table for the Geiger counter. "Okay. Okay. I have it out and on. Now what?"

"Check the implant needle sources."

"What? Are you kidding?"

Miller stepped off his stool and stood right in front of Buzz. "Do I look like I'm kidding? Do it now."

Buzz shook his head and began checking the needle with the Geiger counter. "Holy shit. I guess you're not kidding."

No sounds came from the counter, and Miller looked over Buzz's shoulder to see the readings on the counter. "No activity? Right?"

"Right." He placed the Geiger counter on the table. "But, how did you know?"

"I didn't know for sure. Until now." He looked around at the OR staff who had been essentially silent and mystified with the whole exchange. "We are going to abort the case!"

"Abort the—" said Buzz.

Miller turned quickly back at Buzz. "Yes. Abort the case now! There is no radiation in the needles, so we have to get the patient off the table for now."

"Miller, what do you mean 'no radiation'?" said the anesthesiologist who had risen from his place behind the drape covering the patient at the head of the table.

"Like I just said. There isn't any radiation in the needles. They're what we call dummy sources. So wake him up and get him off the table." Miller then looked around at everyone. "Listen, everyone, I'm sorry. I know this seems crazy, and frankly it is, but I'll explain everything later."

One of the nurses stepped forward. "But, Dr. Miller, what are we going to do about the case?"

"I'm not really sure right now. All I know is that I have to find out what the hell is going on with my patients." Dr. Miller walked over to the OR door, swung it open, and quickly disappeared out into the hallway.

Buzz ran after him and caught up with him just as the elevator door opened and Dr. Miller stepped inside. "Doc. Wait up!"

Dr. Miller hit the Hold button and looked out to see Buzz running down the hall. "Buzz, what are you doing? Trust me, I'll fill you in on everything—though I'm not sure what exactly I know for sure yet. All I know right now is I have to investigate a hunch on what and who is behind what happened at today's case with the radiation sources being missing and quite possibly linked to our other patients who have died unexpectedly."

"What about Bill?" said Buzz.

Miller put a hand on Buzz's shoulder. "Buzz, I need you to help me out on this."

Buzz stepped closer to the door and put one of his feet against the door to hold it open. "No problem. Anything. Just name it."

"I need you to talk with Bill and his family to try to explain that something was wrong with the equipment, so we have to reschedule. Whatever you do, don't talk about the missing radiation seeds."

"Got it,. Not to worry."

"And page me when the patient is stable and out of recovery. I want to talk with him as soon as I can get back. He won't be happy, but I think

I know him well enough that he'll understand. The bigger problem is how to explain to them why I aborted it in the first place."

"Does this have something to do with the pattern you mentioned earlier to me? Maybe I can help."

"Yes, I believe it does. And thank you for offering, but I don't want to get you or anyone else involved until I'm more sure about things. Now, I need to call someone who may be able to help us understand what happened here today. I'll call you later today. Okay?"

"Okay. But, I gotta tell you that you're making me nervous. This seems pretty serious and even dangerous. Whatever you're going to do, you be careful. You hear me?" Buzz then stepped back and away from the door.

Miller stepped back into the elevator and let go of the Hold button. "I hear you, my friend, and thanks again. I promise I'll be careful." These were the last words he said as the elevator door slowly closed in front of him.

CHAPTER 6: THE SHOWDOWN

DR. MILLER RUSHED OUT OF THE HOSPITAL TO HIS CAR PARKED in the garage and pulled out his cell phone to call Ahzid. When he did not answer, Miller called his home. Ahzid's wife answered, and she told him that he had left to go to prayers at his mosque. When she asked if everything was all right, Miller didn't let on anything was wrong, as it was obvious to him that Ahzid did not tell his wife of anything that was going on between them.

He followed the directions she had given him to the mosque. The day was a gray, overcast one, with rain called for later. The streets were mostly empty of people. He waited for Ahzid outside in his car, for he knew it would be better not to go inside to raise suspicion. After several minutes, the doors of the mosque opened and men began to exit. Miller watched carefully, and when he saw Ahzid coming out, he left his car and walked to the expansive granite stairs leading to the front of the mosque.

Ahzid walked down the stairs and talked with men on either side of him. When he looked down and saw Miller standing there looking up at him, he slowed to a complete stop and turned to one of the men by his side and continued talking. He obviously was trying to avoid Miller.

Miller began to walk up the stairs toward him. "Ahzid," he shouted.

Ahzid did not turn but kept on talking to the man to his right.

Miller continued up the steps until he was standing next to Ahzid. He tapped Ahzid on the shoulder. "Hello, Ahzid."

Ahzid turned to Miller. "Jake! What are you doing here?"

Miller climbed the next step to be at eye level with him. "I came to talk with you. Your wife was kind enough to tell me where I could find you and how to get here. Can we talk?"

"Well … I don't know. I was —"

"Come on, Ahzid. As you yourself have said, you and I go way back. How many times did I protect you when we were at St. Pete's together? And when nobody else would hire you when you came back to the States, I did. I put my neck on the line to defend you and get you this job." Miller moved closer to him. "And this is how you act? You betray everyone, the staff, the patients, and even me and my trust for you."

Ahzid folded his lower lip under his upper and stared off into the distance in thought.

"Hey, knucklehead," said one of the bullies. "I'm gonna give you a break since you just got here at the orphanage." He grabbed Ahzid by the collar. "You gots any money on ya?"

"Ahhhh. No. I don't have any money."

Jacob appeared from behind the building. "Leave him alone."

The boy let go of Ahzid. "Hey, Miller, you ain't going to be around to protect him forever." He and the other boys with him walked away.

Jacob walked up to Ahzid. "You okay?"

"Ah, I think so. Thanks for helping me out."

"No problem. We have to stick together to get through being at this place."

"Hey, Ahzid. Did you hear anything I just said?"

Ahzid shook his head. "Now wait a minute, Jake. Don't jump to conclusions. I will talk with you. I do owe you that much." Ahzid turned to the man he had been talking with. "Mohammed, I need to talk to this man for a minute. The other two can wait nearby. Wait for me in the car." He then turned back to Miller. "All right, Jake, tell me what's on your mind."

"Ahzid, I know you are at least involved with the missing seeds. The case today had no active radiation in the needles. My theory is correct. Isn't it?"

Ahzid put his hands on his hips. "Theory? What theory is that?"

"You're stealing the radiation. But why? I can't believe you would do this!"

"You're very perceptive," said Ahzid. He folded his arms across his chest. "I cannot tell you anything about this. But, as an old friend, I would tell you only not to look into this any further."

Miller grabbed Ahmed's arms and shook him once. "Why, Ahzid? Of all the people that I know, I thought you were one of the few people I could truly trust."

Suddenly, two very large Middle Eastern men appeared, grabbed Miller, and held him tightly.

He resisted, trying to get away from them, and yelled. "Where are the seeds? Why are they being stolen? Who's doing this with you?"

Ahzid stepped forward and looked into Miller's eyes. "My old friend. You had better be careful with what you say and what you do. Yes, I did take them, and I cannot tell you any more than that. I tell you this, so you can know that it is not you or your skill involved with the deaths of your patients. You are correct in that those who died did so because they had no radiation in them."

"But why, Ahmed? Why would you do such a thing? Do you need money?"

Ahzid guffawed. "You Americans always think in terms of money. No, my friend. You would not understand." He turned to walk away but then turned back around. "I can tell you only that they are needed for a much bigger purpose than saving a few lives here on earth."

Miller tried shaking the arms off him again but to no avail. "Listen, I'm going to find out what's going on. I have to get those radiation seeds back to prove how they died. You know me. I'll find out, and I'll have to come after you and whoever else is behind this."

Ahzid chuckled. "My friend, I do not want any harm to come of you, so listen to me and the words I am about to speak." He again went close enough to Miller to feel his breath. "If you come after me, if you come after anyone, if you get involved with any of this ... you will surely die." They stared at each other for a moment. "I tell you this not because I hate you. But because I love you." He looked at the two men holding Miller. "Let him go."

The two men holding Miller hesitated for a moment and looked at each other.

Ahzid looked up at them. "It's okay. I'll be all right."

They let go of Miller, and he brushed his arms off, stood up straight, and extended his arms out to Ahzid. "I love you too, Ahzid. How about a hug?"

Ahzid smiled and nodded. "My dear friend."

They then hugged and patted each other on the back. For a moment, time seemed to stand still. Dr. Miller remembered that they would do the same thing as kids in the orphanage when they needed affection and love that no one else could or would give to them. They both pulled their heads backward and looked at each other while in an embrace and smiled. Miller thought how normally he would be uncomfortable embracing another man. It was definitely outside his comfort zone.

They turned with arms around each other and walked down the steep steps of the mosque. Suddenly they heard what sounded like popcorn popping. Two cars raced by them with men hanging out the windows. One of them had something in his hands and shouted, "You fucking towel heads, get the fuck out of here and America before we kill all of you." They gave the finger to them, laughed hysterically, and fired the guns they held.

"Get down! They're shooting at us!" yelled Ahzid.

Miller dove to the ground with everyone else and scraped his face, hands, and legs on the cement. "Who were they shooting at?" said Miller, after they drove by.

"Us! Muslims. Who else? We're harassed all the time," said Ahzid.

They were lying on the ground together panting, with Miller and Ahzid looking at each other. "It seemed to me that the gun was pointed right at me," said Jake.

One of Ahzid's bodyguards stood up, pulled a pistol from inside his coat, and fired it at the cars, hitting the back of one as they sped away.

"No, put the gun away," said Ahmed. He then turned quickly to Miller. "Do you see how misunderstood and hated we are, and what we have to deal with just for practicing our faith?"

"I see it now. I see and feel it now." Miller looked back at the one bodyguard who stood there silently with his hands folded in front of him. Miller now realized that he had seen him someplace earlier. With his being over six feet tall and broader at the shoulders than at his waist, he stood out among all of the other Muslim men. He also had linear scars across his cheeks that were somewhat obscured under his scruffy beard.

"My friend, it is true that we share a bond that nothing can ever sever," said Ahzid. He stood up, extended an arm, and helped Miller to his feet. "As you say, we both lost our families, and we found each other at a time when we both needed somebody we could trust. But when we escaped, we escaped only to this earthly world. I have now found a way to heaven. We both made it out of the orphanage, but mostly with God's help and the talent he gave us. I did not know why I lost my parents until many years later when I researched it."

"What did you find out?"

"My father died for the jihad, fighting for our holy land, and my mother gave her life as well in the cause for Allah and to avenge the infidels."

"What is this jihad?'" said Miller.

"Jihad can mean something different for different people. In general, it is Arabic meaning 'to struggle, to fight,' depending on the context. In my father's case, it was a holy war."

From down the street, sirens began blaring, and lights flashed from police, fire, and emergency vehicles screaming into the area of the mosque. Miller turned to watch them swarm the area. He then turned back to see Ahzid being rushed into a car by his two bodyguards.

The emergency medical team ran to attend first to those involved with the drive-by shooting, including Miller. While he was being attended to for any wounds, mostly cuts and bruising, a man with thick, black 1950s-looking glasses approached him, holding out his detective badge.

"Dr. Miller?"

Sitting on a bench being bandaged on his face, arms, and legs for abrasions, Miller looked up at him and wiped his eyes clear to see the badge better. "Yes. I'm Dr. Miller."

"I'm Detective Fifer. Are you doing okay?"

Miller patted himself. "Yes, I think so. Just a bit shook up. It's not every day I get shot at." He looked down at the EMT attending to his wounds.

The EMT looked up at Miller, winked and then looked over at the detective. "He'll be okay. Just some minor abrasions and cuts."

Miller winked back at him. "Nice job. I think I'll make it after all."

The detective gestured to sit down next to him. "May I?"

"Yes, please, sit down." Miller chuckled. "These seats are not in demand much today."

"Thank you, and, no, I wouldn't think you would be shot at very often. Do you mind if I ask you a few questions?"

"No. Go ahead."

The EMT interrupted them. "I have to go attend to others. I think everything looks fine. If you have any problems or questions, please call your doctor or go to the nearest emergency room."

Miller looked up at him out of the corner of his eye. "I'll do that. Thanks."

"Dr. Miller, what exactly did you see?" asked the detective.

"A couple of cars shooting at us."

"Okay. Did you see any of those doing the shooting, enough to recognize them?"

Miller chuckled. "Ahhh, no. I was being shot at, remember? Maybe you're different, but for me, the last thing I care about when a gun is pointed at me and bullets are flying out of it is to see if the shooter's tie and shirt match."

Fifer chuckled also. "Okay. Good point. But you never know. You would be surprised at what people see. Even when being attacked."

"I did see Ahzid, the person I came to see and was talking with, being hustled into a black SUV limo by others with him."

"Ahzid? Henchman? We'll get to that in a minute. Anything else? Plates on the car? Other faces inside it?"

"Unfortunately, no. Guess I was still in kind of shock at the whole thing. Surreal, if you know what I mean."

"I can understand. I have been shot at a few—"

Miller snapped his fingers. "Wait. There was something strange that I remember about the car."

Fifer leaned closer to Miller. "What? What was strange about it?"

"Mud."

Fifer looked askance. "What do you mean?"

"The SUV. It was covered in mud, mostly dried, but it looked like one of those jeeps the kids take to go off-roading. I remember thinking how odd that an expensive SUV limo would have all that dirt covering it."

"Hmm. Interesting," said the detective as he jotted all this onto his little notepad.

A dark sedan, rusted and dented everywhere, then pulled up along the curb where Miller and Fifer sat. It stopped with a sudden jerk forward. The front passenger side door swung open, and a glob of spit flew onto the side walk. "Jesus fuckin' Christ. You trying to get me sick, Schtinkcoff?" yelled an unkempt man wearing a wrinkled trench coat, sitting in the passenger front seat. He had a haggard face and silver hair with yellowed streaks greased back, and half of a cigar hanging off his lower lip. He swung his legs out of the car, grabbed the handle overhead, and ducked his head as he stepped out and onto the street. He then truned around and looked back into the car at the driver. " You keep driving like that, Schtinkcoff, and I will get me a new driver." He turned back around. He was rather tall, bean-pole appearing, and walked straight toward them with a slight gimp. "Fifer, whatcha got? I hear we had a real Wild West-type shootin' here, Matt Dillon style. Anybody hurt? Or for that matter, dead?"

"No, sir, fortunately no one was seriously hurt." Fifer gestured to Miller. "Sir, this is Dr. Miller." Then he gestured to his boss. "Dr. Miller, this is Lieutenant Detective Crusky."

Miller extended his hand to him and got a quick, barely-touching-his-hand rub back. But it was enough time for Miller to notice the yellowing and clubbing of his nails. And his bluish lips. *Blue bloater.* "Nice to meet you—"

The lieutenant turned away and looked around the surrounding area. "Yeah, yeah. Same here." He turned back to look at Miller and spat on the ground out of one corner of his mouth. "Were you involved with the shooting?"

Miller looked annoyingly at the glob of spit on the ground, not a foot from his feet. "Yes. If you mean being a target as being involved. It sure looked like they were shooting at me and the others with me that had just come out of the mosque."

The lieutenant turned, hocked up a big chunk of saliva, turned to his head to face the street, and spat it out like he was trying to win a distance contest with it. He stared at it like he was satisfied with his efforts and turned back to Miller. "Pardon me, young fella, for saying so, but you don't look like all the others here. You know. No robe or head towel. What were you doing here anyway? Were you in the mosque?"

Miller's face still wore the cringe it had from the other man's spitting. "No, I was waiting for someone I know."

"Excuse me," said the lieutenant. He turned around and blew out of one side of his nose, while pressing on the other nostril with his finger. "Damn sinus congestion." The lieutenant chuckled. "My mom always taught me to be polite and say excuse me before using the air hanky." Fifer looked curiously at Miller. "So why were you waiting for him ... this friend of yours?"

"I needed to talk with him."

"About what?"

Miller threw down his hands to his sides. "Something very personal. I would rather not say."

The lieutenant turned to look at Detective Fifer. "You getting all this on your little notepad there, Fifer?"

Fifer nodded and raised the pad and pen he was using to jot down notes.

"Good." He straightened his back and turned back to face Miller. "Personal, huh. What is his name?" He looked at him with his thick eyebrows raised. "Or is that something you would rather not say either?"

"Ahzid. His name is Ahzid."

"First or last name?"

"First. His full name is Ahzid Mohammed Ahzeez."

"I should have figured. Half these guys have 'Mohammed' somewhere in their name."

Miller stood up and brushed himself off. "Look, Lieutenant. I really need to get back to the hospital."

"Hospital? So you are a real doctor? Not one of those 'Phd-ers'?"

Fifer stepped in front of Miller to semi-block him from Crusky's view. "Sir, I can finish my interview with Dr. Miller and go over my findings with you later if you like."

"Yeah. Yeah. You do that, Fifer." Suddenly a big sneeze came out of the lieutenant's mouth and nostrils, as loud as could be.

"Sir, here's a hankie," said Fifer.

"Nah, I got my own," he said as he leaned to one side, blowing his nose one side at a time into the air. He chuckled. "Remember? It's called an air hankie. Does just fine. And keeps the laundry bill down and the landfills less full."

Miller and Fifer both raised one corner of their lips and raised eyebrows in dismay.

"I'll take another look around here and see what I can come with." He swirled the cigar around in his mouth with the total control of a circus juggler. "Dr. Miller, we may want to go over your statement with you in the future, so let my office know if you plan to leave town. Okay?"

Miller shot a surprised look at him. "Sure. No problem. " Miller looked in disbelief as the detective walked away. *Is he for real?*

Detective Fifer walked up to Miller. "I see you look a bit dismayed. Don't be too hard on him. His been doing this for years, and he really knows his stuff."

"He's a bit judgmental, don't you think, Detective?"

"The years can make a person jaded. His divorce, I'm told, took a lot out of him. And the alcohol and tobacco can be like waves crashing on the rocks. It may take years, but it gradually wears them down. I'm told he was quite an athlete and man's man at one time."

Miller stood there in thought. *Stress? Drinking? Smoking? Is that where I'm headed with all this stress and abuse of myself?*

Fifer reached in his pocket and took out one of his business cards. "Dr. Miller, take this and call me if you think of anything else. We'll be in touch to go over things that happened in more detail. Be careful if you really think the bullets were after you. I tend to doubt it though. There is a lot of hatred for the Muslims around here after 9/11, the Boston bombings a few years ago, and the wars going on. I think it was some hotheads just trying to scare them, particularly with the racial slurs they were yelling."

Miller looked at him, though appearing to look right through him.

Fifer waved his hand in front of Miller's face. "Dr. Miller?"

"Huh, oh, yes." He took the business card from Fifer. "Thank you, Lieutenant. I'll call you if I need to."

Fifer walked away, leaving Miller standing there in thought. *I think those guys were after me and no one else. But why? And for what reason? Is this what Ahzid meant when he said not to investigate this? Could I be getting close to something about the stolen radiation that someone does not want me to find?*

CHAPTER 7: ST FRANCIS HOMECOMING

WHEN MILLER BEGAN HYPERVENTILATING, THINKING OF THE shooting, he thought about what the therapist he had been seeing years before had told him. *When stress overcomes you, and you feel as though you are under attack, close your eyes and picture yourself surrounded by only those who are on your side, those who tell you that you are a good person and that everything will be okay. Your circle of trust.*

He then left the mosque area and drove to the only place where he could find people he knew like that—St. Francis House. He had worked there as a medical student helping with mostly the medical care of the clients there, and he knew Father O'Brien, its director, was still there, as well as many of the clients he had worked with.

When he got to the St. Francis House, he parked across the street, sat, and stared at it for a while. He watched the homeless loiter in front and go in and out. He almost had forgotten how busy a place it could be. It was lunchtime, which was a very active time. Many of the homeless would come for their lunch and then relax inside for a while, to watch the television or play table games, read a book, or visit the medical clinic. After several minutes of watching, he got out of his car and walked up to the front door.

As he got closer to it, his breathing increased, and his palms moistened. A bolus of acid blasted up to the back of his throat, giving him nausea. And when he finally reached it, the stench of urine, beer, and puke filled the air and burned his nostrils. The staccato banging of a nearby jackhammer tearing up the street dominated all the surrounding sounds; it reverberated in his head such that he could barely hear the taxi drivers honking their horns with the voices of nearby pedestrians mixed in. Nothing had changed from the earlier years that he worked there. And why should it? Few cared about the place. It was an area of the downtrodden. The forgotten.

Fifteen years before, while a medical student at Harvard, he'd worked at the St. Francis House taking care of the homeless patients. It had been one of the most eye-opening and rewarding experiences of his life. He'd witnessed, firsthand, human suffering and tragedy.

Now, as he stood at the front door, the sad memories of the people, good people that had fallen down to the bottom of the barrel, flashed in his head. There was the former president of a big Boston bank and a former cop, to list a couple. He and some of those hanging around outside shared passing glances, but he did not see anybody he recognized. That all changed when he walked through the door. Not ten feet away stood Father O'Brien talking with someone. Despite having more silver in his beard and hair, he wore the same wire-rimmed glasses on the tip of his nose. Jacob gasped. "Father!" said Jacob. They both sprung looks of surprise and joy and approached each other with extended arms. They embraced tightly for a moment and gave pats on each other's backs. They then loosened their grip, enough for them to look at each other.

"You look fantastic, Jacob," said Father O'Brien. He showed so much teeth when he smiled that the room seemed to light up.

"You too, Father."

When they finally stopped hugging, Father Obrien put his hands on Miller's shoulders. "Tell me, son. What brings you down here? Not that I'm not excited to see you whatever the reason. And how are things going for you?" Father O'Brien shook his head. "I'm sorry, son. I'll stop asking questions and let you answer. I'm just so excited to see you and I have so many questions to ask you."

Miller nodded. "I'm doing great, Father. Things couldn't be better."

Father O'Brien slid his hands off Miller's shoulders, stepped a half-step backward, and lowered his head while not taking his eyes off him. "Jacob … I don't mean just your work."

Miller tilted his head slightly, raised his eyebrows, and smiled. "Father, I know what you mean."

Father O'Brien then put one hand again on Jake's shoulder and smiled again. "So you're still in therapy then?"

Miller now backed up a step, causing Father O'Brien's arm to fall off his shoulder. "Actually, no."

Father O'Brien folded his arms and looked askance. "Really, son. Why?"

Miller looked around him to see who was nearby, then back at Father O'Brien. "I don't think I need it anymore."

"Oh? And why—"

Miller put his hands in his pockets and looked down to the ground. "I know. I know. You think that it's a lifelong thing that's needed." He looked up at O'Brien. "But I disagree."

Father O'Brien moved a sofa chair closer to one in the corner nearby and gestured for him to sit down. None of the clients sat near them, so they had privacy to talk.

Jake sat first. "Thank you, Father."

"Well then. How are you doing with other things?"

"Well, I've been able to avoid some things but am still struggling with others."

O'Brien leaned forward. "Like what?"

"I still need an occasional cigarette and an occasional scotch to get me through the day. But that's not such bad vices to have, considering everything I've been through and what I could be doing."

Father O'Brien gave an agreeing nod of his head and patted him on the hand. "That is true. Lord knows, things can always be worse."

"But this is not what I came here to talk to you about. I want to talk with someone who can help, but only someone whom I can trust." Jake leaned closer to O'Brien. " Father, I need your advice on something." Miller looked around them. "Something that may involve bad things."

Father smiled, moved closer, and hunched over to Jacob's ear. "First, I am ecstatic that you chose me as the one you can trust. Because you always can. And second, how bad is bad?"

"Very bad." Miller looked around them. "Robbery, for example."

Father O'Brien straightened up. "What?"

"And murder."

Father O'Brien's eyes opened wide. "Perhaps we should go somewhere more private." He stood up and waved for him to follow.

They went upstairs to his office off the hallway, opened the door, went in with Miller behind him, then gestured for Miller to sit in one of the chairs at a table in the middle of the office. The office was of modest size and simple. A couch was at one end and a small refrigerator, sink, stove, and desk at the other. "I'll close the door to give us some privacy."

They sat across from each other. "Father, obviously you're trained in Catholicism. But do you know anything about the Muslim faith?"

He leaned onto the table. "Well of course I'm not formally trained in the faith, but I do know a fair amount through my interactions with the church and learning on my own. And I have friends and know others who are of that faith." Father Obrien smiled. "Son, why do you ask that?"

"I know little about it, but I have this sense—a hunch— I know why Ahzid's been acting differently since he returned from the Middle East. He returned from Pakistan about a year ago to come work with me after he had left his position at MIT as a physicist about a year earlier to work in his home country of Pakistan. And the missing—stolen—radiation seeds and the shooting at the mosque all are connected somehow." Jake took in a deep breath, leaned forward, and put his hands on his forehead.

Father O'Brien looked at Jacob with his mouth open. He then stood up, walked to the sink, and poured himself a glass of water. He took a deep breath and sat back down.

"Father, I know that I mentioned some of these things quickly on my way here today over the phone to you, but I really needed to talk to you in person about all this."

O'Brien took a big gulp of water from his glass. "How are they connected?"

Miller looked up and sat back. "I remembered a lecture I attended at one of our radiation oncology meetings on terrorism that discussed the potential for using radiation to build bombs, what they called 'dirty bombs', using various types of radiation isotopes."

"And you think Ahzid is involved with something like that?"

"Not the Ahzid that you and I know. Not the Ahzid I grew up with at St. Pete's, but if you met the Ahzid I know now, he's very different. I'm not absolutely sure about anything, but his recent behavior is alarming.

And the fact that I believe—no, I know for a fact that he's involved with stealing the radiation seeds-- is very disturbing."

"How do you know for sure that he's involved? Did Ahzid tell you that?"

Miller leaned forward, put his arms on the table, and looked directly at Father O'Brien. "Yes, as a matter of fact, he did, when I was with him at his mosque."

"Jacob, this doesn't sound like you."

"Me? What do you mean, Father?"

"Well, I'm not in your shoes, so maybe I shouldn't be saying anything."

The table was small so he did not have to reach very far, but Miller reached over and put a hand on Father O'Brien's shoulder. "No, no. I value your opinion. This is why I came here. You're in my circle of trusting friends."

Father O'Brien smiled at him. "Well. You need to do what your heart is telling you. And it sounds to me like it's telling you to find out what exactly is going on—and to stop it if it is something bad."

"Yes, you're right." Miller sat up straight, then stood up and walked a few feet away. He turned back around. "But ..."

Father O'Brien stood and stepped closer to Miller. "But what?" he said, raising his eyebrows.

"But part of me feels everything I have worked for, building my practice, my research and my reputation—it could all be destroyed." Miller walked back to the table, flopped back into the chair, and laid his head down on his folded arms that covered up almost the whole table. An anxious quiet took over.

O'Brien's voice broke the tension. "What about others?"

Miller looked up at him without actually lifting his head off his folded arms. His eyelids alone rose so that he could see above his arms.

Father O'Brien sat back down and looked over at Miller. "The things you said are all important things, indeed. But they're all things that deal with you. What about others that will be impacted by your not doing something—anything—to stop it?"

Miller got up, poured himself water from the sink, and sat back down. "Father, what about my life? What about my practice? All my life, I've tried to help others, whether it was helping to teach or protect others at the orphanage, or now, taking care of my patients, more than I take care of myself. My work is much, if not all, of my life. I cannot separate work and outside of work very well. And let's not forget they tried to kill me."

"Are you positive it was you they were shooting at? From what you told me, the police think it may be some threat against the Muslims."

Miller sipped at his water, checked his arms with the cuts and abrasions on them, and looked back at Father O'brien. . "Trust me. I know they were shooting at me. One just knows that when one is being shot at." He looked away and thought for a moment. "Father, my brain tries to override my inside feelings. It seems as I get older, I try to look at things more practically. I'm asking myself questions like the following: Do I gain more by standing down now to fight other battles, like caring for my patients, and fighting other battles another day? Or do I lose everything that I am, and stand for, by avoiding something that I can't help but feel has bigger implications?" He gulped about an ounce of his water.

Father O'Brien reached out to put his hand over Jake's. "These are very thoughtful questions, my son. Questions that only you can answer. Only you are in a position to choose. Sometimes in life, things you believe in … things that truly matter in this world are worth that sacrifice." He then took a drink of his water. "I can tell you that those I know of the Muslim faith are good, kind, and decent people. Obviously those that plot and carry out destruction in the name of their faith are, I believe, the exception, and like others of other faiths or beliefs that do similar things, there can be no accepting that." Father O'Brien turned to the side and crossed his legs. They both sighed and sat in silence.

Miller became pensive, and his eyes looked everywhere while he thought.

O'Brien turned in his seat to face back at Miller. "So, son. What are you going to do?"

Jacob stood up and looked down at him. "I'm not sure yet, Father, but I think I'm going to meet with someone who may help me decide."

Father O'Brien rose, looked into Miller's eyes, and placed his hands on his shoulders. "I know this is something that you must sort out, but please keep in touch, son. I want to be informed. And let me and the others at the house know if we can be of any help."

"Thank you for listening to me and, as always, your sound advice, Father. And not to worry. I'll keep in touch and won't hesitate to ask for your help."

They gave each other a big hug and a pat on the back.

"Love you, Father."

"Love you too, son."

As Miller approached the door, he heard footsteps scuffling from the hallway outside. He quickly opened the door and looked down the hallway each way, but no one was there. He then turned to look at Father O'Brien. "I thought I heard someone out here, but whoever it was, took off. Who could have been listening?" Father O'Brien merely shrugged his shoulders, and they gave a wave good-bye to each other.

Miller went downstairs, and on his way out, he passed two men sitting at a table playing chess in the recreation area. Miller recognized one of them. *Frenchy?* He walked back to the table to get a closer look. "Frenchy!"

The unkempt, older gentleman looked up at Miller slowly. "Do I know you, young man?"

Miller sat down next to him. "Bonjour, Frenchy. It's me, Miller. Jacob Miller. Comment vas—tu? I almost didn't recognize you without your gray beard."

The older man looked him up and down. "Jacob, hmm, Jacob Miller? Well if my eyes don't deceive me, it must be you. I don't know anyone else who speaks with such horrible French." They both laughed. "It's good to see you. What brings you here? Coming back to work here?"

"No. But I wouldn't mind if I had the time. I have many good memories of this place though—including you." He slapped Frenchy's knee.

"You must be lonely and desperate to have me as a good memory," said Frenchy.

Miller didn't have the time to volunteer at St. Francis anymore after medical school because, as a resident, he worked practically every waking hour. After his residency, he would visit from time to time and enjoyed keeping in touch with the staff members and, in particular, a few of the clients he had cared for while in medical school. He had become especially close to Frenchy. Perhaps close wasn't the correct word; more like "connected." He wasn't quite sure, but when he volunteered as a medical student, there was something about Frenchy that would make Miller want to spend time with him and listen to his stories. He had not been back to visit the last few years, as he had no time as the medical director at Boston General Cancer Center.

Frenchy threw the cards he had been holding onto the table. "Bullshit," said Frenchy. He then looked at the man seated across from him that he had been playing cards with. "Fred, I think this game is over for now. We can play a little later." Fred nodded in agreement, got up, and left them alone.

As a young man, Frenchy was one of the wealthiest and most influential men in Boston. He had fallen far years ago, and he had been homeless since. He wore baggy clothes that were stained and torn with worn sneakers held together with duct tape. He still carried a briefcase, now tattered and faded over the years, along with a shopping bag. Alcohol and gambling had taken away everything. Miller sat down next to him.

Frenchy bowed his head in acknowledgment. "Bonjour, Dr. Miller. Tres bien, et tu?" he said.

"Nice to see you as well, Frenchy. I remember you had some problems with weight and diabetes that we managed in the clinic. How are you doing with that?"

"My weight? I'm just a biscuit over three hundred, I would say. But I'm staying away from that A-bomb juice. You look pretty good yourself. Haircut? Lost some weight perhaps?"

Miller smiled affectionately at Frenchy. "Thanks. Yes to both questions. Frenchy, I'm curious. Where did you learn to speak French?"

"Well, you know, I learned it when I was much younger, as a kid. Before they got rid of us kids, we spoke it at the house. Then where I was sent to live, they spoke French."

"Tell me, are you getting ready for the marathon? I remember the city always gave you a hard time about living outside near the race each year."

"Yeah, yeah. Good memory. You should be a doctor or something. Oh, yeah, you are." Frenchy laughed at his own joke. "They make us move our shelters for it because they don't want anybody to know that Boston has a homeless problem. But something funny has been going on around the park this year. Something that to me is suspicious."

Miller moved a little closer to him. "What do you mean, Frenchy?"

"Not positive, but I'm not stupid. Though I may have drunk much of my brain away, I still have the sheepskins to prove that I once had a brain—a damn good one at that."

"Yes, I know," said Miller.

"Anyway, I've seen these guys who are no doubt Muslim. You know, the way they dress, the skin color, the conversations. Anyway, I watch the news about the terrorists and have read quite a bit in the public library."

Miller nodded in agreement. "I know you're very well read, Frenchy. So, what do you think is funny or suspicious?"

"Well where they meet, which seems almost daily, is just a few yards away from my home tucked behind the bushes near the bench, and I can hear very clearly the things they say."

Miller questioned him. "Like what? What kinds of things do they say?"

"They always talk about the upcoming marathon and how they need to make sure they get into the proper positions to watch it and to be sure to have the timing correct on that day. And as strange as it may be, I think they're farmers."

Miller gave him a questioning look. "Farmers! What makes you think they're farmers? Is it the way they dress?"

"As I said, they dress like they still live in Pakistan or one of the other countries there with the towel around the head and in normal slacks and shirts. It's more some of the things they talk about. Like one time they were talking about pigs and that the delivery of them is going well and they expect all the pigs to be delivered on time. I think they're expecting to do a lot of planting of crops also because they also talked one time quite a lot about getting different types of seeds to do the job. The other guy talking with him, just the other day, wondered if it mattered to mix the seeds together and if it would affect the results."

"Really? Did they say what crops they were growing?"

"Nope. And that seemed odd to me. They only said mixing of the seeds may give a better outcome with some effects happening at different times and maybe making it more difficult for others to deal with rather than having only one type."

"Frenchy, did they say anything about time of delivery of anything?"

Frenchy leaned over to Miller and licked his lips. "You know, I'm getting thirsty with all this talking, and my memory works better with a little something to drink. Just a little. You know. To wet my whistle."

"Frenchy, you know I won't do that, but I'll be happy to take you out for a good meal. Anything you like to eat. And some good coffee too."

Frenchy sat up and shook his head in disappointment. "I just ate with the other fellas here not that long ago. I'll take a rain check on that. But the only other thing I can remember is that they expect a big harvest soon. They said something like a big effect, which I took to mean a big crop, but they did talk oddly in my opinion." Frenchy looked off into the distance. "I think that is—oh, yeah. And something about preparing dinner, I think. I know it was definitely about food 'cause my stomach started aching just thinking about it. It made me so hungry. 'Pigs in a blanket.' Yeah, that was it. 'Pigs in a blanket.' I remember now picturing those little wieners all dressed up with fixings in a warm bun, ready to meet their new home—my stomach!"

Miller patted Frenchy on the shoulder. "Thanks, Frenchy. You've been a big help to me. Let me know if you hear anything else, or you can let Father O'Brien know. I expect to be back here real soon."

"Will do, chief. See ya soon."

"Take care of yourself out there, you hear?"

"You know me. I'm a survivor."

Miller smiled and shook Frenchy's hand. "Yes, I know you are."

Miller then left St. Francis House and went directly to his car parked across the street. The sky had turned from a sea blue when he had gotten there to a darker gray, as the sun was setting off in the distance. He got into his car, took out his phone, and called Detective Fifer. While waiting for the phone to connect, he thought about what Frenchy had said to him. *Hmm. Pigs in a blanket. What the hell could that be about? And harvesting. Harvesting what?*

CHAPTER 8: A CALL FOR HELP

MILLER SAT ALONE IN HIS CAR WAITING FOR DETECTIVE FIFER to answer his phone. "Hello. Detective? It's Dr. Miller. I'm good. How are you? Good. Good. Listen, I'm calling to ask if you could meet with me. Why? Well, I'm not sure, but I may know a link to the shooting at the mosque. Great. How about now? Behind the St. Francis House. Do you know where it is? That's right, in the Combat Zone. Oh and, Detective? Come alone."

As soon as he hung up with the detective, his next call was to Buzz. "Buzz, it's me."

"Doc? Are you okay? You sound a bit frazzled. I've been worried about ya. I thought you were going to call me earlier."

"I'm fine. Listen to me. I don't want to talk long. We need to talk about what happened in the operating room today."

"Yeah. Go ahead. I have time. What the hell happened up there in the OR? What's going on? Why were there no radiation readings on the Geiger counter? And how did you know it was empty?"

"No, not now. In person. I'm not sure what's going on, but I have an educated hunch. Meet me tomorrow morning at six in the department when no one's around."

"Okay. You got it. And I'm going to ask Bridget if she wants to come. If that's all right with you?"

"Bridget? Why?"

"She came up to me later, after the implant, and asked what was going on. I told her I wasn't sure but funny things were happening to our patients. She said she wants to help any way she can."

"All right. She can come. She's bright, and I believe we can trust her."

"Great. I agree and think she can be of help to us."

Miller hung up and drove into the alleyway in the back of St. Francis House and waited in his car.

Within thirty minutes, Fifer drove into the alley, parked, and sat in his unmarked car waiting for Dr. Miller.

Miller saw Fifer drive in and park. He walked over to Fifer's car and knocked on his window, which made Fifer jump. "What the—" shouted Fifer. He spilled his coffee in his lap, pulled his gun out from its holster inside of his coat, and pointed it at the window, with the gun barrel pointed right between Miller's eyes. Only an inch of air and glass separated the two.

Miller put his hands up. "Hey, don't shoot, Detective. It's me. Miller."

Fifer looked both scared and angry, with the gun shaking in his hand. "Get in the car," he said as he put the gun back into its holster inside his coat.

Miller ran around the car, opened the door, and looked inside at Fifer. "Sorry about that, Detective. I didn't mean to scare you."

"What? Scare me? Don't be ridiculous. I … I was just startled a little. That's all. Get in, will ya." Fifer wiped the coffee off his pants with a napkin. "Shit, just had 'em washed the other day."

Miller looked inside the car and then plopped down onto the passenger side.

Fifer frowned and looked sternly at Miller. "You should know better than to sneak up on someone like that. Especially someone who packs a loaded gun. And look at the area we're in. Empty buildings. Prostitution. Drug dealing."

Miller kept looking outside the windows, turning his head from front to back, then side to side. "I'm sorry, Detective. I just had to be sure it was you." Fifer was nonplussed, shaking his head. "What are you looking for? What is all this secrecy about?"

"I'm not sure, but I may be being followed."

Fifer took off his glasses, wiped them with a tissue in his pocket, and gave a curious look at Miller. "Followed? Really, why?"

"Yes. Followed," said Miller, nodding. "And thanks again, Detective, for meeting with me. I'm sure your boss wouldn't appreciate your coming here."

Fifer took a sip of coffee, wiping his chin after. "Sure. But why meet here? We could have gone to my office where it's more private and safer?"

"Why this place? St. Francis House? It may not look like very much but ... well, it's hard to explain. For me, it's a place that's safe and where I can trust the people here. No fakes. No fronts. No hidden agendas."

Fifer scratched the top of his head where the hair was thinned and looked like it had not seen a comb in a while. "Okay. Fine. Whatever works for you. As for your comment about my boss, I know he can come across as an—well, let's be honest. An asshole. Trust me. No one knows that better than me. But when it comes down to it, he really means well and does know a thing or two about criminal investigations."

Miller extended his arms forward partially. "I only meant—"

Fifer waved him off. "Never mind that. You said you had a connection, or link, to the shooting at the mosque."

Miller nodded. "I couldn't say too much on the phone. But several of my patients, whom I treated for their cancer, have died from their cancer."

Fifer rubbed his chin with his thumb and forefinger, enlarging the already large dimple in his chin. "Hm. I'm not feeling any less confused. Help me out here again, will ya. Cancer does kill people even when treated for it. Correct?"

"Yes, but these patients were not expected to die. Their treatment should have cured them. I believe someone killed them, and I believe I figured out how it was done and by whom."

Fifer gulped some of his coffee. "Have you mentioned this to anyone else yet?"

"Well actually, yes. I confronted Ahzid today about it at the mosque. But I didn't want to say anything to anyone else until I can prove it without a doubt. And I need your help to do that."

Fifer pointed his hands to his chest. "Me? How can I help you? If you think someone murdered your patients, you need to report it to the police."

Miller chuckled. "Forgive me, Detective. But isn't that what I'm doing now by telling you?"

"No. No. I mean reporting it first to the police, so it can go through the proper investigation."

"Well, I don't know if, based on the information I have, I can actually say they were murdered."

Fifer's head dropped a rung down. "Listen. Why don't you just tell me exactly who you think did what to whom."

Miller took in a deep breath and leaned toward Fifer. "I'm worried that something bad, really, really bad, might be going on, with the way my patients are dying."

Fifer put up an index finger at Miller. Then he reached into the inner pocket of his thin trench coat, tugged out a notebook, and grabbed a pen from his shirt pocket. "Say that again. You treat cancer patients. Cancer patients die. Believe me, I know what it's like to lose someone to cancer. Lost both my mom and dad to it."

Miller looked intently at Fifer. "Detective, I'm very sorry about your parents. But can we please focus on why I asked you here?"

Fifer stared at him curiously for several seconds, squinting his eyes as if trying to look inside of Miller to measure him with a truth meter hidden in his pocket. He then waved him on with his hand. "Go ahead. You have my attention."

"Let me give you an example of what I'm talking about. The last patient that I did an implant on, just this morning, I found that the radiation I was going to implant had been replaced with fake seeds."

Fifer stopped writing and looked up at Miller. "What do you mean fake seeds?"

"They had no radiation in them. In other words, the seeds were not real." Miller then went on to explain that the one connection to all the patients who died was Ahzid, his physicist.

After listening to Miller, Fifer, who had been looking at Miller the whole time, now turned and looked straight ahead, through the windshield into the now thick, black night, lit only by a single spotlight on a nearby warehouse, his head nodding, having absorbed and digested all of what had been said. He took another sip of his coffee. The cup had dried coffee stains along the top rim and down its side, suggesting it had likely been there most of the day. Fifer turned to look at Miller. "Before we go any further, Dr. Miller, answer me this. What the hell were you doing down at the mosque?"

Miller took a deep breath. "It's a long story, Detective."

Fifer snorted with laughter. "I'm off duty, got no kids, and live alone with no video games on the TV. So go ahead."

"I went to the mosque to meet Ahzid."

"The physics guy who works with you?"

"Yes, that's right."

Fifer turned the page of his pocket-sized notebook. "Sorry. Now, you mentioned something at the mosque shooting about you and Ahzid in an orphanage, but tell me again how you two originally met." He licked the end of his pencil and held it above the page, like he was a runner waiting for the starting gun to go off.

Miller sat quietly for a few seconds, staring out the window into the blackness. He began to rub his right arm up and down slowly, like he was petting the fur of a cat sitting on his lap. Gently but with some pressure to flatten what hairs remained. "We grew up together at St. Peters," he spouted out.

"St. Peters?"

"That's the orphanage I mentioned."

"Oh. Yes. Where the 'bad' boys would be sent before the era of reform schools and teen detention centers. What did you two do to be put there anyway?"

"Oh, yes. It was like a prison for bad kids, all right." He rubbed his right arm a bit faster, for a few seconds like he was trying to sooth an itch. "But it also was the only place where other kids, who were not trouble, could go until a foster home could be found. Kids like me and Ahzid."

Fifer held his notepad and pen tightly and didn't take his eyes off Miller. "So how did you guys end up in there in the first place?"

Miller turned slightly in his seat toward Fifer. "As I just said, unlike most of the other kids, we didn't do anything bad to be placed there. We were actually put there because we were truly orphans. Let's just say we both lost our parents and had no family that would or could take us in. And we were stuck in there for a very long time."

Fifer stopped writing again and looked slowly up at Miller from his notebook. "That sounds god-awful. Something out of a movie."

Miller nodded. "Yeah. Like *Nightmare on Elm Street* ... but we were close, and we always had each other's back. We trusted each other and only each other."

Fifer licked the end of his pencil again and held it over the page in anticipation. "So, go on."

"Let me fast forward. We both were fortunate enough to have had the support of the priests who worked there and did Mass on Sundays. One, in particular, Father O'Brien, saw our potential and fostered it, and we both ended up able to go on to college. Good colleges. Harvard and MIT. I became a physician, and Ahzid became a physicist."

"Wow! That is amazing. So ... tell me. How did you two end up working together now?" Fifer grabbed his cup from the console and finished the rest of his coffee in one big gulp.

"Well. Again. Another long story. We kept in touch after leaving the orphanage and got together often all during our college years. Even after graduation, he stayed on at MIT as a researcher and professor of physics, and I stayed on doing my research and patient care, teaching here at Harvard."

"So you guys were close."

"Oh, yes. Very. Until ..."

"Until?"

Miller sucked in a breath and shrugged his shoulders. "A few years ago, he—Ahzid, that is—suddenly quit his position at MIT and went back to his birthplace in Pakistan to work. He called me one day to tell me he was leaving to take a position there. I tried to keep in contact with him, but I didn't hear from him until about a year ago when he contacted me to ask if there might be a position for him to work in medical physics."

"Did that surprise you?"

"Hell, yes. I was very excited, at least at first. Not having heard from him for a few years and to have someone with his talent working with me. But I was surprised that he would want to make such a change given his talents in physics. He had potential to be a Nobel Prize winner some day. Taking a medical physics position, though a well-respected position, was viewed by other physicists in academics as a step down."

"How did things go after he came to work for you?"

Miller looked away from Fifer and down at the floor in front of him. "Ahzid was not the same person I had known prior to his leaving for Pakistan."

Fifer held his pen up with one end in the corner of his mouth. "How so?"

"He was always on the quiet side. But he was different. He was more distant. Kept much more to himself. At first, I thought he was getting acclimated to his new life. But over time, he only seemed to get more withdrawn. He would always have an excuse not to get together for coffee or dinner with me."

"And how did you connect your patients that were dying—unexpectedly that is-- to him?"

"After I analyzed all of the factors involved with each patient that died, but who should not have, Ahzid was the only common factor involved."

Fifer stopped jotting down his notes and looked at Miller with a puzzled look. "But how does this connect to what you said to me about radiation being stolen from your department?"

"As I mentioned already, I discovered that the last patient planned for a radiation implant had no active radiation in the needles."

Fifer puckered his lips and squinted. "And Ahzid worked on that patient?"

Miller raised his index finger. "Yes, and he acted very nervous prior to the case when I confronted him about my linking him, and him alone, to the patients who had died."

Fifer took in a breath and looked away in thought for a few seconds, then looked back at Miller. "Yes, but—"

Miller raised his finger again to Fifer, using it like it was a 'stop' sign. "Hold on, Detective. And he took off after that in a hurry, not showing up for the case later that day in the OR. And he has not been seen at the hospital since."

"And you think this is connected to your being shot at?"

71

"Yes. I'm not sure exactly how. But I went to the Mosque to talk with him about all this."

"How did he know you were coming, and how did you know he would be there? Did you call him beforehand?" Fifer turned the page. "Damn!"

Miller looked over at Fifer. "What is it, Detective?"

"Oh, nothing. Just realized I used up my last page in the notebook."

"Do you have another?"

"No. Never needed more than one before. Guess we talked enough for now. I think I got enough of what I need as far as background at least. We can always meet again if we need to." Fifer took out one of his business cards in his wallet, wrote his cell number on the back, and handed it to him. "Use the cell first if it can't wait."

"Got it. Thanks. Oh, Detective, before you go, I have to be honest with you; the way your boss acted toward me, I can't help but feel like I'm a suspect with the shooting at the mosque."

"Well, I'll be honest with you. You are. But. So is everyone that was involved with the case, until either someone is found to be involved or we can rule them out conclusively."

"I understand all that; he just seemed so accusatory."

"Like I said, he can be an ass. But you know the old saying."

"What's that?"

"You can't turn an ass into a donkey." Fifer guffawed, cracking himself up.

Miller raised his eyebrows, staring at him, barely able to get a curve upward of his upper lip.

Fifer cleared his throat when he realized he was the only one laughing. "So, ah, Miller, what are your plans for now?"

"Not sure. Meeting with a couple of people I work with at the hospital to talk about all this."

"Thought you didn't trust anyone."

Miller smiled. "Deep down, I don't. Except maybe these two. Maybe. I'm not sure yet. Not even sure about you yet, Detective."

"Well, whatever you do, don't get too involved on your own. If what you say is correct, all the evil that is stealing radiation—this could involve very powerfully bad people. People who don't care about life, particularly yours."

"Detective, I've got to do something. This is my reputation ... but even more importantly, these were—are— my patients. My job, my duty, hell, I'll admit it, my calling is to help them and sure as hell not allow them to be harmed."

"Whether you trust me or not, believe me when I say to you, don't do anything stupid. I will look into this further. Just give me some time."

"You promise?"

"Yeah, yeah. Promise, cross my heart." He made the symbol of a cross over his chest while rolling his eyes.

Miller smiled, got out of the car, and stuck his head back in. "I think I'm beginning to trust you, Detective." Miller shut the door and began looking around the area as if it were an autonomic response for him. "Beginning," he whispered.

Fifer started the car, and the headlights came on. Miller thought he saw something move beyond the dimly lit garbage cans. He squinted and leaned forward. The area suddenly turned black again.

Miller turned around. "Fifer, did you see something?" But then he realized that Fifer had already backed up and left. Miller stood in a darkness so deep he could barely see his shoes or his hand in front of his face. A chill ran down his back.

He crept toward the garbage cans where he thought his saw something move. His heart thumped faster. As he got closer to the cans, the lighting had gotten somewhat better from the hanging lightbulb off the St. Francis House porch across the alley. He bent down to get a better look around the cans. Out popped a cat, screeching, causing Miller to jump sideways into the can to his left. Some nearby windows lit up. The loud sound must have woken up some of those who still had apartments in a few of the rundown brick buildings. He picked himself up and brushed off some of the garbage that had fallen out onto him.

"Damn cat." He then looked up to see the silhouette of a car down the end of the alleyway, with its lights off, start up and drive off.

CHAPTER 9: MEETING OF THE MINDS

THE NEXT MORNING CAME EARLY FOR DR. MILLER, WHO HAD a difficult time getting to sleep with his thinking of his meeting with the detective. And that car was on his mind. He wondered how long it had been there with whoever was inside, watching the detective and him, before he spotted it. What did whoever was in it want?

At six in the morning, the Radiation Department seemed eerily empty. No patients or staff would be expected there since it was a Saturday and radiation treatments were not given on the weekends, except for emergencies. However, Buzz and Bridget were already waiting in Dr. Miller's office for their meeting with him when he got there. They exchanged "good mornings," and Miller sat down in front, on his desk. He was no more than a few lengths of his shoes from Buzz and Bridget. He leaned forward and exchanged looks with both. "I can't tell you enough how I appreciate your both meeting me here. I'm not sure where to begin."

"Doc, you know I'll do anything to help," said Buzz.

Miller looked at him eye to eye, pushed his lower lip under his upper. "I know you would."

Buzz turned to Bridget, seated on his left. "And how do you feel about all this, Bridget?"

Bridget nodded to both of them. "Of course I want to help in any way I can. I wouldn't be here otherwise."

"Even though we haven't known each other long, Bridget, I believe you. That's why I asked you both to meet me here. I trust you both." Miller stood up, paced in front of his desk, and rubbed his forearm with the palm of his other hand. "As you both know, I discovered that our last radiation seed case appears to have had no radiation placed into the needles, and I therefore aborted it."

Both Buzz and Bridget followed him pacing, first left then right with their eyes, and then they turned to look at each other.

Miller stopped pacing and looked down at them. "This is not going to be easy. In fact, it's going to be fraught with danger. You don't have to do this. I would totally understand and wouldn't respect either of you any less. Buzz, you and I go way back. You have been an excellent colleague and friend."

"Ain't it the truth. But this is personal. Whoever's behind it has messed with the wrong people. Count me in, You and I are connected at the hip. We're like Moe and Curly, like Abbott and Costello, like—"

Miller raised a hand, gesturing for him to stop. "Okay. Okay. I get it, Buzz. I think." He added a wink and a nod.

Miller looked over at Bridget, who had been absorbing the conversation with her arms folded and head down. She looked up at Miller and said, "My turn?"

He sat back down on the desk in front of them. "Bridget, although I've known you for a short time, I trust you. But you have no reason to feel you need to do any of this."

She nodded. "I understand all that."

"Buzz. Bridget. What I'm about to say to you is very serious. I believe that Ahzid stole our radiation isotopes, and our patients died as a result of that, but I was not positive. Until he actually told me that he had."

Buzz nodded rapidly. "He did act very strange the other day when he ran out of the building. Very nervous and all. But why do you think he would be doing that?"

Dr. Miller looked down and shook his head. "I'm not sure … yet. But I think it's terrorist related."

Buzz sat up, leaned forward, and opened his eyes wide. "Really. You mean like 9/11?"

"Perhaps. I need to investigate things more, and I'm counting on you both to help keep things quiet at the hospital until I can get more information."

"I want to help you also," said Buzz. "I know some people and have a very good friend I have known for years from the neighborhood. We grew up together and—"

Miller jumped to his feet. "Buzz, I appreciate it, but I think we should keep it to as few people as possible for now."

Buzz looked forlorn. "But,—"

"Please. Do as I say. I need you to keep things orderly at the hospital for now and work with the staff to reschedule things for the next week or so. I need some time to get information. I'm counting on you to do this for me."

Buzz sat in the chair, looking down at the ground with a pouty look on his face.

"Buzz? Buddy?" Dr. Miller moved toward him, put his hands on Buzz's shoulders, and looked down at him with a tilt of his head. Buzz slowly raised his head to look into Miller's eyes. "Buzz, what do you say? Can you help me out this way?"

Buzz nodded.

Dr. Miller patted him on the shoulder. "Thanks. I'll contact you later today or tonight. I need to meet with that old friend I mentioned, later this morning." He began walking back to the front.

Buzz suddenly stood up. "But, I really, really have a good buddy who works for the FBI in Boston. He may know things about this already. I can have him help us, and I know he would keep it quiet."

Miller stopped, turned back around, and looked intently at Buzz. He thought for a minute.

Buzz looked around nervously and sat back down. He shook one of his legs up and down.

Dr. Miller walked up to Buzz and leaned down at him. "Okay, Buzz. Tell me more about your FBI connection."

Buzz exhaled and slumped in his chair. "Phew. I thought you were going to give it to me for a minute there." He sat back up straight, and his color returned to his face. "Well, we go way back. We hit it off in high school right away on the football team as rookie freshman. We both got picked on by the seniors—"

"Buzz, I mean tell me more about your relationship now with him and why you think he can help us."

Buzz gave a puzzled look while crossing his legs. "Oh … sure, sure.

I gotcha. Well, we've kept in touch through the years. I talked with him just the other week. He works out of Boston."

Dr. Miller leaned forward. "But what makes you think he can help us—and would he want to or be able to?"

"As I said, we go way back. We're tight. He would do anything he could to help out."

"Does he work in any special area?"

"He works out of Boston mainly."

"No, I mean does he work in a particular area of crime investigation. You know. Like organized crime or bank robberies."

"Oh, yeah. I see whatcha mean. He does a lot looking into anybody doing anything they think may be related to terrorism."

Miller, who had been looking off into the distance in thought, not expecting much of an answer to his question, slowly lowered his arms to his sides, turned his head back toward Buzz, and walked back over to him. He leaned forward and opened his eyes wide. "What did you just say, Buzz?"

"About my buddy?"

"Yes, yes, your buddy."

"I said he works in Boston on things to prevent any terrorists from trying to attack us. You know, like—"

"Yes I think I know what you mean." Miller then grew a smile from ear to ear. "Now he's someone we need in our corner. When can you talk with him?"

"I can give him a call right now."

"Perfect. Why don't you go do that. Talk with him in private though. Do it outside the hospital in your car. And don't tell him anything too specific over the phone. I'm beginning to worry that we may be being watched and listened to."

Buzz stood, put on his down parka, and walked toward the door.

"Oh, Buzz," said Miller.

He turned back around, "Yeah, Doc?"

"Call me on my cell after you talk with him."

"Sure thing." Then he left.

Miller stopped pacing and sat back down next to Bridget. He clasped his hands together, rested his head on them, and took in a deep breath.

He looked over at Bridget. "So … I really appreciate your wanting to help, Bridget. I feel bad getting you involved in all this. I'm not sure what you can do at this point. Perhaps just be my eyes and ears here at the hospital while I'm not able to be in the clinic."

Bridget slid forward on her chair, sitting on its edge. "Please, Dr. Miller. I want to help. Of course I'll be your eyes and ears in the clinic, but I think I know how I may be able to help in another way also."

Miller sat back in his chair and folded his arms. "I'm all ears," he said with a curious look.

Bridget moved a little closer, leaned forward, and placed her hand on top of Dr. Miller's.

He looked at her green-blue eyes, like that of the ocean, inviting him in with their seemingly endless depth. He looked deeper and saw beyond her superficial beauty to see a sincere goodness and honesty inside. "You know, I feel like we're connected somehow. I feel I really know you and can trust you."

She smiled, showing off her bright white teeth. "You can."

Buzz then walked back in, startling them both.

He walked over to where he had been sitting. "Ah. There it is." He bent down to pick up something. "My cell," he said, showing it to them. "Sorry to interrupt ya. I'll call you later after I meet with my friend Dave to let you know how I made out."

Miller raised one of his hands in acknowledgment. "Sounds good, Buzz."

After he left again, Miller and Bridget looked at each other, and the sheer surprise of his coming back made them burst out with laughter that they couldn't hold inside.

CHAPTER 10: FIRST DATE

//

MILLER AND BRIDGET CONTINUED TO TALK ABOUT ALL THE craziness at the hospital, namely their patients dying. Bridget really opened up to Dr. Miller, and he to her.

"I would love to keep talking with you, Bridget. How about if we meet to talk across the street at the Coffee Connection for some coffee? This way we won't get interrupted in case Buzz decides to come back for something else he forgot."

She smiled and nodded. "I would love that."

"I have one patient that I need to call, and I need to check test results on a few others. Let's say nine o'clock?"

Bridget stood gently and grabbed her purse. "Sounds good. See you at nine."

Miller broke a happy smile. "Perfect."

When Bridget turned and walked away, Miller found himself staring at her walk. He had to admit that she looked rather good with her hourglass shape and toned, long legs in her midthigh-cut dress. *How did I not notice those big, green -blue eyes and that thick, black hair before?*

After she left, he called one of his radiation implant patients whom he had recently had repeat follow-up laboratory and radiographic imaging to assess his status after completing his treatment. He had to tell him the news was not good, and he and his wife wanted to come in to talk with him. Although he cared about all his patients, George was someone he somehow felt closer to. And after he hung up with George, he sat there at his desk staring at his diplomas on the wall. He thought for a while. *With all my degrees, all my awards and certificates, with all the studying, training, and experience, I still couldn't keep George from failing his treatment. And even worse, with his cancer having spread to other parts of the body, I can't even offer George any salvage treatment that would offer him a second chance for a cure.*

His pager went off, breaking his thoughts. He read the name of the caller, "Bridget!" and looked at his watch. "Oh, shit." He was almost twenty minutes late for his coffee date with her. He quickly picked up the phone. "Bridget, I'm so sorry. I lost track of time talking on the phone with a patient of mine … Thanks for understanding. I'll be right over."

Jacob hung up and sprinted out the door, through the hospital corridor, and across the street to the Coffee Connection. A cab nearly hit him when he jumped off the curb without looking into the street. Panting from his sprint, he sucked air as he walked up the outside stairs and saw Bridget sitting alone at one of the outdoor café tables. A Boston morning, early-spring chill kept all the other tables empty. He walked over to her. "Hi, Bridget," he blurted out in between his pants while resting his hands on his knees. "I'm so very sorry to be late. I had a lengthy and difficult talk with a patient over the phone and—"

Bridget stood up. "Catch your breath? Are you okay?"

Miller nodded.

She walked over to him and put a hand on his back. "That's okay. I understand. I was worried you might be standing me up."

"Oh, no. I would never do that." He took in a deep breath, exhaled, and stood up straight. "By the way, you look awesome." They allowed themselves to give a hug to each other that lasted several seconds, then sat down at the table.

"Thank you. You look good too, as always."

He just smiled. "I'm so glad you wanted to meet me for coffee. It's so much easier for us to talk outside the office. Though I wasn't so sure you would feel comfortable meeting me."

Bridget turned her head just slightly and frowned. "I'm not sure what you mean … 'that I wouldn't feel comfortable.' Why would you think that?"

Miller sat back in his seat. "Honestly?"

Bridget leaned forward, reached out, and held his hand. "Yes, I would want nothing less from you."

"Well, I have to admit that I may have an attraction to you beyond you as a professional medical person."

Bridget sat up with a slight eyebrow raise. "Really. I didn't think—I mean—I did assume you didn't ask me to have coffee to talk only about medical things. But I never would have guessed that." Bridget looked around. All the other tables were still empty. "In fact, I must admit—if we're doing true confessions here—that as much as I may have been physically attracted to you, I didn't think at first that you were my type."

Dr. Miller sat up tall and cleared his throat. "What do you mean by 'not your type'?"

Bridget reached across the table, grabbed Miller's hands, and leaned forward with a frown. "Well, remember that I didn't say 'now.' I said 'at first.' And second, I'm not sure how to say this easily—and please don't get me wrong—you're a fantastic doctor, doing what you do with radiation and implants and all that ... but when I first met you, I thought you were kind of 'full of yourself.' And I like someone who's more humble; self-confidence is good, but not conceited or cocky."

Miller sat, mouth open, his eyes blinking slowly. "Oh ... I see."

"But let me finish. My working with you daily and seeing how you treat your patients and staff—and I don't mean just me, because that certainly could be easily feigned for other reasons, which I even thought at first—made me see you differently. I saw a man who, for whatever reason, when he let his outer walls down had a very kind, caring, and warm feeling inside of him that he willingly shared with anyone needing him."

Miller gulped the coffee he had just sipped and coughed a bit. "Wow. You saw and felt all that?" Miller stared at her for a moment. "I don't know what to say."

"You don't have to say anything. You asked me why I changed my mind about you, and that's why. I decided that the man underneath was someone I would love to share a cup of coffee with and possibly get to know better."

Miller folded his lower lip up under his upper lip and nodded a few times. "Fair enough."

"So why the interest in me, Jake—I feel funny calling you Dr. Miller now. Do you give such special attention to all your female staff?"

Miller chuckled. "I agree. Outside the hospital, please call me Jake or Jacob. And as far as my seeing others at work, that would never happen. Up until now, I never let things like that interfere with my work."

"Okay. Well that makes me feel special. By the way, I like your name, Jacob. But it may take me a while to feel totally comfortable with that. After all, you are my boss."

"I hate that word, 'boss.' I prefer to look at us as colleagues."

Bridget smiled. "So, to get back to my question: why did you ask me for coffee?"

"You are attractive, and I'm human after all. Like you, my reasons would have been very different had I asked you when I first met you— which obviously I didn't do."

Bridget's high cheekbones reddened as she sat forward, clasped her hands under her chin, and glared at Miller with glassy eyes. "Go on. I'm more than a little intrigued."

Miller's pager went off. He checked it and sighed. "Bridget, I'm sorry, but I have to get back to the office."

"Nothing urgent, I hope," said Bridget.

Dr. Miller stood up and brushed off his pants. "That patient I told you about that I talked with on the phone wanted to come in to see me, so I have to go meet with him, but I've really enjoyed talking with you." He pressed his lips together. "I really hate to have it end. You have a way to make me forget about things." Miller put his index finger up in the air. "Hey, are you doing anything this afternoon?"

Bridget thought for a moment. "No, I don't have any plans. Why do you ask?"

Dr. Miller felt the excitement of that of a seven-year-old who was just asked if he wanted to go to the carnival. "Well, I was just thinking about how much I would like to show you a very special place. It's called Nubble Point, in York, Maine, and it's less than an hour from here. It's beautiful there. The rocky coast, the view of the ocean, the quaintness."

"Oh, that does sound like a beautiful place. I would love to go. How about in an hour or so? I just need to take care of a few things."

"That's perfect. I need to meet with my patient and finish a few things at the hospital. So where should I pick you up?"

"My apartment would be fine. It's not far from here. Down on Fruit Street across from the Boston Medical Hospital Cox building."

"Got it. Know exactly where it is. See you in an hour." Miller stood up and walked over to Bridget, bent over, and they gave each other a hug. He also snuck in a kiss on her cheek, which made her blush again.

When Miller walked into his office, George and his wife Margaret were already waiting in the consult room.

George got up when Miller walked in. "Hey, Doc. Good to see ya. No one was around, so the security guard let us in to wait when we told him we were meeting you here. We didn't know the department was closed." He was a chubby guy who looked like he earned all of his seventy-two years of age. Margaret sat next to him and looked up at Miller with squinting eyes. She looked equally worn as George.

Miller walked over to them. "Hi, George. Good to see you. You too, Margaret."

"Well it's always good to be seen, you know," said George, with his usual chuckle out of one side of his mouth.

Margaret looked up at him and rolled her eyes, then looked back at Dr. Miller. "Why did you need us to come down here? It's bad results, isn't it?"

Miller looked over at her. "Well, yes. I wanted to talk with you in person because the tests show that the cancer has come back."

George looked down.

Margaret looked right at Dr. Miller and said, "You said he would be cured with his treatment. How could this happen? Tell us. How could this happen?" Her breathing became rapid, and her face reddened.

Miller took in a deep breath. "I know this is a shock. The tests shocked me too. It was not expected. His treatment for his stage should have taken care of the cancer."

George then looked up at Dr. Miller with saddened eyes. "Doc, listen, I know we did the right thing. Nothing can be 100 percent."

"So, Doctor, what do we do now?" interjected Margaret.

"The first thing I would like to do is to have George see a medical oncologist I work with, and his urologist."

"And what are they going to do for George?"

Dr. Miller sat down across from them and looked directly into Margaret's eyes. "The tests show his cancer not only involves the prostate area but also apparently has spread to other areas of the body. Hormone treatment and sometimes chemotherapy can be used for metastatic disease—and even biologics are playing a bigger role now."

Margaret snapped to her feet, which startled Dr. Miller and made him lean back a few inches. "What? You mean his cancer has spread already?"

George stood and put his arm around her. "Please, Margaret," said George. "Calm down. I know you're upset."

"Calm down." She pointed her finger at Dr. Miller and said, "We were told by him that you were absolutely going to be cured. Now he tells us your cancer is back and spread everywhere. I'm sorry, but I can't and won't calm down." She picked up her handbag off the floor and stormed out of the room.

George turned to Dr. Miller. "She's just upset. We'll be all right."

He started walking out after her, and Dr. Miller said, "George."

George stopped and turned around. "Yeah, Doc?"

Miller walked over to him, put his hand on his shoulder and looked at him with soft eyes. "I'm sorry, George. Truly sorry. I'll have my office be in touch with you about having you see the medical oncologist I spoke about and your urologist to discuss possible treatments."

"Doc, it's not your fault." George pointed to the trophy case near them. "I remember when we first met for my consult and saw your boxing and martial arts trophies there. As a former boxer myself, I knew you were someone I could trust. Still feel that way." They exchanged a nod, and George then left the office.

Dr. Miller took a big sigh and collapsed in his chair, exhausted from the exchange. He wanted to cry, but that was not his mechanism to deal with stress from sadness, though his eyes did water, and he did become nauseous about the whole exchange with George and his wife. He looked over at the clock on the wall. "Oh, crap. Not again. I can't believe I'm going to be late three times in one day—twice on our first date," he mumbled to himself, then rushed out to the parking garage and drove to meet Bridget. Along the way, he almost ran two red lights and nearly hit a pedestrian. He pulled up to Bridget's apartment building and screeched to a stop. Bridget was outside waiting on the steps to her apartment. She waved with a welcoming smile and ran down the stairs, excited.

Dr. Miller looked up to her. "Hi, Bridget."

She got into the car. "Hello again."

Boy, she looks so good. Smiling, Miller looked at her with please-forgive-me eyes. "Bridget, I just wanted to say how sorry I am for being late to pick you up."

"Listen, I understand. Really I do. My dad was a doctor, so I know what it is you go through."

"Really? Then I guess you would have a unique understanding. Did he specialize in anything?'

"Yes. Psychiatry."

"Interesting." *Psychiatry. Hmm.*

They headed out to the Tobin Bridge to Route 95, heading north. Bridget alternated between looking out at the road and scenery along the way and watching Jacob drive. They turned off 95 and drove up route 1A along the coast toward York. With the top down on his Mercedes convertible, the wind with its ocean smells blew through her hair. The automatic CD player covered the range of music from AC/DC and Black Sabbath to classical Mozart and Beethoven to finish with Celtic. Then they drove through the town of York and up to Nubble Point.

It was midafternoon when they finally arrived in York. He pointed to Long Sands Beach as they passed it on their way to Nubble Point, only a few miles up the coast. When they got there, he parked the car facing the Nubble lighthouse. "Well, here we are at God's backyard. Nubble Point is one of my favorite places. I hope you didn't mind the music selection on the way up."

"Oh, no. I like the eclectic selection of music."

"This is the place where God lets me forget about everything for a time."

"How do you mean, Dr. Mill—"

Dr. Miller looked at her and frowned.

She laughed. "Oops, I mean Jake."

Jake patted her thigh just above the knee. "That sounds better,

Bridget. How does it make me feel this way, you ask? The simplicity of it all lets me escape from the pressures of patient care and discovery in the lab. I feel like a kid again, living only for the moment, not worried about the next week or day, or next hour, for that matter. Just focusing on the sand, rocky coast, and vast ocean in front of us." He waved his hand across the scenery in front of them.

"I know exactly how you feel. I've always loved the beach and ocean."

They got out of the car and sat next to each other on one of the flatter, grayish boulders and stared out at the Atlantic Ocean. It was a hot spot during the summer tourist season, people walking, talking, and taking pictures of the rocks, ocean and, of course, the lighthouse. But now it was mostly empty, with it being early spring and a weekday.

"I can sit here for hours … just staring out at the vastness of the ocean," said Miller. He took in a deep, slow breath and exhaled. "And the smells of the ocean. It's darkness, depth, and awesome power. I feel so helpless against it … yet so at peace watching the powerful whitecaps pounding against Maine's rocky coast. Look at how the lighthouse stands strong as it overlooks the ocean, serving as a guide to ships on stormy nights." Dr. Miller finally turned his head away from the vast ocean in front of him and toward Bridget, who sat not two feet away to his right. "It is here actually where the idea of my lab research took an important turn."

Bridget turned to look at him. "Really? I'd love to hear more about that."

"Well, I realized that in many ways our bodies are as complicated as anything in nature and that it's not one thing alone that controls functions, but it's the product of many events or actions working in concert that brings about the desired effect or response in a controlled and orderly way."

Bridget nodded. "Oh, I understand. We spend too much time looking for that magic bullet to cure cancer."

"Exactly. I knew you would get it. Anything as complex as cancer requires more than just one thing to overcome it. It's multiple things, multiple pathways and connections that allow it to protect itself against other things trying to kill it and avoid attacks all together. This is why I got the idea of using a cocktail as an anti-cancer serum, a mixture of several things that work all at once to overwhelm the cancer cell, so that it's unable to hide or protect itself. In addition, there is one new element that I have added."

Bridget sat up straight and adjusted herself on the rock. "Oh. And what might that be?"

"I'd tell you, but I would have to kill you," said Miller, laughing softly.

She stood, put her hands on her hips, and looked down at Jake. "Well you better not tell me then."

Jake stood and grabbed her hands in his. They laughed together. "I love your sense of humor. I tell you what, let's talk more over a late lunch/early dinner at Fox's and then ice cream at Brown's.

"Fox's? Brown's?"

"Yes, to eat lunch, then ice cream." He pointed in their direction. "Brown's is just down past Fox's over there, and around the corner and up the hill. We can burn a few calories walking over and not feel guilty after we eat. I think they opened just last weekend."

"Sounds good. I'm game." They left the car parked where it was, since there were few others sightseeing, and continued their conversation as they strolled, side by side, down the road a few hundred feet away from the lighthouse.

"So, Jacob—see, I called you by your first name." They both laughed. "How did you get into medicine, and particularly what made you want to go into treating cancer patients?"

He stopped when they reached the corner next to Fox's and the road that led up to Brown's. He stared outward at the vastness of the ocean, noting the wide vista of the rocky coast that stretched out very far to the get to the ocean's edge, and then slowly turned to look at Bridget. "Do you want the long or the short version?"

"Whatever you like. I have no place to go."

"Great. Let's go inside then and eat. I just love the lobster stew, lobster rolls, and just plain lobster," said Miller. "Then, I'll give you the short version. I don't want us to talk about only me today."

"I was going to ask what you recommended, but I would take a wild guess at that being lobster."

They laughed and went inside and sat at a table with an ocean view.

These were difficult to get during the busy tourist season, but Miller got excited when he saw that there were a few available. They ordered their lobster lunches and talked in between bites.

"First, before we talk more about each other, tell me more about why you asked me out again, but this time can you be more specific?"

"Now, why did I ask you out?" He placed one hand under his jaw. "You know, if I had to say just one thing, and I really hate to use a cliché, but when the shoe fits ... but to use a better one, it would be being around you has been like a breath of fresh air to me."

Bridget folded her arms together in front of her and leaned forward across the table closer to Miller. "Really. How so?"

"Well the type of woman I have gone out with all seem to be like you, very beautiful." Bridget's corners of her mouth lifted. "But unlike you, they don't have much going on deeper than the looks that's stimulating. I guess I'm one of those hopeless romantics."

She adjusted her position in her seat and sipped at her coffee. "And what deeper things do you see?"

"Well, for one thing, you have a self-assurance that I haven't been accustomed to. And I actually feel I can talk to you—I mean talk to you about things more than just the weather or what concert you saw."

"Okay, I like your reasoning for asking me out. Now tell me more about you."

"Basically, I have worked my whole life either as a student or a doctor since getting out of the orphanage," said Miller.

"Ah. Orphanage? I felt as though you had an interesting past."

"Interesting? Yes, all of that, to say the least. I was raised in an orphanage, so I can identify with those having nothing—no money, no clothes, no food, and no education. But I also identify with those who have everything. I have been in both worlds, rich and poor. In medical school, I often felt alone. I couldn't stand the snobs born with the silver spoon in their mouths. Yet, I admit, I loved the intellectual challenges that I shared with them."

As she ate her lunch, Bridget listened intently to Miller. "I was blessed by being able to take college classes outside the orphanage when I was very young. It was arranged by Father O'Brien, one of the priests who worked at the orphanage. I owe him everything. He saw my talents in science and math and nurtured them. He allowed me to take classes outside the orphanage beginning in sixth grade. By age sixteen, I was in the MD PhD program at Harvard Medical School." He leaned forward and took one of her hands resting on the table. "What about you? I feel like I've been talking all about me."

"Wow. You overcame a lot to get to where you are now. I admire that." She inhaled deeply. "Well, unlike you, I was fortunate to have had loving parents. They were great. They supported me with whatever I decided to pursue."

"They sound like terrific parents." Miller leaned forward and grabbed her other hand. "Hey, I got a fun idea. Do you like taffy?"

"Love it."

"Good. Then we can talk more after lunch at Golden Rods down the street and pick up some. I'd like to hear more about you and your family. They sound like very loving parents."

After finishing lunch, Jacob and Bridget walked passed Brown's Ice Cream to Golden Rods across from Short Sands beach. When they got there, Jacob rubbed his hands together. "Not to worry, we can get ice cream after the taffy." And when they got to Golden Rods, they stood for several minutes in front watching the machines turn and twist the thick bands of taffy. "I just love watching them make the saltwater taffy," said Miller. "Isn't it the coolest thing?"

Bridget nodded. "Yes, it's awesome."

After watching the taffy making and buying a box of it, they went across the street to Short Sands Beach and talked while walking on the beach. Then they sat to watch the sun set and eat some of the taffy. Jake put his arm around Bridget, leaned closer to her, and kissed her on the lips. She wrapped her arms around him and kissed him back. They held their kiss for several seconds, then released their embrace and held onto each other's hands.

"That was a nice surprise," said Bridget.

"I'm glad you liked it."

"Very much so."

"So tell me more about your family, Bridget."

"Well, we're a close family. Very supportive and nurturing to one another."

"Any sisters or brothers?"

"Two brothers, one older and one younger." She suddenly became teary and choked up.

Jake held her shoulders tightly. "Are you okay, Bridget? What's the matter?"

She grabbed a tissue out of her pocketbook and wiped her eyes dry and blew her nose. "I'm sorry. I get emotional talking about my family. You see, my older brother and parents were killed in the Twin Towers on 9/11. They had been visiting New York City to see my brother who worked as a broker in the Towers."

"Oh my God. I'm so sorry." Jake hugged her tightly. When they let go of their embrace, Jake held onto her hands in her lap. "Bridget, you don't have to talk any more about it if you don't want to."

She patted her eyes again with the tissue still in her hand. "No, I'll be all right. I need to learn to become more comfortable when talking about it. I was so angry after that happened that I even considered joining the military branch that deals with covert activities against terrorism or the CIA—anyone that would allow me to fight against terrorism." She described how she felt the need to do something about it too, fighting terrorism so her parents and brother wouldn't have lost their lives for nothing. She also talked about her younger brother who had recently finished college and joined the military to fight terrorism and avenge the loss of their parents and brother. "He's in Afghanistan currently to stop them from killing others like they did to those on 9/11."

Miller reached out and took one of her hands in his and squeezed it tightly. "I'm so sorry to hear about the loss of your parents and brother. I cannot imagine the hurt you must feel. And I admire your motivation to do something to contribute to the fight against terrorism. I get so angry when I think about 9/11 and how screwed up things are in the world with all the fighting going on. But, Bridget, please try to focus on the positive things you have had, and still do, as difficult as it may be. You are lucky to have had such a home life. I had none of that and lived in a hell hole for years."

"You are absolutely right, and I do appreciate everything I've had. I perhaps don't understand growing up the way you did, and I had loving parents. I thank you for reminding me of that. Sometimes I let the hurt make me so bitter and filled with hate that I lose sight of the good things in my life and life in general."

After stuffing themselves with as much Taffy as they could, they walked to Brown's up the hill and sat at one of the picnic tables across from each other eating their ice-cream cones. Miller continued talking, and Bridget sat forward, looking riveted. "Wow, Jacob, that's amazing to come from the orphanage to MIT and Har—"

"Over there." Miller had turned away from Bridget and was staring off down the road. He had noticed a man leaning outside a car a few hundred feet down the road and staring at them, holding either a camera or binoculars.

Bridget turned to look behind her. "What? I don't see much of anything."

"That car parked down the road on the left facing toward us, just at the bottom of the hill." Miller pointed at the car. "See the man getting inside on the driver's side?"

"Yeah. What about him?"

"He's been following us and watching us."

"How do you know that? And why would he be doing that?"

"Watch." Miller got up from the bench and started to walk toward the car. Within a few seconds, the car started up, whipped a U-turn, and sped off out of sight.

Miller then turned to look at Bridget. Her mouth hung open. Miller walked back to her. "Coincidence that he just had to leave at that second? Perhaps, but I don't think so," he said. Miller sat back down on the bench.

"Wow. How strange was that?" said Bridget.

"I think I've seen him before, and in that very same car. He and others have followed me before." Miller had turned away from Bridget and was staring off down the road. "It's a detective, I think."

"A detective? Why would a detective be following you?"

"They think I'm involved with the shooting at the mosque. Can you believe that? Me." Miller slammed his fist onto the table. "How nuts is that?"

Bridget squinted her eyes at him. "Why would they think you did it or are involved?"

"I don't know. They say they have to investigate everyone. Maybe it's just my overreacting."

Bridget looked at him sympathetically. "I'm sure you're right in that they're just investigating everyone."

"I try not to think about it, but it's difficult." Miller looked off to the ocean then back at Bridget. "I've had a wonderful time today. I really hate to have it end."

"I feel the same way."

Miller leaned forward excitedly. "Well, if you mean it, we don't have to let it end."

Bridget smirked. "Okay, what do you have in mind this time?"

"How about if we head back into Boston and have a few drinks in a really nice pub I know near the hospital?"

"Again you make an offer that I just can't say no to."

Miller jumped up from sitting. "Great."

They headed back to Boston to have a few drinks at O'Rouks, an Irish pub on the same block as Dr. Miller's condominium on Beacon Hill, not far from Boston's General Hospital. There they played a game of pool and darts and had a few drinks and lots of laughs. Though reluctant at first, Miller asked Bridget if she wanted to go to his place to look at the moonlight shining off the Charles River from the rooftop of his building. She accepted the offer without hesitating.

They climbed the stairs to the rooftop deck. "The view is breathtaking," said Bridget.

"Isn't it though? I come up here often late at night and early in the morning to sit and look out at the moonlight dancing on the river. Similar to Maine, looking out over the ocean, the vastness, beauty, and silence. Like now at one in the morning. It's kind of like going to see an orchestra with only me in the audience to soak in the beauty and emotions."

"Jake, I feel like I'm closer to you more and more each moment we're together. I'm not sure how to explain it, but I feel as though we have so much in common. We both lost our parents, and we both have the same romantic yearnings, like to be near the ocean and the stars."

"And I feel the same way. Like we were meant to find each other."

"Like soul mates," said Bridget.

"Yes, that's it. Soul mates." They embraced tightly and then kissed.

"I have another crazy idea," said Jake.

"What's that?"

"Let's go downstairs and have a drink in my place in front of a nice fire."

"That's not crazy. Let's go."

He poured them both a glass of red wine, and in front of a roaring fire, he sat on the couch and raised his glass. "Here's to finally finding our soul mate."

Bridget raised her glass to tap his. "I second that."

While they drank the wine, Jake opened up to Bridget even more about his past and his struggles, his goals and desires. "I love my work," said Jake. "I don't view any of it as a job. It's more like a calling. I truly care for each of my patients."

"I can see that, even though we haven't worked together that long."

But I love the research side as much. The learning. The discovery."

"I like that side of you too. Jake, I would love to see your lab and learn more about what exactly you're working on."

Jake wrapped his arms around her, and she reciprocated. "I think that can be arranged for you." Miller loosened his embrace and looked into Bridget's eyes. "I have searched for someone that I can truly trust, and I think that person may be you." They kissed a long kiss. When they stopped, Jake continued, and Bridget listened intently. "For the first time, I feel I can let down my walls and be myself."

"Jake, you are so cute when you show your shy and boyish, naïve side. I like that side of you much better than the cocky doctor I first met at the hospital."

"Well, that's very sweet of you to say, but I didn't realize I had been so cocky to you."

"Oh, yes, you were, but then I saw how you were with your patients. You are such a kind and caring person. That's the side I can't resist."

The fire burned a bright yellow with a mixture of blue and green tints. For a moment, he felt a bit empty for words. He felt spent from purging. He had not talked to anyone about himself at the orphanage and his work like he had done with Bridget. He moved closer to her and wrapped his hands around hers. "I'm sorry, Bridget, but I'm mentally exhausted right now. I'm planning on visiting one of my favorite patients, George, tomorrow. He has suddenly taken a turn for the worst. How about if we continue talking another time about me and my past? I promise I'll tell you anything you want to know about me."

She looked into his eyes. "That's fine. I understand and feel the same way. But, Jacob, you have to stop beating yourself up. You cannot cure everybody. Strange things happen."

"I know. You're right."

"No one wants to lose a patient. You have to learn to let it go. Maybe it would make you feel better if you kept a scrapbook of your patients to remember them by."

"A scrapbook? Hmm. Never thought about that."

"Yes, a scrapbook. And be sure to put the many ones you have cured over the years, not just the ones you have lost."

Their eyes locked. "That a great idea, Bridget. I've focused only on the bad outcomes. No wonder it's all been a downer. And I can't stop thinking about Ahzid being involved and perhaps behind everything. The last patient I treated with no active radiation, Ahzid's confession to me at the shooting at the mosque, and now his disappearance. I can't help but feel they were shooting at me. I just have to figure out what the hell is going on."

Bridget put her finger up to his lips. "Sh. No more talking or thinking about those things. Remember?"

"Yes, you're so right." He looked deeper into her eyes and moved slowly and ever closer to her, where he could feel her warm breath on his face. "Now you wouldn't say all this unless you meant it, right?"

"What? Of course. Why would you—"

"Never mind. I sometimes have issues of trust. That's all."

He gently pressed his lips to hers, and they kissed a long, passionate kiss. They soon moved to the floor in front of the fireplace without letting go of their embrace and kiss.

"One more thing I need to tell you, Jake."

"Yes. What is it?"

"I need to be careful."

"What do you mean?"

"I need to be careful because I can become vulnerable when I have a few drinks."

"I understand. I will be careful too."

Then they held each other tightly and passed out in each other's arms.

CHAPTER 11: THE FBI CONNECTION

BUZZ WAS HOME WATCHING TELEVISION AND DRINKING A BEER, when Dave, his FBI friend, called him. "Hey, Dave, how's it—what? You changed your mind? But you made it clear when I called you yesterday morning that you couldn't talk with me about anything involving your work and that you couldn't meet with me for at least a few weeks because you were so busy at work. Okay. Okay. That's great. I'll meet you at Bubba's for coffee and breakfast in an hour."

The morning had barely woken up with the sun still low in the sky as he drove in his rusted, 1968 Lincoln to meet Dave, with his golf bag and clubs in the backseat and wrappers from Burger King and McDonalds covering the front passenger seat and floor. Driving through his old neighborhood brought back memories of when they were kids. He saw the grain mill storage house where they had released one of the train's box car's air brakes so that it rolled down and off the tracks. If they weren't all under sixteen, they may have gone to jail for that. Then he passed the shoe mill parking lot where they played baseball and football. Not far from there, he saw the Swenson's dilapidated house still standing at the far end of the parking lot. He remembered hitting the longest hit he ever made and the baseball going right through old man Swenson's front window. Boy, how he was so mad and came running out after them, swearing the whole time.

When Buzz arrived at Bubba's and saw Dave waiting for him, he ran right over to him to greet him. They gave each other a big bear hug and several pats on the back.

"Buzz, man. You old bastard. Let me look at ya. You look great. Not a day over eighty."

"Gee, thanks, Dave. I wish I could say the same about you."

"How the hell are you?" said Dave.

"Doing good." He shook his hand, and then they both gave each other another big bear hug and a pat on the back.

"Come on, let's sit."

"Thanks for meeting me, Dave. Buzz raised and lowered one leg nervously. "What was it, Dave, that you said when I asked you what made you change your mind? Oh, yes, 'revenge' you said. Now what's that supposed to mean?"

Dave leaned over the table toward Buzz. "Listen to me very carefully." Dave looked around them to make sure no one else sat at the outdoor café. He then looked under the table and under the overhead table umbrella. "I wanted to sit outside so no one else can hear us. I could be fired for this—possibly even go to prison."

Buzz nearly spit out his coffee and began choking. "What are you talking about, man?" He put his cup down and wiped his mouth with his sleeve.

"Sorry, Buzz. Didn't mean to startle you. You okay?" He handed Buzz his napkin. "When you called me at work and told me you needed help in getting information on possible terrorists in the area and how they were stealing radiation from hospitals, I almost shit my pants."

Buzz adjusted himself, looked around, and sat forward to listen more closely. "Go ahead. I don't see anyone around."

"I've just got to tell you that your calling me to meet to talk about this surprised me—no, shocked me."

Buzz looked puzzled. "How do you mean?"

"I'm going to tell you something that happened to me the other day—the day you called me to be exact. But you cannot tell this to anybody, or I'll have to kill you."

Buzz chuckled. "Ah, ha. Sure. No problem."

"No. Seriously. Your life really may be in danger just being involved at all."

Buzz raised his eyebrows and snapped his head back with surprise. "Okay. I get it, man. I understand. You can trust me, buddy."

"There were some things that were being said during my work that made me think of something you had said about what was going on in the hospital. And the day of your call, I lost two of my partners."

Buzz squinted. "Ahhh. I'm so sorry to hear that, man."

Dave nodded and patted his eyes with his napkin. "Thanks."

"How'd it happen? If you can tell me, that is."

"We were on a surveillance mission outside a Boston apartment. We were a team of three. Members of an antiterrorist unit. We were assigned to follow and monitor those suspected of being homegrown terrorist cells. We were keeping watch on a few college students from Canada because we had gotten a tip earlier about them and became suspicious when, believe it or not, one of the kid's own fathers reported them to local police."

Buzz took a gulp out of his coffee cup. "Really!" Buzz gave a quick look around. "His own dad?" he whispered.

"Yup. He had noticed his son having meetings in his garage with others from their mosque and had overheard them talking about killing people for Allah. And that they would all be able to be glorified by fighting against the Westerners. I have a recording of the surveillance from when my partners were killed. I want you to listen to it and tell me if there's anything on it that in any way sounds like something you've heard before or rings any bells. The mood was tense; you'll hear that we were getting on each other's nerves from being together for days."

Buzz took another sip of his coffee, not taking his eyes off of Dave. "Sure. Sure. I understand."

"We had been staked out for days, taking breaks only to eat, go to the bathroom, and to sleep at a nearby hotel. Stakeouts are tough. Hunger, fatigue, anxiety. It all built up. We all hung in there because we felt we were about to get a break in the case." Dave handed Buzz a set of headphones. "Here, put these on."

Buzz looked surprised but put them on.

"I don't want anyone else to hear this," said Dave.

Buzz listened for a few minutes before making a frown. "What did he just say? Pigs in a blanket? Boy I could eat right about now, myself."

"Shut up, will ya. I'm trying to listen too." Dave turned up the volume to both his and Buzz's headphones.

Another voice came on. "Mohammed, the seeds have been ordered and are on the way."

Buzz's eyes opened wide when he heard the name.

The conversation continued. "That is good, my brother, for we are expecting a big harvest this spring."

"Did you take care of the noisy neighbors at the farm?"

"Not yet, but soon. Especially the woman."

"Make sure you do it before they try to tell someone about the seeds and pigs at the farm."

Buzz looked up at Dave. "What the hell? Are they farmers?"

Dave shut off the recorder. "I don't want to have to tell you again to shut up," replied Dave with a stern look at Buzz. Then he turned it back on.

On the recording, a cell phone began to ring: "Hello? Buzz? Oh my god. How long has it been?"

Buzz then took his headphones off and looked at Dave. "Hey, Dave, this is when I called you."

Dave sighed loudly, clicked off the recording, and looked annoyingly at Buzz. "Yes, no shit, Sherlock." He smirked and put the recording back on.

"Hey, why don't you take that outside," a voice said to Dave on the recorder.

"Okay. Okay. I will. Take it easy, it's getting a little hot in here. I think I need some air anyway."

Dave clicked off the recorder again. "Buzz, that's when I stepped out of the van to light up a cigarette." He then turned the recorder back on, and the other voices in the van continued after Dave left the van. "Not sure what this seed talk is about. Very strange. I think we should make today's messages a priority three level. What do you think, Dave?"

"I think you're right, Joe. It sounds very weird that these young guys would have such an interest in farming. Do you think they could be into growing pot? They could use this money to help any radical causes."

Buzz reached out, turned off the recorder, and looked at Dave. "Dave, what's the difference between one, two, and three in priority?"

Dave took off his headphones. "Communications are classified by levels of priority: one being the highest that would require immediate action by the team and notification to supervisors; two being significant but not urgent, and it would be sent to the supervisor by the end of the shift; three meaning suspicious but notified in writing at the end of the twelve- to twenty-four-hour shift as a log, to be submitted to the supervisor, who was to get it on his desk the next day; four being not suspicious but reviewed at the end of the week by a supervisor.

"Now, Buzz, please, let's continue with the recording. This is where I returned to the van after finishing my cigarette." Dave turned the recorder back on.

"Hey, guys, any more updates on our farmers?"

"Yes, Dave, as a matter of fact. They indicated that they are expecting a shipment of pigs within the next few weeks."

"Pigs? Man, they really are into farming. They don't know how much work is involved with raising pigs. I had an uncle who raised them and—"

"Listen, will ya, Dave," said Joe. "How did you get this job, anyway? Do you have a relative that hired you?"

"I don't think this is just about seeds and pigs. I think this is some type of code they're using. But code for what is the question," said Dave. "I think it's about pot, if you ask me. Lots of money in growing and selling it."

"Could be. Could be," said Joe. "Even if you're correct, it's such a strange thing that I still think it's a level three. Perhaps even two."

"Level two? Nah. Not that high. Level three?" replied Dave.

"Yeah, I suppose," said Joe.

"Well if you want to know what I think," said Dave.

"No I don't," darted out of Joe's mouths.

Dave jumped back a bit, hitting his back on the van door. "Okay then, screw you guys." Joe chuckled.

Dave then opened the van door, quickly stepped out, and slammed the door behind him.

"He's probably going to go have a good cry," said Joe.

Dave explained to Buzz what happened outside the van, that he had walked around the block to cool off and have another smoke, that his cell phone then went off, but there was no answer, and the phone quickly clicked off. He had noticed the number was the code from the van.

Dave leaned forward toward Buzz. "I thought it strange they would call me and then hang up, so I thought I better get back and see what that was about. When I got within several feet of the van, I noticed some reddish liquid dripping from under the van's back door. I crept up to the door, grabbed the handle, and opened it. The sight made be gasp, then gag. I saw both my partners lying dead on the floor and the van equipment all destroyed. Blood was everywhere. Both of them had had their throats slashed."

Dave then described to Buzz that he grabbed his phone and dialed 1 on the speed dial while he checked both of them out. He spoke with the FBI operator, telling her what had happened and asking for help.

Buzz looked up at Dave, his mouth agape, horror written all over his face. "Oh, man. You poor guy."

"Me? My poor partners, you mean. It was awful, to say the least." Dave put the headphones and equipment back into his backpack. "So, anything about any of this strike you at all?"

"Don't know if it means anything but—"

Dave shut the bag and placed it on the table. "But what, Buzz?"

"The stuff about pigs and farms."

"What? Did you hear about that before?"

"Yeah. That's what Ahzid, our physicist, blurted out to me the last day I saw him—when he ran off on the day of that seed case that I mentioned to you with the missing seeds. Do you know who did it?"

He gulped the last of his coffee. "Not yet. But I can assure you that this whole investigation is top priority."

"What happened after you called for help?" asked Buzz.

"Well our team supervising-agent, along with several other agents, came to help. As I recall, the conversation went something like this:"

Agent Dave. What the hell went down here?

I left the van to have a cigarette and was gone only for five minutes or so and came back to find them like this. No one else was around.

So no one else was on surveillance then. We're checking any local street cameras that were in the area but haven't got anything yet. However, it looks like they both were involved with listening to something. Neither was up near the outside monitor to keep an eye on the area.

I feel awful about this. If only I had been there to help.

Do you know what they had last communicated?

Yes, it was about pigs. The pig farm—

Just then, Dave's phone rang. "Buzz, excuse me. I need to take this call." He took the phone out of his pocket, and it indicated there was an encrypted message sent to him. "Holy shit," said Dave.

Buzz stood up and walked over to Dave. "What is it?"

"Looks like the agents transmitted their last conversation to my phone. Likely just before they were attacked—or during perhaps the attack."

"Quick. Let's decode what it says." Buzz leaned forward to watch Dave enter various codes to get it translated. "So what did it say?"

"Patriot's Day, all die," said Dave.

"Did you say Patriot's Day?" asked Buzz.

"Yeah, why—"

"Holy shit. That's when the marathon happens."

"Yeah. Okay. So What does that have to do with any of this?"

"Don't you see, Dave? The bombings occurred just a few years ago in Boston. There could be a link to the upcoming marathon and terrorists trying to repeat it but this time perhaps even bigger. I've got to tell Doc. He may be able to put the dots together better than I."

CHAPTER 12: SPACE AND TIME

BRIDGET HAD TRIED CALLING MILLER WHEN HE SAID HE WAS going to be visiting his patient, George. She became worried when he didn't return her calls. Early the next morning when he still didn't answer his phone, she went into the department to see if she could catch him there and talk with him in his office.

Bridget knocked on Miller's office door, but there was no answer. She tried a few more times, each with a louder knock than before. She finally tried the handle, and to her surprise, the door opened. She stuck her head in, said "hello," and waited a few seconds but didn't hear any response, so she walked inside. When she approached his desk, she gasped to see the back of Jacob's head as he sat in his chair with his back to her. "Jacob!"

Jake jumped and spun the chair around to face her. "Oh, hi, Bridget. I didn't hear you come in." He rubbed his eyes with his closed fists.

Bridget peered at the wall in front of Jake as she marched around the desk and stood in front of him. "I guess the hell you didn't. What's going on? You scared me half to death. I tried calling you day and night yesterday, and then this morning."

Miller looked away from her, lowering his head in his lap. "I'm sorry, Bridget," he softly said.

"Jake, what's wrong with you? You look so down—and tired. Have you been here all night?"

Miller looked back up at Bridget. "Yes, I have been here all night. Listen, I didn't want to burden you, but I've been down because of my patients dying."

103

Bridget knelt next to Jack and held his hand. "I'm so sorry. I know how difficult it has been for you, losing your patients and all. I know you care for all of them so much." She then wrapped her arms around him and squeezed. She gave him a kiss on the lips but got no response. ?She snapped her head back. "Well I thought I might at least get a kiss from you."

Miller gave her a blank look, void of any expression. "What? Oh. I'm sorry, Bridget. I guess it's just everything that's going on … it's got me down so."

"I understand, but you can't let this—"

Miller reached out to grab her arm with one of his hands and raised his other with the index finger pointed upward. "I do have some good news though. Buzz called me last night to tell me he thinks his friend who works in the FBI may be able to help us. He couldn't talk much over the phone, but he seemed very excited to work on some information he had." He looked at Bridget, who didn't say anything. "Oh, did I just cut you off?"

Bridget pouted but didn't say anything.

"I'm so sorry. I apologize. This whole thing feels like an elephant sitting on my chest, stabbing me with pins—no, knives."

Bridget stood up and walked over to the papers hanging on the wall that she had noticed when first walking in. "What have you done to the wall?"

"What? I'm sorry, Bridget. What did you say?"

Bridget pointed at the obituaries hanging on the wall and looked at him sternly. "Your wall, I said. What have you done to this wall?" She pointed to the wall and stepped closer to it. "All these … obituaries? Up here. They had you frozen like a statue staring at them a moment ago when I walked in."

"Oh … oh that, the wall."

She stepped toward Jake, bent down to his eye level, and raised her eyebrows. "Hello! Yes, the wall. Those are obituaries. Are they not?" She moved back toward the wall for a closer look at them. "They are obituaries! Seriously, are you okay? You've been down in your office every night for hours the past few days after dinner. What's going on?"

"I'm sorry. I should have talked with you about this."

Bridget pulled a chair from the front of his desk around to sit next to him. "Talked to me about what, Jake?"

"As you know, I have been flogging myself about my patients dying."

Bridget leaned over to him and held his hands. "Oh, honey. Of course you have. You are a very caring doctor. You never like to lose a patient."

"I know. But what I mean is that these particular patients should not be dying."

"I know. I know. You've said that over and over again, but in the end, everybody dies, and you cannot save everyone."

Jake pulled his hands away from her grip and pounded the desk a few times. "No. No. You just don't get it. They should have been cured."

Bridget sat up and looked surprised and annoyed at Jake's behavior. "Yes. I know. You have told me so, and I believe you. You don't need to get angry about it. So what are we going to do about it?"

Jake turned his chair to face Bridget. He finally smiled to animate his face and erase his stone-like expression. "Glad you asked me that question. I think I've found a pattern." Jacob swiveled 180 degrees in his chair and pointed to the wall off to the side. "Look over there."

"Oh, yes! That wall. I remember it well from when you had me and Buzz and Ahzid here together to look at those flow charts and Venn diagrams you made."

"Yes, indeed. But now you may notice I added something to the charts. I followed your advice about looking at not only those who failed treatment but also those who were cured. I now compare the patients dying unexpectedly on one side to others treated during the same time period with a similar diagnosis and stage, those that didn't die unexpectedly, on the other side. In this particular permutation, I used the same radiation technique, brachytherapy, to keep the variables as small as possible."

He stood and walked over to the wall. "Bridget, notice anything unusual about one side compared to the other?"

She walked the entire length of the wall, scanning it up and down. After she finished, she turned back to Jacob, who stood next to her.

"And? What about those that failed?"

"Two words. Ahzid and brachytherapy are only involved for all those that failed treatment."

He made a fist and shook his arm. "Exactly. I knew you would pick up on that pattern. Each and every one of these patients that died, what I call unexpectedly, was treated by radiation alone, using brachytherapy, and by one physicist each time, Ahzid."

"Chance? Coincidence?" Bridget asked. Her head always tilted to her right with a cute little corner-of-the-mouth smile when she was playing devil's advocate.

"Ahhhh. Naturally one has to consider that." Jacob sat back in his thick leather chair, which made a swishing sound.

"Which I did. But this is unlikely. Why, you might ask. Let me show you something, and I think you'll agree with me."

Bridget sat back down next to him at the desk. "Jake, so you're telling me that you used the same radioisotopes for all your implants, either permanent or temporary, into the tumors directly, which gave a high dose of radiation right into the tumor and minimized treating any normal tissues or structures near the tumor. Just like the case you helped me with that first day of ours in the OR with doing the prostate seed implant?"

"Well there are different ways of putting the radiation sources into the tumor. But I use this technique most often to treat breast cancers, gynecologic cancers like cervical or endometrial, and prostate cancers. And it can and has been used for others as well." Miller stood and walked to the other side of the wall. "Now, look closely at this newer diagram of the other patients, next to the ones we first looked at. Anything jump out at you within the categories I have set up, that are like the other patients?"

Bridget walked over next to Jake and, again, took her time. As much as she could be impulsive with her thoughts, she could be equally as pensive when called for. She again swept her eyes over the patient information. "Only one thing different this time."

Jake smiled. "And what might that be?"

"Different dosimetrist. Buzz. Not Ahzid. Only Buzz was the dosimetrist with you on these particular patients listed as cured."

"Bingo!" Miller walked over to her and gave her a high-five.

Bridget sighed. "This is all well and good, Jake, but I'm still not convinced that it's the radiation, or lack thereof, that's killing all the patients. Could Ahzid have stolen all the seeds alone? I doubt it. So stop beating yourself up. Strange things happen. No one wants to lose a patient."

Miller leaned in closer and gave her a big kiss on her forehead. He rubbed his arms excitedly.

"What is? You're scaring me."

Miller jumped up and out of his chair. "No. No. I'm fine. I just get a little 'hyper' when I'm thinking rapidly."

"So now what are you going to do? Try going to the police again?"

"No, I need to do a lot more digging into this. I have to be sure about things before I say anything to anybody. Please keep this to yourself."

Bridget frowned. "Of course. Of course I will. You know you don't even need to ask me that."

Miller bit at the inside of his mouth and looked away from Bridget. *I'm not sure what the next step is. I need to find out the exact link between Ahzid and these patients.*

Bridget took a deep breath. "Jake, I do care about you. Very much. But I have to be honest with you I think we need some time and space apart. I have been meaning to talk with you about this, but I was not sure about it until today. Your outburst has made me more convinced than ever."

Jake jerked his head around to face Bridget. "What do you mean?"

"Jake, I don't like the person you are right now. To be frank, I think you have some type of mental illness. The horrible experiences you had at the orphanage probably have something to do with it. I have the name of a good—"

Miller pounded the desk with his fist. Then he slowly turned his head to look directly at Bridget. "Are you calling me mentally ill? I'm not mentally ill! And I don't need any help. I tried that type of mental illness therapy before, after I got out of the orphanage, and it did nothing for me."

Bridget backed away. "You see. The way you snap at me. And I'm only trying to help you."

"Help me? Right! Just like those nuns who kept saying that they were only trying to help me. The beatings were for my own good, they would say. They never loved me. Are you sure how you feel about me? Look at me. I'm a very successful doctor and scientist. I don't need anyone. I have made it on my own. And my patients love me too."

Bridget shook her head. "Look at how you snap without any reason, or, like the other night, when you asked me if I really meant it when I said I could fall in love you. Honestly, I think you also have tendencies toward depression and mania. Certainly with trust and abandonment. I care enough about you to be honest with you, to help you get the help you need, but you have to want it."

Miller threw the pencil in his hand at the wall. "If you really loved me, you would understand."

Bridget reached for Jake's hand, but he yanked it away from her. "Jake, do you hear yourself? Look at how you're acting toward me. Listen to what you're saying." Bridget wiped her tears with a tissue she took out of her purse, stood up cautiously, and looked down at Miller, who sat slumped over in his chair, looking at the floor, his hands clasped and twirling his thumbs rapidly. "Jake, I have enjoyed our brief time together, but you need to resolve your inner conflicts created from your past so you can move forward and let go of those trust issues." Bridget stared down at Jake, waiting for a response. None came. "Jake, you need to get therapy." She turned and began to walk away.

Jake suddenly sat up straight and turned his chair to face his desk, and Bridget. "Wait!"

Bridget stopped and turned around. "Yes, Jake, what is it?"

He peered at her for a moment with squinted eyes. "I don't need any therapy." He then reached into the bottom desk drawer to grab a bottle of scotch, pulled it out, and thumped it on top of his desk. "This is all the therapy I need. Therapists are just people who can't work out their own head problems but try to do it by helping others. I can work anything out on my own. And with the help of my little friend here, Scottie." He tapped the top of the bottle of scotch. "By the way, he's a damn good listener, too."

Bridget peered back at him, shook her head side to side again, and waved her finger at him. "You see. The fact that you don't even see or admit that you need professional help from your past puts me off.

It's obvious that your past creates problems with your work and your patients—relationships as a whole. I can tell you regress under stress. It's almost as if you become another person and are reliving the past—or something evil from the past takes over."

"Damn it. I'm not nuts!" He whipped the shot glass that he had just poured against the wall, shattering it. The overhead lights shined on the tiny pieces, each acting like a prism. It would have been a beautiful sight, like a Disney light show, if it had not been the result of smashed glass during an argument. He stared at the broken pieces of glass on the floor.

Bridget stepped toward Jake with her arms out to touch him. "Calm down," she said. "I never said you were nuts. I merely said you need to get professional help to deal with how your past is affecting you now." She placed a hand on his shoulder and over him. "Let me help you pick up the glass."

Miller snapped at her. He pushed her hand off his shoulder and looked up at her. "No! Leave me alone! I'll take care of it. I don't need your help—or anybody else's."

Bridget grabbed at the wrist and held onto her arm that he had pushed. "You see. It's like a dark side of you is coming out from your past."

He stood and walked up to her. Only inches from her face. "Look, if I'm so evil, why don't you just get the hell out of here."

Bridget leaned back, staring at him. "Don't you swear at me, Jake. I don't deserve that, and you know it."

Jake whipped back around, sat back down in his chair, and threw his arms up in the air. "Just get out of here. Will you? Just go!"

Bridget walked over to him and looked down at him. "You know, you're right. Like I said before, the time apart will do us both good. But in our short time together, I also do believe our souls are connected." She reached into her pants pocket and pulled out one of her business cards and wrote a phone number and name on the back of it. "This is the name and number of a therapist that helped me get through my family losses and can help you too—if you allow him." Miller rested his head in his cupped hands and didn't move. She placed the card down on his desk, grabbed her coat that she had laid on the chair near the door, and walked out without saying another word. She slammed the door behind her on the way out.

Damn! I can't believe this. How could she just up and leave like that? Should I go after her? God. How could this happen to me? He began rubbing his right forearm. Back and forth. Back and forth. After a solid minute of it, he stopped. It looked like a ripe tomato with barely any hair on it from all of the rubbing done over the years. *Okay, let's see, what did those therapists used to say to me. Oh, yeah, whenever I feel like I'm out of control and angry, I close my eyes and think about the people that make me feel secure. That's it. Deep breaths. Deep breaths. In. Out. In. Out. She'll come back. I can't take this anymore. I need to stop pushing the people I love and care for away. It's got to stop.* His realizing that Bridget may be right about his needing help brought pain and emptiness deep into his viscera. He stood and threw the rubber ball he had been squeezing in his hand against the wall, walked to the door, and opened it. He looked down the hallway to see if Bridget was still there, but she had already left the departme

His cell phone began to ring. Miller took it off his belt, smirked, and answered it. "Well, it didn't take you long to say 'I'm sorry.'"

"Sorry? Sorry about what, Doc?"

"Buzz?" said Miller. "I thought you were someone else."

"Who'd ya think I was? Bridget?"

"Yes … I just assumed it and didn't check the number. We had a little tiff. I thought it was her realizing she made a mistake by leaving."

"Yeah. Good luck with that, big guy. A woman admitting she made a mistake. You'll be waiting a long time to hear that, my friend."

"I'm so worked up right now. I just have to go to the gym down the street to get some frustration out of me. With everything going on, I haven't had the time to work out the way I used to. I need to release some of this built-up frustration. A good fight sounds good right about now."

"I'll come over to watch ya. You know how I like to watch you in those amateur matches they have at the gym. Maybe we can get a bite to eat after."

"Sure. And a few stiff drinks to go with it."

CHAPTER 13: RAGING BULL

MILLER HAD NOT BEEN WORKING OUT THE WAY HE HAD BEEN prior to all the stress from his patients dying and the stolen radiation. At one time, he had been working out every day, up at five am for a run down the Charles, then to the gym for weights, and then another hour stretching and practicing his mixed martial arts moves. Judo, tai kwon do, and boxing were the main ones, with kicking and boxing on the heavy bag. He had often competed in the regular amateur matches the gym had, but he had not competed in a kickboxing or karate match now for over a year. He called over to the gym and signed up for the matches to be held early that evening.

The gym where he worked out was about a mile from the hospital, and he thought the walk there would be invigorating for him. There was a definite late-afternoon chill in the air that time in late March, but no snow at least. On his way there, he couldn't help but notice a dark SUV that seemed to be following him as he walked down the street. To test whether he was right, he tried losing the car on foot. First he ran about a block and hid in an alleyway. He waited for a minute then looked back out of the alleyway onto the street. No SUV. So he continued walking to Max's gym.

He didn't see the SUV again until, before going inside, he turned around one last time to see behind him. There across the street sat the SUV. He knew it was the same one because of the government-looking plates on it. He stopped and stared at it. He couldn't see who was inside with its tinted windows. He thought for a moment, then decided to walk over to it, more out of annoyance than curiosity, but as soon as he took a few steps toward it, the SUV took off.

He watched it drive away. *Very weird.* He then went inside the gym to warm up and look at the fight competition list. The matches were based on fighting level experience and weight class. The competition was held upstairs. A very large mat covered the center of the gym for the fights, with ropes around the perimeter to keep the fighters inside them. The crowd sat mostly above the gym floor in the stands, but there were also people outside the ropes that were related to the fighters or VIPs. There was a big crowd for the night with about one hundred people sitting and many more standing behind them.

"Doc! Hey, Doc," Buzz said as he walked hurriedly toward Miller.

Miller turned to Buzz now standing beside him in his corner. "Hey, Buzz. Glad you could make it."

"Are you kidding, Doc? Have I ever missed any of your matches?"

Miller smiled. "No, I guess you haven't. Listen, I have to change. I'll be right out."

Buzz patted him on the back. "Sure. Sure. I'll wait here for ya."

Miller came back out dressed for the fight within a few minutes. "Buzz, not sure how I'll do. I haven't done one of these in a while and am not in the best of shape." They walked over to the warm-up area, and Miller started to alternate jumping rope, shadow boxing, and hitting the speed bag.

Max came over to talk with Miller. "Hi ya, Buzz."

"Hi ya, Max. Expect Jake to kick some butt out there."

"I agree. Now, Jake, Butch is tough. But he's a brawler, so use finesse out there, and he's yours. When you told me you were into a good fight after you and Bridget had a beef, I knew exactly what you meant. Listen, I'm going to get some stuff ready for your corner. I'll see you over there. Okay?"

"You bet, Max." Miller stopped jumping rope and turned to Buzz. "I feel pretty good, even though, like I said, it has been a while since I competed. I was so damn frustrated though; things were building up inside of me, and I thought I was going to explode. And when I called Max, who, as you know, is my friend and the owner, he invited me to compete to get it out of my system. I just couldn't say no. He will be in my corner today also. He's the best." He went back to shadow boxing.

"Hey, Doc? Do you think I could sit with you and Max in your corner?"

Miller gave one last big punch at the bag, then stopped. "Buzz, I don't know. Remember what happened the last time you did?"

"I know. I know. I promise, I won't yell or anything like I did to distract you."

"I appreciate your support, but you can't be throwing things at my opponent and swearing at him, just because you feel he did something illegal or dirty, like you did before."

"I know. I promise. I just want to be there for you. Close to you to give support. Drinks will be on me after the fight."

"Well, all right, if you promise you'll behave."

"I promise. I promise. Thanks, Doc. Really. Thanks. I mean it. I won't let you down. You watch and see."

When it was time for Miller's match, he and his opponent, Butch, were called out to the center of the mat where the referee waited. Butch had a few teeth and cauliflower ears, a flattened nose, and small, deep-set eyes from the scarred tissue around them. After the rules were outlined for them, they exchanged glove tapping and commenced fighting. It was slow at first, with each one not wanting to commit too much at the beginning. They circled each other, giving half-hearted kicks and punches periodically. Miller found himself not as aggressive as he used to be, not timid, just more cautions. Max was now yelling from the corner, "Wake up. Move. What are you doing? Get your hands up, start moving, don't just stand there. Go get him. Come on. You got this fight."

The crowds were beginning to yell negative things like "stop dancing and fight." The referee even warned Miller to "fight." He clearly had lost round one.

Miller's attitude and aggressiveness changed, however, when he came out of his corner for round two and his opponent began to laugh and taunt him with things like "come on, chicken, fight me." And when he said, "I guess you got no problem with letting your patients die when they can't fight back at cha, but you ain't so tough, huh? When you got fists and legs comin' at cha, huh?"

Miller's heart raced. The fight-or-flight response kicked in, and he chose fight. Something snapped inside. Miller saw red, and it was all Butch, and he became the bull. He began to kick and punch like a machine with the stop switch broken on it, knocking his opponent down several times. With only a few seconds left in the round, he snapped a powerful spinning kick, catching his opponent's left temple, sending him hard to the mat. The sound of both the bone-to-bone contact and then his head hitting the mat echoed throughout the gym. The crowd immediately stood and gasped at the sound of it and the sight of his opponent laying motionless on the mat. Blood began to pour out of his nose.

Miller had not only won round two, but if not for the bell sounding the end of round two, the fight may have been over, for it looked as though the referee came close to stopping it when it looked so one sided. As Miller walked back to his corner for the one-minute inter-round break, he saw how the crowd had changed toward him. They were cheering him on and chanting, "Miller, Miller." Many if not all stood with their fists waving in the air. He now felt like a Roman gladiator with the crowd cheering for him and wanting blood. In an instant, he had gone from the bum to the hero.

When the bell rang for the start of the third round, Miller came out fighting like a bull with his opponent being the red flag waving in front of him. Within less than a minute, Miller again pummeled him so much that the referee stepped in to see if the fighter could go on. He told Miller to stand back and away, over near the ropes, while he counted to ten. The other fighter looked as though he didn't know where he was, and the referee stopped the fight immediately. He went over and raised Miller's arm to signify he had won. Buzz and Max hugged him and congratulated him when he came over to his corner.

* * *

Later at O'Rouke's Bar and Grill, where Miller liked to go in his neighborhood to mingle with the regular dirt-under-the-nails folks,

Miller and Buzz had been celebrating for hours. They ate. They drank. And they drank some more.

"I've seen you workout and fight before but never like tonight. Where did you learn to fight like that?"

"Hey. Buzzie, Wuzzie, my dear friend. I grew up fighting. I had to fight to survive. I fight only in these local matches to keep in shape, and occasionally a few ego-building trophies. I never wanted to hurt anyone. I never let my anger fuel my fighting like I did when I had to—when I was younger, that is, and trying to survive every day in the orphanage— until tonight. I had a lot of frustration built up from the quarrel with Bridget, as you know, and when that guy brought up my patients' dying and blaming me, I just lost it. Especially after just spending time at my patients' funerals."

"He deserved what he got tonight in the ring. He was an asshole to say those things." Buzz stood and put his hand on Miller's shoulder while they sat at the bar. "But the families and friends of the ones who've died need to know that it's not your fault. You hear me? Not your fault. And by the way, I knew you were good at mixed martial arts, but I didn't think you were another Bruce Lee."

"Bruce Lee!" Miller slapped the edge of the bar, and his hand slipped off, almost pulling him off of his stool. Buzz reached over to prop him up. "Ha, ha, that's a good one." Miller gulped another shot of scotch, put his arm around Buzz, and looked into his eyes with his half-opened. "Buzz, I do believe you may be someone I can trust. I get so damn depressed whenever I go to one of my patient's funerals. And I'll be visiting my patient and pal, George, at his home again."

"How's he doing?"

"Not so good. I just can't believe that our patients are dying this way. We have to find out exactly what is going on and who's behind it. It can't be Ahzid acting alone."

"I'm not sure about that, but I do know that even months before he took off, he didn't act the same. He kept to himself all the time. And I noticed Ahzid and our technician spent a lot of time together in his office—and in the radiation storage room."

"Buzzy, I couldn't agree more. I even became suspicious and asked him about it."

"What did he say when you asked him?"

"All he said was that he needed to update records and quality-check forms with him."

"Yeah, I remember one day joking with him about his driving a new metallic black Mercedes coupe and that the seed company must be paying technicians pretty well these days. He didn't even smile."

"We should have cured all those people. Do you hear me? Cured them!" said Miller.

After a few more drinks, Buzz brought Miller back to his apartment. He had to help support him into the building and to his door. Miller grabbed Buzz's shirt when they reached the door and pulled him toward him. He almost pulled Buzz to the ground when he lost his balance. "Buzz, I miss Bridget. I miss her so much. I never realized how much till she left. I don't know if I can ever get over it or get her back. I feel she is the first woman I can really trust and is honest to me with her thoughts. Yet I might have scared her away permanently."

"The orphanage shit again, huh?"

"Yeah. And it's really got me down. Like the therapists have said, and it's true—I finally admit it—I can't let people get too close to me, especially women."

"What did they say to ya?"

"My mom." Miller hiccupped. "I trusted her ... more than anything. The abuse, physical and emotional, by the nuns at the orphanage—they gave me a huge mistrust of everyone, especially women."

Buzz stared at Miller and nodded.

Miller repeated his thoughts with a lecturing look. "Buzz, I don't let women get close to me because I believe they will leave me, no matter what they say and do."

Buzz's eyes widened. "Oh. I gotcha. Come on. Let's get you inside. We don't want everyone knowing your business." Buzz opened the door to Miller's condominium and brought him inside, straining to hold him vertical the whole time.

"Buzz, I miss Bridget. I miss her so much."

"I know you do. You told me already."

"I did?"

"Only about a million times so far."

He looked into Buzz's eyes and blinked his very heavy eyelids. "Buzz. I guess I'll have to focus on my lab research and patients, like I always have."

Buzz helped Miller into bed. "Doc, you need to sleep this off. Tomorrow is another day."

Miller looked up at Buzz and blinked to focus his vision. "Buzzie Wuzzie?"

Buzz smiled, rolled his eyes, and leaned over him. "Yeah? What is it?"

"Bridget and I had so much fun just talking and hanging out, and seemed to have so much in common. We both loved the beaches and mountains of New Hampshire and Maine, Nubble Point, one of my favorite places … and watching them make the taffy." Miller sighed and then drifted off to sleep.

Buzz tucked him in. "Goodnight, buddy. We'll talk more tomorrow. And great fight again." Buzz let himself out.

CHAPTER 14: DIGGING UP SEEDS

THE NEXT MORNING, MILLER AWOKE IN HIS BED WITH A MAJOR hangover. His head pounded, and he tasted bile acid in the back of his throat with each belch, which occurred every few minutes. He thought a little alcohol would help, so he poured a glass of single malt, gulped it down, and got dressed. He looked out the bay window of his Beacon Street condo at the Charles River below, then lit up a fire with the few pieces of wood still remaining from the night he and Bridget cuddled on the floor in front of the fire the whole night. He couldn't remember all the details of that night but what he did remember, particularly their waking up without their clothes on, brought a warm feeling inside of him and a wide smile on his face. He wondered was else they did that evening, but couldn't remember. Then he flopped onto the couch to relax until he felt his headache soften and the nausea go away. He grabbed a Pop-Tart out of the kitchen pantry for breakfast and walked over to the Radiation Department.

When he got to his office, he flopped in his desk chair and swiveled right then left, rapidly at first, then he slowed to a full stop. His mind began to race. He realized Bridget was right about the things she had said to him. He needed to get control of his thoughts, feelings, and actions. He wanted to overcome his struggles with trust—trust he lost when he was abandoned at the orphanage. He decided he needed to seek counseling, to deal with his not being able to let go of the orphanage and its memories of the beatings and torture he endured there.

He looked at the pictures of him and patients on the walls of his office, the certificates of all his research and clinical awards, and then the trophies on the shelves of his athletic achievements, including his martial arts awards. Suddenly, he realized that he was sweating profusely. He grabbed a towel off of a nearby chair, dried himself off, and called the therapist's number on the card that Bridget had placed on his desk.

* * *

Jacob drove slowly around the block to check out the building where the therapist's office was. He was careful to look around at the area and the people walking on the streets. Late morning in Boston was a relatively busy time for pedestrian traffic, which he thought was both good and bad—lower chance that anyone paid attention to anyone else walking by them, but also a higher chance that there might be someone who would recognize him. The last thing he wanted was to be seen going in to see a psychotherapist at a mental health center.

He managed to find a parking spot a block away from the office. He dressed with a hat pulled down over his forehead and sunglasses. With the gusts of wind that day, he held onto the brim to make sure it wouldn't blow away and expose him, and he managed to sneak into the building without seeing anyone he knew. Once inside the office, he felt somewhat relieved. *I have to do this. I have to see if what's happening to me is related to anything else in my life, past or present. But for something that's supposed to help me with things like my anxiety, this visit sure makes me feel anxious.*

He walked down the hall to the therapist's office, opened the door, and poked his head inside. No one else was there. He walked inside and noticed that Enya music played and incense candles burned. He looked around the waiting room. Books lined a nearby bookcase, and he looked closely at the selection. "Hm. Interesting." One title read *Modern Psychotherapy*, and another read, *A Guide to Self-Help and Self-Healing*. He sat down on a sofa and looked through the magazines laid out on the coffee table in front of him. He noticed a door off to his left that said 'Office' on the glass with a little sign underneath it that said 'Therapy in Session'.

After a few minutes, Jacob put down the magazine he had been thumbing through, folded his arms, and began to tap his foot. He shook his head. *Maybe I shouldn't have come here. The whole thing is stupid.*

119

I'm so out of here. He pushed himself up and off the couch and began to walk to the exit. But just as Miller reached for the door handle, a soft-spoken voice came from behind him, "Hello, can I help you?"

Miller stopped and turned around. "Are you the psychotherapist? I was waiting for my appoint—"

"Ah. " He smiled widely. "You must be Dr. Miller, my twelve o'clock. Please. Do come in." He waved him on and turned to enter his inner office.

Dr. Miller raised his eyebrows and one corner of his mouth, shrugged his shoulders, and followed him to his inner office. *I came this far. What the hell else do I have to lose?*

"Please, please. Come in and sit down. I'm Dr. Lazlow. Sorry to be a few minutes late, but I lost track of time with my patient."

Miller looked at him. "Patient? I didn't see anybody come out of your office."

"Oh, that's because they can use the back entrance you see over there." He pointed to the door at the back of the office. "Some feel anxious about being seen leaving the office so choose to go out the back."

Miller nodded in agreement. "Really. That's cool. I can see how some may feel that way." Miller waved his hands, palms down. "Not that I feel that way, mind you."

"Of course not. But if you did, that would be fine too." Lazlow sat back in his office chair, clasped his hands, and began twirling his thumbs. "So, Dr. Miller. What do you seek from me?"

Miller pouted his lips and shrugged his shoulders.

"In other words, what troubles you?"

"Well, Dr. Lazlow, to tell you the truth, I'm not sure … well … I mean, I do have things that have been troubling me, but I'm not sure if there's anything you could do about them. I called because someone suggested I need help. And I thought about her comments."

"And?" said Lazlow. He pressed Miller to respond with his eyes pointing at him.

"And I think she may right."

"Tell me then what things are troubling you now, and we can go from there."

Jake sighed. "Let's see, where do I begin? My patients die when they shouldn't be dying, my girlfriend broke up with me; I have been told I build walls around myself to keep others out and that I need mental health help. Should I continue?"

"Wow," said Lazlow. He leaned forward and rested his arms on the desk. "Jacob. May I address you with your first name?"

"Yes, please, and I go by Jake."

Lazlow smiled and nodded. "Jake, you certainly should feel stress, at the very least, from any one of those things. Who told you that you needed help?"

"Most recently, my girl—ex-girlfriend. She thought I have problems with control because of things that happened to me in the past. Like being raised in an orphanage."

"Orphanage? Oh, I see. And you build walls around yourself? Or you have been told that anyway. Correct?"

"I don't know, I'm not sure. Well, yes, I suppose so. I would describe them perhaps as not walls that keep everyone out of—let's call it my castle—or everyone out completely."

"Is anybody ever allowed inside the castle itself?"

"Yes, on occasion, but to continue the metaphor, I don't let them into the most intimate parts of the castle, and certainly not in my secret room."

Dr. Lazlow sat up straight and shot a curious look at him. "What do you mean by secret room?"

Jake leaned forward, looked left to right with only his eyes. "It is a place where only I can go, and even I sometimes don't even let myself go there. It's a place where my deepest, darkest secrets are. Where I'm sometimes afraid to deal with them or are afraid to find out what they really are."

"Do you mean it's a place where things are kept that bother you?"

"I think I have mixed feelings about it. I feel I go there to try to understand things, try to ask myself, 'Who am I?' or why I'm the way I am about things or in general. It's a place that I try to confront the truth."

"Jacob, that can be a scary place for anybody. We all have those places in one form or another. Tell me, who are the people, if there are any, you would trust with your innermost thoughts? Maybe not all of

121

them, but at least some of them. For example, your mother perhaps. Most people feel that's someone they can trust."

Jake began rubbing his right arm. "My mother? Huh! I never really got to know my mother for very long. And from the little bit I know from others, I certainly don't think she cared to know me; otherwise, why would she have abandoned me there? All I know for sure is what Sister Asshole at the orphanage would tell me, often during one of her rants and beatings."

Dr. Lazlow looked down and swung his head left to right. "How awful. And what did she tell you, Jake?"

"She would say awful things like, 'Your mother dumped you here because she didn't want to deal with her bastard child.'"

Dr. Lazlow got up, sat next to Jake on one of the chairs, and handed him the set of headphones off of a nearby shelf. Jake noticed one leg of Lazlow's seemed shorter than the other, so that when he walked, he had a very noticeable limp that made him bob up and down. *Perhaps an accident. Or maybe a birth defect.*

"Jake, I would like to have you try to relax and listen to this CD with the headphones on while we talk. He connected the headphones to the nearby CD player and looked over at Jake. "It's just a very low sound of a click that will go from one of your ears to the other. Studies show that this can open up the subconscious mind, which allows you to recall things that you may not otherwise."

Miller looked at them skeptically. "Okay. I guess you know what you're doing."

"Now, Jacob, I want you to listen to the clicking sounds going from one ear to the other as I mentioned. Let yourself relax and go with your thoughts. I'll ask you questions, and just give me your first thoughts that come to mind. Don't question it. Let things flow outward. You mentioned to me your being sent to the orphanage as a boy."

"Yes. I would say that was one of the worst experiences of my life. I was about five years old."

Dr. Lazlow poured himself and Miller glasses of water. "Why don't you try closing your eyes and relaxing. The clicking sounds will eventually reach a faster tempo."

"I hear them. It sounds like someone snapping their fingers in my ears."

"Exactly. This will help us go a bit deeper into your subconscious. Now, try picturing what you can remember. Can you remember the day you went to the orphanage? If so, picture it and try, if you can, going through that experience. Go back and be that little boy on the day you first went to the orphanage."

Jacob began taking deep breaths, then began talking about his experiences at St. Peter's Orphanage. While he talked, he sometimes appeared like an observer of the events, as if he were actually back at the orphanage, describing the scenes, and sometimes he would speak as though he were actually living in the past, as Jacob, at that very moment. He became that boy again going through what he had gone through back then.

"I see Jacob as a scared little boy sitting in the backseat of a big car. His mother sat in the front on the passenger side looking back at him. Jacob couldn't stop crying during the trip. 'Please, please, I don't want to go. Why can't I stay with you?' 'Mommy just needs time in the hospital to get well,' said his mother. 'I promise, as soon as I'm feeling better, the first thing I'll do is come get you. I promise.' But she never came back to get Jacob."

Dr. Lazlow stood up, walked over to Jake, and put his hand on his shoulder. "I'm so sorry, Jacob."

Jacob continued talking as a real-time observer again. "He would never be able to forget his very first morning at breakfast. Sister Blackenstein couldn't wait to demonstrate her power to all the new kids. She seemed to derive an extra special thrill by being mean and nasty to those who didn't know her as yet, and certainly didn't know the rules—her rules. The oatmeal tasted awful. His stomach turned at the sight of it. He couldn't eat another bite after his first, put down the spoon, and stared at it, occasionally lifting his eyes to look around at the other boys to see if they were eating. Suddenly, his scalp burned. Sister Blackenstein had snuck up behind him and pulled so hard on his hair that she lifted him out of his seat. The pain radiated down his spine."

"'What hand do you eat with?' she shouted at him.

"'M-my right,' he responded.

"'Put it out,' she demanded.

He slowly raised it out to her. She grabbed it before he could even straighten it. She then began hitting it repeatedly with a hardwood stick that she held in her other hand. He tried pulling away, but that only infuriated her, making her hit him even harder. He then began to cry and rub it, as it hurt so much. It swelled and bruised terribly. The rubbing gave him some comfort when no one else offered any. He looked at the others either snickering or looking away with fear that they could be next.

Jacob shook his head and suddenly blurted out, "I can't talk about it now." He pulled out his earplugs, threw them on the table, and jumped up from the couch. He grabbed Dr. Lazlow by the shirt collar and pulled him toward him so that their noses almost touched. "Listen, Sister, you're not going to ever hurt me again. You hear me?"

Lazlow coughed, grabbed Miller's wrists, and tried to pull them away. "Jacob, it's me, Dr. Lazlow. Not Sister Blackenstein."

"What? Who are you?" Miller's eyes opened widely.

"It's okay. It's okay, Jacob. You don't have to talk about it now. Just, please, let go of me and sit back down," he said in a mousy voice like he had just inhaled helium gas, from his larynx being compressed.

Jacob looked down at his hands clawing onto Lazlow's shirt so tightly that it pinched the underlying skin of his neck. He quickly let go of his shirt, almost like trying to shoo it away, like some nasty spider had crawled on his hands. "I'm so sorry. I guess I lost control. Being back there frightens me so." He flopped back down on the couch. "Screw those bitches and bastards at the orphanage. I think I told you already that I still have night terrors about that place."

Laslow coughed a few times to clear his throat, took a few deep breaths and then a gulp of water. "I understand. I really do. We don't have to continue today if you are upset."

Miller moved to the edge of his seat. He sat in thought for a moment, staring down at his feet, kicking their sides together, then lifted his head. "No. I want to try again. It's draining, but it's also cathartic."

Lazlow rubbed the skin over his larynx, as though he was checking to make sure he still had some there covering his voice box. "Okay then. Let's do it." He brushed himself off, cleared his throat again, and sat back in his chair. "Tell me of positive experiences you had or positive people you knew at the orphanage, or both." He held his pen over the pad of paper he held in anticipation.

"Well. Yes. There is, of course, my friend Ahzid."

Dr. Lazlow stood up and turned on the ceiling fan. "Jake, I'm a bit hot. Do you mind if I turn this on?"

Jake shook his head.

"Thank you." He sat back in his chair across from Jake. "Why don't you sit back on the couch to totally relax."

Jack nodded and sat back.

"Good. Now, tell me about Ahzid." Lazlow handed him the earplugs. "Here, put the ear plugs back into your ears. I'll turn on the tape. Listen to the alternating tones again. Relax. Take deep breaths. In and out. Slowly. That's it. Slowly. In and out. Good. When you feel loose and relaxed, tell me about Ahzid."

Jake took in several deep breaths, exhaled each slowly, and began talking in the third person right away, as the outside observer again. "Ahzid and Jacob had common ground for sure. Neither had parents. Ahzid's father died in the Arab-Israel war, and, according to Ahzid, his mother died as a suicide bomber and gave the money she earned for it to her family in the States for him to go live with his uncle and aunt who owned a gas station/mart. They had some type of accident later, or just became too ill, and he was take to the orphanage because there was no one else he could live with." Miller sat up on the couch like he had just awoken from a bad dream. "I need a drink of water, Dr. Lazlow. We hit it off immediately; we both liked to discover and learn. Mathematics and science came easy to both of us, and we used it to entertain ourselves and to keep secrets between us."

"Of course." Lazlow poured more water into Jacob's glass. "Jacob, that sounds like you and Ahzid were close. That's so good that you two were able to connect that way. If you don't mind, I would like to move on to something that I think may help you when you leave here today to get through stressful events that cause you anxiety and trigger uncontrolled behavior. Let's try a technique that you can you use anytime, anyplace when you sense you are losing control or feeling out of body. First, tell me of a person or persons that make you feel secure, that make you feel good about yourself, and most of all a person or persons that you trust. If there is a place that you can go to, you can use that also, to go to that place. Although it sounds like you had a trusting relationship with Ahzid, it seems to be associated with a time and place that stirs up too many bad feelings, so I think until you can separate that better, you should not try to think of it. Is there anybody or anyplace else that you could think of that made you feel good about yourself, and you knew they cared about you?"

Miller sat up with a straight back, turned to the right, then to the left, and then looked directly at Dr. Lazlow. " I got to tell you that I had therapy some time ago, and they had me doing similar things. And I have tried it from time to time. But I'll be honest with you, it doesn't seem to help me all that much overall."

"That's okay. Did they use the sound therapy with the headphones also?"

Jake shook his head.

"No? I didn't think so, as this is relatively new. Let's continue, shall we anyway, as I think it works better with the sound therapy."

"Okay. I'm game," said Dr. Miller. "Well, there was this one priest at the orphanage. Out of all of those that gave us Mass, he was the only one who took the time to talk to me. One time I heard him say to one of the nuns to look after me and make sure I was okay."

"What would he say when he talked to you?"

"Just little things, nice things. He asked how am I doing, made sure I study my lessons to become smart, that I eat enough, no matter how awful it may taste, and told me to exercise so I get big and strong to protect myself. That kind of stuff."

"Sounds as though he acted like a surrogate father to you," said Lazlow.

Miller scratched underneath his chin and looked upward. "Never thought of it that way before. But, yes, I guess so, now that you mention it. He did always come to my sporting events and academic events, at the orphanage and later in high school and college. But I'm not sure I can trust anybody right now."

"Nobody? Anybody? Close your eyes and relax. Don't rush."

He closed his eyes, and he took in some deep breaths. Several minutes passed. Not a word. He didn't move a muscle.

Lazlow raised his eyebrows and looked intently at Miller, then looked at his wristwatch. "If you cannot think of anybody or anyplace, not to worry. This is something that we can work on perhaps the next time, if you would like to come back."

Miller opened his eyes and raised his hand. "Wait. Wait. Aside from Ahzid, I just thought of some people at a place where I can feel secure, and I truly trust them."

"Oh? Who are they, and where is this place?"

"St. Francis House. A place I did volunteer work in downtown Boston for the homeless while I was in medical school, and later during my post-graduate training, but less so. There were and still are some real characters there. I really loved going there though. It felt good to care for those who couldn't or wouldn't care for themselves."

"So the experience made you feel good about yourself?"

Miller smiled and nodded. "Yes. Very much so."

"And you trusted the people there?"

"Yes, both my coworkers and the homeless patients I would take care of. There were no hidden agendas. Nothing to gain by their playing games with me—though some may have tried at first as part of the survival skills they learned. As a medical student, I worked there during the summer between my first and second years while working full-time in the laboratory as well." Miller looked off into the distance, romancing about the people and place. "I really became close to a few of the clients. In fact, I recently went back there to visit with the clients and Father O'Brien. I needed to talk with someone I could trust." Miller gave a look of sudden realization. "In that case, I *did* use the technique of surrounding myself with a circle of trust."

"Very good. Excellent. Glad to hear you're using it. And did it work for you?"

Miller tilted his head, shrugged his shoulders, then nodded. "I believe it did."

"Good. And what about your girlfriend, or I guess you said your ex-girlfriend?"

Miller stood up and paced a bit. "I guess I would include her," said

Miller. He stopped and looked down at Lazlow. "To be honest, I never have felt this way about any woman before. In such a short time, I've opened up to her more than I have ever done. I guess I feel comfortable with her. We're alike in many ways.

"She's the first woman I have felt an immediate connection to. We can talk about serious stuff, like life and death with our patients, rather than just sex and having a good time. Don't get me wrong. That has a place in a relationship too." Miller raised his eyebrows a few times like Groucho Marx. "But ..." Miller became silent and looked down at Lazlow.

Lazlow's eyes opened wide, and he leaned closer to Jake, like he could will it out of him. "But?"

"But." He looked at Lazlow and blinked his eyes. "I had an outburst and kind of told her that did I didn't need her." Miller squirmed to be more comfortable and crossed his legs. "I can't wait to make up with her and tell her about visiting you. I don't know if I mentioned to you that she really wanted me to go to a therapist and get help."

"She sounds very compatible with you. Why don't you include her in your circle of trust—at least for now, until you see how things go when you see her again."

Miller looked away in thought and nodded his head. He looked back at Lazlow. "Good idea,doc. Hey, isn't that funny? I'm so used to being called 'doc' by everyone, and here I am, saying it to you. Just sounds kind of weird to me, being on the other side of the couch—if you know what I mean?"

Dr. Lazlow smiled, reached out, and patted him a few times on his knee. "I know exactly what you mean, Jake. Well, I think we have made some very good progress and covered some very important issues. I think your experience with being dropped off, basically abandoned, by your mother and left to grow up there in the orphanage the way you did created deep-seated conflict and problems with trust. In short, you have a type of post-traumatic stress disorder. If you have problems with relationships and trust, it likely stems from this. It's truly amazing that you have become the person you are today. You can be thankful for good genes and being nurtured by a few."

Miller jerked his head back, stood up, and stepped toward Lazlow.

Lazlow put his hands in front of his face, twisted to his right, and bent over as if to protect himself.

"Post-traumatic syndrome! Isn't that associated with serving in wars? I never served in war. What in the hell are you talking about?"

Lazlow extended a hand in front of him. "Jake, please, relax. You don't have to have served in war to have it. It can be due to any serious, traumatic, or perceived traumatic event or events that occur to you."

Miller thought for a moment, sighed, and placed his hands on Lazlow's shoulders. "I'm sorry, Dr. Lazlow. I didn't mean to alarm you." Miller sat back down, put his face in his hands for a few seconds, then looked up at Lazlow. "Yes, I suppose I knew that but didn't want to believe it when I heard it."

Dr. Lazlow approached him and placed a hand on Miller's shoulder. "It's okay. I understand. You push everyone away ultimately because you want to avoid being hurt. It's a very natural, human response to the early childhood assault on your trust. So we have talked for over an hour now. Perhaps we should—"

"Wow! I have talked for over an hour now? So what do you think? Can I overcome this?"

"I'm sure it will take more than one session together for me to even begin to understand you, and in particular, why you are who you are."

Miller nodded in agreement. "I understand, but is there anything at all you can tell me that could help me to understand myself better? Just something to hang my hat on when I go out that door."

"I can say this much. You definitely experienced things in your earlier life that affected you in serious ways. Seeds have been planted in you that can either germinate and, if you feed it the sustenance they need to grow, take hold, or they can be stifled if starved of those things. I like to call these things the Seeds of Destruction. But we can pick up on this more at your next session—that is, if you would like another session."

"Oh, yes. Most definitely," said Miller.

"Good. But for now, when you feel that you're going in a bad place, close your eyes and picture yourself with the people at the St. Francis House that would make you feel good about yourself and secure."

After Jacob left the therapist's office, he tried calling Bridget to tell her about his visit with the therapist. He felt proud of doing so and knew she would feel the same. He wanted her to know that his wanting their relationship to continue made him realize that he needed to deal with the psychological issues created from early childhood that polluted his mind and poisoned his ability to have trusting relationships.

What the hell is going on? Why doesn't she answer her phone? Hey, you dummy. Maybe it has something to do with the fact that you told her to get lost and that you didn't need her. I know. I'll go over to her place if I don't hear back from her. But first, I have to get back to the hospital. And then visit George at his home.

As he stepped out of the therapist's building onto the sidewalk, a car parked in the front suddenly pulled out and sped off. The man on the passenger side was taking pictures of him as they drove away. "Who the hell was that and why was he taking pictures of me?"

CHAPTER 15: GEORGE'S SONG

WHERE IS THIS PLACE? THE GPS SAID IT WAS 1.2 MILES FROM THAT last exit.

For just over two weeks, each evening after finishing his rounds at the hospital, Dr. Miller drove to visit George at his house, ever since he had been declared eligible for hospice care, which allowed him to be transferred from the hospital to his own home for his care. Yet each time he drove there, he felt lost. Lost internally, with an out-of-control feeling that he couldn't put his finger on. His thoughts ran wild as he drove from work, to his house, and back to work again. And each time, he became, literally, lost—externally also. This particular evening, he almost missed the turn off the highway onto the long and tortuous dirt road that led to the old farmhouse. And each time he would visit, he felt he didn't know exactly what to say to George, what to do for him, or what to feel.

But on this trip, he had a different feeling inside. There was a sense of knowing inside of him—knowing how he felt about George; a connection to him. It was not completely clear to him what it all meant, but it was becoming a slightly sharper image to him. Something about this visit tonight was different.

As he traveled to visit him, he became more aware of his surroundings and noticed how the sky was very deep and dark, like a giant black hole. Empty of stars. It had begun to rain when Jake finally found the road off the highway. It had no streetlights. Only vast darkness surrounded him as he traveled down the empty, tortuous dirt road. It was the only road that led to George's house, and it was full of potholes. Some were wide and deep enough that a small car could be swallowed whole.

As he came around the last bend of the road, he saw George's house in front of him. It stood there overlooking everyone and everything. The house where George went to die was big, but empty. It sat all by itself up on a hill, surrounded by a vast, open field. It was devoid of life. No trees, no green grass. In the evening light from the three-quarter moon that became uncovered when the clouds moved across the sky, the silhouette of the house set up high with its surrounding emptiness, dominating the landscape and reminding him of St. Peter's Orphanage.

He slammed on the car's brakes, shoved the gear into park, and turned the motor off. His chin fell to his chest. Waves of nausea ebbed and flowed; with one wave, a bolus of bile shot up from his stomach into the back of his mouth. He tried to keep it down, but then a second wave came, causing him to projectile vomit onto the passenger floor in the front seat next to him. His heart rate increased. His chest wall pounded from inside with each heartbeat. He looked into his rearview mirror and saw his jugular veins pulsating. He took deeper and deeper breaths. Each one closer to the next. Things around him spun. His whole body became cold and wet. The outpouring of adrenaline caused him to soak his clothes through and through. He sunk down and sideways onto the seat, losing consciousness.

Miller couldn't stop crying in his dreams, and he was so scared that he shook uncontrollably. *Please, please, I don't want to go to the orphanage. I'll behave. I promise. I'll be a good boy. Why can't I stay with you, Mommy?* He awoke to the silence of the night, coughing and sweating profusely. Checking his watch, he realized he must have passed out for at least ten minutes. The experience exhausted him, like the feeling he would get at the end of a marathon; each muscle lay flaccid. He was still sick but not to the degree he felt before passing out. He realized he had had a panic attack. And he knew why. He had had these before but had not had one in a while. George's house brought back nightmares of St. Peter's Orphanage, a place that wouldn't stop haunting him.

Post-traumatic stress. That's what the psychiatrist called it. That's what's been happening to me. I can't take this much more. Miller grabbed

132

a gym towel from the backseat and wiped as much as he could of the mess and went inside the house to visit with George. George had warned Miller that his wife had left the house before he came that night, so she didn't have to talk with Miller. She still blamed him for George's cancer failure and now his impending death. He had been told by George over the phone to let himself inside with the key under the doormat.

When Jake peaked inside the first-floor bedroom, he thought he saw a living corpse. George lay in his bed, being eaten alive by his cancer, and there was not a damn thing that anyone could do about it. His own cells that had given him life for so many years had now turned against him. They had become independent of the normal restrictions for growth (the sine qua non of a cancer) and now starved his healthy normal cells of the vital nutrients and oxygen they needed, causing them to enter the state of programmed cell death.

George had told Miller previously that death no longer scared him. Indeed, he welcomed it with open arms. It was the process of dying that scared him; for every minute of every day he remained alive, he would have to experience the constant feelings of pain, nausea, fatigue, weakness, helplessness, hopelessness, and sadness. He had told Jake he wished it didn't have to be such a slow, painful death.

Now bedridden, George had accepted hospice care a few weeks earlier. One might have considered him a yokel, but Miller's knowing him for so long revealed his having a much deeper understanding of the world. His bedroom had the smell of death. Musky, stale air. Not even the dozen or so bouquets placed around the room could mask it. He lay in bed wasting away. Waiting to die. He was now too frail to do most daily living activities, even things like going to the bathroom. His bed served him like his mother's womb had prior to his birth, with everything going in or out of his body done within the confines of his bed rails. He had failed his cancer treatment with a radiation implant and subsequently exhausted all available salvage treatments and was now placed under home hospice care. No explanation could be found for his failure, which was nothing less than a shock to everyone involved with his care. No explanation, until Dr. Miller realized that he was on the list of patients treated by Ahzid, and likely had no or less radiation than needed to kill his cancer, placed in the seeds implanted into his prostate.

And it was so hard for Dr. Miller to see George, watching him die the way he was. He was now a mere fraction of the man he was on the outside when he had first met him, his broad biceps now reduced to bone with skin hanging off of his arms. His once trunk-like fingers that felt like shaking a vice grip now reduced to squeezing a sponge with bones inside of it. His former salt and pepper, wavy, thick head of hair, now a snow-white, thin patchwork on his scalp. Now the scars were showing off the wounds he had talked about that were formed when the medics pulled shrapnel out of his skull during WWII. Now he lay in his ICU-style bed with tubes of all shapes and sizes appearing to dance around him, filling practically every orifice in his body and making some extra ones too. One to monitor heart function, another to check his urine output, and others to provide needed medicines and fluids to him. He also noticed a notebook but with a hardcover and no pictures or writing on the cover on the table next to him. He wondered if he had begun a journal.

Jake knew full well that dying from prostate cancer never is welcome, though when the time is near, everyone wishes it would come quickly. "George, how's your level of pain? Any better than the other day?"

"Not really. Still can be an eleven or twelve out of ten."

His bones, liver, and lungs were now packed with cancer cells. Those fentanyl pain patches controlled it about half the time.

"Sorry, George. You are now getting the highest amounts you can tolerate. We have to limit your breakthrough oral pain pills because they made you so lethargic."

"Well, some days are better than others, though the good ones are becoming fewer. Today seems to be a good one so far." George tried to clear his throat to speak but could only muster a weak dry, hacking cough, the type with one-syllable sounds.

Miller noticed George fighting back the tears. Miller was too. But George was losing his battle. His bloodshot eyes, sunken into his skull, began to glisten, well up, and bubble over the lower eyelids, first one tear at a time, then a steady stream.

Miller didn't say a word. Neither did George.

They couldn't.

There was nothing left to say.

Miller had always seemed to have the answers to questions and the solution to problems. Not this time. Miller wanted, needed, so badly to reach for something to give him, or to do for him—or to him. He knew there was nothing he could say that would comfort him, nothing he could do that would relieve his suffering. George looked away from Jake and wiped his face with his baggy hospital garb hanging off his shoulders. Miller pursed his lips, folded his eyes downward, and lowered his chin into his chest. Silence was all there was for the next few minutes, but it felt more like an eternity to Miller.

Though George had become clearly weaker and smaller on the outside, his attitude showed him to be a much stronger and bigger man on the inside. Dr. Miller had noticed his becoming more introspective and having more philosophical discussions over the past year. George, for example, had pointed out to him the fine detail of the molding around the top of the walls of his room. "Do you know the work involved with making each of the flowers that was in relief around the wall?"

"I can only imagine it's a lot, George."

"All those memories of growing up here pop into my head." He moved the pencil he held through his fingers. "My brothers and sisters running around, dogs barking, and farm tractors humming. Now it's nothing but a place for, instead of people coming into the world and living, for dying and leaving this world." George wiped his eyes again with his sleeve. "All the fights, the playing, the tears, and happy times with laughter." He threw the pencil onto the floor. "Now, only pain and suffering."

Miller sat on the edge of George's bed. Neither spoke for several minutes.

Jake broke the creepy silence. "I'm so sorry, George."

George turned to face Miller. "You did everything you could. My failing the treatment. My dying. It's not your fault. None of it. I believed in you and trusted that you did the right thing the right way. It's not like you were trying to kill me or anything … right?"

Miller turned to look at George, at first with a blank look.

George tried to sit up. "Doc? I said ain't that right?"

"Right! Of course not. George, thank you for your understanding. But as much as your understanding means to me, I never like to fail—I mean, I never like to have my patients fail. I don't think I'll ever be able to forgive myself for your dying like this." Miller threw the pen he had been twirling in his hand down on the floor. "It simply didn't need to happen." He stood up and paced around the room. "Damn it! It should not have happened. You had nearly a 100 percent chance of cure." He pulled his chair over to the nearby window, sat, and stared out at the midnight sky. He wiped under both eyes with his arm sleeve. He knew that since he could not prove his theory yet about Ahzid's stealing the seeds that he should not bring it up to him at this point. What good would it do him.

"Now you listen to me, and listen good. You stop those tears and get over here near me."

Miller didn't respond. He kept staring out the window.

"Hey. Doc!" George weakly raised his arms and snapped his fingers at Miller. "Yoohoo. Over here," said George, in his now raspy and horse voice. "Remember me?"

Surprised, Miller jumped in his chair, lifted his chin off his chest, and adjusted his collar. "What? What? Oh ... sorry, George, I must have drifted off for a minute."

"Drifted? You looked more like you were flying. Anywho, I want you to know that I appreciate your visiting me. I really do. But I would appreciate it more if you would try to stay a bit more awake when I'm talking with ya. Now you listen to me, and listen good. Hey, I'm beginning to sound like the Duke. You know. John Wayne. They called him the Duke."

Miller looked at him with questioning eyes. "Duke?"

"Oh you're too young to understand, any how. You stop that foul language and get the fuck over here near me." George reached out to grab Miller's arm to pull him closer.

Miller then grabbed underneath the seat of his chair, raised it off the floor, and slid it over to the bed.

George leaned forward, looking directly into his face. "Not your fault. Not your fault. Got it? Besides, dying isn't so bad, when you think of the alternative."

Miller looked at him, puzzled. "George, what do you mean by—the alternative?"

"Lying here the way I have been has given me a lot of time to think. And I have been thinking. Thinking a lot. *What do I mean?* you ask. I mean having to live the way I am now. I just lie here day in and day out depending on everybody for just about everything. And, I mean life, living on this planet, it's fucking hard. Think about it. We struggle through each day, and for what? Just to exist. Just to fill our gut with crap, like Twinkies or fries."

George then reached for the urine basin hanging on the side bed rail and tried to lift it off but could not. It was too heavy for him to lift it up and over the rail. Even that bit of effort expended so much of his energy that he fell back onto his pillow, panting and breaking a sweat. After catching his breath again, George began to speak. "You know, I was once a star athlete in high school. I played football, basketball, and baseball. I could lift the back end of a VW Beatle, for God's sake. Look at me now. I can't even take a good piss on my own anymore."

Miller stood and reached for the urine basin. "Hey, let me help you with that urine basin, George."

"No! I can do it myself. I didn't notice it was still half full. Didn't know my piss was that heavy. Probably all those blood clots mixed in don't help neither. Don't much have to take a leak now anywho."

George panted more heavily, hungering for air. His anxiety and anger no doubt had increased his blood pressure, stressing both his circulation and respiration. It was not only his muscle wasting affecting his breathing but also the cancer itself was now filling up his lungs, blocking the remaining few good alveoli from much-needed oxygen-enriched blood and filling more air sacs with fluid, which prevented air from getting into the lungs. He looked so defeated as he looked away from Miller, trying to hide his feelings of desperation. His frustration was in large part from having been an independent man. A man of dignity, which was now all but lost.

George again finally broke the deafening quiet that had developed in the room. "Hey, I almost forgot to tell you about the book I wrote this morning. Doc? There you go again. Are you sure you're not sneaking some of my pain meds for yourself, behind my back? You sure seem kinda dopey today."

Miller smiled at George. " I heard you. I heard you. Wow. A book you wrote? And in just one morning?"

"Yeah. No shit. Me. Writing a book. Fancy that."

"What is it about.? May I look at it?"

"Of course, well, I mean, not exactly. You can listen to it though."

"Listen to it?" I don't understand.

George leaned over to the table next to his bed, opened the drawer, and pulled out what looked to be a photo album. He fell back into his bed, exhausted just from that little movement.

Miller put his hand on George's shoulder. "Catch your breath, George. Take your time before speaking."

George, using his accessory muscles, sucked in a few slow, deep breaths, wheezing the whole time, with the help of his neck and chest muscles assisting his diaphragm. Miller reached behind his bed and adjusted the oxygen level higher to his nasal cannula wrapped around his head and over his ears. His color turned for a few seconds from a faint yellow because of his jaundice to an ashen hue from his low blood-oxygen level, but then it returned back to normal, for him, after a few minutes with the higher level.

"Yeah, yeah, I'm okay now. Just got a little winded. Happens every time I turn to my left. They told me it's cause of the fluid in the lungs and the pressure that increases in my abdomen that prevents my lungs from being able to expand. Anywho, here it is," he said, with a shit-eating grin. "My first book." He handed it to him with a proud glow on his face.

Miller gently took it from George's hands, which were able to almost fit around the book. He looked at George, then the book, then back at George. He seemed reluctant to open it, almost scared to find out what was inside.

George waved with the back of his hand to signal him to open it. "Go ahead. Open it. Ain't nothing inside going to bite ya. What cha waiting for? Open it."

Jake slowly pulled open the cover, and immediately a recording began playing with George's voice on it. Miller jumped back, startled at first, and quickly closed the cover.

"Jesus, Doc, it's one of those recording books. I made it for my grandkids so when they get older they'll know more about their gramps. I have also taken care of some of the funeral arrangements. I had a good friend visit me the other day, Mary. She and the missus helped me with the book. She—Mary that is, not my wife—has a wonderful voice and sings in the church choir. I have heard her on occasion, when I have gone from time to time. You know, whenever my sins built up enough that I needed to make a clean slate of things with the man upstairs."

Miller slowly moved his head up and down. "Yeah, I know all about that method of cleansing yourself. I have known many who do that."

George frowned at Miller, not certain how to respond to him. "So. My friend. She agreed to sing a couple of songs at my funeral that I picked out. I asked for *Ave Maria*, 'cause I really liked it from me and the wife's wedding day—and I know it will be a tear-jerker. I only wish I could see the faces of those hard-ass friends of mine weeping like babies."

"And what is the other song, although I'm afraid to ask."

"Oh, this is a beaut. This one will be at the end of the funeral to get people all pumped back up for the party at the house. 'Are You Ready for This?'"

"I'm ready. Go ahead. I think."

George stared at him in disbelief. "No, no. What I mean is 'Are You Ready for This?' is the song. For someone so smart, you sure can be, with all respect, kinda dumb sometimes, to real-world kinda things, I mean."

"Oh, I get you, it's the name of the hip-hop song from the 1990s." They both laughed.

George then reached down and grabbed Miller's forearm. "Doc, I also want you to speak at the funeral."

Miller snapped his head back. "Me?"

"No, the guy behind you. Yeah, you. And I want it from the heart and how you really felt about me. I want it to be real. Don't be afraid to tell it like it is. No BS. Believe me, the folks there can take it."

Dr. Miller sat there at the edge of the bed, holding the singing book, and staring as if he were watching someone off in the distance. The images of a father whom he had never known flashed in his head. He imagined that his father would have been a strong man, like George. A man who must have had something terrible happen in his life to want to leave him all alone like he had. George, for that moment in time, became his father, who now was laying in his hospital bed, at his home, in his own bedroom, and a mere skeleton of what he once was. Dr. Miller actually saw what he believed was his father laying on the bed next to him, dying. He saved people for a living, he thought to himself, but here in front of him lay his father dying, and there was nothing he could do to help him.

He imagined himself jumping up and climbing into what he thought was his dad's bed next to him and hugging him gently. Dr. Miller had longed to hear his father tell him he loved him. Just once to have heard those words spoken by his father would have lifted him to heights unknown.

But he knew, deep inside him, both his real father, and also George, had loved him. It was just not in them to show it easily by words or by touch. Dr. Miller never remembered his supposed, real father ever hugging or kissing him. He never remembered him much at all, for that matter. Perhaps he had done those things before he was sent to the orphanage. Perhaps. Jake was too young to remember if he had. Now, another person, George, that he had let himself be close to, was leaving him. He had failed at love and relationships his whole life. This time it felt even more painful.

"Doc? Hey, Doc! There you go again, drifting off into outer space. You all right? You'd think you were the one who was sick. Remember. I'm the one dying here."

Dr. Miller shook his head as if he had just been woken and blurted out, with tears rolling down his face and a crackling in his voice, "You know that I love you, don't you?"

George jumped a bit in his bed, raised his eyebrows, and darted his eyes left to right a few times to see if anyone else was around. Both George and Miller seemed uncomfortable, and each squirmed a bit. Then there were a few seconds of silence, but those seconds somehow seemed like hours.

George stroked his chin with one hand, looked at Miller out of the corner of his eye, and again broke the uncomfortable silence in the room. "Hey ah, Doc. You're not getting queer on me or anything like that, are ya?"

Miller tilted his head, raised his eyebrows, and blinked his eyes a few times. "No, nothing like that, George. I simply wanted you to know that I care about you ... just like I do all my patients."

George waved one arm at Miller. "Oh, is that all you meant? You had me worried for a minute there. I had always thought of you as sort of a man's man and was kinda taken back, thinking maybe you were from the south side of town." George then slowly leaned a few inches closer to Miller. "If you catch my drift? Loving your patients ... well ... good. That's a good thing. To tell you the truth, me and the missus kinda felt that way toward you all along. And she still does, no matter how she acts. We often heard many of your other patients saying how they felt you treated them like they were your family, and to tell you the truth, we have felt that you were part of ours too."

They went on to talk a bit more about things, some sports, some women, but mostly poking fun at some of the hospital staff that they both knew well. After a few hours had passed, and Miller began to yawn and George began to close his eyes, they said their usual evening good-byes, but this time they exchanged an awkward hug, something they'd not done before. On his way home though, Miller wished that he had given George a bigger hug.

George passed the very next day with his loving family surrounding him. Dr. Miller was given the news while he was in his office going over George's chart, as he had done so many times before. He was looking for anything that could have been odd that would point to Ahzid's stealing the seeds. He knew that's what had to have happened after they proved he had been given dummy seeds. *But how to prove it.* He also was looking at several other charts of patients that had undergone brachytherapy implants around the same time as George and had recently failed treatment. *Did they all have dummy sources? Could he check them all?*

His concentration was off though, as he couldn't get out of his head the conversation he had had with George the day before his passing. The things they had both said. The things he wished he had said. He wondered if George had really felt the same as he did before he passed.

141

I do care for all my patients like they were my family or at least the family I often wish I had. Is it really my fault that he's dead? Should I have seen things going on in the OR? And how could I speak at his funeral with the feeling that I could be somehow responsible for his death? George didn't have to die with such a curable cancer. Is Ahzid truly the only common thread among these patients?

"Dr. Miller. Dr. Miller," said Jennifer, his nurse.

Miller blinked his eyes a few times to focus on the voice. "Oh, yes, Jennifer, please come in."

"I have those updated bone scan and CT scans."

"Scans? Whose scans?'"

"You know. On those patients you asked me about that you will be seeing next week."

"Oh, yes. Of course. Great. Let me see them." He took the films from her and held them overhead toward the office lights. His eyes widened as he scanned them up and down. The scans lit up like a Christmas tree with blastic and sclerotic lesions throughout the skeleton.

"Oh, God! Please. This can't be happening."

CHAPTER 16: DEATH'S TOLL

AFTER THE NEWS OF GEORGE'S PASSING AND THE UPDATED films on other patients showing failure of their cancer treatment, he went straight back to his condo and poured himself a big glass of scotch. He went into his bedroom, took one sip of it, and lay down on his bed. He felt mentally exhausted from his visit and the recent patient scans showing yet more failures from treatment. He soon drifted off to sleep.

Miller awoke to a knock on his door and got up to answer it. When he opened it, Bridget stood there with a smirk on her face.

"Well are you going to just stand there or are you going to let me in?"

"Oh, sorry. I'm just surprised to see you. That's all."

"Listen, why don't we go out and get a bite and talk. We can come back here later for a few drinks if we want."

"Ah, yeah. Sure. That sounds good."

After they went downstairs to have dinner at the bar, they came back to his condominium for a drink and to continue talking. Earlier during dinner, he undressed her with his eyes while they sat across from each other at dinner. Now he wondered if what he had imagined earlier would come true. Her breasts were perfect, sensually curved, perfectly proportional to her body. He wanted so badly to press his lips against hers.

They began kissing and soon moved onto the bed, and didn't even bother to get inside the covers. Bridget lay down first, and Jake thought he saw lust in her eyes. Her eye orbits curved gently downward, giving her a puppy-dog look that gave not only an excited feeling but also a calming one; her gorgeous figure lying there before him was simply stunning. Her curvaceous and voluptuous body was more than he could stand. He wanted to touch her, to hold her. His longing for her after they had broken up was painful enough, but now to have her here and her wanting him as much as he wanted her was almost too much to handle. *I knew you would come back to me. I knew it.* And when they later made love, they couldn't do it fast enough. Pulling and practically tearing off their clothes, all the while continuing with their passionate kissing.

They later collapsed, both spent after making passionate love for hours. When he awoke some hours later, he watched Bridget with her back to him as she lay next to him on her side, and listened to her gentle rhythmic breathing. He reached out to stroke her shoulder-length hair, then glided his hand over her back, ever so lightly, so as not to wake her. Lower and lower his hand slid, flowing over her curves, first upward then downward over her hips, then down further to her thighs. He rubbed her gently, squeezing her thighs, moving ever so slowly, first over the outer thighs, then moving to her inner thighs.

He reached up again to touch her long, shiny hair when suddenly loud, rattling noises woke him, and he then realized he had been dreaming. *Shit. It felt so real.* He punched his pillow. *Damn you, Bridget, for leaving me!* Sprawled onto the bed, half-dazed, quarter-dressed, he looked over to where Bridget had been laying so still next to him. She was gone, his image of her anyway. Jacob realized he was alone in his Beacon Hill apartment and had been all along.

He got up and shuffled over to look out his bedroom window and saw several pigeons camped on the ledge outside. They squawked and flew away. *When they woke me up, they must have been flapping their wings.*

He sat back down and grabbed a bottle of scotch from table next to his bed and began to drink again. He wanted to forget the pain of it all. He began talking out loud, though no one was around him to hear him. "Just a dream." He turned to punch the pillow again, got up and out of bed, and shuffled again over to his bedroom window that overlooked the Charles River. The clouds hung low and heavy that day. Rain poured, splashing off the windowsill in big drops. The background sky was gray, like the color of Miller's feelings.

"I had everything … everything … a successful medical practice. A successful research lab. My patients loved me. I finally found a woman who truly cared about me. Cared enough to be honest with me. Not to tell me just what I wanted to hear but what I needed to hear. Damn this mental illness, this PTSD, or whatever the hell it is. Damn my stubbornness."

The phone began to ring, but he ignored it. It kept ringing and ringing. "Stop it!" He grabbed the phone and ripped it out of the wall. His breathing rate increased, and his blood pressure skyrocketed. His thoughts were pounding in his head, rapid-fire like a machine gun. His legs became as heavy as lead-filled buckets. Everything crashed down around him. He was stuck, sitting all alone on a runaway rollercoaster. Thoughts of the loss of his patients and how it could lead to his losing his clinical position at the hospital, and now of Bridget repeated. Over and over and over.

Miller shook off the movies in his head going fast forward, distracted himself, and stared at the obituaries of his oncology patients that, like that of his office, lined the wall of his bedroom. Profiles in courage of those who succumbed to their cancer but who should be instead now living, eating, and laughing.

He thought of the Captain, as he liked to be called, with a head and neck cancer, who forever wore his sailor's hat, scruffy beard, boat shoes, and a sea-weathered face. He had a dry sense of humor and a hidden intelligence. "Doc, how am I doin'?" he would ask each week at his clinic visits. He would inevitably have something to show him about boating; one week it was a cut out of "rules of the sea to survive," and another it was a copy of a boating manual.

Many thought he either exaggerated or even made up some of his sea stories. Until one day he said, "Hey, Doc, have I ever showed you some of the sharks I tangled with out to sea?"

"No you haven't," thinking that would be the end of it, but then he pulled out several pictures from his shirt pocket with him standing next to two dead sharks standing taller than he was.

Miller then went right down the wall of the obituaries—the hunter, the cook, the ballet dancer …

He stopped when he got a sinking feeling, thinking about telling a few of his patients the other day about the tests showing return of their cancer. David, in particular. He recalled how the tests that were gotten the previous week showed his not only having a recurrence in the lung region that had been treated but also that the cancer had now spread to other parts of his body. David was truly a character. He had thinning, sandy-blond hair that hung forward over his forehead, like that of a twelve-year-old boy. He had sunken brown eyes, barely seen underneath his hair, and a prominent overhanging forehead. His large jowl jutted underneath his thickened lips. And in many ways it was befitting him, as his personality was very much that of a child. He was into cars. Not just any cars, 'muscle cars'. He raced dragsters and had several muscle cars that he would talk so proudly about when he came in for his radiation implant treatments. Miller remembered the conversation in his office they had to review the scans showing the return of his cancer.

"*Doc, I know my time is getting short.*"

"*What makes you say that, David?*"

David's eyes began to well up. Trust me, I just know it. If you were me, you would just know it … You just … know … it."

He thought of how they sat there in the exam room, across from each other. An uncomfortable silence took over. Dr. Miller tried to find words to say. Any words. But none came. Simultaneously they both broke a one-sided smile, as if to say to each other that they had a tacit understanding. They both knew that David was quite right about his feelings, but from that point on, neither would talk about it again. They both stood, shook hands, and hugged. After David left, he slammed the door of the exam room.

Miller slowly turned his head from staring upward at the wall to that of a bottle of sleeping pills on his nightstand next to his bed. Next to it, the bottle of scotch. He thought of it for a moment. It was the bottle that Bridget had given him. Tears began to run down his cheeks. He shuffled over to it and reached for the bottle of scotch and filled the shot glass. He sat on the edge of the bed, gulped it, and lay down.

The imaging studies didn't lie. More patients were dying, and others would also. The bone scans, the CTs, the MRIs. All showing disease burning holes through bones and organs alike. And like George, these patients were not expected to fail. And like George, they had very early cancer—a small area with pathology showing very low-grade disease,

disease that was as close to normal cells as one could get and still be considered a cancer.

Why didn't I see this going on? Many thought of me as their savior; I wasn't even their protector.

His eyes shifted over to George's recent obituary. George appeared to be looking at him with his sad, brown, cow-like eyes. As the tears began to run down his cheeks, Miller reached for the bottle of pills, poured a drinking glass halfway, and guzzled it down.

He looked disdainfully at the bottle of pills. "Pills are the cowardly way out." He threw the pill bottle onto the floor and reached over to open the top drawer of his nightstand. There was the .38-caliber pistol he kept at home for security. He shoved a full clip of cartridges into the bottom of the pistol grip, sighed, and slowly raised the gun to his right temple. He pressed the cold steel against his skin and bit down hard. *Please, God, forgive me.*

CHAPTER 17: THE ENEMY WITHIN

BRIDGET KNOCKED ON MILLER'S CONDOMINIUM DOOR RATHER softly with two or three taps. She waited for a response. When she got none, she leaned her ear to the door. She heard nothing from the inside, so she stepped back, looked at the door up and down, and shouted, "Jake ... Jake, open up. It's Bridget." She waited another minute, which felt like an eternity. She paced a few steps in front of the door, then stopped and rapped on the door, staccato-like, and waited again with her ear turned toward the door ... nothing. Not a sound.

She paced again with short steps, abruptly stopped, sucked in a deep breath, and leaned toward the door as if she were trying to will an answer from the other side. No answer again, so this time, she pounded with her fists. "Miller! Are you in there? It's Bridget ... open up." A dog began to yap a few doors down, and she could hear shuffling inside the condo across the hall. She worried that she had woken up the others with her knocking and yelling. Soon, another dog barked from a floor beneath, then another on the floor above.

Again she listened close to the door with head down and one ear turned toward the door. She folded her hands and tapped her fingers together. *Keys! The keys he gave me.* She had forgotten about the set of keys Miller had given her. She had never used them before because she never wanted to go to his apartment without his being there. She dug through her pocketbook, pulled out a set of keys, and fumbled to find the correct one, dropping them twice before finding it.

With fine tremors of her hands and beads of sweat creeping down her temples, she opened it on the third try, poked her head inside, and looked around the living room.

"Jake?" She crept though the apartment, scanning everything in sight, going from the front of the condo to the back, where, down the hallway, she saw his bedroom door closed, but a light shot out from underneath it. She skulked ever closer to it. Pink Floyd permeated the door. This time she didn't knock or speak. Instead, she squeezed the doorknob, inhaled deeply, and swung open the door.

In front of her sat Dr. Miller on the edge of his bed, next to his nightstand, his back to her, looking up at the window that overlooked the walking bridge crossing the Charles River to Cambridge and MIT. At first she felt relieved to see him sitting there. She stepped inside and crept closer to him. She noticed his eyes were closed and assumed that he didn't hear her with the music and what she hoped was his meditating. Her eyes widened as she got closer to him, and she shrieked when she saw the pistol in his right hand resting on his thigh.

Miller jumped like he had touched a hot stove and turned sharply toward her. "Bridget! What are you doing here?"

Bridget stepped sideways, directly in front of him, and frowned. "What am I doing here? I think the question should be what the hell are you doing here? And with that thing next to you." She pointed to the gun against his thigh. "I've been banging on your door. Didn't you hear me?"

Miller shook his head and looked down at the gun. He picked it up. "What? This old thing?"

Bridget folded her arms tightly and looked sternly at Miller. "Yes. That. And please put it on the bed."

"Sure. No problem." He placed the gun down on the bed by his side. "Listen. I'll be honest with you. I went to see a therapist like you suggested, and initially I felt good about it and that I could overcome my issues. But after I visited George the next day—who died the very next day after I visited—I began thinking about my patients … how I failed them … how despite everything I stood for and worked hard for, it all seemed to be crashing down around me."

She looked around the room and saw the obituaries hanging from the wall. She walked to only a foot away from him and looked down at him. He looked as though he hadn't showered for a week, and he smelled of alcohol. He had bloodshot eyes, and she noticed the half-empty bottle of scotch on the table. "You didn't fail anyone, especially your patients. And I'm proud of you for going to the therapist. You'll have to tell me more about it, if you feel up to it."

Miller kept looking down at the ground, hunched over with his head resting in his hands. She bent over, inches away from him. "Jake, do you hear me?"

Miller raised his head, like a heavy chain anchored it down to the floor, to look up at her. "Bridget, thank you for saying that. And thank you for coming over." He tilted his head curiously. "What made you come over anyway, now especially?"

"Buzz called me to tell me he had concerns about you. He said you seemed pretty down after going to a few of your patients' funerals, and then he couldn't reach you on the phone this morning, so he wanted me to come check on you."

"Just *he* wanted to check on me?"

"Okay, I wanted to check on you too. Is that all right with you?"

Miller slapped his knee like Jed Clampett on the *Hillbillies* and grew a smile out of proportion to his face. "So you do care about me!"

Bridget reached down and picked up the gun with her thumb and forefinger, holding it like a smelly diaper, and put it on top of the nightstand. She sat down next to him and put her hand on his. "Are you kidding? Of course I care for you. I care for you deeply."

He raised his head, and light radiated from his face. He turned to face her and placed his other hand on top of hers.

She frowned at him and looked deep into his eyes. "I don't understand. Why would you want to take your life? You are so important to everyone."

Miller turned away from her to scan the patients' obituaries hanging on the wall in front of them, then looked back at Bridget. "I felt I let everyone down. A big part of my life, as you know, has been caring for my patients, fighting against their cancers, both in the clinic and in the lab. Instead of feeling good about all that, I felt like I lost everything, my patients, my research and even ..."

Bridget squeezed his hands. "What? Even what?" She moved to

within inches of his face, looking right into his eyes and sandwiched his hand between hers on his thigh.

Miller looked back at her, and a tear rolled down his cheek. "Even you."

Bridget looked deeper into his eyes. She saw the depth of his feelings for her in his blue eyes. They leaned slowly closer to each other, until their lips touched. Then they wrapped their arms around each other tightly and pressed their lips together in a passionate kiss. They kissed for a few minutes, and when Miller began to kiss her neck, Bridget opened her eyes, stopped hugging him, and let her arms down to her side. She took a deep breath, exhaled, and pushed him away. "Wait," she said.

Miller shot back, wide-eyed, "What? I remember the last time we did this. As you may recall, it didn't turn out so well." He leaned a few inches more toward her. "I do love you, you know."

Bridget stood and turned to look down at Jake. "No. It's nothing like that this time. I know you love me. And I love you. And I want to make love with you, but I have to meet someone."

Miller sat up straight. "Right now? Who?"

"A friend of my brother's in the military. Remember our talk in Maine? The people I told you about that he worked with in Afghanistan?"

Miller nodded. "Yes, I remember."

"Well, he called me earlier today and said he had to meet me this morning. My brother had contacted him from his base in Afghanistan and said that it was urgent, but he couldn't say much more over the phone. But he did say he believed it had something to do with the radiation and that terrorists are involved. Even more importantly, he said that some high-ranking military may be involved as well."

Miller grabbed her hands. "Are you serious! You didn't tell me you told your brother about any of this."

"Yes, very serious. I know I should have told you that I had mentioned what we thought was going on with our patients and all, but I never thought he would ever contact me about anything dealing with it."

Jake stood up. "Bridget, I have to go with you."

She sat back down, breaking his grip. "No you can't come with me."

Jake sat down next to her and put his arm around her. "But why? I'm more involved than anyone else with all of this."

"I realize that, but I'm meeting him on a military base that requires special clearance."

"How did you get—"

"Clearance? Because I'm his sister, my brother can request I be allowed to go onto the air force base, where his friend is, as a visitor to pick up a package from my brother."

"Isn't there some way that—"

Bridget stood back up, paced in front of him, and shook her head. "No. My friend can request only visitors to this specific site on the base, if they themselves have military clearance. Which, I said, I have as his sister. The guards will be expecting only me. I'm sorry. I would want nothing more than for you to be with me. But if they suspect anything going on, I—we—could be arrested on the spot."

Miller stood up and walked over to her. He held her hands, leaned into her to give her a long kiss, then looked into her eyes. "I understand. I appreciate everything you're doing—and your brother and his friend—to help with all this insanity."

Bridget picked up her handbag off the end of the bed. "It's important that we get to the bottom of all this. For you, me, our patients, and their families. They were all our patients. And for our country. I can't help but feel this is part of something a lot bigger, especially from what Private Peter Singer, my brother's friend, told me over the phone about higher army personnel being involved." She walked back over to give him, and they hugged and kissed again. "You're going to be all right ... right?"

Miller looked up at her with a reassuring smirk, grabbed the pistol on the nightstand, and put it back in the drawer. "Yes, I'll be fine. No worries. Besides, I like to think we'll have a long time ahead of us to be together."

She gave a reassuring smile back. "Yes, I like to think of having a very long time together too. I'll call you to let you know how my meeting went."

"I'll be waiting. In the meantime, I'll give Buzz a call back. He has tried to reach me it looks like three or four times on my phone, and left messages.

They embraced and kissed again.

Miller smiled. "Now that, I missed."

Bridget smiled back. "Yes, me too."

Bridget was anxious to go to the special units site at Camp Irving down on the Cape in Massachusetts to review the video images that had been sent from Afghanistan by her brother. When she finally arrived, the guard posted at the main entrance asked her a lot of questions but eventually, if reluctantly, let her through. She went straight to the communications center of the camp where she met her brother's friend and told him about her encounter with the guard at the entrance, but he didn't seem to worry much about his behavior.

He took her straight to the viewing library, where he had access, to look at the CD he had made with the secret information her brother had sent to him.

"Your brother and I go way back to basic training together. We've watched each other's back while in the military."

"I know. He's often talked about you and him being best friends through his letters and phone calls. He told me he trusts you as much as he trusts me. That's why I'm here now."

"He told me the same about you. I guess that's why I'm willing to do this."

When they got to the communication center, they went inside and quickly began looking at it, and he narrated as they viewed the images shot by the drones of the terrorists at their camp.

"Private, go back over that last bit of footage."

"No problem."

"There. Stop it there. Zoom in to Personal ID level." She was amazed by the close-up detail that could be captured by the drones flying above.

"Wow! Good eye. That's our general, General Ringer, the commander of all the military antiterrorism units in the Middle East."

"What do you think he's doing standing next to the terrorist leaders?"

"They're in one of the hidden camps in the mountains." He pointed to the computer screen. "Look at this. Like your brother said, he's meeting with Omarh Sharrid, the former assistant to Bin Laden. This isn't right. To me it looks as though he has unauthorized and likely crooked dealings going on. He actually shook the hands of one of them before they disappeared into that hole in the side of the mountain, no doubt a cave used by the Taliban. I wouldn't have believed it if I hadn't seen it with my own eyes."

Bridget gawked at the computer screen, then turned to the private. "We can't make any definitive statements and certainly can't go to anybody without being certain."

"But what else could it be?" said the private. "We caught this on film unsuspectingly with one of our drones. Could he be working secretly with them? But this wouldn't be handled by a general going to one of their secret hideouts. He must be doing something with them. And doing something not right. What am I going to do? Who can I talk with?"

"We talk with no one. Do you hear me? No one," said Bridget.

Peter snapped back, "Sure. Sure. If you think so. Most of your brother's work involved organizing, coordinating, and analyzing intelligence information gathered by spy-drone planes as well as spoken and written communications on airways and through the Internet. This is how he captured this, from one of the drones out scouting in that area on that day. It's just by pure luck that it caught this. I can see why he wanted you to see it right away. It makes sense now with all the rumors—"

She turned her head quickly away from the screen and toward the private. "Rumors? What rumors?"

"Bridget, your brother and I were—are—close. I, myself, just got back from Afghanistan. We heard rumors over there that our commander was crooked, and these photos prove it."

The private who had screened her earlier at the gate walked into the viewing room. "Is everything all right? Do you need any help?" he asked.

Startled, she jumped at hearing his voice and turned quickly to see him standing in the doorway. "No, Private. I'm fine. Private Singer has been a big help to me. You both have been a big help."

"Okay, but let me know if I can do anything," said the private. He then left and shut the door behind him.

She looked at Peter next to her. "I really need to go now." She pushed the eject button and took the CD out, put it in her pocket, and looked around to make sure she was not being watched. She got up quickly and opened the door, only to find the private who had just left waiting outside. She smiled at him and kept walking with Peter, following close behind her.

Halfway down the hallway, she looked back to see the private walk back into the viewing room and looking at the computer she had been using. She and Peter ran to her car, and as they drove away, she noticed that the private had come outside behind them and was talking on his cell phone. She realized that he probably had been watching them the whole time. Her thoughts raced about what, if anything, she was going to do. "Private, I can drop you off anywhere you want, but here's my cell number and where I'll be if you need to reach me with anything else."

"Better yet. I'm off duty now and will come with you. Your brother asked me to keep an eye on you anyway."

"Perfect. I could use the company on the drive home."

"Where are we going anyway?"

"I want to go to my apartment to hide this CD where my friend, Dr. Miller, can find it. After that, I'm not sure."

They sped back to Boston to her apartment. "Private, park it on the street rather than in the garage, so we can take off quicker if we need to." They were lucky not to get a speeding ticket, so Bridget thought that maybe her luck had changed. When they finally got inside the apartment, she couldn't put the CD into the computer fast enough. "So, Private, tell me more about those rumors you started to talk about."

Peter sat down next to her. "There are rumors that we all heard when I was overseas and still hear from my buddies over there, including your brother. Things like that the general drives a Mercedes there that the Taliban gave him. And he acts like a king, having massages, and sex with prostitutes daily, and he eats and drinks the best of foods. His family in the US has everything; they have vacation homes, cars, clothes, and his wife has the best of jewelry. Worse than all that though, a buddy of mine who works at the desk of the general overheard him with others talking about stolen weapons and radiation and manipulating the stock market to make lots and lots of money."

Suddenly, a screech, from what sounded like the tires of a car skidding radiated through the apartment from an open kitchen window in the next room. The private went into the kitchen to look out the window that overlooked the alleyway behind the apartment building and saw two men getting out of a van. The private ran back into the living room. "Bridget, this looks very suspicious. I don't recognize them, but those guys out there don't look like they're here to sell Girl Scout cookies. I'll go downstairs to see who they are and what they want. Lock the door behind me until I come back."

"Okay. I'll quickly make a copy of this CD for Jake and wait for you right here."

After the private left to go down the back stairs to the alleyway, she locked the door and called Jake, but she had to leave a message when he didn't answer. "Jake, I placed a CD for you in our secret hiding place. The general is in it, is crooked, and, I think, behind the radiation being stolen from our patients."

She quickly placed the CD in a hidden compartment under the table, then went to the kitchen to check on the private outside. She heard multiple footsteps coming closer in the back hall. She stuffed her cell phone into her bra and began to move out of the kitchen as two large men wearing trench coats and black masks burst into her apartment through the kitchen door. She tried to run into the next room, but one of them grabbed her and held her tightly while the other duct taped her mouth, hands, and feet.

"Take her downstairs and have Mohammed help you put her in the van while I check the place out," said one of the men.

"Don't be long. Someone may have heard the shots and called the cops," replied the other man. He then half-dragged and half-carried her downstairs. Muffled screams came from her mouth when they passed the private lying next to the dumpster in the alleyway near the van. Blood covered his face and soaked his uniform.

CHAPTER 18: KIDNAPPED

BRIDGET'S ABDUCTORS THREW HER IN THE AIR, AND SHE LANDED face down on the cold floor of the van. Her ankles slammed the doorway's edge, and a nasty gash sprang up, bleeding through her socks. Her head whiplashed and then pounded from the force of her body's weight coming to a full stop. She heard her nose break first, snapping loudly from the force of its hitting the floor, and blood began running out of her nostrils, and then she felt the fiery pain. She became lightheaded and nauseous. Her carotid pulse bounded with each heartbeat from the pressure of someone's hand pressing on her neck and pushing it into the steel floor. Her skin felt like wet ice under her clothes from the adrenaline pouring out of her glands.

One of the men ripped the duct tape off her mouth, and she began yelling. "Ow! You bastards. Get off me. Get off me. Let go of me. Let go of me. Stop! You're hurting me." She was having some difficulty getting her breath with the nose bleeding profusely and began to choke on the blood that leaked into the back of her nose down into her throat.

"Shut up, you bitch, or I'll hurt you more than that," said one of the abductors, and he proceeded to put more of his weight onto her with the foot he had placed on her back to hold her down.

"Stop, please. You're crushing me." Bridget gasped for air, and the pain seared into her back with the heal of the boot digging deeper into her spine. Sharp, lightning-like burning ran down both of the back of her legs.

"Mohammed, get off her and let her up," shouted another's voice from behind them. "She cannot hurt us or escape being tied up. Put her onto the pull-down cot."

He did as he was told. He took his large boot off her back, bent over her, lifted her up in one fell swoop from underneath her armpits, and swung her over to the cot. She landed on her back, facing her assailants.

Bridget looked up at him. He stared down at her and frowned. She then noticed the other man who had ordered her off the floor. Her jaw dropped, and her eyes widened. "Ahzid! I don't believe this. You're involved?"

Ahzid rubbed the blood off her nose with a towel, took the duct tape off of her hands, and handed the towel to her. "Bridget, I truly apologize if you are uncomfortable, but we need to keep you tied up. You will bear witness to a great event soon. We are all going to find eternal peace, happiness, and love. Patriot's Day is a perfect symbolic day for attacking the enemy at the heart of their elitist belief. Don't you think?" Ahzid handed her a towel. "Here, use this to stop the nose bleed."

"What the hell does Patriot's Day have to do with anything?" she said.

"Don't you see? We are revolutionists, just like those that Patriot's Day is celebrated for. The marathon was held on Patriot's Day, a holiday to commemorate the start of the Revolutionary War. But this year the people celebrating are in for a very big surprise."

Bridget looked askance at him. "What surprise?"

Ahzid laughed. "Oh, you will see soon enough."

"You're working with that general, aren't you?" said Bridget.

Ahzid and Mohammed looked at each other and then back at her simultaneously.

"I knew it. That's why I'm here, isn't it?"

Ahzid looked down at her. "What are you talking about?"

She looked away and didn't answer. *That was stupid of me. I shouldn't have said anything.*

"See, she knows too much. We must kill her now," said Mohammed.

"Relax, Mohammed. She's not going anywhere. Bridget, since it doesn't matter now, I don't mind showing you everything anyway."

"Ahzid, we are getting close to the farm. She should not see it," said Mohammed.

"Don't worry, my brother, for I want her to see all that we are doing." Ahzid taped her hands in front of her. "Bridget, remember when you said it was a shame that I didn't live up to the expectations everyone had for me. Well, I want you to see just how well I have lived up to them. I'll have created a weapon that will make the world see how well I have done. I'll be creating one of the greatest destructions of our enemies, in the name of Allah, not seen since the planes attacked the Twin Towers in 2001."

"But, Ahzid, that's not what I meant when I said that. I meant using your talents for good, not evil."

"So you say. Many more will see it differently after tomorrow," said Ahzid.

After driving for about an hour, they drove off the main road onto a dirt road leading to the farm. They were tossed up and down as the van hit the potholes staggered along the road. Ahzid reached out to grab onto Bridget's shoulder to keep her from falling off the cot.

Bridget looked out the side window to see the farmhouse up ahead. They drove around it into a large barn behind the house and pulled inside.

Ahzid leaned over and looked into Bridget's face. "I do apologize again. I'm sure it's not as comfy as your apartment. But you will be staying here as our guest for a bit."

"Ahzid, I really need to go to the bathroom," said Bridget.

"Let her piss her pants like the dog she is," said Mohammed.

"You want the van to smell like urine?" said Ahzid. "I don't think so."

Mohammed gave a conciliatory look. "But we should keep her blindfolded."

They stepped outside, and Ahzid called his daughter over to him. "Answar, take her to the bathroom and bring her right back. Her name is Bridget, and she will be our guest for a while."

"Yes, Father."

Bridget followed Answar outside the barn along a path into the nearby woods. She was a pretty girl of sixteen, with big, brown eyes, soft skin, and dark hair. "Answar, thank you for helping me."

"You are welcome," she answered without turning around to look at Bridget.

"Do you know that your father is going to kill many innocent lives? Think of it," said Bridget.

Answar stopped, turned partially around, and frowned at her. Just as quickly, she turned back around and kept walking to an outhouse up ahead of them. She pointed to the house. "Here it is. I'll wait out here for you," said Answar.

"I'll need my arms untied," said Bridget. Answar accommodated her. Once inside, she looked outside through the cracks of the tiny outhouse. She saw men with semiautomatic weapons patrolling the ground. They were smoking and laughing as they were looking over at Answar. Some were also hiding up in trees with makeshift stands. She even saw a few on top of the barn roof with their guns. When Bridget came back outside, she saw the men glaring at them both.

Answar was shy, not wanting to look at them, as they obviously were looking at her and snickering. Answar then began wrapping the tape around Bridget's hands.

"Please don't tie them as tight as they were. It hurts."

Answar did as she asked.

On the way back, Bridget looked at the surroundings and noted the outside layout of the place and the location of the van and an ambulance at the other end of the barn. Men were standing around it while others were taking things out of big metal containers and putting them into the ambulance. She saw Mohammed looking at them, his head and eyes tracking them like prey as Answar escorted her back into the van. Bridget put one foot onto the steps set next to the van, turned to Answar, and bent down to her ear. "Can you help me?" said Bridget softly.

Answar stepped backward. "I cannot. I cannot go against my father."

"Please, can you at least untie my hands?"

"I'll untie them but will need to keep your feet tied, and I'll tie one of your hands to the rail."

After Answar left and closed the door to the van, Bridget reached into her bra with her untied hand and pulled out her cell phone to call Jake.

He didn't answer his phone again, so she left a brief message, breathing rapidly the whole time. "Jake, I don't have much time. I've been kidnapped, but I'm okay. For now, anyway. I'm being held somewhere outside Boston, in the country, on a farm—I believe in New Hampshire, because some of the cars here have New Hampshire plates. There are many armed men here. Ahzid, your physicist is involved. Go to my apartment. Get the CD that I left you—I mentioned it on my earlier voice message to you. These people are planning some type of major explosion, worse than 9/11—something to do with Patriot's Day. In Boston. Ahzid told me so himself. Jake, I was so wrong. I'm so sorry. Listen, there is something else that I need to tell you. I—" Just then the door to the van swung open, and there stood Mohammed. She screamed as he approached her. "Ahhhhh. Get away from me! No! No! You bastard! Stop—" The phone went dead.

CHAPTER 19: SEARCH FOR TRUTH

EVER SINCE THE INCIDENT OF AHZID'S RUNNING AWAY ON THE
day of the last seed implant, Buzz became obsessed with finding out
exactly what Ahzid's involvement with the missing radiation sources was.
The information that his friend in the FBI had given him recently only
further gave cause to link Ahzid to things. Although he was suspected
of stealing the radiation sources, and even admitted it to Dr. Miller, it
couldn't be proven. So, Buzz thought perhaps going through his office,
which had been essentially left untouched, could lead to some clues.
No one had used it since the day Ahzid bumped into him when he
was running out of the department, so perhaps there was something,
anything, that could give information about the radiation sources.

But he knew he had to act soon to find out anything he could. He
and Jake knew time was running out and something bad was going to
happen if they couldn't get to the bottom of it. Buzz waited until Friday,
after everyone had left the department, so the office was empty. Except
for skeletal weekend crews, most of the hospital would be deserted. It was
a good chance to investigate the radioactive sources in the storage lab.

Finally, with no one around, Buzz left the patient waiting room
area and made his way down the tortuous, darkened hallway. First,
down past the clinical treatment areas, where the high-energy linear
accelerators were housed in their "bunkers." These are the rooms with
no windows and concrete walls several feet thick to shield those outside
them from the X-rays being generated to treat the patients with cancer.
Then down a more narrow corridor that had all the industrial-sized
piping and wiring exposed on the ceiling, with the sounds of water

running through them. It was lit dimly, as these halls were rarely used except for maintenance people and Ahzid, who had his office next to the radiation source storage room. Radiation oncology clinics were historically kept in the basements of hospitals—otherwise known as the bowels of the hospital, and this one was no exception. This was one way to keep the radiation away from the general population and to use the underground as a protective shielding effect that was cost effective.

Buzz stopped for a moment, sensing something behind him, but when he turned around, there was no one there. He walked back down the hallway to look around, and when satisfied that no one was around, he continued back down the corridor another thirty feet or so to where it turned sharply to the left. There around the corner straight down the remaining corridor where it ended was a big, yellow and red Radioactive sign covering the heavy metal door to the radiation isotope storage room. To the right was a sign next to the closed office door that read Chief of Physics.

Buzz stepped forward as if he were walking barefoot on broken glass, opened the door cautiously, and poked his head slowly into Ahzid's office. Buzz gave a cursory look around the office, looking behind the door, before stepping inside. It felt eerie. The room was cold, with no natural light and no air movement. A deafening silence filled the lifeless room. The shelves were filled with stacks of scientific papers and journals and pictures of Ahzid. The air had a stale smell because of no windows in the office or in this whole section of the department. He knew Ahzid was not in the habit of shutting his door before he disappeared but still was surprised to find it open since it was no longer being used. He had not seen anyone around but still felt uneasy about being there alone in the darkness.

At first he was reluctant to turn any lights on, for he didn't want to attract attention, but since no one would likely see them on, he decided to turn on the overhead lights in the office to see better. He noticed the lab coat hung on the back of the door with the insignia on the upper left label, Dr. Ahzid M. Ahzeed, PhD, Chief of Physics, faded from years of use. The desk itself had few items on it aside from a few pens and pencils and a couple of physics textbooks. On the walls were a few pictures of his homeland in Pakistan. But the odd-looking sword, two sided, shorter than what a sword normally is, was gone. He remembered asking Ahzid about it one day when he first saw it in the case, but Ahzid only replied, "It's like Allah looking over me and protecting me."

Perhaps I'm letting my imagination run wild; maybe I should just forget the whole thing. He turned around, started back to the door, then stopped. *No, I have come this far. I need to find anything I can to help solve this nightmare for Doc and all of us. It's just so strange what's happening with the patients—and now Ahzid's disappearance.*

He crept behind the desk and quickly began trying to open the desk drawers. They were all unlocked, except for one. The open drawers were essentially empty, so he took out his pocket knife and jimmied the lock on the locked drawer until it popped open. Inside were a few newspaper clippings on Al-Qaeda terrorist groups being caught and a folded piece of paper with a crude drawing of a map on it. He studied the map closely and noted that it was a drawing of an area in New Hampshire, north of the cancer center, and by the measurement scale in the corner of it, about an hour away. He then noticed a notebook way in the back of the drawer. He pulled it out, opened it, and found lists of names, with radiation sources, amount of radiation, as well as dollar amounts.

Just then, he heard voices coming down the hall and getting closer; one sounded like Ahzid's, and the other was familiar, but Buzz couldn't quite place it. As the voices became louder, Buzz's heart jumped, and he hyperventilated. He looked to his left then his right. He took a step toward the door. *No, that won't work.* The voices got louder as they got closer. He had only seconds to decide. Quickly he stuffed the notebook down the front of his pants and darted under the desk, hitting his forehead on the metal top on the way underneath. He pressed on it to quell the pain and felt the warmth of blood running down. He tried desperately to keep from breathing loudly, struggling to exhale slowly and quietly. He felt his heart pounding and worried that others could hear it as well, beating like a drum on the inside of the walls of his chest.

"Well, how many sources do you have for me?" said a voice sounding like Ahzid's, just outside the office door.

"Like I told you over the phone, it's getting tougher to get the sources," said the person with him. "The company is starting to nose around a bit more and questioning our deliveries. That's why I'm down on my supply side. I'm not sure, Ahzid, but I think someone from some government agency was snooping around the other day asking questions. He wore a shiny badge inside his suit jacket."

Buzz covered his mouth to keep him from screeching. *It's Ahzid. I knew it.*

"Okay, okay. Bart, tell me, how much more money do you want?"

Buzz nodded. *And Bart. The seed delivery guy. I should have guessed.*

"I'm serious, Ahzid, it's not just about money."

"I'm prepared to double your fee," said Ahzid.

Bart didn't respond at first. "Double, you said?"

"Double. Well, how many sources do you have today for me anyway?"

"Listen, we shouldn't even be here like this. Why did you want to meet here anyway? This is the worst place for us to be right now. Everyone knows about the missing seeds. Dr. Miller and even the police are also now asking questions. I am going to leave."

"Wait! Don't go."

Bart stomped his foot on the floor. "Ahzid, are you listening to anything I have said? They want to meet with me next week to talk. I think they know about us."

"Calm down, my friend. They know nothing. I needed to come here to pick up a few things. I'm prepared to pay you handsomely for more sources."

"Ahzid, what exactly are you doing with the sources anyway?"

"I already told you that. We need the sources for medical treatment in our countries in the Middle East. We don't have access to them, like in America."

"Well there's more and more talk about using these sources for other purposes."

"Okay, okay, I understand. You 'westerners'. How much more money do you want?"

"Damn it, Ahzid. I'm serious. Like I told you already, it's not just about money. It's my job. Even going to jail. And what do you mean, 'you Westerners'?"

Ahzid chuckled. "It is always about the money. You did bring more sources today?"

"Yes, but I just don't know if this is worth it anymore. I have the sources in the company van for two cases on Monday." He shook his head again in doubt. "Ahzid, I just don't know."

"Okay, my friend, let's go to your vehicle to talk about it; I think you're right. It's better not to keep talking here. You go ahead of me. I'll be right there. I just have to go to the bathroom."

After hearing them leave, walk down the hall, and the shut the back exit door, Buzz slowly moved out from under the desk. His clothes were soaked, and his heart was still pounding. He leaned over, poked his head out from under the desk, and listened intently. No sound. He got on all fours and crawled slowly out, stopping every few inches to listen for any sounds, until he made his way out completely. He peaked his head over the top of the desk and looked around. Nothing. He got up and sat back in the chair, exhausted; every muscle in his body was spent. He felt he had just run a marathon.

Until then, he had not realized that he had left the drawer open and was clutching the notebook so hard that his fingertips had left imprints on the cover. He didn't remember taking it out of his pants while under the desk, but he thought he must have, and he began again to look inside. He now noticed that there were other sections of the book with other names. He knew this was important and pulled out his cell phone, hitting the speed dial for Dr. Miller.

Come on, Doc … answer. When he didn't pick up, he left him a message. "Listen, Doc, I'm in the department and sitting in Ahzid's office. I opened a locked drawer in his desk and found a notebook." Buzz looked down at the notebook, holding it tightly to his chest. He flipped the pages and then shoved it down his shirt. "You need to get over here now. It looks like a list of radiation sources, amounts, monies paid, including from our department, going back at least a year, maybe two, and also names of people in different sections, even a name with 'General' in front of it. They must be all the seeds stolen from us, and likely others too. And I overheard Ahzid and the seed vendor guy talking about buying and selling seeds, I gotta go… I think I hear something--"

Buzz sensed something behind him, turned around, and shouted, "Ahzid, no, don't!" as he turned to get away. He heard the crack of the back of his skull and felt a burning that pierced his entire body. Still in the desk chair, he fell forward, hit the desk, and the phone fell out of his hand onto the floor. He was semiconscious, drifting in and out, and could taste the warm fluid running down his face into his mouth. He mumbled, "Ahhhhh."

Ahzid put the knife-like-sword back into his belt and looked down at Buzz. He turned his head left to right. "What a shame, my friend. I liked you. But you should have stayed out of this business. This is bigger than you and me. We are soon going to spread such panic, and we will bring down the US once and for all."

Ahzid squatted down next to Buzz. "Did you actually think you were smarter than me? That I didn't smell you, hear you, and see you under the desk. I had to take care of the seed vendor before I came back for you—and my book." Buzz felt him pull the book out of his shirt and heard him grabbing everything out of the top drawer. He heard his steps move away from him. He heard the footsteps suddenly stop and then continue, but this time they were getting closer to Buzz, and then they stopped right next to him.

"I first need to make a call," Buzz heard Ahzid say.

Buzz peaked out of his nearly closed eyes to see Ahzid pick up the phone on the floor in front of him, and then he heard him call the police.

"If Doctor Miller is coming to see you, Buzz, then I think the police should be here to see him also. This way they will think he did all this to you," Buzz heard him say.

"Hello, Is this the Boston Police Department? Good. And, yes, you can help me. I think something funny is going on in the Radiation Department at the Boston General Hospital. I saw some strange people when I was driving by, and it looked like someone had a gun or knife with them. Please hurry, I didn't want to get involved, but I'm very worried someone might be hurt."

Buzz raised his head and opened his eyes again to see Ahzid run out of the department. He sighed, then collapsed back onto the desk. But before losing complete consciousness, he moved his right arm slowly to write out with his finger the letter A onto the desk, using his own puddle of blood.

CHAPTER 20: JAKE'S ESCAPE

AFTER BRIDGET LEFT HIS CONDOMINIUM TO GO TO THE AIR force base, Jake noticed the blinking light on his phone and remembered that Buzz had called him earlier a few times. "Damn, I forgot to check the voice messages." All the messages were from Buzz. In the first few, he wanted to know if there were any updates on anything. The last one, however, spooked Miller: "Doc, it's Buzz, pick up if you're there. Please pick up. I'm in the department… There are people here, I think trying to steal our radiation sources. An, one of them, I believe, is Ahzid. I'm hiding under the desk in Ahzid's office right now, so they don't find me. Get down here as soon as you get this. Please."

Miller snapped the phone shut, grabbed his coat, and ran to his car. All the way to the hospital, his thoughts raced. *Is it really Ahzid in the department? Who else could be there? I hope Buzz is all right.*

When he pulled up to the entrance of the Radiation Oncology Department, he noticed the seed vendor company van in the parking lot. He went directly to the doorway that entered into the registration area for the patients treated daily with radiation. The crisp morning air with overcast skies made him shiver as he approached the building. The door was unlocked, and all the lights were still off. *Odd. Buzz turns everything on when he's the first in and certainly would have turned everything off and locked the door had he left already.*

He went inside, flipped the light switches on, and walked throughout the department looking everywhere for Buzz. " Hello, Buzz," he yelled as he walked down the hallway leading to the offices in the back. "Buzz? " he said repeatedly as he poked his head into each office along the way. He then heard what sounded like the departmental door that he had just come through close again. *Could that be Buzz?* "Buzz?" He hustled back to the patient waiting area but didn't see anyone. He rushed outside to see a car pull out of the parking lot and race down the road. He scratched his head. *Who the hell was that?*

He hustled back inside and down the hallway again to the last office that he had not checked yet, Ahzid's office. He pushed the door open and saw Buzz sprawled out on Ahzid's desk, laying in what looked like pooled blood.

"Holy shit!" He darted over to him, placed his hand onto his back, and shook him, hoping he would wake up. "Buzz ! Buzz! Oh my God!" He checked for a radial pulse. "Shit, barely a pulse." He grabbed a nearby rag, and pressed it over his neck and scalp where the bleeding became obvious to him. He leaned down closer to his head and saw that his skull had been bludgeoned, with blood oozing out of the wound. He looked up at the desk with blood all over it and leaned closer to it. Something looked weird. *What is that? The letter A carved out on the desk. He must be telling us who attacked him. Hmm. A? Could it be Ahzid? Buzz did say on the phone he heard someone sounding like Ahzid. But he wouldn't do something like this. Not the Ahzid I know. Or maybe he was the Ahzid that I thought I knew.* Miller heard the sound of running footsteps and shouting.

Within minutes, the police arrived and started asking questions of Miller. One of the policeman called the station to request backup and homicide as soon as he saw Buzz on the desk with blood all over him and the desk. And within another several minutes, backup arrived, followed by Lieutenant Detective Crusky, who began introducing himself as he entered Ahzid's office. "Dr. Miller!" shouted the lieutenant when they caught each other's eye. "We really have to stop meeting like this. Your being around these sort of things is really getting to be too much."

Dr. Miller gave a one-sided smile back. Blood covered his shirt, face, and hands. "Detective Crusky!" Shortly behind him was Detective Fifer. "Detective Fifer! Oh, thank God you're here. I barely found a pulse on him. Help me get him to the emergency room here at the hospital, or it may be quicker to call 911 to get EMTs to stabilize him," said Jacob.

The backup police and the detectives walked toward Buzz and Miller. "So what the hell happened here?" asked Crusky.

Miller felt exhausted. " I don't know. Please call 911."

Crusky turned first to the policemen standing in the office with them. "You guys check out the department for anyone else that may be here and tell the guys outside to make a perimeter around the building. Don't let anyone in or out. He then turned to Fifer. " Fifer, call—"

"Already on it, sir." The detective quickly called 911 for the ambulance. "Lieutenant, look at this." Fifer pointed to the desk surface.

Crusky looked over at the desk. "What, Fifer? What is it?"

"I'm not sure but, near his hand, it looks like the letter—"

Miller looked up at Fifer. "A," said Miller. "I thought it looked like it myself. He must have drawn it in his blood before he passed out."

The lieutenant snickered. "Oh, you guys are good. Are you sure though that he didn't draw it after he died?"

"He's not dead yet, so please don't say he's dead, " said Dr. Miller, who was now pressing Ahzid's lab coat on Buzz's neck wound.

Crusky moved over to the desk and leaned down to take a closer look at the wound on Buzz's head. "The wound on the head is strange looking." He then leaned down to look closer at the coagulated blood on the desk. "Hmm. Fifer—and Miller—you may be right. It does look like the letter A." Crusky stood up and looked over at Miller. "Any thoughts about what this may represent? Miller?"

Miller looked up at Crusky. "What? I'm sorry. When is the ambulance coming? He may not have much time."

"Listen, Miller, not to bust your bubble, but I have seen a lot of dead people in my line of work, and he fits the bill to me. Ahhh. I hear the sirens now. So what do you make of this letter A on the desk here?"

"I ... I'm not sure. It may be he's trying to tell us who attacked him."

"No shit. Brilliant. You sound like Fifer now. Of course he was trying to do that. What I need to know is what, or likely, who do you think the A stands for?"

"I'm sorry, but my attention is on Buzz right now." He focused back to Buzz and helped get him onto the stretcher as the EMTs arrived. They secured him on the stretcher, checked his vitals, and stuck an IV line into him to begin running fluids and blood. "Quick, let's get him to the hospital," said Miller, who started to move with them out of the room.

Crusky put his arm across Miller's path. "Hold on just a minute, Dr. Miller. I need you to stay here with us. I have a few more questions to ask you."

Everyone stopped in their tracks.

"But, I—"

"No buts. You stay here for now, with us."

Miller then turned to the EMTs and held Buzz's hand. "Okay. But be careful with him. It looks as though he has two wounds, one on the top of the scalp and the other on the nape of the neck. Not sure what type. I have been trying to keep pressure on his neck."

Detective Fifer walked over to Miller and placed a hand on his shoulder. "Miller, let them go. They'll take good care of him."

"Okay. Okay."

"We understand," said one of the EMTs as they whisked Buzz out of the office, down the hallway toward the exit to the ambulance outside waiting for them.

As they wheeled him down the hallway, Miller yelled out to them, "I don't know about any other medical problems! Get as many lines in him as you can. You may have to do a cut down since he hasn't perfused for while. And be careful with the intubation with his neck wound. I would just bag him until you get him in the ER—if his oxygenation is good, that is. With his being overweight, he's obviously Pickwickian. I'll be right behind you and meet you in the ER, which is right around the corner in the next building, and—"

At the end of the hallway, one of the EMTs yelled back, "Thank you, but we know how to do our job. Now let us do it."

Miller put his head down. "Sorry. He's a good buddy of mine. That's all," he said softly.

Detective Fifer stood with his arms folded across his chest outside the door near him. "Dr. Miller, we need you to come back inside."

Miller looked at him with a confused look. "Huh? Oh yeah. Sorry, Detective. I guess I'm in kind of a shock about the whole thing." They walked back down the hall together.

171

"That's totally understandable," said Fifer. "Here, let's sit down." They both sat down, and Crusky joined them.

Miller looked down at the floor and slowly moved his head left to right in disbelief. "Who could have done this?"

"I was about to ask you the same question," asked Crusky.

Miller pointed at himself. "Me? I really don't know. Buzz was—is— such a good guy. He had no enemies that I know of."

Crusky pulled his chair closer to them. "So then, Dr. Miller, how is it that you happened to be here today? And what was he doing here? Did you see anything? Was anyone else here with you?"

Exasperated, Miller looked up at the lieutenant. "Slow down. I can barely think after all this."

Fifer again put his hand on Miller's shoulder. "It's ok. Take your time. One question at a time. Do you need some water?"

Crusky rolled his eyes. "Get me a Bud also, will ya, Fifer. And make it a lite."

Miller smiled at Fifer. "No, thanks. I'm okay. So to answer your first question, Buzz actually called me, telling me to come meet him here. He said he had found something that he thought was important to the investigation of our missing radiation sources. When I got here, I found him like this on the desk, not long before you came."

"So, he was like this when you came in?"

Jake tilted his head and rolled his eyes. "Yes, that's what I just said, isn't it?"

Crusky pursed his lips and frowned. "Yeah, so, was anybody else around?"

Miller sighed. "No, I didn't see anyone. Though I thought I might have heard someone leaving after I got here."

"Really. We'll come back to that one in a minute. Did you touch anything other than the body?"

"No, I don't think so."

Detective Fifer leaned forward to Jake. "What do you make of the letter A that we assume Buzz drew?"

"Not sure ... wait a minute ... maybe the name Ahzid?"

"What? Did you say Amen?" said Crusky.

"No, I said Ahzid. The physicist who worked here with me. The one we talked about that I was suspicious was stealing the radiation sources from the hospital and perhaps others. He must have been trying to say that Ahzid was the one who attacked him." Just then Dr. Miller's cell phone started to ring. The ringer played the song "Fallen," by Alicia Keys, that Bridget had put on his ringer with her picture, so he would know when it was her calling. He excused himself, stood up, and walked to a corner of the room to answer the phone.

Crusky followed him. "Wait, Miller, where are you going?"

Miller turned to face him. "I'm just answering this call. That's all."

"That's okay, but come back near us to answer it."

Fifer got up and scurried to the door. "Lieutenant, I really have to go take a wiz. I'll be right back."

"Hurry back. I gotta go after you," said Crusky.

By the time Miller dug the phone out of his pocket, it had stopped ringing, but two voice messages had been left. They were both from Bridget. He listened intently to the earlier one and the other message she had just sent, and then sat and stared. His mouth hung open.

Crusky stared at Miller. "Miller, you all right? You look as white as a ghost."

"What?" Miller shook his head to snap himself out of his disbelief. "That was Bridget? I listened to the messages. I didn't realize it, but she had left an earlier one too, when she went to the base. She said someone followed her to her apartment and was coming to get her. Then this one just left ... she sounded terrified, even screamed at the end ... listen, I have to go. I'll talk more with you later."

"Oh, just hold on now," said Crusky. "We have a lot more to talk about, and I think maybe we should continue this downtown. The forensic guys will be here shortly, so we'll let them work on the murder scene."

Miller turned to Crusky. "Murder. We don't know for sure Buzz is dead yet."

"I've been doing this for over thirty years. He looked dead to me."

"I can't stay. I gotta go. Bridget needs me. I know she's in trouble."

"You ain't goin' nowhere." The lieutenant grabbed at Millers arm, but he tore it out from his grip.

"Look, I'm sorry, but—" Miller then turned around and ran off down the hallway.

"Stop!" shouted Crusky. He pulled out his revolver from inside his coat and aimed it at Miller. "Stop or I'll shoot," he yelled again.

Suddenly Detective Fifer stumbled out from one of the bathrooms down the hall into the path between Miller and Crusky's .357 magnum barrel.

"Fifer, get out of the way, you idiot!"

Fifer froze, with his mouth wide open.

"Get down, you idiot!" said Crusky.

Fifer jumped to his right, hit the concrete wall with his shoulder, and slid to the floor.

"Miller, last chance—stop or I'll shoot." Miller stopped and turned around to see the barrel of Crusky's barrel aimed right between his eyes. As he started to turn back around, he saw Crusky take a deep breath and cock the hammer back.

CHAPTER 21: RACE TO BRIDGET

JAKE KNEW HE HAD DODGED A BULLET, LITERALLY. HE HAD heard the gunshot from behind him, that sounded like a firecracker going off, and the bullet smash the lightbulb inches above his head. It showered pieces of glass on him and around him just as he turned the corner leading down the hallway. He sprinted to his car like he was in the Olympics and drove with the gas peddle pressed practically to the floor the whole way back to Bridget's apartment. On the way there, he weaved in and out of traffic, trying to avoid getting stopped for speeding, or worse, getting into an accident.

He felt the pounding of his heart against his chest wall the whole time he raced from the hospital to Bridget's apartment. Darting in between the cars on Storrow Drive, crossing the Charles River from the Cambridge side to the Boston side, he knew something was wrong the minute he pulled up to her apartment building. He drove slowly, noting all the front shades to her apartment were closed, something Bridget wouldn't do until dark, and her car was in the street parking, not in the garage as it usually was. He maneuvered the car into a spot on the street, not far behind Bridget's, and cautiously approached the building.

Once inside, he looked for anything unusual as he made his way down the hallway to her apartment. Nothing seemed out of the ordinary as he walked along, looking all around him, to her door. He rapped on the door and waited a long minute. Then he rapped again, this time harder. When no one answered, he debated going in on his own for a few seconds. He fumbled to get his cell phone out of its case on his belt, quickly opened it, and punched number one to speed dial Bridget. He held the phone with his head tilted toward his shoulder to free his arm so he could rub his forearm while waiting. When she didn't answer, he played her voice message again in his head and became worried, so he turned the doorknob. To his surprise, the door was unlocked, so he threw open the door and burst inside. The apartment looked trashed, in total disarray. The cabinets and drawers were all open with dishes and silverware strewn across the countertop and floor in the kitchen. "What the hell? Bridget! Bridget!" He ran through the kitchen, stepping on broken dishes, and then into the living room. It also had been ransacked, sofa cushions thrown on the floor, with knifelike tears across both the sofa and chair covers, and bookshelves emptied onto the floor. "Oh my God. Bridget!" He ran upstairs, checked in each bedroom, and opened all the closets and bathroom doors. Bridget was nowhere to be found, and like the downstairs, all the drawers had been emptied onto the floors, and the furniture and beds torn apart. He ran back downstairs, desperately hoping he would somehow find Bridget standing there with a good explanation for what had gone on there.

When she was not standing there waiting for him, he began to think very bad thoughts. *I don't see any blood, at least gross blood. But I know that something terrible has happened to her.* He sat down at the computer desk looking for anything. Something that might help him understand what went on there. He looked on the computer and noticed the computer itself looked as though it had been worked over. *What the hell.* He looked for any sign of whoever did this. *What have they done to my Bridget.* He then remembered Bridget's voice message telling him that she put a CD in the secret compartment. He remembered she had told him earlier that this was under her desk, so he slid off the chair, crawled underneath, and pushed up on the secret compartment under the desk to release the locking mechanism. The cover popped open. He put his hand inside, felt a CD case, grabbed it, and sat back in the seat to look it over. Something cryptic was written on it. "Drone 183 General P," said Miller with a questioning look. Taped on the other side was a note. He ripped it off and read it.

Jacob, this is the CD I told you about on your phone message of the general behind the stealing of the radiation; men are coming to find it and me. Let the authorities know LU.

He held the CD to his chest, over his heart, looked up to heaven, and prayed. "Please, let her be all right—" His prayers were interrupted by moans that echoed through the open kitchen window from the back alleyway. He opened the window wide, leaned out far to look around the alley, and saw boots projecting out from behind the garbage dumpster. He shoved the CD into his breast pocket, ran out the kitchen door, and down the backstairs to the alleyway exit.

He opened the exit door, looked at each end of the alleyway, and darted over the dumpster to find a soldier on the ground. He again looked both ways. The alleyway was empty except for the soldier and him. He bent over him, rolled him on his back, and checked his pulse. It was barely palpable, and he saw that blood soaked his shirt. He again checked for a carotid pulse and for any breathing. The soldier suddenly popped his eyelids opened and began to mumble softly. "Bridget put the CD under computer desk … It's about terrorists and General … corruption … attacks planned. I brought it to her to look at before they shot me … and grabbed her."

Miller put his hand over the soldier's mouth. "Don't speak. Save your energy. You'll be all right. I'll call an ambulance," said Dr. Miller as he opened his phone.

The soldier reached up to grab Miller's wrist and again spoke softly, struggling to get the words out.

Miller leaned closer to him. "What? What is it?" said Miller.

"Not going to make it." He panted shallow breaths. "Heard them say, 'Going to Boston to blow it up … at marathon.' You need to stop it." He panted again. "Uggh," he moaned and curled into a fetal position. "The pain." He coughed up bloody sputum, then gasped for air. "Getting more … difficult … to breathe."

Miller squeezed the soldier's hand. "Okay. Okay. You be quiet now. I'll take care of things. You just … rest." He wiped the perspiration off the soldier's face, sighed, and looked at him with saddened eyes. The soldier gasped a few times, then took his last breath. Miller knew he was gone when he heard the slow exhale of air being squeezed out of every last alveoli with his diaphragm relaxing. He didn't need to check his carotid pulse to know, but he did so anyway out of habit as a doctor.

Off in the distance, he heard sirens. And they were getting louder. *Someone must have seen what happened and called the police.* He jumped up, ran to his car, and drove out of sight before the police arrived. Once he felt no one was following him, he quickly slid the CD into the player and crossed the bridge back onto Storrow Drive. He knew he needed help if he had any chance of finding Bridget and stopping whatever was planned for the marathon. A lightbulb then went off in his head. *My circle of friends. Indeed. I need Father O'Brien and my homeless friends to help me out. Maybe they've seen or heard something.* Bridget's voice interrupted his thoughts on the car speakers. He kept his eyes on the highway and checked for any local or state police on the way. He went above the speed limit but not so much that he would be at high risk to get pulled over. As he drove, he listened intently to her voice. She sounded nervous, using rapid, shallow breaths as she worked to get her words out.

"Whoever is listening to this—I hope it's you, Jake—you have a CD that's highly government sensitive and requires your full attention and urgency. You must pass this information to the local police, FBI, and any other law enforcement agency you can. The people behind all this are important and powerful people. They'll do anything to get this CD and destroy it—and all of us who have seen it. It shows footage taken by a US drone showing military personnel meeting secretly with terrorists in their mountain hideouts in Afghanistan. General Ringer has been selling weapons to the terrorists, and this has included facilitating the stealing of radiation sources in the United States."

"Holy shit! This can't be happening!" Miller slammed his fist onto the dashboard. "I can't believe it. That son of a bitch. I remember that name. He's one of the brass I met several years ago at the Pentagon to discuss my defense research—funding. So, he's the one responsible for the deaths of my patients, stealing the seeds that were supposed to save their lives. He can't get away with this. But whom should I contact? Who will believe me? I need to think." Jacob kept driving and looked at the cars he passed. Everyone seemed suspicious to him. He felt he was constantly being watched. *Am I becoming paranoid? But anyone could be involved.* He began to rub his right forearm, all the while looking around him for anything that looked unusual or suspicious.

His eyes began to glisten and his eyesight became a little blurry. *Where could she be? I need to find her, to rescue her—and Boston.*

CHAPTER 22: PLANNING THE RESCUE

HE THOUGHT FOR A MOMENT. *WHERE CAN I GO? AND TO WHOM for help? My circle of trust.* Miller pulled his cell phone out of his pocket and hit the St. Francis House number. "Hello, Father. It's me, Jacob. I need your help, more than ever. I need to speak to you now."

"Are you all right? You sound out of breath. I'm with several of the clients you know sitting around the kitchen table."

"It's Jacob," Father said to them. "Jacob, they want to know if you are coming to visit."

"Yes, I'm coming now."

"Okay. Good. You sound nervous. Now I want you to calm down, son. Don't worry. All the clients are eager to be involved. Of course, we will help you."

Miller then swerved around a car that pulled in front of him. "Damn! Listen, I don't know if anyone is following me or even listening to this call."

"Make it to Russit Street—remember, where we would go to provide medical care to those who wouldn't come to the house? I'll get a few of the guys to help you out there."

"Yes, of course I remember. I spent many an all-nighter caring for the homeless there. But are you sure about getting anyone involved, Father? I don't want to—"

"You just get there, and we will see to it that you make it to the house. Drive through the alley to the back, and I'll be there to let you in the garage. Call me back when you're within ten minutes."

He hung up and turned sharply onto Boyston Street, toward the theatre district. He found himself again looking around. Everyone seemed suspicious. Those in the cars looking at him. He even questioned whether a woman pushing a baby carriage was truly a woman and if pushing the carriage was all a disguise. He became paranoid. *If a general could be involved, then anyone could be.* He thought how ironic that one of the biggest and longest-running shelters for the poor and homeless for men, in the heart of Boston and its theatre district, was where the rich and famous would gather and hang out.

As he entered China Town, a Boston Police car came up behind him with lights flashing. He didn't know if they were after him because of the incident at the apartment or because of his racing recklessly through Boston, or for some other matter all together. But it didn't matter now. All that mattered was that he needed to get away from him and to St. Francis House. Up ahead he saw signs for the Callahan Tunnel. He sped up and turned sharply, almost a U-turn, onto the exit, cutting off several cars, scraping one of them as he entered the tunnel.

At first he thought he lost the police car, but within a minute, he saw it coming up behind him again in the tunnel. They both zigzagged between cars, changing lanes to cut off cars that made them stop short, causing fender benders along the way. Horns glared relentlessly and echoed through the tunnel. Miller came out the other end of the tunnel, said a Hail Mary, and whipped the car across an open section in the meridian back onto Highway 93 south to head back in the tunnel, back to Boston and St. Francis House. He looked behind him to see if the cop had been crazy enough to follow him. No cop behind him, only a pile of wrecked cars he had caused when he cut them off to get back into the Callahan Tunnel.

He had not noticed until then how much he had pushed his body to the limits, driving the way he had. In the mirror, he could see his jugular veins pulsing and shiny beads of sweat covering his face. Within a few minutes, he turned back onto Boyston Street, wiped his brow with his shirt sleeve, and noted the street sign for Russit Street up ahead. He managed to pull up the corners of his mouth for a brief smile, in between deep breaths during his oxygen recovery. He called Father O'Brien again. "Father, I should be there in ten minutes or less."

"Got it. Anybody following you?"

"I lost a police car earlier in the Callahan Tunnel." He looked up in the rearview mirror. "I don't think anybody else—oh. Wait a second. Shit! I spoke too soon. Another patrol car, coming up behind me—and fast. Father, I don't want to put you or anyone at the house in danger—"

"Stop that talk and listen to me now. You should see Pappy and Grumpy on the side of the street with their carts just a few blocks before your turn to the alley way to the house. Flash your lights when you see them."

"Got it, Father. I see them now, just up ahead. Will see you shortly," he said and hung up.

He saw the two shopping carts with Pappy and Grumpy standing behind them. He flashed his lights like he was told. Immediately they waved back, and they started to push their carts into the road. He beeped and waved just as he passed them, and they continued into the middle of the street after he had passed them. He looked in the rearview mirror to see that they had turned their carts over to block the street and started pushing each other as though they were arguing.

Behind him, the police car, with its flashing lights on and siren blaring, slammed on its brakes and swooped sideways. Miller kept driving the next few blocks into the combat zone and turned into the alleyway that separated the poor and homeless district from the theatre district, and led to the back of St. Francis House. He drove straight to it and saw Father O'Brien standing outside next to the garage in the back. Miller looked all around him in the alleyway behind the St. Francis House to see if anyone had followed him there. Father waved him into the garage and pulled the steel door down behind him and quickly padlocked it from inside.

The car filled the garage so much so that when Miller squeezed out of the car door, he practically fell into Father O'Brien's waiting arms. They hugged and patted each other on the back, and hugged and patted some more.

"Jacob, it's so good to see you again, my son."

"So good to see you too, Father."

"Despite the troubling circumstances, I'm glad you didn't wait as long as the last time to come visit."

Miller nodded and smiled while they embraced.

Father O'Brien let go to put his hands on Miller's shoulders. In the dimly lit garage, he scanned him up and down. "My, how good you look. Come on, let's get upstairs. Some of the guys are up there waiting to see you." He gave one last look around the garage and a quick listen to outside the alleyway behind the garage door. "Looks as though you made a clean getaway."

"Thanks to Pappy and Grumpy. I don't think anyone followed me to here."

Father O'Brien started up the stairs, then turned to Miller. "Watch your step. These stairs are old and not used much." Father O'Brien then continued up the squeaky stairs to the door in the back of the kitchen and pressed the buzzer.

Following behind him, Miller thought of how, after all these years, nothing had changed about the building, not even the retched sound of the backdoor garage buzzer. He also thought how ironic it was that Catholic organizations had given him some of his worst life experiences, like at St. Peter's Orphanage, and some of the best, with life and people, like at the St. Francis House.

The door soon opened, and there stood Frenchy in his usual gray sweats that Miller remembered he would always wear to bed. "Good to see yuz. What brings ya here so late? And why are ya—"

Miller climbed the last step and moved into the kitchen. "Hi ya, Frenchy. I need to talk with Father, and you guys of course." He opened his arms for a hug. Frenchy obliged him.

Frenchy stepped back a foot and started to turn around. "Well, come on in for crying out loud."

They went into the living room area where the residents who lived and worked at the house sat around watching TV. No one turned as they entered, all glued to a *Welcome Back, Kotter* rerun. Without looking up from the book he was reading, one of the residents said, "Frenchy, who was that at the back door?"

Miller chuckled and looked over at Father O'Brien. "So much for the guys waiting to see me. Guess I'm trumped again by Kotter."

Father O'Brien chucked also. "Some things never change, my son."

Dogger, the hotdog vendor man, then turned to look who was talking. "Doc! Great to see you, son," he said in his thick Irish brogue.

He slapped both of his thighs, got up to give him a big hug, and stepped back to look him over. "If you don't mind my sayin', you look a bit weathered and frazzled. Is everything all right with ya?"

"I wish I could say otherwise, but no, actually there is much wrong. I need your help more than ever. I hesitated to come here, for I didn't want to put any of you in danger."

"Danger?" interjected Frenchy, with his eyes snapping wide open.

"Yes, Frenchy. Danger. But I had nowhere else to go. No one else to turn to."

Father O'Brien put his arm around Miller's shoulders. "No worries, son. Come in and sit down in the kitchen. I'll make you my favorite tea. You remember it, don't you?"

Miller smiled. "How could I forget? Do you still make it with single malt?"

"Oh, yes. Indeed. That's what makes it so good. Let's have a chat, you and me. We'll let the boys sit here for now entertaining themselves."

Father O'Brien whispered into his ear while they walked into the kitchen. "What was it exactly that you wanted to talk to me about?"

"Father, I believe there is going to be a terrorist attack in Boston. And soon. But as I've said, I don't want to put you or anyone at the house in danger."

Father gestured for Miller to sit in one of the chairs around the table. "Let's sit in here, in the kitchen, for now and talk." There they sat and talked for well over an hour as Miller explained everything that had happened up to this point. Aside from a few quick questions, Father O'Brien barely moved, riveted to his seat. Miller, normally prone to giving only outlines, gave details of the people and events within this whole nightmare. He also explained that he was concerned about going to the authorities since they had suspicions about him with the events at the mosque and later with Buzz's being attacked and the police and detectives currently after him. "I believe they're planning to use a dirty bomb at the marathon, and it's going to be up to me—with the help of you—to stop it." He ended and sat back in his chair.

After Miller finished, Father O'Brien sat frozen. After a minute or so, he began to thaw. "Son, now I feel frazzled after hearing all that. It's unbelievable. He stood up and walked over to the kitchen counter. "I need another cup of tea after hearing all that."

"You do believe me, Father?"

"Of course I do. Hell, even the best fiction writers couldn't make that up."

"I didn't know where to turn. I came here because I trust you and know you would understand. Can you? Will you help me?"

"Of course. The bigger questions is not *if* I can but *how* can I help you. We need to brainstorm a little. You're good at charting. I remember that from when you helped here. Do you think you could make some charts of all these events you just rattled off in that brilliant brain of yours, so we less brainy folks can better understand things?"

"Of course. My charting actually is what made me stumble onto who was involved with the deaths of my patients, which led to the unraveling of all these other things." Miller then went to work on the charts and within twenty minutes had Venn diagrams and flow charts all neatly made, all with various colors and shapes to highlight and show better various connections between events and the people involved.

Father O'Brien had watched him work in amazement. "Your brain has not skipped a beat in all these years, my son. I'll make us another cup of tea, and we can decide what we should do and whom we should contact and when."

"Yes. I guess I could use more tea. Maybe it will lower some of this anxiety. Do you have any Tums? My stomach acid feels like it's burning a hole through my esophagus."

Father pointed to the other side of the kitchen near the door leading to the garage downstairs. "Sure thing. Try the medicine cabinet in the bathroom over there."

Miller got up and noticed that both Pappy and Dogger were standing in the doorway behind them, staring at the charts and diagrams that Miller had made and taped on the kitchen walls and cabinets. Others stood on counters. They both just smiled at Miller as he passed them to go to the bathroom. He shot a smile back at them, winked, and said, "Hey, guys. Didn't know you were standing there. How you doing?"

They smiled at him. "Looks complicated, Jake," said Frenchy.

"I'll explain everything to you when I get out." He went inside the bathroom.

After about thirty seconds of staring at all the charts in front of him, Pappy turned to Dogger. "You see there, Dogger, on the charts, that guy Ahzid knew Dr. Miller and the general."

"Yeah, I see that," replied Dogger. He pointed to a different chart. "And look. Those pigs those guys kept mentioning are there too on the charts."

Miller swung open the bathroom door, stood at the doorway with his mouth hanging wide open, and gawked at Pappy and Dogger. "Did you guys just say you know about Ahzid and the general and the pigs?"

They tilted their heads together in harmony, like they had rehearsed it, and looked at Miller. "Yeah," said Dogger. "We both have seen guys almost every day at the park, standing and sitting around and talking about things like pigs." We saw them taking measurements around the Boston Common the other day with some type of distance-measuring device. I overheard them say they needed to be precise for the location."

The back door suddenly began to shake from someone banging on it from outside. Everyone froze.

CHAPTER 23: DELIVERING THE PIGS

4:00 A.M. PATRIOT'S DAY

AHZID HAD BEEN AWAKE ALL NIGHT WITH THOUGHTS RACING IN his head. He chose to sleep inside the barn the last night, wanting to breathe the fresh night air; he had stared at the inside of the barn roof so long, trying to fall asleep, that in the morning he could draw its layout solely from the image in his head. Thoughts about growing up with Miller in the orphanage crept in and out of his brainwaves all night long. Thoughts about the good times they had, the friendship and bond they had developed over those years, despite their terrible living circumstances. He chuckled when thinking about the games they set up with each other using mathematics. Thoughts about the present, such as the time spent with his family, the events soon to unfold that day. And also thoughts about his future. In particular, the belief in the promise of an afterlife with what he was about to do.

But questions he had about leaving his family persisted and tore at the depths of his viscera. How could he live without them, even in an afterlife? Would they truly be fine without his being here for them? How much he had hoped for a relationship with his children, the kind he had never had with his parents. He felt torn to leave his family, especially his young, impressionable son, Ahmed. He shot up quickly on his feet and went to awaken him. To tell him how much he loved him and how much he depended on him to take care of his mother and sister if anything should ever happen to him. But when he went to wake him, his bed was empty. His mouth dried up instantly, and his heart raced.

He looked about the property, inside and outside the barn. Ahmed was nowhere to be found.

He went inside the trailer where he and his wife slept. He shook her gently. "Have you seen Ahmed? He is not in his bed, and I haven't been able to find him," he asked her.

She moaned, rolled over, and wiped the sleep from her eyes to focus better. "Ahzid? No I haven't seen him. It's not like him to be up and about this early."

"No, it's not; that's why I'm worried. I'm going to look again, but this time everywhere on the compound." After searching everywhere he could think to search, he finally found him in the secluded part of the barn, next to the ambulance, watching the men loading the radiation sources into the heavy, lead pigs labeled with Medical Emergency Supplies on the outside. Ahzid's face turned an angry red. "Ahmed, come here now!"

Ahmed turned quickly around. "Father!" He ran with his arms raised and hugged his father at his waist.

Ahzid didn't return the hug. He grabbed Ahmed's arms and pulled him in front of him. He assumed a coaching stance, bending over to within a few inches of Ahmed's face, with his hands on his knees. "Son, I've been looking for you everywhere. From now on, I don't want you near the ambulance and those men working over there."

"But, Father, did you see the shiny, green rocks that they have in those metal boxes?" His face glowed like he had discovered a mountain of gold.

Ahzid worried about his son's curiosity, a curiosity that reminded him of himself when he was that age, but he knew how dangerous the radioisotopes like the shiny, greenish, powdery rocks of cobalt were. He grabbed Ahmed by the shoulders and looked intently into his eyes. "You stay away from them, you hear me?"

"Yes, Father. If you say not to, I will not." Ahmed looked up at Ahzid with questioning eyes. "But why?"

"You never mind why. Just do what I say."

Ahmed looked down at the ground and kicked some of the dirt. "Yes, Father."

Ahzid saw his son's disappointment and squatted down to look his son at his eye level and smiled. "Son. I have to go now, but I want you to know how much I love you and am proud of you. You have gotten so big. You are ten years old now and will be a man before you know it."

"Father, are you going to do Allah's work like you said?"

Ahzid nodded and gave a gentle, reassuring smile. "Yes, my son."

"When you come back, can you play catch with me?"

"Yes, of course. But I may be gone a while this time."

Ahmed bore a forlorn look. "How long, Father?"

"I'm not sure. That's what I wanted to talk to you about." Ahzid sat on the ground and put Ahmed on his lap. "While I'm away, I need you to be the man of the house. You will need to be kind to your mother, and if you see her cry, I want you to give her a big hug. Like this." Ahzid wrapped his arms around Ahmed and squeezed him into his chest. He put his hands on Ahmed's shoulders and looked directly in his eyes.

Ahmed reached to wipe a tear running down Ahzid's cheek. "Father, please don't cry."

"My son. Can you do that for me … and your mother and sister?"

Ahmed nodded affirmatively. "Yes, Father. I will not let you down."

"Good. While I'm away, you are the protector of our family. And our name."

Ahmed proudly pulled his shoulders back and grinned.

"Ahzid," shouted one of the men from across the barn who was transferring the isotopes into the ambulance and wore a surgical mask and thickened gloves.

Ahzid hugged Ahmed once more. "I'll always love you, my son." He then stood, cupped his hands around his mouth to act like a megaphone, and shouted back, "Are we all ready to transfer?"

"Just a few more to go."

Ahzid gave him a thumbs-up sign and looked down at Ahmed. "Ahmed, I must go now and say good-bye to your mother."

Ahmed smiled. " Okay, Father. I love you too." He then ran outside the barn.

Ahzid walked to the trailer to talk with his wife. He noticed her face looked worn from crying. "I have said good-bye to Ahmed."

"How was he?"

"He is a brave boy. He will take care of you and Answar." They hugged and kissed. "I love you and will be waiting for you."

"I love you too. We will be all right. I know Ahmed will grow big and strong and take care of us until we are together again."

5:45 A.M.

IT WAS AN EERILY CALM MORNING, BEFORE THE ONCOMING storm. Inside the ambulance, Bridget sat quietly. Ahzid and Mohammed and Ahkmed accompanied her. No one said a word for the first few miles. Ahkmed, the younger brother of Mohammed, looked to be in his late teens or early twenties. He had come to the States via Canada and prior to that from Yemen. He had left his native country of Yemen a few years earlier to study engineering in Canada but had soon left to join others he had met at his mosque to enter the United States through the Niagara Falls and Buffalo, New York, area to form terror cells. "Mohammed, you and the others did a great job of transporting the radiation sources to the farm in New Hampshire," said Ahzid. "And also everyone who later helped to assemble the bomb and transfer it into the ambulance."

"Thank you, Ahzid. You and the others also did a great job to keep it hidden in one of the old barns until the dirty bomb is delivered and detonated on the day of the Boston Marathon, Patriot's Day."

Ahzid explained to them the design of the ambulance on the way to Boston. The ambulance itself was reinforced with heavy-duty shocks, the kind for large dump trucks to keep it supported from the heavy weight of the bomb. Ahzid showed the inside of the bomb itself. He opened the container. Bridget scooted down the bed to peak at the bomb. "You see the complex mechanism of the bomb—the timing unit along with all the radiation sources. There is a manual switch attached to explode the bomb should the handheld electronic device fail to do so. When it goes off, the world will hear it. It's hardly recognizable, because of its being contained within a lead-lined box labeled First Aid. That's why it makes the ambulance so heavy that we had to place it into the ambulance by a special lift in the barn."

* * *

When they were about two miles outside the city, Ahzid saw the Boston skyline come into view. The ambulance traveled down Highway 95, passing many cars, motorcycles, and trucks. Ahzid stared at each one as they passed. "They are all clueless about us; they think we are just an ordinary ambulance. But we know this ambulance and what we carry will destroy their way of life in the Boston area and, depending how extensive the ultimate blast is and the strength of the radiation sources that enter the air afterward, potentially areas hundreds and even thousands of miles away could be affected," said Ahzid.

Ahzid noticed that the traffic on the highway had been thin until they crossed over the Newberry Port Bridge just after crossing from the New Hampshire border into Massachusetts. Then the traffic thickened as the cars coming down from New Hampshire joined with the Massachusetts towns feeding into the highway. He called ahead to let those already in position at various locations at the marathon know. "Hello, seeds on way for harvesting."

"We are ready for mother pig," was the reply.

"It's a roadblock!" shouted Mohammed. He hit the brakes, which jerked the ambulance forward, along with everything and everyone in it. Ahzid slid forward, hitting his head on the dashboard, and the paperwork on his lap flew onto the floor. Bridget fell off the stretcher onto the floor.

Ahzid held one hand on his forehead and with the other gestured to Mohammed to keep moving the ambulance. "Mohammed, it's okay. It's okay. Calm down," said Ahzid. "We prepared for this, remember? So, do just like we practiced."

Mohammed made rapid, shallow breaths. "Yeah, yeah. Okay, I remember. It just caught me by surprise. I had not pictured it with so many lights and police cars. That's all. I'm good now."

Ahzid patted him on the thigh. "Good. I knew you would be okay."

The normally dark and dreary Tobin Bridge leading into Boston looked more like Faneuil Hall during Christmas season. State trooper cars with lights flashing were parked on both sides of the toll booths. Some of them were sitting in their vehicles; others could be seen walking about the area as cars pulled up to the booths. A few cars had been stopped ahead of the toll booths to be inspected by individuals wearing jackets with either bright green or orange letters on the back, DEA or HLS.

Ahzid poked his head behind him and through the open door leading to the back of the ambulance. "Ahkmed, checkpoint ahead. Be calm. And quiet."

When Ahkmed noticed Bridget trying to look through the doorway and out the front windows, he pulled out his pistol and pointed at her head. "You bitch. You want me to kill you? Huh? Huh?"

"Ahkmed, take it easy," said Ahzid. "We will be fine, if we all stay calm. Keep her gagged and tied, and both of you stay behind the curtain."

Ahkmed poked his head into the front cab. "What do we do now, Ahzid? Should I get the guns out?"

"No. Do nothing. Stay calm. We can and will get through this. Let me do the talking."

The ambulance approached the toll booth slowly. Normally they would let all ambulances go through without even a check if their yellow lights were on to indicate they needed to get to a place in a hurry. Not today. Every vehicle was checked regardless of their purpose.

In his rearview mirror, Ahzid noticed a police officer step from behind the booth and look inside the back window of the ambulance. Then he walked slowly around to the front on the passenger side. Ahzid's heart pounded and his body chilled from the cold sweat forming between his skin and underclothes. The officer tapped on his window with his baton. Ahzid smiled at him and rolled the window down. "Good morning, Officer," he said with an innocent smile, showing the dimples under his scruffy beard.

"Transporting anything?"

"Ah, no. Not really, officer"

The officer looked at Ahzid curiously.

"What I mean is nothing other than what we always carry. First aid stuff. Oxygen. You know. Like that."

"Where ya headed?"

"To the race ... the marathon. We're part of the support team for the runners."

He squinted his eyes at Ahzid, curled his lower lip under his upper, looked over at Mohammed, then back at him. He chomped on his gum. "Hmm. I see ... a bit early, ain't cha?"

"Well, you know. Need to get there early because of the traffic and crowds and—"

"We get help for the race from all parts. Can't say I've ever seen you folks come down to help from New Hampshire."

A clanging sound like metal hitting metal rang out from the back of inside the ambulance.

The officer snapped a look behind Ahzid at the sliding door into the ambulance. "What was that?" The officer poked his head through the window for a closer look.

Ahzid's tenseness grew; his arms and legs tightened, and sweat bubbled out his temples. He unhooked the cover over the gun on his right hip, hidden under his shirt, and gripped it in a ready position to pull out for use. He then chuckled. "Oh, Officer, it must be that special oxygen tank for the runners at the marathon. It has concentrated oxygen, which makes it very top heavy and difficult to strap in."

The officer looked down at Ahzid and raised his eyebrows. "Just to be sure. Let's have a look see. Okay?"

"Sure, Officer ..." Ahzid looked up at the officer.

"O'Mally. Officer O'Mally." He then adjusted his hand to grip his holstered revolver.

Ahzid pushed his pistol deep into the side of the seat to keep it hidden, then turned to open the door to the back of the ambulance behind him. The door suddenly slid open on its own, and out popped Ahkmed's head with a shit-eating smile. "They must not have tied that oxygen tank properly again," he said to Ahzid. He then turned to O'Mally who was staring at him. "Oh, hello, Officer. How are things?"

"I thought that was the problem," said Ahzid. He then turned back to O'Malley. "When we get through the toll, we'll pull over, and I'll personally get back there to tie that up."

"Sure. That should be fine. Do you need a hand with anything?" asked O'Mally.

"Ah, no, Officer. It's not a big deal. But thank you anyway."

O'Mally stepped away from the ambulance and saw the line of cars building up and waiting behind them at the toll booth. "All right then, you guys better get going. They need you in Boston more than here to take care of those runners, I'm sure. Oh, and—"

"Yes, Officer."

"And take care of the tank. I don't want any accidents to happen because of it."

The officer closely watched them drive slowly through the toll booth checkpoint. Ahzid could hear Bridget scream in the back, muffled by the tape over her mouth. The ambulance drove about a hundred yards, then pulled over onto the right breakdown lane, still very much in sight of the toll booth. Ahzid turned and threw open the sliding door to see Bridget lying on her side on the floor, and Ahkmed with his boot on her neck holding her down with his pistol to her temple. "You fucking whore. I should blow your fucking head off."

Bridget's eyes were opened wide with fear. Ahzid darted through the doorway into the back of the ambulance. "No, Ahkmed." He put his hand on his arm to stop. "We don't harm her. Now, please put the gun away."

Ahkmed looked up at Ahzid but kept the pistol to her temple. "She is nothing but trouble. She kicked the tank over and almost got us caught back there."

"Listen to me, Ahkmed. We need her alive for now. If the police see us sitting here too long, they will become suspicious. Help me put her back on the bed and take the tape off her mouth."

Ahkmed frowned at him. "What? No. She may scream."

"No, she won't. Right, Bridget? She knows better. Besides, with the windows closed, this ambulance with its reinforced walls to shield the radiation sources is as sound proof as it gets."

Ahkmed reached down, practically flipped her over onto her back, and ripped the tape off her mouth. He smiled insidiously and seemed to take pleasure in doing it.

"Ow!" she screamed. Her eyes watered as she fought back tears from the pain.

"Sorry," said Ahzid and looked at her apologetically.

"Thank you," she said with a struggle to move her bloodied and raw lips.

Ahkmed looked at her with disdain. "If she tries anything else, I'm going to kill her. I swear." He grabbed her head and turned it like opening a bottle of water to face him and put the gun barrel between her eyes. "Do you hear me, bitch? Try something again, and I'll blow your head off." He sat back down across from her. Ahzid pleaded with Bridget with his eyes and went back to the front passenger seat.

"We all set?" said Mohammed.

Ahzid looked behind him to check out things in the back and then back at Mohammed. "We better be. Let's get moving."

Ahzid leaned forward, picked the papers off the floor, and looked them over as they continued down the highway to Boston. And when they got there, they traveled through the streets without any problem. Any police that they saw ignored them. It was common to have many ambulances in the area the day of the marathon, and within a relatively short time, they were near the marathon finish line. He followed the face of *Mona Lisa* that lay on his lap with a transparent map layered over it.

Ahzid pointed to a small alleyway. "There. Over there. It's the perfect spot, hidden yet close enough for serious damage. The crowds are just on the other side of that building on the left and down the other end of the alley. Park in front of that sign." They pulled into the alley and in front of the Loading Zone sign.

So far, everything went as they had planned. Now they waited. And unlike the noise and excitement of the marathon only a few blocks away, the silence inside the ambulance painfully gnawed away at those who were waiting.

Mohammed frowned at Ahzid. "Are you sure we park here, Ahzid?" he asked.

"No deliveries here today because of the race. The streets are blocked off all around us for blocks. We're good."

"You don't have to do this. Your wife and son need you here on earth more than ever," said Bridget.

Ahzid's face showed the strain building inside of him. "Quiet. Don't talk about that anymore."

"Let me kill her now, Ahzid. She is trouble," said Ahkmed.

"No. No. Leave her be. Now please, everyone, be quiet." Ahzid grabbed a pair of headphones from his bag. "I'm going to listen to the police and Secret Service channels for chatter." A smile pushed across his face. "Hey, it sounds like they're taking the bait on the president as the target. Means fewer police at the race. Ahkmed, call the others. Let them know that we are here."

"Ahzid, for once you have a good idea." Ahkmed called on his cell and left only a brief message to whomever answered. "Hello, the mother pig has arrived." Then he hung up.

Now they waited some more. *The hourglass keeps on running.* Ahzid knew he was at a crossroads, where doing the right thing was now not so crystal clear to him. He looked in his rearview mirror to see a tall, dark uniformed man staring at them about two hundred yards away. His mouth fell open like a set of pull-down stairs.

CHAPTER 24: HUNT FOR THE BOMB

NO ONE AT ST. FRANCIS HOUSE DARED MOVE A MUSCLE TO SEE
who was knocking at the front door. They all looked like mannequins
with only their eyes shifting left to right, looking to see if anyone would
do or say something.

"Who … who is that?" said Frenchy softly.

Father O'Brien broke the ice and turned to look at Frenchy at the
other end of the table. "I don't know," said Father O'Brien. "But maybe
we should take a look. This early in the morning, anyone who knows
this place should know that we are not open."

"Maybe someone should answer the door, Father." Miller stood up
and bent over near Father O'Brien's ear. "I should hide while you look
to see who it is," he whispered.

"Wait. Let's look out the window first." Frenchy got up to peek out
the front window. Frenchy turned to look at Father O'Brien and Miller.
"Uh, oh, Father, it's the police." He turned back again to look. "Uh, oh."
He looked back at Father O'Brien. "And they got Pappy and Grumpy
with them."

"Jacob, maybe you should hide in the back room over there off the
kitchen while I go deal with the police." He went over and opened the
back room door, and Miller slipped inside.

Father O'Brien turned to those in the kitchen and in the living
room. "Listen, everyone, I have to speak with the policemen downstairs.
Please don't make a lot of noise. I'll be right back."

Everyone nodded. A few barely took their eyes off the television set.

Father went downstairs to the front door and opened the door.

"Hello, Officers. Can I help y—" He stopped short, and his eyes popped open when he saw the police on either side of Pappy and Grumpy.

"These two here yours?" said one of the officers, chomping on a wad of gum and pointing to Grumpy and Pappy. He took off his hat, revealing a bright orange crew cut, wiped his brow with his shirt sleeve, and looked down at Father O'Brien, who was not accustomed to having to look up at others.

Father looked first at Pappy up and down, then checked out Grumpy the same way, then looked back at the officer. "Well, sort of, Officer."

Both of them gave Father O'Brien a look of surprise at his answer.

The officer raised his eyebrows to him. "Well, they claim they live here."

Father O'Brien looked over and down at them. "You two in some sort of trouble?"

They didn't answer but put on guilty looks.

Father crossed his fingers behind his back and glanced up to the sky. *God, please forgive the lie I'm about to tell.* "Officer, no one officially lives here on a permanent basis, but we do have many who spend much of the day here, and some even do stay periodically."

"They impeded a police chase."

Father looked back and forth at them sternly. "They did what?"

Grumpy shook his fist. "Father, he pushed me first."

Pappy stepped forward. "But he tried to cut me off in the street, Father."

The officer stepped in between them. "Okay. Okay. Settle down, you two, or this time you'll be going downtown to the station."

Father O'Brien waved for them to follow him inside. "Please, why don't we all go inside to talk." They followed him in. Father O'Brien turned to look at the policeman directly behind him. "Officer?"

"Higgens. Officer Higgens."

Father O'Brien smiled. "Pleased to meet you." He raised his eyebrows at them. "Officer Higgens and Officer ..."

The other officer smiled. "Officer Madley." He was obviously the younger of the two and the junior partner, letting Higgens do all the talking.

"Well, Officers, if you please, I'm sure we can sort out this misunderstanding." Father turned to Grumpy and Pappy. "Isn't that right, you two?"

Officer Higgens looked at the two of them in disgust. They both had quieted down and were looking at the ground.

"Guess it wouldn't do them much good to be put in the clinker," said Officer Higgins. "Or would it?"

They looked up at Father O'Brien simultaneously, and their eyes nearly popped out of their sockets.

"In fact, if I didn't know better, I would say they did it on purpose. But now why would they do that. Right?" The officer looked first at one, then the other.

They didn't respond, but Father O'Brien interjected, to speak for them, reaching up to put his arm around the officer, and walked him back to the door. "I'm sure that's right, Officer. Going to jail wouldn't do much except take up space for real criminals. I'm sure they simply lost patience with each other, as they always are doing when they're alone together. I'll have a talk with them, and if there's anything else that I think you should know, I'll certainly give you a call."

The officers nodded, turned, and started to walk away. "I suppose you're right. Especially today with the race and all. And with all the talk about terrorists since the bombings a few years ago, we need to spend our time on other things today and not on chasing things like these two fighting each other."

"Have a good day, Officers," said Pappy and Grumpy in stereo. They stood in the doorway and smiled.

Officer Higgens stopped, turned around, and gave a long look at them. "Yeah, sure. You two ... behave now. You hear?"

They nodded up and down rapidly. "Yes, sir, Officers," they said in stereo.

After the police left, they all went up the stairs. Pappy, Frenchy, and Grumpy all began to snicker under their breath. When they got upstairs into the kitchen, the whole group that had waited inside quietly and patiently for them started to high-five them as they entered the kitchen.

Father O'Brien put his finger over his mouth, moved around the kitchen, and looked at each and every one there. "Shhhhhhhh. Now, boys, calm down before they hear you and come back."

Everyone became silent and humble.

"But. Pappy and Grumpy," he said.

They both looked at each other, then at Father O'Brien.

Father O'Brien walked up to them. They were sitting next to each other, looking up at him timidly.

"Yes, Father," they both said.

Father O'Brien looked at them sternly. "You two."

"Yes, Father," they said, now with sad looks on their faces.

He raised his right arm in front of them above his head. They both cowered at first, as if they thought he was going to hit them.

"You two ... you two did a good—no—a great—no—a terrific job today," said Father. He high-fived them, and patted them on their heads and shoulders.

They both smiled and laughed, and then everyone came up to them to high-five.

"Jacob! I almost forgot about him." He hustled over to the back room door and opened it. "Sorry, you can come out now, son."

Miller laughed. "Sounds like you're having a party out here. Everything went okay with the police, I gather."

Father O'Brien draped his arm over his shoulders and looked down at him and smiled. "Yes, my son, God watched over us on this one. Although I had to fib a little to them."

Jacob winked at him. "I'm sure 'He' understands and will forgive you at your next confession, Father." They both chuckled and went into the kitchen. Jake rubbed his eyes. "Man, that gets real dark in there," he said.

As soon as they saw Jake enter the kitchen, Pappy and Grumpy darted up to greet him. They did a three-way hug. Then everyone in the room broke out again in cheers.

"Nice job, you guys," said Jake. He looked at them. "I really owe you."

"No problem. You us nothing. We owe you, if anyone owes anything, for all you have done for us through the years. Just glad we could help," said Pappy. "Stupid here had to tell the cops where we lived. That's why they brought us back here."

"Oh, yeah," said Grumpy. "Well, at least I didn't tell them we didn't see them driving at us because you were waving at a friend."

Father O'Brien chuckled and stepped in between them. "Okay. Okay. You two settle down and have a seat over there at the kitchen table. Jacob wants to talk to us to see if we can offer him any help on a problem he wants to tell us about."

Pappy and Grumpy gave Father a questioning look and sat down with the others.

Miller leaned against the kitchen counter to address the group. "You guys have already helped me a great deal by blocking the police, which allowed me to get me here." He looked over at Pappy and Grumpy and winked.

They both smiled proudly.

Father O'Brien went into the living room to get the others who still sat watching the television during the whole time the police were there. "Hey, any of you guys want to come out here in the kitchen? We're going to talk with Jacob about a problem he needs help with. I told him that we would all be happy to listen and help, if we can. But understand, no one has to help with anything if you don't want to."

A few of the guys got up and walked into the kitchen; the other few remained seated, staring at the television.

The two who came into the kitchen were Cabby and Nam. Jacob recognized them immediately. "Great to see you guys. It's been a long time." They each gave Miller a hug before sitting down at the table.

Cabby once served as a cop, and then a detective, but alcohol and drugs got the best of him. "Until St. Francis opened, I was living on the street. Thanks to the care I got from Father O'Brien and others, including you, Dr. Miller, I'm alive and doing well driving my Boston cab. So anything I can do to help, count me in."

Nam spoke up next. He also became a St. Francis client in its beginning after getting back from the war. It was not kind to him, taking both of his legs below his knees, but he walked with his artificial limbs so well that most couldn't tell the difference. "Yes, I feel the same way as Cab," said Nam. "If not for this place and you guys, I hate to think where I would be—probably I should say where I would be buried. I was proud to serve my country in Vietnam—and still would today, if I could. But now look at me. I'm not complaining, mind you; in fact, I'm doing pretty well despite losing my legs and still dealing with the post-traumatic stress disorder."

The last few guys in the living room finally trickled into the kitchen, Boss and Kid, and pulled up chairs.

"Hello, Boss," said Miller. Jacob remembered well his sad story. He had been the CEO of a large Boston investment firm, but as with many, alcohol and later embezzling got the better of him, landing him in the streets of homelessness, until St. Francis saved him.

Jacob smiled affectionately at the last one to join them. "Hi, Kid," he said.

"Hey, Doc. How are ya?" responded kid with some twists of his arms and legs, in his usual shy mannerism. Kid got his name because he had been on the streets for most of his life, in between being in and out of orphanages, mental institutions, and foster homes. Miller felt a connection to him right away when he first worked at St. Francis, with his having also lived in orphanages. Abandoned at a young age, No one would hire him, so he was a beggar most of his life, living on the streets. Now, he had become a helper at St. Francis. And he was proud of it.

"Glad you two could join us," said Father O'Brien.

Boss sat and nodded at him but didn't say a word.

Kid, on the other hand, beamed with excitement carrying his forever, ongoing smile. "Father. That's okay. We're happy to join you. Besides, *Welcome Back, Kotter* was ending and—"

"That's fine, Kid," said Father O'Brien. "Look who's come to visit with us today. Doctor Miller."

Kid nodded, still smiling, said hello, and all at once, a cacophony of sounds erupted in the room.

Father O'Brien made a loud throat-clearing sound. "Okay, everyone, what do you say we settle down and give Dr. Miller, or as we like to call him, Doc, or Jake or Jacob, a chance to speak?"

Jacob looked over at Father O'Brien and everyone now sitting around the kitchen table. "Listen, I remember each and every one of you. I want you to know how much your wanting to help me means to me. But don't feel any obligation to do anything. I don't want anybody to get hurt or get into trouble."

"We remember all that you did for us when you helped here and how you continue to help with sending money to help. We all want to help you," said Cabby. All the others nodded in agreement.

Miller smiled and looked over at Father O'Brien.

"Jacob," said Father O'Brien, "I know you asked me not to say anything to anybody, but before you came, I thought I needed to remind them of how much you have done to help St. Francis. I also felt it would help to brief them on the problems with which you need our assistance. Namely finding Bridget and stopping the terrorist from exploding their bomb in the city. Our city. Boston."

Obviously touched by the gratitude and willingness of the offers to help, Jacob cracked a smile, and a tear fell out of one eye and rolled down the side of his face.

Kid handed him a tissue. He always carried loose ones in his shirt pocket to wipe his constant nasal congestion. "Here you go, Jake."

Jake took it from Kid. "Thanks." He wiped the tear away, grew a soft smile, and looked up again to the entire group. "And thank all of you for wanting to help me find my Bridget but also find the terrorists and stop whatever it is they plan to do, which everything indicates is to explode a large bomb in Boston. What they call a dirty bomb."

Everyone around the table gasped at the thought of it all.

"I know it's scary stuff," said Miller. "Let me highlight the events for you to help you understand how I got to this point." He pointed to the Venn diagrams and flow charts that still hung on the kitchen walls and against the counters behind him. He referred to them when relevant while he explained the events that led up to his coming to visit them. The suspicion and discovery of Ahzid stealing the seeds used to treat the cancer patients and the resulting deaths from it, Buzz being attacked in the department, the police suspecting him, and his escaping only to discover the soldier murdered in Bridget's apartment, then her being kidnapped, and lastly, how the evidence pointed to terrorists involved with the whole thing, planning to use the radiation as a dirty bomb to explode in Boston, quite possibly to repeat the terrorist bombs that occurred a few years prior.

Not a one sitting around the table said a word the whole time he talked, riveted to their seats, and most had their mouths hanging open while staring at him. Jake looked around the table. "Well does anyone have any questions? Or thoughts?" He raised his eyebrows and looked around again at each individual. "Or, how about even a comment?"

Father O'Brien broke the silence. "Well. That certainly is an amazing tale of events. Kind of like a book one does not want to put down."

"Yeah, I felt I was watching a movie," said Frenchy. "One of those action movies. You know. Like *The Terminator.*"

"Yeah. *The Terminator,*" echoed Kid. He bounced up and down in his seat in excitement. "Remember when he took that guys clothes and—"

"Okay. Okay, guys. If there are no other comments, let's move on, shall we," said Father O'Brien.

Boss raised his hand. "Boss, do you have a question?" asked Jacob.

"Yes, I get how you linked the missing seeds to …"

"Ahzid."

"Yes, Ahzid, your physicist, and how Bridget left you the CD which told you how they may be planning to use the seeds for a dirty bomb to explode in Boston to destroy life, limb, and our way of life."

Jake and the others leaned toward Boss, as if trying to pull the question out of him. They waited and waited. "Yes, that's good you understand all that, Boss, but?"

"But. What I don't get is how we are going to find them and when this is supposed to happen. I mean, let's face it. Boston is a big place, and the marathon is an all-day and night affair, at least."

"Yes, I realize that—"

"Wait a minute," snapped Dogger. "I run one of the busiest hotdog stands in the Boston Commons, and I remember seeing more men in the park the past week or so. I thought it strange. Maybe a convention, or wedding, or something like that. They were walking along different routes of the park. I also remember seeing some of them outside the park."

"Where outside the park, Dogger?" asked Jacob.

"Along where the race ends. In that area of all the restaurants. They had just put up the road block signs and blockades on the street, and I remember thinking how some of them were taking pictures of mostly empty streets, early yesterday morning, in fact, before much traffic. I thought it strange then but figured they were tourists, especially with those sheets around their bodies and heads, taking shots of where the race was going to happen."

Jacob looked at Father O'Brien with wide-open eyes, like a lightbulb had just gone off in his head. "Father, are you thinking what I'm thinking?"

"Casing the area?" answered Father.

"Exactly. Why else would anyone be interested in where traffic was going to be held up and where all the people would be allowed to stand?"

"Maximum effect."

"Exactly."

"Hey. I just thought of something too," said Cab.

Everyone turned to cab. "Yes, Cab," said Father.

"I also have taken a lot more men than usual, dressed in those middle Eastern garbs, in the cab the past week. Many to and many from the park and race area."

Jacob and Father O'Brien pursed their lips and nodded at each other in acknowledgment of the implications of what Cab had just said.

Frenchy then gave a big yawn like a lion roaring and stretched his arms out at the same time. One after the other, each at the table began to yawn as if they were programmed to do so after the one before them finished.

"It's been almost four hours and is close to two in the morning. Perhaps we should get some shuteye and get up early to investigate this more," said Father.

"Investigate what? Who? Maybe we should just call the cops?" said Grumpy.

"Call the cops? Are you nuts? What good will they do?" said Pappy.

Grumpy looked at him angrily. "At least I gave an idea. Do you got one? Let's hear it, if you do."

"Guys. Guys. Come on now. No use in arguing with each other. That won't help us out. It's getting late, and we could all use some rest before tomorrow. Besides, I agree with Pappy. The police will only try to stop us from looking for the ambulance at the marathon. They don't understand everything that we'll be doing, and moreover, will not believe us. Would you, if someone came to you and said they were looking for a kidnapped woman being held in an ambulance—which is not really an ambulance—and by the way, it also carries a dirty bomb, which if we don't find it and stop the men, the terrorists, they will blow it up and kill who knows how many people and potentially destroy half the city and their way of life?" Jake raised his eyebrows and looked around at everyone. "I sure as hell don't know if I would if I were them. That's why all along I haven't approached the police on this, in addition to them having suspicions about me that I've mentioned."

"Jake, they'd think we were nuts," said Frenchy.

Jake nodded. "Exactly."

Father O'Brien stood up. "Everyone is welcome to stay, but you will have to sleep on the chairs and couches or the floor. The only bed here is mine, and I'm going to need a good few hours of sleep." Everyone began to stand up and walk into the living room, except Jacob. He stayed in his seat.

Father O'Brien turned as he began to walk out. "Jake, aren't you going to close your eyes? Don't worry, I'll set my alarm to wake us."

"Thank you, Father, but I don't think I could sleep if I tried. I think I'll stay up and go over our plans for going into Boston and the best route to take to minimize attention and maximize our finding the ambulance."

Father smiled and nodded. "As you wish. I understand. I think we have a good idea in general of where to look tomorrow. Beyond that, I must admit I'm not sure where to look for the ambulance."

Jake smiled, blinked his eyes a few times, and gave a short yawn. "I know, but I think the information on the *Mona Lisa* will narrow it down for us. Goodnight, Father."

"Goodnight, my son. I'll pray for all of us to succeed."

Jacob then shuffled through the papers in front of him for several more minutes, looking behind him every now and then at the charts on the wall behind him, as if to verify something he had just read. His yawning was getting wider and more frequent, so he decided to close his eyes and lay his head down on the table, resting it on his arms. He heard the repeated tick tock of the grandfather clock in the living room with each sway of its ticking hand and a few snores coming from the living room as he drifted off to sleep. After about an hour, Miller's cell phone went off, waking him up in a start. His head jerked up off his arms that were stretched out on the kitchen table. Confused, he looked around him but couldn't see anyone. The phone kept ringing, and he felt around for it on the table, but he was in the dark, and his eyes were partially still closed and puffy from sleep.

A few of the guys in the living room woke up and wandered into the kitchen. They all tried talking at the same time to Miller. "Aren't you going to answer it?" someone asked. "Who do you think it is?" asked another.

Soon, the house had gotten so noisy, so quickly, with side discussions and yelling out thoughts that Jacob could not even here the phone ringing. "Quiet. Quiet down, please!" said Jake.

Everyone's talking ground to a halt, and they all looked at Miller. Miller looked at his cell in his hand. He looked over at Father O'Brien, who had come into the kitchen in his bathrobe and flipped on the light. "Father, it's my cell, but I'm not sure who this is. I don't recognize the number."

"Go ahead. Answer it," said Father O'Brien. "What have you got to lose?"

Miller hesitated, then reluctantly pressed the green telephone symbol to answer it. He didn't say anything at first but instead waited nervously to hear a voice on the other end.

"Hello," came through the speaker on the phone.

Miller frowned curiously. "Hello. Who is this?" he responded.

"Detective Fifer."

"Did you say Detective Fifer? Oh, man. It's so good to hear from you. Yes, this is Miller. How did you get this number?"

"Buzz told me."

"Buzz! My Buzz! This no joke, right?"

"No this is no joke, Miller. He's lying right here in his hospital bed beside me, right now, as we speak."

Miller began to pace short, quick steps, back and forth. "Detective, let me speak to him."

"No, you can't. I mean, he can't talk right now."

"Can't talk? Why? What—"

"Not to worry. He took a bad blow to the back of his head, but he is recovering."

"I know. I was there. I saw him, and it looked bad to me … I didn't want to believe he was dead."

"Right now his head is mostly bandaged up, but he's breathing on his own. They took those pipes out of his airway only a few hours ago."

"Will he eventually be able to speak? How is he doing overall?"

"The doctors can't say for sure. He took a bad blow to the back of the brain. That's the area where we see things, they tell me."

"Yes, Detective. I know that. I'm a doctor."

"Oh, yes, of course. But anyway, he is now responding to simple questions with a yes or no with a squeeze of his hand. And all his other vital signs are getting better, they tell me."

"Can I tell him something?"

"Of course. I'll put the phone next to his ear. Tell him to squeeze my hand twice if his answer to anything is a yes. And to squeeze once if it's a no."

"Twice for yes and once for no. Got it. Thanks."

"Okay, the phone is now by his ear. Buzz, this is Dr. Miller on the phone, and he would like to talk to you. Are you up to it? I felt two squeezes, so go ahead and speak to him."

"Buzz it's me, Doc. I thought I lost you, man. I can't tell you how good it feels to know you're alive. I just wanted you to know that. I won't keep you on the phone because I know how hard it must be for you now. But I want you to know that I'm at St. Francis House with the guys here. You remember my telling you about this place and me?"

"He just squeezed my hand twice for a yes," Fifer yelled into the phone.

"Good. They're going to help me find Bridget, who the terrorists kidnapped, and stop them from carrying out the explosion at today's race with the radiation seeds that they stole from us and others."

"Miller, hold up," said Fifer. "There is an FBI agent standing here who is a friend of Buzz's, and he wants to speak with you. By the way, I think I see the hint of a smile on Buzz's face each time you speak."

"Thanks. Yes, go ahead and put him on."

"Hi, Dr. Miller. Dr. Miller?"

"Yes, you must be Dave, the childhood friend of Buzz's that he told me about."

"Yes, Buzz and I go way back. Listen to me. Buzz obviously can't speak, but you'll have to trust me on what I'm about to tell you."

"Sure. Of course. What is it? Anything."

"Well I don't understand most of it, but Buzz told me to tell you this if he ever got hurt and that you might know how to make use of it."

"Please, go ahead," said Miller.

"Well, it involves a picture of the *Mona Lisa*, which I'm sure you're familiar with."

"Yes, of course, who isn't?"

"This is the strange part. He had told me that using a—wait a minute, I wrote this down and put it in my wallet. Oh, yeah. Here it is. Using a right triangle and py ... pyth—"

"Are you trying to say Pythagorean triangle?"

"Yes, that looks like how you would pronounce it."

"Okay. Okay. What else?"

"This is where it gets a little tricky, so forgive me."

"No problem. Go ahead."

"He wrote this down for me. It looks like it says, 'the nose is the right angle, which is also the main gate to the park.' I don't know what all that means but—"

"That's okay. I think I do. Anything else?"

"Like what? I'm not sure I—"

"Like, any numbers or units?"

"Units?"

"I mean like distances. You know feet, yards, meters."

"Oh yeah. That must be what these are on the sides of the triangle."

"Please, tell me what they are. It's important."

"It looks like one side says thirty feet, the one next to it forty feet, and the longest side says ..."

"Says what?"

"Hold on. Hold on. I don't have my reading specs with me, and the ink kind of ran a little. Must be my sweating."

"Does it say fifty feet?"

"Why, yes, that does look like a fifty. How did you know?"

"It's a mathematical formula for the side of a right triangle. No magic of mine, I assure you. That's great, though. Let me speak to Buzz one more."

"Wait. There's something else he wrote on the other side of this."

"What? Go ahead. What else?"

"Oh, yeah. I remember thinking how funny the name sounded when he told me and wrote it down. Intervals of men are a Fibo, Fib, nacchi series to, the … ambulance. Yeah. Ambulance. That's it."

"Thank you, Dave. If there is nothing else to tell me, I really need to ask Buzz one last question."

"Sure. Sure. And don't you worry about Buzz here. We're going to take good care of him. He and I have been buds for a long—"

"Yes, I know. Thank you, Dave."

"Hello. This is Fifer. Dave tells me you want to ask Buzz another question, so I'll hold the phone up to his ear. Go ahead."

"Buzz? This is Doc again. Listen, I just got the information you gave Dave to give me, and I wanted to confirm it with you. I'm going to repeat it and tell you what I think it represents. If you agree, just answer yes. If not, then I'll restate it until I figure it out. The right triangle is a three, four, five with the numbers thirty, forty, and fifty in feet?"

"He squeezed twice for a yes answer," said Fifer to Miller.

"Buzz, the next part is that right angle is on the main gate at the Boston Commons Park with, I assume, the long side, forty, parallel to the park perimeter fence?"

"He squeezed my hand two more times, another yes," said Fifer.

"Okay, great. This is terrific information, Buzz. Based on the layout of the park and running areas, I assume that the point where the shortest side, the thirty-foot side, and the hypotenuse meet is the target area, the ambulance."

"Another two squeezed," said Fifer. "Any more questions? I think he's getting tired because his squeezes are getting weaker and farther between them."

"Just one more, Detective."

"Buzz. Doc has only one more question for you."

"Go ahead. The phone is up to his ear."

"Buzz. Last question. I promise. And you know how important this information is. I'm not even going to ask you where you got it, as I know you. And if it was not from someone or somewhere valuable and reliable, you wouldn't have taken the time to write this down for me. Okay. Last question. I believe it's the Fibonacci series that will be used for the sequencing of either targets or men deployed in the area to do harm and create disruption, death, or destruction. Is that correct?"

"Nothing yet."

Miller began pacing short steps again, this time in little circles. He waited a minute more. "Anything at all?"

"His vitals are all still strong on the machines. He may be just too tired and falling asleep. It has been—oh wait a minute. I feel one squeeze."

"That's it? Just one?"

"I'm afraid that's going to be it. No. Wait! He's squeezing me a second time. Not as strong as the first but definitely a squeeze."

"Great. That's excellent."

"I'm afraid we'll have to stop asking him anything. He looks too tired."

"That's all right. The information will help for sure. Thank you, Dave, and Detective. And please tell Buzz, when you can, how much this is likely going to help and what a hero he is. And, of course, that I love him and will keep praying for his full recovery."

Miller hung up the phone and looked around to see that the whole gang had once again rejoined him around the table. "Guys, what time is it?" Miller asked.

"Five in the morning," answered Father O'Brien. "So how did the call go?"

Miller's smile grew ear to ear. He looked at each of them seated around the table. "Guys, I have good news. First, my friend Buzz that you have heard me talk about is not dead like I had thought. He is very much alive and was able to give me information that I think ..." Miller stopped talking to stare at everyone, noting their anxious-looking faces, then jumped in place, startling everyone, "is going to help us not only find Bridget but also the terrorists planning to blow up a bomb at the marathon."

"Why that's terrific, son. Isn't it, guys?" said Father O'Brien.

"Isn't it though, Father," said Miller. "Guys, I need someone to get me a picture of the *Mona Lisa*, quickly."

"The *Mona Lisa*? The famous painting?" said Kid.

Miller looked over at kid and smiled. "Yes, Kid, that one."

"I'm sorry, but we would have to steal it, and we cannot do that." He looked over at Father O'Brien. "Right, Father? That would be a sin."

Father O'Brien walked over to Kid to stand behind him. He put his hands on his shoulders and started to massage them. "Yes, Kid. Stealing would be a sin. But I think what he meant was for us to get a copy of the *Mona Lisa*. Not the real thing. Isn't that right, Doc?"

"Yes, that's right. I just need a copy. Something from a book."

"Or, how about a printout from the computer?" asked Frenchy, who got up all excited. "If that will work for ya, I can do that on our computer downstairs."

"Perfect, Frenchy. That will work fine. Thank you."

Father O'Brien sat down at the table. "Jake, why do you need a picture of the *Mona Lisa*?"

"Father, it's the key to finding the terrorists' location at the marathon. Buzz was able to give me the coordinates of their location using an algebraic formula that Ahzid is using to communicate with his men."

Father O'Brien looked confused.

"Father, Ahzid and I would use mathematics and science to communicate with each other in the orphanage so no one else would know what we were saying or doing or even thinking. It was just between us."

"Oh, yes, I remember that. You two would always seem to know what the other was thinking, but no one else. And now I understand why."

Miller smiled and nodded.

Everyone in the kitchen then began talking again to one another about how good the news was. The noise level quickly rose, making it difficult to hear. Miller shouted for them to quiet down. "My phone is going off again. This time it's vibrating." He picked it up and noticed it was the same number that Detective Fifer had just called him from at the hospital. He looked at the others with a forlorn look.

"Why would he be calling you again?" asked Father O'Brien.

Miller held the phone and stared at it. His thumb extended over the answer button. It appeared stuck, and his face appeared petrified. The phone kept ringing and was on its fifth ring.

Father O'Brien sat forward and closer to Miller. "Why don't you answer it, son?" he asked.

He had one more ring before it would go to voicemail. "I don't know." He looked up at Father O'Brien. "I'm worried that it may be about Buzz. I have a feeling it's bad news." The phone stopped ringing.

CHAPTER 25: SAVING BOSTON

FATHER O'BRIEN TALKED PRIVATELY WITH JACOB ABOUT THE plan for them to find the ambulance by driving into Boston, and using the mathematical sequences, they would then surprise them in the ambulance to rescue Bridget. They would simultaneously disarm the terrorists and stop them from exploding the bomb, even if it meant having to hurt or kill some of them. Father O'Brien decided it best that he stay at the St. Francis House rather than go into Boston. "I think a priest running around at the Boston Marathon would only draw more attention than you need. Kid and I will need to take care of things here. I'll have my cell on me at all times if you need to call for anything."

"I understand and agree. Thanks, Father," said Miller.

They embraced. Father whispered in his ear. "God's speed and, remember, our father, your father, always loves you and always has."

Miller looked at him curiously and smiled. "Yes, I know he's always watching over me."

Kid had been eavesdropping in the doorway. He stomped his foot. "But I want to go with Doc to help him," he said with a pout.

Miller turned to Kid. "Kid, I would want nothing more than to have you there with me. But I need someone smart and brave like you to help Father O'Brien out. We can't leave him here alone to handle everything." He put his hand on Kid's shoulder and squeezed it. "Now can we."

Kid smiled. "Okay, Doc. If you need me that badly, I'll stay."

They smiled and hugged.

Miller took in a deep breath. "Okay, I guess it's time we should be going."

Father pressed his lips together to control his emotions when he looked over at Miller, and then he nodded.

Miller went downstairs into the garage to the car. It was pitch black, and only a flashlight he held gave him any light to find his way. He noticed Frenchy opening the garage door behind them, who then squeezed into the driver's seat. Miller looked over at Frenchy. "Hey, Frenchy—" Miller's jaw dropped, his eyebrows lifted, and the whites of his eyes grew larger. "Frenchy?"

"Yes, you were expected Lady Godiva?"

"Oh, is that who you're supposed to be? I wasn't sure with the blond wig and big boobs—and that pink dress with flowers on it. I didn't know going in disguise was part of the plan," said Miller.

"I suppose you have issues with my lipstick, eyelashes, and rouge." Frenchy slowly backed the car halfway out of the garage to let the others waiting outside get into the backseat. Nam and Boss got in the car. "They're less likely to pull a woman over," said Frenchy.

Nam looked up over the seat to check out Frenchy. "Yeah maybe if you looked more like a woman and less like Godzilla," said Nam.

"Okay, you guys, please stop it," said Miller. "Nam, Boss, tell Frenchy he doesn't need to dress up like a woman. Tell him that, if anything, it may attract attention." Miller waited for a response from them, but none came. "Nam? Boss?" Miller turned around. "Did you guys hear—oh my God—not you too."

"It was a last-minute decision, and we didn't think you'd go for it," said Frenchy.

"You're right, I wouldn't have."

In the back sat Nam dressed in his old Vietnam soldier outfit, with the colors faded and holes everywhere, and Boss with a 1920s hat and suit looking like Al Capone. Miller tried controlling himself but couldn't and had a guffaw.

"What?" Nam and Boss said in stereo.

Frenchy slowly backed the car out all the way to let Pappy in. "Don't think he'll get the back door open far enough for him if we don't get all the way out." As they backed out, Pappy came into full view, standing outside smoking a cigarette, with black-rimmed glasses and an obviously fake handlebar mustache that covered his lips. When Pappy tried to get in the back, Boss moved closer to Nam, who moved his arms in front of himself to give them more room. After a few minutes and a few huffs and puffs, Pappy finally squeezed inside, having to put his own arms on top of his protuberant abdomen, using it as a table. "Geez, can you guys move over a little? I feel like a sardine," said Pappy.

"Are you kidding me?" said Boss, with several shallow breaths. "I can barely breathe."

Miller turned to look behind him. "Okay, okay, no arguing. Remember, this is serious." He let out another guffaw when he saw them dressed up in their disguises. "I'm sorry to laugh, but you guys look like a bad imitation of those guys on the Papa Gino Pizza sign.

"Ha. Ha. Very funny," said Pappy.

☆ ☆ ☆

As they drove through Boston, Miller's thoughts again began to race. *I hope Bridget is safe. What do I say when I find Ahzid and confront him? I hope all this works out to stop the bombing, rescue Bridget, and go back to treating my cancer patients.* Frenchy drove over a large frost heave in the road, and immediately Miller began speaking. "So, I've been giving this a lot of thought, and it seems to me our main task is to find an ambulance. We find the ambulance, we find Bridget and the bomb. But knowing exactly which ambulance is the key."

"Maybe we should get more help. The police or the army?" blurted Pappy from the back.

"Now, listen, guys. We stick to the plan like we discussed. We are on our own. We cannot be running around looking for anybody to help us. They'll know nothing, and it will raise suspicions. And remember, just because we don't see policemen or other government agents, it does not mean they're not there, hidden from our view, and that there's likely video surveillance everywhere. They'll have full forces out because of the prior Boston bombings and to prevent anything like it again. And when we park, I'm going to figure out from the information we got from Buzz where that ambulance is located and where we have to look out for the other bad people who will be trying to stop us."

"Say again, who is this guy, Ahz … Ahzith—" said Frenchy, puffing on his cigarette with a half inch of curved ashes barely hanging on at the end.

"Ahzid worked for me as my physicist and …" Miller looked forlorn and distant. "He was like a brother to me. We grew up together at St. Peters Orphanage. That's how I met Father O'Brien. He worked there as one of the priests."

"Oh, yeah, I remember Ahzid now," said Boss from the back.

"Because of our bond, part of me struggles to believe that he would be involved with something like this. But looking back over all the events that have happened, it does makes sense now: the stolen seeds; the attempted murder of Buzz; the terrorist communications; he has the brains and energy to put something like this together. It all fits. But what to do first?"

"Notify the FBI?" someone in the back blurted out.

"No, we can't. Like I already said, it's going to be difficult at best to convince the authorities. At best they would want to investigate it their way, which will slow us down and make it impossible to stop the bombing in time." *But I did promise Bridget that I would get help. And the more I think about it, the more I think we will need help.*

Boss looked over at Frenchy. "Hey, Frenchy, better flick those ashes out the window before you catch on fire—"

"And while you're at it, give me one of your cigarettes," said Miller.

Frenchy rolled the window down, flicked the ashes out, and looked over at Miller. "You don't smoke."

"I did give it up, but today I do. What are they, Marlboro?"

"Does it matter?"

"No. Just give me one … please."

"Okay, but I hate to see you start again."

"I know. I know. I promise I'll quit after all this is over. Now, just give me one of those damn cancer sticks." He popped it into his mouth, grabbed the lighter that Frenchy held out to him, and lit it up. "Thanks." He sucked on it until he made half of it into a cylinder of ashes hanging off the end, held the drag for a few seconds, and violently coughed out the smoke.

A few muffled giggles came from the back of the car.

Frenchy turned to look Miller, not taking his eyes off the road. "Ah,,. How was it?"

Miller coughed again, then looked over at him. "Great, Frenchie. Just fucking great."

"Good thing Father O'Brien didn't hear that," said Frenchy.

"Oh I've even heard Father say worse when he gets angry," said Miller.

When they approached Boston Commons, the city that morning looked like any other Boston Marathon race day, with crowds gathering in the streets. Miller noticed a calmness in the air despite being only a few blocks from the center of all the gathering at the race finish line. The wind was mild but picking up. The air was crisp. It was the time of year when winter meets spring. April. The flowers bordering the Boston Commons were still dead, and a few mounds of snow remained on the grassy areas. Other things were being born or coming back to life. He began to think of how much he normally loved coming here. Unlike today.

The race had officially begun a few minutes earlier. Crowds were also building near Fenway Park in anticipation of the baseball game that day. There wasn't a pub with an empty seat that day to be found in Boston. The President himself was in town for a big fundraiser, and rumors had it that he even had plans to meet later with the winner of the marathon that day, if time permitted. Neither the President nor the crowds that were gathering were aware of what was about to unfold on this day. A day that would shock America on a level not seen since 9/11.

As planned, Frenchy followed Cabby, who had driven his cab, and now pulled to the side of the street, just ahead of the Boston Commons, behind Cabby, without a hitch. No one seemed to follow them or to be watching them. They sat in the car for a minute scoping out the area. Boss, Pappy, and Nam sat in the back giving suggestions of what they should do to find the ambulance. They all witnessed a patron try to get into Cabby's cab for a ride, and Cabby then kick him out. Dogger soon arrived and pulled his bicycle cart up next to the cab on the street side of the cab.

"Okay, I need everyone to be quiet for a few minutes," said Miller.

Frenchy looked over at Miller, then down at his lap. "Is that the map and picture of *Mona Lisa* on your lap that we printed out for you?"

"Yes, I need to calculate the point from the gate using the numbers and Pythagorean's Theorem."

"Pythag what?" asked Frenchy.

"It's a simple algebraic equation used in solving problems dealing with right triangles."

"Okay, if you say so," said Frenchy.

Miller had realized the connection between the copies of the *Mona Lisa* and the cryptic writing on the back that all the terrorists were using based on the three-number sequence of Fibonacci.

Pappy leaned over the front seat. "If I can help, I had some training in the military and police with maps and things."

"Yeah, me too," said Nam. "The military anyway. I remember back in Vietnam finding my way through the jungle—"

"Well I never had special training, but I used to be pretty good with the maps on vacations with the family years ago. Boy, you would think it would be easy finding your way around Disney Park," said Boss. "Well let me straighten you out on that—"

Miller stopped staring at the papers on his lap, rolled his eyes, and sighed deeply. "Okay, okay. Thanks, guys. I'll certainly ask for your help if I need it. But right now, I need to focus on this map I have over the picture. A golden rectangle. That's what we're dealing with," said Miller.

"A golden what?" said Frenchy.

Miller pointed to places on the map. "It's a mathematical pattern. And the line about thirteen and fourteen of Fibonacci dates—that has to be the Fibonacci sequence. The numbers at the thirteen and fourteen positions that they will use to set up their men or possibly other explosives." Miller began writing on the map.

Frenchy leaned over for a closer look at the map on his lap. Doc, what are you doing?"

"Writing down the Fibonacci series to see what the thirteenth and fourteenth numbers are."

"You remember all that?"

"Yes, but I want to write it out to be sure of the exact numbers at the positions along the way to what I believe is the target, the ambulance. Got it. It's 144 and 233. That's what I thought," said Miller.

"So now what?" asked Pappy.

"Well, we'll use these numbers and assume units of linear distance of feet to start. This has to be how they're letting the terrorist know where they'll be hiding."

"If you say so. It all sounds Greek to me," said Frenchy.

Dr. Miller then rechecked the calculations he had made the night before on the exact distances and correlated them again on the map of the area. "Now we have to also figure out what the other information means, as this is not enough to tell us the exact spot. It's undoubtedly somewhere within this golden rectangle."

Frenchy looked over at him and rolled his eyes. "Undoubtedly."

"Let's look at the next line; don't take your focus of the unusual left eye. Focus equals focal point," said Miller.

"Uh huh, right. Of course," said Frenchy.

"Sorry, Frenchy. I'm not doing a good job, I guess, of explaining myself."

"Listen. That's okay. You just get us there—and safely. That's all that matters."

"The long and the short is that using other golden rectangles, various focal points can be found. Da Vinci used mathematics and focal points to draw our eyes to these in the painting." Miller began drawing a line with the pencil in his hand. "So if I draw a line to the left eye from say the corner using the left elbow here, we should have a straight shot to—oh no.

Frenchy reached out to Miller. "What? What is it?"

"It looks like they're going to explode the bomb very near to the finish line of the race, which is what I expected, but I didn't think they would be this close, knowing the security would be tight. Likely to get maximum effect with all those people exposed outside and to get maximal terror and panic." Miller took in a deep breath. "All right, guys, we should get moving. The plan is that we will pull out first, and Cabby and Dogger will then follow behind us."

Frenchy then began to pull out of the parking space onto Charles Street. In his rearview mirror, he saw a police car barreling down the street toward them. Then Cabby pulled out fully into the street behind Frenchy, forcing the police car to slow down, stop, and blast its horn. The police spoke on the outside speaker for the cab to pull over and move out of their way.

Dogger peddled his foot cart in front of Cabby, blocking him at the corner of Arlington and Charles. He jumped off his bicycle seat and sprinted over to Cabby's window, yelling at him about how he had hit him with his cab.

Frenchy kept driving down Arlington Street. After a few blocks, Pappy yelled for Frenchy to stop the car. "I think that guy over there on the corner looks suspicious. Why would a Middle Eastern guy be hanging out on that corner in the cold with nobody else around? Not to sound prejudice or anything, but am I right? And look, he keeps looking around himself and at his watch, like he's waiting for something or someone."

Miller looked at the man standing on the corner then back at his map. "His location matches perfectly with one of the locations using the Fibonacci numbers," said Miller.

Pappy leaned forward and put his hand on Frenchy's shoulder. "Let me out here so I can check him out."

"I'll get out with you, just in case you get into trouble," said Nam.

Frenchy stopped and let them both out far enough away that they wouldn't be noticed. The two of them approached the man on the corner and acted like bagmen, begging for money. When they got within a few feet of him, he looked at them disdainfully and said, "Get away from me, you dirty pigs."

Nam walked right up to him, began to turn like he was going to walk away, and then whipped around with a side kick to the man's abdomen, causing him to keel over. Pappy then jumped on top of him, grabbed the gun out of his holster that he found hidden inside his coat, and quickly turned him over to tie his hands and feet and gag him with string and duct tape he had in his pocket.

They waved to Frenchy to move on without them. "We'll catch up to you," yelled Nam.

Dr. Miller signaled back to him with the okay sign, and Frenchy drove down the street cautiously.

"They can sure handle themselves, eh?" said Frenchy.

"I'll say. Nam doesn't look like he's lost a step from his days in Vietnam. They were terrific."

"We are damn lucky that everyone is on the other side of the building at the race and that it looks as though no one saw us," quipped Miller.

"Yeah, lucky so far," added Frenchy. "Let's hope if there are any cameras on this side that the guards were looking the other way."

They drove slowly and looked for anything suspicious. They first looked closer to the finish line, then parked a block away from the first aid and fluid stations. Several ambulances were there ready to assist if needed. Miller pointed to an open area on the street. "Frenchy, let's park the car there. I think if we walk, we'll draw less suspicion. Boss and I can get out here and look for the ambulance with Ahzid and Bridget in it. Frenchy, you stay with the car and wait for Nam and Pappy to catch up, and in case we need the car later to get away on St. James Street." When they got out of the car, Miller noticed a man down the street shuffling his feet back and forth together, like he had to go to the bathroom, and when the man saw Miller, he darted down the alleyway.

"Wait for me, Boss." Miller sprinted after the man. The alleyway was deserted, except for a few stray cats and a big rat. He ran down the alleyway, looking into doorways along the way until he got to the end. He thought he heard something behind him and turned around. Nothing was there, so he turned back and took one more step to enter the cross street.

A two-by-four slammed into his chest, knocking him to the ground. The man wielding it stepped from around the corner and pulled out a knife that was more like a sword.

Miller raised his head to look up at his attacker. *Ahzid's sword.* He recognized the ornate handle in the hand of the man wearing an orange coat with Security written on the front, just before he plunged it down toward Miller's exposed chest. Miller was able to roll quickly to avoid it, jump to his feet, and go into his karate-fighting stance. When the man swung wildly at him with his knife, Miller came down with a blow to his arm to knock the sword to the ground. He grabbed his arm, and flipped him over on his back, knocking the wind out of him.

Half walking, half jogging, Boss finally caught up to him, coming down the alley, huffing and puffing. "Are you okay?"

Miller took a deep breath and patted himself to check for any injuries. "I'm okay. No bleeding or anything broken that I can tell."

Boss pulled out string and duct tape from his pocket. "Hold his arms together while I tie them. I saw what happened when he swung that sword at you. Man, you took him out quickly. You are good. Bruce Lee's got nothing on you."

"Funny but I have heard that recently."

Moans startled them from across the alleyway. Boss looked at Miller with an open mouth. "What was that?"

They crossed the alleyway to check out the source of the moans that continued but at a slower interval and lower volume. Behind a dumpster, they found a policeman on his back with blood covering his chest. "By the pattern of the blood and no pulsing of blood, only oozing, and the entry wound off to the right, it likely hit a vein, not an artery, so I think he can be stabilized with wound pressure to the chest," said Miller. He grabbed a nearby rag and pressed it onto the chest wound. "Boss, you stay here with him. Keep the rag over his shirt so it stays clean. And keep pressure on the wound like I'm doing to help control the bleeding."

"Sure thing." Boss knelt down next to him and pressed down on the chest.

"I've got to look for the ambulance. Time may be running out on us. If the guys arrive or anyone else to help, send them my way."

"Don't you worry about me. I got things covered here. You be careful out there. You hear?"

Miller nodded, turned, and headed onto Dartmouth Street, the street that on the map where, if the Fibonacci numbers were correct, he would find the ambulance—and thus Bridget ... and the bomb. Down the street, perhaps only another fifty yards, Miller noticed an ambulance parked all by itself. It was only a few blocks away from the finish line of the marathon, behind the Boston Public Library on St. James Street, but strangely with almost no one nearby it. It was located in an area practically deserted, with all of the spectators at the race site only a few blocks away.

How strange is that; an ambulance over here by itself and cigarette smoke coming out of the driver side window. It has to be the ambulance with Bridget and the bomb. It has to be. Hoping to avoid being noticed by anyone inside it, he crept up to it from behind. He came within thirty feet of it when his cell phone in his shirt pocket began to ring. "Shit, " he whispered, and darted into a nearly doorway to hide, not fifteen feet from the ambulance.

The driver side door opened, and a rather tall and wide, darker-skinned male dressed in Muslim-looking attire, smoking a cigarette, stepped onto the sidewalk.

"Did you hear that, Mohammed?"

That sounds like Ahzid.

"Yeah, sounded like a bell or something," responded Mohammed.

"More like a ringer on a phone. Take a look around!" the voice from inside the van shouted.

Mohammed looked again at his immediate surroundings. "Ahzid, I don't see anything or anyone out here."

So it's Ahzid in there.

"Walk around and look. And if you see anyone at all, shoot him and get back in quickly. We can't take any chances on being stopped by anyone before we give the message!"

"Okay. Okay. I gotta take a leak anyway."

Mohammed walked around the ambulance and looked again at the surrounding area. "That Ahzid is fuckin' nuts." He then opened the front of his pants and started to relieve himself on the driver's side of the ambulance with his cigarette still hanging out of his mouth.

Jake saw this as an opportunity to take him out so he would have one less terrorist to deal with and perhaps take Ahzid by surprise. He had noticed someone sitting in the passenger side but couldn't see anything else inside the ambulance. There were curtains on the back windows.

Miller crept up to within a few feet of Mohammed, surged at him, and took him out with a single karate blow to the neck. He never knew what hit him. Miller was able to catch him as he fell and laid him down on the ground to dampen the noise. He then slowly sneaked around to the other side of the ambulance to the passenger door.

"Mohammed, do you see anything out there?" came from inside the ambulance.

At that instant, Miller, who had moved to the passenger door, opened it and reached inside to grab Ahzid. "Yeah, he saw me," said Miller.

Ahzid quickly turned and jumped over to the driver's side to see Dr. Miller standing there. He pulled out his pistol and pointed it at Jacob. "Miller!"

Miller jumped back from the ambulance and darted away.

Ahzid reached to grab the door handle and pulled the door shut. Jake hid behind the pillar next to the ambulance and saw the back door open. He gulped a big ball of saliva when he saw Ahzid holding his gun to Bridget's head. "Miller, I know you're out there. If you don't want any harm to come to your girlfriend, you had better get out in the open right now."

Miller, who had taken a position hiding behind one of the marble posts of the back of the public library next to the ambulance, stepped out from behind it to witness Bridget being held by Ahzid. One arm was around her neck, and the other with his gun pointed at her head. Ahzid and Jake locked eyes. Jake's heart was racing. He frowned at Ahzid, then looked back to Bridget. "Bridget, are you okay?" he said with concern.

"Yes, Jake, I'm all right."

Miller frowned. "Ahzid, let her go. She means nothing to you. She doesn't have to be involved with this."

"Never mind all that. What do you think you're doing by being here?" asked Ahzid.

"Ahzid, I know all about your plan with the dirty bomb."

"Well then, you must know that by coming here, you will die."

"No one has to die, Ahzid. It doesn't have to end like this. You and I go way back. We know each other like no else does. We've been through much together. Are you listening to me? You don't have to do this to send a message about your beliefs." Miller then made one step forward.

Ahzid turned his gun on Miller. "Don't take another step."

Miller raised his arms slightly, fully extended with palms upward like the priests would do at the orphanage Masses. "I too now believe there has to be something bigger than us, all of us, and this world in which we live. I'm not sure if it's as you believe, one God, one way only to escape it. But I know for sure that it's too arrogant of me to believe that this is the last stop on the line."

"Ah, I see that you have indeed made progress. You have much further to go, however, but I'm pleased to see you have at least opened your heart and mind to see beyond the world in which you live and the walls you have built to keep others and other ways of thinking out of it."

Miller dropped his hands by his sides, still tightly holding his gun. "Ahzid, would it not be better to try to achieve your goals of spreading your beliefs through living rather than through dying? As I have come to see things in a different light, perhaps you could do the same. Perhaps you too could try to see the world outside of the walls you have also created through the years."

Ahzid dropped his arm down to his side but still gripped the gun tightly. "I have struggled many years to do just that."

"Ahzid, you have my word that if you stop all this, I'll do everything I can to help your cause at getting more of us so-called Western-thinking people to understand our differences and to work to make peace. Do you remember when we drew blood together from our fingers and pressed them together as kids in the orphanage?"

"I do indeed. I still have the scar." He held up his finger. "See."

"Yes, me too." He then held up his finger. "We became blood brothers that day and swore to always look out for each other. That's as good and meaningful today as it was then. You have my word on the things I say and that I'll carry them out."

Ahzid shook his head. "Unfortunately, no one ever listens unless death is involved."

"That's not true! I listened to you and have changed my understanding and beliefs about the things you stand for."

"You are an exception, my friend, because you are very smart and caring."

"Please give me a chance to talk with you. That's all I ask."

Ahzid thought for a moment while still holding onto Bridget. "We have been through much together. About that you are correct. I guess I do owe you the right to talk at least." He let go of Bridget and gently nudged her in the direction of the ambulance. "Bridget, go sit back inside the ambulance. Ahkmed, keep an eye on her, and if anything happens to me, you have my permission to carry out the mission."

Ahkmed leaned out of the ambulance. "Don't waste your time," he said. "Just shoot him now."

Ahzid looked intently back at Ahkmed. "I have to do this. You wouldn't understand. We grew up together. We did everything together at the orphanage. Protected each other. Studied together. Played together. When either of us was punished with no food, the other would steal food to give it to the other. We were like brothers."

Ahkmed kicked the ambulance door. "Ahzid. You are foolish to do this."

Ahzid turned back around to face Miller. "You and I'll make history today, no matter how it turns out."

Ahkmed turned toward Bridget, who was now sitting at the backdoor of the ambulance. He pointed his gun at her. "Try anything, bitch, and I'll blow your head off." She didn't respond. Nor did she take her eyes off of Miller standing just outside the ambulance, watching everything going on.

Jake saw Ahzid wore a belt with explosives taped around him. He walked slowly toward him. "Please drop the belt so I can give you a hug, " said Miller.

"Stop, Jake," who was now only several feet from Ahzid. "I can't do that."

"Then I'll give you a hug anyway." Miller then took one step toward him.

Ahzid raised his pistol, pointing it at Miller. "I wouldn't do that. Don't make me hurt you."

"You won't hurt me." Miller took one more step slowly toward him.

Ahzid raised his head with a slight twist and raised his eyebrows. "I'm warning you. I'll have to either shoot you or set this belt off to explode and take you with me."

But Miller took another step to move within only a few feet of Ahzid and sighed. "Ahzid, remember how we watched out for each other at St. Pete's? Remember how we would warn each other of trouble to keep each other safe?"

Ahzid broke a subtle smile, and his face relaxed. "I remember. Those are memories I have often thought of through the years."

"Ahzid. This is not right and will not help you or your cause. It will only create more anger and distrust, just like the 9/11 attacks or the Boston bombings did. Please, stop this now before it becomes a terrible tragedy. You cannot achieve anything through this senseless violence."

"I wish others could respect my beliefs and get along and live in peace. Believe me. I really do," said Ahzid.

Miller took a another step, this time more like a half step forward with some hesitancy in his motion, like he was about to dip his foot into freezing water. He reached his arms out to Ahzid, gesturing for a hug.

Ahzid stood there looking at Miller, then looked side to side to see what was going on around him, but he didn't move.

Miller then stepped forward to be within inches of Ahzid, wrapped his arms around him and hugged him tightly.

Ahzid had one hand on the side of the belt in position to trigger the detonators and the other holding onto the pistol by his side. He sighed and moved his arms gradually upward and wrapped them around Miller. There they stood in a tight embrace. An almost total silence filled the air, except for the distant, scrambled noise from the gathering of people a few blocks away at the marathon's finish line.

Behind them, in full view of Miller, Ahkmed held his pistol to Bridget's head while he watched Miller and Ahzid first talk and now hug. He paced back and forth and bit at his nails, then began to rant and rave questions to Ahzid. "What is happening? What are you doing? Ahzid, you must stop this craziness and get back here."

Ahzid then reached down in front of his belt toward the detonators it held.

It appeared to Ahkmed that Ahzid's motions were to detonate the bomb. "Yes, yes. Do it now," Ahkmed yelled out. He bowed his head in preparation of the impending explosion, prayed, and calmly prepared to sacrifice himself.

Miller leaned forward to whisper into Ahzid's ear. "Ahzid, we both have suffered from those destructive seeds that were planted within us at a very young age, to no fault of our own. We have let them grow within us over the years and have let them affect us in very negative ways. But we have both been fortunate enough to have our paths cross again and to help each other see that. You have opened my eyes to my narrow mindedness about things, in particular, other religions and beliefs. I hope, and I do believe, I have also done the same for you."

Ahzid pulled his head back to look up and into Miller's eyes and chuckled. "Indeed, yes. I cannot deny that that's true. I am, honestly, now torn between setting off the bomb and trying your way of peaceful dialogue, like Martin Luther King did with racial issues."

"The bottom line is this, Ahzid. I want you to know that I love you, no matter what you do now."

Ahzid slowly raised his head, grew a wide smile, and looked deeply again into Jacob's eyes. "I cannot explain it, Jake, but I suddenly feel a deep inner connection that has gripped me tightly. Perhaps it's seeing you not afraid to die, as I'm not, that has made me realize that perhaps there is more than what we think we know about our beliefs of afterlife and our gods that we each believe in. And your eyes speak a truth to me about your feelings, such that I cannot do this until I understand more." Miller reached out and put his hands onto Ahzid's shoulders. "Ahzid, you are the man I have thought you are. A man of reason. A man with a heart."

Ahzid slowly moved his hands toward the center over the belt holding the bombs and unhooked it, letting it fall to the ground. He and Miller then embraced again, only this time tighter, patting each other on the back.

"Careful or you may squeeze the air out of me," said Ahzid.

They both laughed and loosened their hug.

"Ahzid, it's in your power now to set a powerful example of how other means can be used to get the message of your religion as a peaceful one, one that wants to be less influenced by Western ways.

Ahzid had a chill and shook from it. " I agree with you, my friend and my brother." Ahzid dropped his weapon, and they embraced again.

It had gotten cooler outside with the sun now hidden by the clouds and a slight pick up in the breeze.

When Ahkmed saw them embrace again, he shouted, "Traitor. Traitor." He pulled out his pistol, aimed it directly at Ahzid, and fired. The bullet hit Ahzid in the back. Ahzid sagged violently forward into

Jake's arms, and they both fell to the ground, with Ahzid on top of Jake. He felt warm blood flowing from his friend and looked up and over Ahzid's shoulder at the ambulance. "Ahzid!" Jake cried. He saw Bridget scream "No!" and grab a metal first-aid kit off the wall and hit Ahkmed on the head from behind. He sprawled to the floor. His pistol flew out into the street. She looked delirious but managed to get up, step down onto the street, and stagger over to Miller, who was still covered by Ahzid's body.

Ahzid opened his eyes a crack. "I'm sorry, my friend, that we will not get to be together longer on this earth." He coughed out blood. "I ask only one thing of you." He then coughed again, and more blood came out of his mouth, this time copious with clots.

Miller looked down at him and held him tightly. "What is it, Ahzid? You just tell me, and I'll take care of it. You have my word on that."

He coughed out even more blood and struggled to get out his words, "Please ... help take care of my wife, daughter and son. You will know what having a family is like soon."

"I promise you I'll take care of them like family, as you have been like my brother all these years."

Ahzid nodded his head in agreement, exhaled a long breath, and closed his eyes.

Miller hugged Ahzid tightly, pulling his head into his chest. Tears began to run down his face.

When Bridget finally reached Jake and saw him laying there, covered in soot like a chimney sweep, with dried blood and debris, she fell to her knees, burst out crying, and began to hug them both, rocking back and forth like she was comforting her baby. "Jake, be alive. Oh, God. Please be okay." She began to pull them apart and burst out crying. "Please don't be dead." Streaks of tears covered her swollen face. Jake began moaning from underneath, and she sat up, startled. "Jake? Is that you? Oh my God! She struggled to untangle and roll Ahzid off him. She finally rolled Ahzid off him, straddled him, and bent over to hug him. " Please, Jake, please. Be okay."

He again coughed, trying to clear his lungs. "Where am I ?" He blinked to clear the dust. "Bridget, is that you?" Jake's eyes snapped open. "Bridget? I knew I felt fireworks when you're near me, but this one got out of hand."

She looked directly into his face. "I'd laugh, but I'm too busy crying." She then began kissing him on the face and lips.

Miller sat up and patted himself over his chest and back. "I don't think I'm seriously hurt."

Bridget embraced Miller again like she would never let go. "Thank God. I thought I had lost you forever."

Miller looked over at Ahzid lying on the ground next to them. Blood soaked his shirt, covering the peace sign on the front. "I m not seriously hurt, but it doesn't look as though I can say the same for my friend and brother." Miller shuffled over to Ahzid and lifted his head onto his lap. Blood ran out of the side of Ahzid's mouth. He checked for a carotid pulse. " I think I can palpate a pulse, but barely." Miller waved for an EMT to take Ahzid. "Quick, I think he is still alive, though barely," he said as they took Ahzid away on a stretcher.

Bridget inhaled deeply, then exhaled and shook her head. "It looked like you two were talking to each other. What did he say to you?"

"He asked for me to take care of his wife and son. I promised him that I would. He also said the oddest thing." Miller turned to look at her. "That I would know what having a family is like soon. What do you think he meant by that?"

Bridget kind of smiled and looked away. "Well, I think I may know what he meant."

Miller looked confused, then saw inside the ambulance and noticed Ahkmed moving inside it. He appeared semiconscious, holding and shaking his head, and staggered over to the dirty bomb. When he reached it, he shouted, "I'll do it. I must do it."

A flash, then a popping sound came at that instant from behind a nearby tree, causing Ahkmed to fall on the ambulance floor in front of the bomb. Out from behind a large tree with a very wide trunk, not thirty yards from the ambulance, stepped a SWAT team sharpshooter holding his scoped, high-powered rifle over his shoulder. Detective Crusky followed behind him.

"Detective Crusky?" said Miller.

At that moment, "You can all go to hell," came bellowing from the ambulance.

Miller, Bridget and Detective Crusky, all wide eyed and mouths hanging open, looked over at the ambulance and saw Ahkmed crawling to pull himself up to the manual switch on the dirty bomb, flip it to the on position, and then collapse on it.

CHAPTER 26: Healing

///

MILLER GRABBED BRIDGET. "HIT THE GROUND!" MILLER shouted. Miller pulled her to the ground, and he landed on top of her. They waited, but nothing happened. No massive explosion. Not even a loud bang. The SWAT team members along with Crusky slowly got up. Miller looked up at them. "What happened?"

"Apparently nothing," said Crusky. "My guess is either he missed the manual detonation switch because he died just before or he just plain didn't know what he was doing. In any case, we are alive."

One of the SWAT team members walked slowly to the ambulance and poked inside of it. He went inside for a minute. They all waited anxiously. Saliva pooled in Miller's throat, which he gulped. When the SWAT team member poked his head out and said, "All clear. He's dead," Jake sighed in relief.

"Let's get the hell out of here and get Ahzid to the hospital," said Jake.

"I'm with you," said Bridget.

More police arrived as well as a few ambulances. One of the SWAT team leaders approached Jake. "Sir, we need to take you and your friend in the ambulances."

"Thank you, Sergeant," Miller strained to see his name badge, "Rico. Fortunately, I believe we suffered only cuts and abrasions and maybe minor concussions from being knocked to the ground."

Miller then looked over to Ahzid lying next to him, covered in blood. "He is a brave man. I made a promise to him to take care of his wife and son. A promise I'll forever keep." *How ironic. Ahzid used an ambulance to kill, and one is being used to save his life.*

At that point, emergency medical personnel approached them. "Ma'am, sir, we need to get you over to the hospital to check you over. Are you both okay?"

"Ambulance? No thanks. I've been in enough ambulances to last me a lifetime," said Bridget.

"Ma'am, I don't understand," said the emergency technician.

She pointed to Ahzid lying on the stretcher going into an ambulance. "Never mind, but you need to get that man to the hospital urgently. Except for a bump on the head, I'm okay."

"I'm okay too," said Miller. "But please take good care of our friend."

"Just the same, you and the lady need to go to the hospital to get checked out; my team is headed that way on the way to the president's fundraiser," said the SWAT commander.

"Anything going on there?" asked one of his men next to him.

"No, but we need to provide backup in case, with all this going on."

"I understand, sir. I'll get the team ready to go."

"Make room for two passengers," said the sergeant.

"Yes, sir."

Miller turned to Bridget. "Okay. Okay. Come on, Bridget. No sense arguing. We need to get to the hospital regardless."

Bridget nodded and walked with him to the SWAT team transport vehicle.

They had driven about three miles and were only several blocks away from Boston General Hospital when suddenly Miller saw a bright flash light up the sky. It was off in the distance in the direction of where they had just left, followed soon after with the loudest sound Miller had ever heard, like that of a bass drum going off in his ears and glass bursting inside from the windows imploding. The driver whipped to the curb and stopped. Without a word being said to them, all the SWAT team members began preparing their weapons for anticipation of battle, checking their automatic weapons and placing extra supplies of tear gas and cartridges in their protective jackets and pants.

The radio then began chattering. "Say again, say again, Mother Ship?" said a loud voice.

"I repeat, this is Mother Ship to Eagle I. We have a high-level red alert. Move the president out of there immediately. Use tango red protocol.'"

"I read you, Mother Ship. Level-one red alert, follow tango red protocol. Eagle I out."

"What's going on, Sergeant?" asked Miller.

"Not sure." The sergeant received a call on his ear receiver. The sergeant nodded and replied to the caller, "Yes, sir," several times before hanging up. He then turned to address his team.

"Okay, listen up. I just got a call from the commander. The bomb apparently went off, which, not surprisingly, was what we just felt. They don't have specifics at this time on its effects, but we are being diverted to get to the President's fundraiser. He looked at Jake and Bridget. "Sorry, but you two have to come along. This is a red alert, as you heard, so the President takes all priority. I'm sure you understand." He then turned back and shot orders to the driver.

Jake reached over and held Bridget's hand, shrugged his shoulders, and smiled softly to her.

"At least we're together," said Bridget.

They arrived within several minutes of the call to the fundraiser for the President, which was only a few miles away from the hospital. The SWAT team began filing out of their vehicle. The sergeant turned to Miller. "You need to come with us. You'll be safer until we find out what's going on."

Jake and Bridget followed them in with one of the SWAT team members staying behind them. When they got inside the building, they all went immediately to the back of the stage area where the President would give his speech. Jake overhead the sergeant talking with one of the Secret Service agents. "What's going on? How can we help?" said the sergeant.

"We just asked the President to finish, but he refused."

"What? He needs to get out of here."

"We know. The lead agent is afraid to piss him off because so many of those here are big donors to his election. I don't think the agent told him the magnitude of this, so we're trying to get his special assistant to listen to us."

"So what happened with the explosion" We had just left the site and thought everything was secured," asked the sergeant.

"From our sources on the ground and air, the ambulance exploded flooding the air with a deafening sound wave. It ejected damaging metal debris and spewed thick, black smoke above its burning flames. The pressure wave toppled anything standing in the immediate area to the ground and generated a giant sucking sound, with air rushing back into the vacuum created by the blast. The fire and heat from it instantly set nearby trees on fire."

Miller turned to Bridget by his side. "Did you hear all that?"

With her eyes wide open, Bridget nodded.

"So how bad is the damage?"

"We haven't been able to send more people into the site yet, but what we've been told is that only death and destruction remain where life existed a moment earlier. The explosion destroyed people and property for a two-block radius from its epicenter. And following its spherical path, bodies lay everywhere; one of the guys on the ground reported some moaning and groaning that showed life still remained within some, but many others remained still, most covered in blood and debris."

A rumbling sound began, and the building began to shake. People standing were knocked to the ground, and the sounds of furniture falling and glass shattering radiated in all directions. The continuing secondary explosions from the fires and gas mains created aftershocks that hit buildings for miles from the epicenter, causing everyone on the stage to sway like they were surfing on a big wave.

The lead Secret Service agent, Harold Evens, who had just gotten the call from the command center, went into the motions he had been so well trained to do. It was the day all agents who protect the President train for, one they hope never happens. "Get the President's ass out of there now," he shouted to his staff. The Secret Service agents swarmed the President and rushed him off from the platform in the middle of his fundraiser speech.

"This is Eagle calling from the field; this is a priority level-one call. Please connect me to Joint Operations Center linked directly to Pentagon Central Command and the Federal Aviation Administration," said Evens. Off stage, Evens briefed the president. "Mr. President, sir, you will need to activate ICS, the Incident Command, so that we can employ all military, governmental, and civilian resources."

In a state of shock, the President nodded but didn't reply. He looked around at the chaos unfolding within the building that hosted the fundraiser. "So what happened, Evans?" said the President.

"Mr. President, our worst nightmare. We think a dirty bomb detonated in Boston about five miles from here. The explosion itself was felt and heard for miles around. We have all federal, state, and local agencies involved with protecting the people and property of Boston in action. The CIA, FBI, Massachusetts and Boston Police forces have swarmed the city like locusts on crops. But for now we need to get you out of here and to the airport. I'll brief you further on everything we know to date and what we have done so far to contain the damage. Right now, sir, you need to enter the codes for the nuclear standby silos," said agent Evans.

But the President didn't respond.

Agent Evans looked into the president's eyes. "Mr. President?" He moved the briefcase he was carrying from next to the president's thigh to the president's lap. One Secret Service agent always carried it by the president's side.

"Sir, the protocol for such a potential national emergency requires you to enter the codes."

The President then slowly turned his head to look at Agent Evans. "Yes, of course." He then slowly, methodically, punched in the codes hidden on the top of the briefcase.

When a secondary major explosion occurred and its shockwave hit the building, three large Secret Service agents, standing right next to the President, piled on top of him for his protection. "What the hell was that?" said the President, muffled by the layers of bodies above him.

Evans then put his hand over his ear piece to focus the sound better. "Mr. President, we are detecting radiation levels moving out toward the ocean, so we are changing our planned flight."

The President acknowledged him with a nod. "What is the initial assessment of the risk?" asked the President. "I hope to God this is not another 9/11 attack." The President shoved a few sticks of gum into his mouth and began to chew rapidly.

"This is a level-one red alert, sir. I have talked with our men on the ground. We're not certain of the full extent of the attack, which we believe at least one terrorist group is behind, but we recommend we treat it as though other potential attacks are imminent. We have to be prepared for the worst, sir, and that's why we have scrambled the fighters and also have our offshore submarines readied. We have secured the borders of the city limits with both a mile- and a fifty-mile perimeter and have the entire city in lock down. No one enters. No one leaves. We recommend the National Guard be activated immediately for protection and assistance. The Pentagon communicated all service branches are on high alert as are all intelligence agencies."

"I totally agree. Get the governor of Massachusetts on the phone to activate the Mass National Guard. I want up-to-the-minute briefings. We will use my office for central planning. And, Agent Evans ..."

"Sir?"

Put me through on a conference call with the heads of the military at the Pentagon, the Secretaries of Defense, and Homeland Security."

Evans nodded once. "Yes, sir." He spoke in his ear piece. "Is everything all clear now in the streets to remove the President? Good." Evans and several others then lifted the president, carried him to the waiting limousines outside, and whisked him away to the waiting *Air Force One* at Boston's Logan Airport.

Miller and Bridget followed several feet behind them outside. Helicopters and scrambled fighter jets flew everywhere above Boston's skies. They went back inside the building and Miller saw Sergeant Rico helping to organize the crown. "Sergeant, I need your help to get to the hospital."

"Can't you see that I'm rather busy right now?"

"Yes, but I overheard that there may be radiation released from the bomb when it exploded. I'm Dr. Miller, the head of radiation at BGH and the radiation safety officer also. I need to talk to the antiterrorist squad and radiation disaster leaders about what to do for the contamination."

"I understand. Let me talk with the commander here for a moment and let them know your situation."

"Thank you, Sergeant."

Within a few minutes after the sergeant left, a uniformed military officer sauntered over to him. "Hello, I'm Captain Ignacious, in charge of the antiterrorism unit in Boston. I have been told you were asking to talk with someone about decontamination. Is that correct?"

"Yes, Captain, do you have the dirty bomb kits available?" asked Miller.

"Yes we do. We are setting up our main base closer to the epicenter but came here first to make sure the President was safe. Now that he's on his way—excuse me, but who are you?"

"I'm Doctor Miller, and I know all about the radiation that has been released by the explosion of the dirty bomb. I can help with the decontamination needs."

The captain turned to walk away. "That's very kind of you, Dr. Miller, but we have this under control."

Miller grabbed his shirt sleeve. "Listen to me, Captain. I don't think you know everything that you're dealing with here. I can help you. This is what I do."

"I don't know who you think you are, but I'm in charge of things here, and I will—"

At that instant, a deep voice barreled out from behind the captain. "What's going on here, Captain?"

The captain turned around, somewhat surprised. He immediately snapped to attention and saluted. "General, I didn't know you were in the area, particularly here."

"Captain, I came to make sure the President was safe but understand he has made good his escape and is now on his way to *Air Force One*. Is this Dr. Miller I hear your arguing with?"

"Well, yes, but—"

The general stepped in front of the captain and reached out to shake Miller's hand with his gloved hand. "Dr. Miller, I'm General Simon, head of all the military antiterrorism activities in the US. I have been briefed on everything to date. I would like you to lead our efforts with controlling the radiation and help us understand what we are dealing with."

"Sir, I'm more than happy to do so," replied Miller. "What is the status of things after the explosion?"

"Well, the President seems to have made good his escape, at least for the moment anyway. Those on the ground near the blast zone were not so lucky. Things within a few hundred yards from ground zero were horrific. Bodies lay everywhere. Most didn't move and were covered in bloody soot and debris. Only a burned-out and melted metal hull remained of what was the ambulance. And debris was everywhere from collapsed buildings with fires self-ignited, which caused further explosions, blown out windows, and busted gas and water mains."

"And are other agencies already assisting?"

"Oh, yes. Police, FBI, CIA, DEA, Homeland security, specialized governmental antiterrorism units—we have every branch of the military covering the epicenter and surrounding region for up to a mile in every direction. The city went into chaos after the explosion with panic setting in everywhere. People trying to figure out what had happened and many attempting to escape the city. While the chaos grew everywhere within the city, the Boston Police, along with help from neighboring police and the National Guard, tried to control the crowds and keep things safe and orderly."

"How far has the news gotten out?"

"All local and regional television and radio stations, within minutes, covered the disaster and the drama that followed, and within the first hour, the national and international news organizations arrived on the scene. They initially showed the governor address the local Boston residents, updating them on the events and trying to keep everyone calm. They have also focused on the antiterrorism and radiation disaster teams swarming all around, attending to those injured, arresting looters, and hunting for terrorists."

"General, what's being done to control things at and treat anyone near the blast site?"

"At ground zero, those with protective gear worked to put out the fires and spray decontamination foam on the ambulance and surrounding contaminated areas. Anyone exposed, even potentially, was taken to Boston General Hospital, which was becoming overwhelmed with those needing care from injuries both from the bomb itself or the radiation, and also secondary from the panic that occurred once people became aware of the dirty bomb and the radiation. And by the way, Dr. Miller, there has been an emergency command station along with a treatment center set up at BGH, and I want you to join me there and head up radiation operations."

"Happy to do so, sir."

"Good. And, Captain, you will follow Dr. Miller's recommendations."

Captain Ignatious looked at the general with his mouth and eyes wide. "Sir?"

The general turned around quickly and looked down at the captain. "You understand me, Captain?"

"Yes, sir."

"Good. Now I have to get downtown to BGH. We need to control the chaos that's breaking loose in the city and find those involved with this nightmare."

"General?"

"Yes, Dr. Miller."

"General, are you tracking the weather, and in particular the wind, to follow any contamination that may have spread from the dirty bomb?"

The general chuckled. "Brain already working on things. I like that. And, yes, we are on top of it. And we will keep you updated. For now, we need to get you checked out so that you can help with the decontamination efforts and treating those who have been exposed."

Miller smiled back. "General, I totally agree and am more than happy to help anyway I can."

Dr. Miller then directed his attention to the captain and other soldiers dressed in their decontamination gear who had now gathered around him, waiting for their orders. "Captain, I know you and your team are well trained for these situations, but I do have a few suggestions."

The captain sighed. "Dr. Miller, what do you suggest we do first?"

"You will need to make risk zones from the epicenter, based on blast extend, weather, and type of isotopes. I'll give you the isotopes that were likely in the dirty bomb, but we will need to gather the radiation information from the detectors to know all the types they may have used. They must have used plastic explosives for the explosion itself. Also have your men with the Geiger counters scan the area in concentric circles of one hundred meters to record the levels in the immediate area."

The captain nodded affirmatively, turned to the lieutenant next to him, and spouted off orders. "Lieutenant, you heard the man. Take your men and join the others at ground zero and begin the sweeps with the Geiger counters and then give regular reports in to the central command every five minutes."

Miller coughed and cleared his throat. "And, Captain."

"The captain sighed and turned back around to face Miller with an annoyed look. "Yes, Doctor Miller."

Miller half smiled and raised his eyebrows. "You will need to have everyone that was in the several hundred meters of blast area remove their clothes and shower."

The captain looked askance at Miller. "All their clothes?"

"Yes. Completely undressed, Captain. This will remove approximately 80 percent of any radiation carried by the dust particles in the air. Then set up portable showers with shampoo and soap. And give them clean blankets to cover themselves."

"Completely." The captain thought for a moment, then sighed. "Okay, you're the boss here."

A private then ran up to the captain and saluted. "Sir, the general called and said they need Dr. Miller down at the hospital now."

"Thank you, Private." The captain saluted the private again and turned to Miller. "Okay, Doctor, you heard the man. We have to get you down to the hospital, pronto."

"Captain, you and your team are doing a great job. Please have anybody that undergoes your treatment taken to the hospital, where we can do more specific testing and treatments."

The captain rolled his eyes behind Miller's back. "Yes, sir. Is there anything else, Dr. Miller?"

"Yes. Pray for winds to blow the radiation out to the ocean."

As Dr. Miller was being taken outside to go to the hospital, he heard a voice calling to him and looked over to a man in a tattered trench coat with dirt over his face. He was walking toward him with the aid of a SWAT team officer on either side of him. Miller squinted to focus better.

It was Detective Crusky, and even for him, he clearly looked shook up and disheveled, much more than normal.

The detective pointed to Miller and waved. "There he is, over there. Hey, Miller!" shouted Crusky.

Miller saw him coming straight toward him with the policeman on either side of him. "Oh no. Not the detective." He turned to the soldiers assigned to assist and protect him. "Guys, hurry, get me to the hospital." Miller saw him gaining on them. "Seriously, there's an extra twenty in it for you both if you get me out of here before that guy catches up to us."

The soldiers looked at him and then each other and laughed.

"I'm not joking. I'm very serious," said Miller, looking both frustrated and angry.

"Wait! Miller! " Detective Crusky walked even faster toward Miller and caught up to him. "Miller, I need to tell you something." He bent over and supported himself with his hand on his knees to catch his breath. "I know," he said, and took in one more deep breath. He stood up and looked directly at Miller. "I know you didn't try to murder anyone. I have the whole story now. The feds captured a terrorist and the general behind everything."

Miller squinted at him with a doubtful look. "So, Detective, you know that they, the terrorists, have just exploded a dirty bomb here?"

"Oh, yeah. Fortunately, we had left, like you, only minutes before the blast. Others, like some of the members of the SWAT team that were closing down on the ambulance, were not so lucky; sadly, there were many of them in the high blast range."

Miller grew a forlorn look. "Detective, I'm sad to hear about the SWAT team and others who made the ultimate sacrifice, but I'm happy that you now know what really happened before all this with me. Really I am, but what exactly do you mean by 'we' when you said 'we had left'?" asked Miller.

"Who else? Fifer. Me and Fifer came together. Fifer actually guided us to where the ambulance was and the SWAT team right to the terrorist bastard and shot him, but unfortunately he was not dead and blew himself up when setting off the bomb. Word has it that he must have triggered another remote somewhere in the ambulance." Crusky looked down and sighed. "Fifer, unfortunately, didn't make it."

Miller's lips turned down at the news. "No. Not Detective Fifer. He was such a good guy." *One of the few people that I learned I could trust.*

Crusky put his hand on Miller's shoulder. "You got that right. I only wish I had told him earlier just how good he was at his job, and a good guy. The best I ever worked with. If not for him, we wouldn't have been here as quickly as we were, and many more may have died."

"So, Detective, one of the generals here just told me that we have many agencies on the ground already?"

"Oh yeah. With something like this, we probably got every fuckin' fed here or on his way. By the way, I'm sorry to have been after you, thinking you were, if not behind the murders, somehow involved. " He put his hand again on Miller's shoulder. "You understand? Just doing my job."

Miller pushed Crusky's hand off his shoulder. "Yeah, I understand. Everybody has to have an asshole in their life. And you're mine."

Detective Crusky extended his arm to shake hands with Miller. "I guess I deserve that," he said.

Miller then extended his, and they shook hands. "Never mind that now. I have to get to the hospital, where they're taking anyone injured or exposed to radiation."

Bridget, who up until then had quietly stood next to Jacob, grabbed his hand as they began to get into the lead-lined antiterrorism vehicle. She smiled at him. "Jacob, there's something I have been meaning to tell you."

"Yes, what is it?"

One of the soldiers interrupted them. "Dr. Miller, we have to take you in a separate vehicle to get you to the hospital faster because they called to say that they think several of the patients were exposed to radiation."

Miller turned his head toward the soldier. "What? Okay. I'll be right with you." He turned back toward Bridget. "Bridget, what were you going to tell me?"

Bridget pulled her hand away and feigned a smile. "Oh, nothing. It can wait. You need to get to the hospital to help those sick people. I'll join you there as soon as this tank can get me there."

Miller reached for her hand. "Are you sure?"

Bridget gave him a kiss on the lips. "Yes, I'm sure. I'll join you at the hospital and can talk more to you there."

* * *

When Miller entered Boston General Hospital, the general was going over plans for caring for the sick and injured. Miller entered the room as the general was speaking. "And when Dr. Miller arrives, he will be in charge of decontamination operations and the treatment of those exposed to the radiation or suspected of being exposed; anyone potentially exposed will be separated on the east wing of the hospital."

Miller approached the general from the back of the room. "Already here, sir," said Miller, wearing only a blanket.

"Dr. Miller. Glad you could make it and perfect timing. Someone please get the man some clothes to wear," said the general with raised eyebrows.

"Thank you, General. Trust me, I would much prefer clothes. On the way here, I was briefed on the status of the patients admitted, and I—"

CEO Dinkus got up from his front-row seat and walked directly to Dr. Miller. "Excuse me, Dr. Miller," said Dinkus. "First let me say how happy we all are that you're all right. And second, how pleased I am that the general has put you in charge of the radiation injury operations here."

Miller looked at Dinkus with disdain, sizing him up and down. He didn't say a word and turned to look back at the general. Miller then saw Bridget come in the back of the room. He waved for her to come up to the front with him. "Bridget, are you all right?"

"Yes, I'm fine now that I'm with you." She gave him another kiss on the lips.

Dinkus grinned. "Oh, how sweet you two are. And, by the way, I have good news for you, Jake. I have convinced the board that there was a misunderstanding about things between us in my office that day, and as a result, we are willing to forget all that happened and take a risk to allow you to come back to work for us at (our) hospital and, when all this emergency stuff is over, continue the fight against cancer with us."

Miller turned back around and stood in Dinkus's face, put his hands on his hips. "Is that a fact?" Miller laughed. "Dinkus, you can't be serious. How generous of you and the board, since you know I had nothing to do with any of the missing radiation and my patients' deaths and you had no ability to actually fire me anyway."

The general stepped forward and addressed the crowd, who watched the interaction between Dr. Miller and the CEO intently. "For now, that's all for this briefing. We will announce any further updates, and in the meantime, please, all of you go to your assignments. And thank you for all your hard work." He then stepped next to Miller and looked at Dinkus. "And let's not forget that Dr. Miller by his actions here has literally saved at least thousands of lives and perhaps even our city. Including your sorry ass, Dinkus."

"And having a national hero on your staff can only be the best public relations move you have ever made," interjected Bridget.

Miller grabbed Bridget's hand and leaned to her ear. "Thank you, but I think I'll take pleasure to handle this one."

Dinkus, who was now dripping in nervous sweat from head to toe, frowned at Bridget and then looked over at Miller. "Hey, listen, I'm not stupid. Remember, I went to West Point." He looked over at the general and smiled proudly.

"Yes, I know. Dishonorable discharge—wasn't it, Dinkus?" remarked the general.

Dinkus turned a ripe tomato shade of red, coughed, and cleared his throat. "Excuse me? Listen, Miller, I know you've gotten a few bruises today, so take the night to think about coming back to BGH to your old position, and let's talk in the morning."

Miller leaned forward to within inches of touching noses. "Dinkus, I tell you what. I don't give a shit what you and the board think or do."

Dinkus covered his upper lip with his lower one. "Well, I think you should—"

"Dinkus, I have only one thing left to say to you."

"Oh, and what—"

"Kiss my ass." Miller then punched Dinkus in the face, sending him to the ground.

Dinkus lay flat on his back, grabbed his bloody mouth, and looked up at the general. "Are you just going to stand there?"

The general reached down, took Dinkus's hand, and pulled him up. "You're right, I'm not just going to stand here." The general looked at one of his men. "Soldier, take this poor excuse for a man to our interrogation room for questioning."

"Yes, sir," said the soldier. He saluted and then handcuffed Dinkus.

Dinkus dropped three inches closer to the floor. "You mean to tell me, General, that you are interrogating me? For what? What did I do? He's the one who hit me!"

"Give me a minute. I'll think of something," said the general.

The soldier walked Dinkus out, who kept mumbling.

The general turned to Miller. "We have concerns about his involvement with the terrorists and others behind today's attack, so I felt it was good opportunity to bring him in for questioning. Don't you think, Dr. Miller?"

Miller smiled. "Totally agree, General, sir."

"Good. Now is there nothing else we can do?" said the general. "For example, is there any type of antidote available for this situation that my men could distribute to the masses?"

"I'm afraid all we can do is treat for the sources we know have been used and for symptoms that they cause."

The general sat down with a forlorn look and folded his arms across his chest. "No magic bullets up your sleeves then, Miller?"

He sat down next to the general. "No, I'm afraid not. There are no proven antidotes for post-exposure to radiation to eradicate all the effects. Patients exposed will get certain treatments, like I already said, to try to counteract the radiation, but none to fully protect, and certainly, none exits that will correct damage already done. However, my patients that look as though they are acutely dying could be given experimental-type treatments."

One of the nurses then came up to Miller and the general. "I know we're testing the air, water, and explosion site, but what types of radiation do you think we're dealing with here?"

"I suspect at a minimum a mixture of isotopes, including of cobalt, strontium, iridium, and iodine; these were the types used for cancer treatment and stolen from my and other radiation therapy departments. But I'm not sure if there are other types as well."

The nurse took Miller's hand. "By the way, and I speak for the entire hospital staff, we are all glad you're back here at the hospital and leading us through this. None of us ever thought you did anything wrong with our patients."

Miller looked down at the nurse and smiled. "Thank you. That means a lot to me." They gave each other a big hug.

"What do you want us to do first, Dr. Miller?" said the nurse.

"First we need to give anyone in the surrounding region calcium, as the strontium will get into the bones. Also, they all need aggressive fluid and electrolytes for any tritium. And give stable iodine to block any radioactive iodine. Administer bronchial lavage for any alpha- admitters from cesium that might have been inhaled, to help prevent pulmonary fibrosis. After that, place them all on oxygen at high concentration, using hyperbaric chambers."

"Doctor, excuse me for asking, but why do they need high oxygen concentrations?"

"Some of the research in my lab has shown that high concentrations of oxygen help mitigate the damaging effects from radiation exposure. We need the hyperbaric chambers to treat those with more progressive disease or higher exposures. The others seem to respond to oxygen by face masks, kept at the 100 percent level."

"Thank you, Doctor." The nurse began walking away.

"Wait. Nurse? That reminds me. We need to assess current and projected weather forecasts to determine direction and speed of winds. We need to know where this may spread to."

The general stood up and put his hand up, as if to signal 'stop right there'. "Excuse me, Nurse, but I got that one." He then put his hand on Miller's shoulder. "From the most recent satellite updates, the weather appears in our favor. The winds appear to be tracking out to sea, so the potential radiation exposure over the city should be minimal. The radar images show that most of the radiation will be taken out high in the stratosphere and therefore should have a low impact on plant and animal life. But, as always, this can change in a minute's notice." The general laughed. "After all, we are in New England."

They all laughed and nodded in agreement. The nurse started to walk away again but stopped and turned around. "Doctor?"

Miller looked up and over at her. "Yes. What is it?"

"I almost forgot to tell you that a few of the patients asked to speak with you when you arrived. They said they knew you."

"Do you recall their names?" Miller asked with a curious look.

"One I do because he was so funny—and flirtatious. Buzz, I think he called himself."

Miller's smile grew wide, and his face glowed. "Buzz? Really?"

"Yes. But the other, I can't recall. But he has his wife, daughter, and son in the room with him."

Who could that be? The only one I know with—but no. That can't be him. He must be in the ICU.

The nurse took a step toward Miller. "Doctor Miller?"

Miller snapped out of his gaze and opened his eyes to see the nurse looking up at him from underneath. He jerked his head up. "Oh, okay. Thank you, Nurse. I was just going to go up to the wings to check on the patients."

When Miller got to the wing with the radiation-exposed patients, he checked on Buzz first. But when he got to his hospital room, he stood outside his room in the hallway at first. Calming himself with deep breathing for a minute, he stuck his head far enough in the doorway to see Buzz laying in bed talking to someone. It was with one of the nurses. *Figures.* He noticed the bandages that covered the top of his head, and he was afraid of the damage Buzz may have suffered. *Look, he's flirting like his old self, so how much damage could he have suffered?* He took a deep breath and stepped into the room. "Always chatting with the women, aren't you," were the first words out of Miller's mouth.

Buzz turned to see who was talking. When he saw who it was, he grew a smile ear to ear and threw his arms up in the air. "Doc, oh man, it's good to see you." He was so excited that he couldn't control himself and started to get out of bed.

The nurse sitting on the bed reached to restrain him. "Now, Buzz, you know that you're not supposed to get out of bed without help."

Miller rushed over to him to stop him. He held him on the bed at first, and then they hugged each other with several pats on the backs. "You stay right where you are, Buzz! Man, it's so good to see you though. I thought you didn't make it with that wound you took on the head— And you can speak now. That's terrific. I was so worried about you, man."

"Yeah, but still hoarse, as you can tell, and slow, but I'm comin' around."

"Buzz, I should get back to my other patients now. I can see you need to catch up with your friend, so I'll come by later." She blew him a kiss and walked out.

"Okay, sweety. Later." And he blew a kiss back to her.

After she left the room, Miller gave him a high-five, and Buzz slapped it. "Buzz, I could tell when I saw you working on that nurse that you were back to your old self."

Buzz snickered like the wild dog on the Bugs Bunny cartoons. "Oh yeah. Very cute nurse. Howze about a script for Viagra?"

They both laughed.

"I still struggle to believe it was Ahzid involved with all this, but it must be true. It was definitely him who attacked me."

"Buzz, you're right, but you should know that before the explosion, Ahzid changed his mind. He tried to stop it, but Ahkmed, another terrorist, set off the bomb. Not Ahzid. And we were lucky, because Ahkmed couldn't set it off using the timing device. He had to hit it manually or another remote, which for some reason didn't have the full impact. As a result, it blew up incompletely, which helped reduce the amount of radiation sent into the atmosphere. And because of the way they designed it with the plastic explosives all on one side of the bomb and where the bomb itself was placed in the ambulance, it apparently blew mostly in one direction, toward the library."

Buzz looked up with a questioning look at Miller. "So, I guess Ahzid was not as bad a guy in the end. Huh?"

Miller looked down and pursed his lips while he thought for a moment. "Listen, I'm not sure what to think right now, Buzz. I have to go now, but I'll be back to talk with you later."

"Can't wait. I heard all about how you've been saving lives—and the world. You're awesome, Doc. The best."

Miller and Buzz high-fived each other again. "Thanks, Buzz. That means a lot to me. By the way, thank you for giving me that information you got from Ahzid's stuff—and the way you did."

Buzz smiled and bashfully looked away for a second. "Glad it helped."

Miller put his hands onto Buzz's shoulders and looked him straight in the eyes. "Buzz, my friend, it didn't just help; it made all the difference in the world. Because of it—and you, I found the ambulance and the points along the way, right away. I didn't have to waste time searching for the ambulance."

They hugged again, and Miller started to walk away.

Buzz raised a hand, pointing his index finger in the air. "Doc, just one more thing before you go."

Miller stopped and turned around. "Yeah, Buzz. What is it?"

"I just want you to know that I never doubted for one minute that you were innocent of everything."

Miller smiled and struggled to hold back his emotions. "I know, Buzz. And for that, I thank you. I'll be back shortly. I promise. I need to check on the other patients exposed to the radiation."

One of the nurses was waiting in the hallway for him. "I'm here to take you to another." Ahzid came to mind. Since he'd initially thought Buzz was dead, maybe Ahzid too had survived? The images of the bullet wounds and blood flashed in his head.

The nurse escorted him directly to the room with the patient. Miller peaked inside the doorway, ahead of actually entering, then did so slowly. He feared what he might see or do. His heart nearly stopped when he saw Ahzid's wife sitting at the side of the bed with her daughter and son standing next to her. Her face was drawn. Dark rings encircled her eyes. Tears filled them, ran down her cheeks, and dripped off her nose. The boy and girl didn't say anything. Their eyes were fixed on the bed and who occupied it, just in front of them.

When Miller looked at the man on the bed and did a double take, he couldn't help but shout his name from the shock. "Ahzid!"

Ahzid's wife, daughter, and son turned quickly to look at him. "Dr. Miller," she said.

Miller walked over to her and her children, all the while forcing himself to smile. "The tests so far show he is stable. But how is he doing in your eyes?"

"Well he's alive," said his wife. "We don't know for sure as yet how he will be. They took him to emergency surgery and are now giving him blood. He has not woken up yet." She wiped her tears with the hankie she held.

"He is a lucky man. That's why I was surprised to see him alive and shouted his name. I have been told that all blood tests show no high levels of radiation exposure. And although there are no names used, since no one else exposed has had a high level, all of you are in the clear also.

She turned to her son and daughter, put her palms onto their heads, and began stroking their hair. She looked up to the ceiling. "Oh, thank you, Allah," she said and hugged them. "What about Ahzid? And us? We are in trouble, aren't we?"

Miller looked at her and gestured to the side of Ahzid's bed. "May I sit?" he said. After she nodded yes, he sat down on the bed in front of them. "I wish I could give you better news. But yes, the authorities have and will continue to take this very seriously. They will get to the bottom of all of it and punish anyone responsible and, I suspect, even remotely involved."

She cupped her hands over her face, began to sob, and fell back into her chair. "I never wanted any of this."

"But what I also know is, with the little I have discussed with the authorities, including the general downstairs, based on the details I have given them so far, especially Ahzid's deciding not to explode the bomb, they will take all that into consideration when it comes time for any punishment."

She then stood up. Still sobbing, she gave Miller a hug. "Bless you, Dr. Miller. I knew you were a good and decent man."

He hugged her back. "I have to go know to check on the other patients. I'll be back to check on him regularly." He gave her a reassuring smile and left the room.

When Miller stepped out into the hallway, one of the soldiers waiting outside the room approached him. "Dr. Miller, you are wanted down in the news briefing room."

"I can't come now. I still have other patients to check on."

The soldier put his hand gently on Miller's shoulder. "Sorry, sir, that's an order from the general."

The lead floor nurse standing next to them overheard them and turned around. "You go ahead, Dr. Miller. We'll keep all the patients stabilized until you get back."

Miller stared at her.

She smiled at him. "I promise."

"Thank you, Nurse." He turned back to the soldier. "Okay then. Can't argue with a nurse when she means business. Lead the way, soldier."

Downstairs in the large, temporary briefing and meeting room, the mayor of Boston and its chiefs of Police and Fire Departments, and heads of the local FBI, Antiterrorism and Military Units and local experts were about to discuss on the national and international media the damage, treatment of victims, and concerns and efforts for spread of the radiation.

The general looked up and saw Dr. Miller enter the room. He signaled for him to sit in the front. "Okay, everyone, please sit down and listen up. Here's where we stand," were the first words out of the general's mouth. He then proceeded to outline what had been done so far and what was planned for containing the radiation, capturing terrorists, dealing with other possible strikes, and treating those exposed or potentially exposed to the radiation. "I have just come from an update briefing in our command center in the next room, which gave new information from our field units. At this time, we have located and secured the base camp of the terrorists, which was a farm located in upstate New Hampshire. Unfortunately, they found one person dead, a woman whose name we will not disclose yet until she is completely identified and her family notified, as is our usual policy. But she apparently was a neighbor who had stumbled onto the terrorists' property. One of the terrorists confessed to this. We also found lots of evidence of stolen radiation sources, computers with information on the whole operation. We have also captured several remaining terrorists there at the camp and those that were trying to escape into Canada through Buffalo, New York.

A hand popped up from someone from one of the national broadcasting stations, and the general pointed at him to talk. "Sir, what was the town in New York where they were found?"

The general wiped sweat off his brow before answering. "Can you believe it? These guys were sitting around having a beer at a local tavern called the Barbill in a small town outside of Buffalo, called East Aurora. They were showing off pictures of the *Mona Lisa* they had and bragging loudly about how they were going to blow up other places besides Boston." One of the aides behind the general came up behind him to whisper in his ear. "I'm told that a local patron, actually a local hero named John Spooner, called in what he heard at the bar after watching the news of the Boston explosion."

The general then pointed to another reporter jumping up and down with his hand waving. "Yes, you there with the ants in the pants." The room broke out in laughter.

"What is the current status of the city of Boston?" asked a local Boston newspaper reporter.

The general again wiped his brow. "I'll be straight with you, but I cannot give you specifics, as I'm sure you can appreciate. We are taking action from the highest levels. The city is in total lockdown surrounded by both antiterrorism units and military units. The National Guard has been activated and, among other things, is helping our citizens by directing them to designated shelters and keeping others inside buildings. We have emergency medical teams flying in as well from all over the country, and local teams helping with triaging to get people properly evaluated, tested, and treated. All high-risk exposures are designated to come to this hospital or transferred here as our highest priority."

"How about the president? He was speaking at a big fundraiser not far from the blast."

Before he answered the question, the general drank water from his cup, downing almost the entire thing. "I'm pleased to report that the president is fine and not in any danger. He flew out of the area ahead of the explosion and is safe and sound, and as commander in chief, he is leading all branches of the military from a secret location. Other than as authorized, all air travel is grounded for now, but let me stress, at this time, we don't think the threat is outside this area or related to use of airplanes. We are just taking precautionary measures."

The general pointed at one of the reporters in the sea of waving arms in front of him. "What are the concerns for exposure to the radiation from the bomb, General?" she asked.

"Great question," said the general. "Fortunately for us, the winds have taken the radiation dust out to sea for the most part. We believe we have it under control and have given anyone with any exposure, or suspected of it, treatment with the medications they need to combat the radiation effects. And I'm happy to report that except for those killed at the ambulance, the scene of ground zero, everyone has survived."

Miller had been riveted to his seat and began looking for Bridget in the room. When he saw her sitting in the back, half asleep on a chair, he walked up to her and took her hand in his. "How about you and I take a little walk down to one of the empty patient-consult rooms at the end of the hall, sit in a comfortable chair, and talk—or sleep, if you prefer?"

Bridget's eyelids opened and she blossomed a smile. "That sounds real good to me." Hand in hand, they snuck out the back of the room, not to draw attention to themselves.

They sat alone in one of the consult rooms down the hall. Miller put his arm around her, pulled her close, and held her other hand in her lap. She rested her head on his chest. Miller had begun to close his eyes but then quickly opened them. "With all this craziness, I keep forgetting to ask you what it was you wanted to tell me before," said Miller.

Bridget lifted her head off his shoulder, sat up, and looked directly at him. "Oh, nothing big. Just that I'm pregnant with your child."

"Oh, is that all—what! You're pregnant! With my, I mean our child? Are you sure? Well of course you're sure. I mean, how far along? That's so cool, I mean so neat, I mean so beautiful." He hugged and kissed her and kept giving her hugs and kisses. "I cannot believe we're going to have a baby and I'm going to be a daddy."

Bridget sat up straight. "And I'm going to be a mother? But tell me, and be honest with me. With all this radiation, the baby will be all right, don't you think? Right? We don't have to worry about the baby."

Miller reached out and hugged her, pulling her tightly to his chest. "Absolutely not. Not to worry. I checked on our exposure risks, and your exposure was not high. And even if it was, it's still unlikely anything crossed the placenta at this early stage, which is not a high-risk time for the fetus."

Bridget let out a very big sigh. "Oh, that makes me feel so much better. You have no idea how worried I have been."

They were interrupted by the door opening behind them and then a voice traveling through the darkness. "Excuse me, sir, but, Dr. Miller, you have a phone call?" The soldier stepped toward them and handed him a military phone.

Miller answered back with an annoyed look and tone, "Soldier, who is it?"

"Sir, it's the President"

"Our president? Of the United States? For me. A patient named Buzz didn't put you up to this, did he?"

"No, sir," said the soldier, who started walking away. "I'll be right outside the door if you need me, Dr. Miller."

"Hello, Mr President".... Miller and the president then talked for several minutes. "I agree, Mr. President, we were lucky with this one and also that we have to find ways to bring each other together before it comes to tragedies like this. To educate each other so as to prevent these terrible atrocities, not just react to it when it happens. I'm so glad that it appears the radiation exposure has been at a minimum thanks to the winds. Mr. President, I have some important work to finish right this minute, so if you don't mind, I would like it if we could talk more later. What? An invitation to the White House? Well, yes, of course, I would love that. Would I consider an appointment as a radiation expert on your national security panel? I would love to talk to you more about that. Thank you. Look forward to my visit to the White House." After Jake hung up, he slapped his knee and shouted, "Oh, yeah, baby, I'm going to the White House!" He turned and gave Bridget a big kiss and hug.

"Wow, that was quite a kiss," said Bridget.

"You ain't seen nothing yet. Soldier," he called out.

The door opened. "Yes, Dr. Miller."

"Please take the phone back." He handed it to him. "Thank you again. Please tell the general or anyone else that's asking about me that I'm busy and that I plan to join them shortly."

"Yes, sir. Everything all right?"

"Things couldn't be better." The soldier left with the phone, closing the door behind him.

Bridget looked puzzled at Miller. " What could be more important than talking with the president of the United States?"

"You're being all dressed up, holding onto my arm while we walk up those steps together to the White House. That's what."

"Ah." She smiled. "That does sound nice. Really nice." They went back to hugging and kissing.

EPILOGUE: REFLECTIONS AND A LOOK AHEAD TO THE FUTURE

TWO WEEKS AFTER THE DIRTY BOMB EXPLOSION, THE BOSTON area and its people still suffered, but most everything had returned to normal. The prayers regarding the weather that Miller had requested were answered with the winds blowing out to the ocean and away from the city. Very few people had any significant exposure, and for those that had any amount above normal, they were treated at the hospital. Except for superficial radiation burns, most didn't suffer any major organ problems.

The sunset over the Charles River in the fall was moving in. The pinkish-blue clouds hung low in the sky, and the ripples of the water sparkled and twinkled with scullers cutting across the grain of the waves twenty yards off the embankment. There on a bench overlooking the river, Jacob and Bridget sat, looking out across the river to the Cambridge side with Storrow Drive and the Boston General Hospital directly behind them, with the walkers, runners, and bikers riding up and down the path along the river's edge. Across from them on the Cambridge side of the river shined the golden dome of an MIT building and the silhouette of a sailboat, big enough only for two, sailing upstream against a gentle breeze.

"Can you believe the crooked general behind all this ranted and raved about you? They said he cussed your name as they escorted him off the base. Why do you think he hated you so much?" said Bridget.

"I have no idea why. What's really strange is why he apparently took cyanide and killed himself. And even stranger is that they put his body in a temporary morgue, and when they went to pick his body up for the forensic autopsy, it was missing." Miller began to rub his right forearm. "But, I promise you this, I plan to find out more about our crooked general."

"There you go again," said Bridget.

"What?"

"Rubbing that right arm of yours. You do that a lot, you know."

"Do I?"

"Give it to me." Miller turned toward her and placed his arm on her thigh. She began to rub it gently with her hand. "There. Does that feel better?"

"Actually yes. It does."

"Why do you do that? It has to be a nervous habit."

"One psychologist said it was probably my projection of painful thoughts because that's where that evil sister used to burn her cigarettes on me and beat me with her ruler. I do it without even realizing I'm doing it."

Bridget bent down and kissed his forearm. "Is that better?"

"Much." Miller pulled his arm away and sat up. "Let's not talk about that stuff."

"Okay with me."

"Let's talk about the silver linings of this tragic event."

"Silver linings? I like that. Such as?"

"For example, I just spoke with Father O'Brien about how he and the guys at St. Francis are doing. With all the risk they took to help me, I'm so glad that none of them got hurt."

"Good point. What other silver linings?"

Miller put his arm around Bridget, with her head resting on his chest. "We have been through a lot, to say the least. The best silver lining that I can see is that you and I are together."

"Ah, that's so sweet. And I couldn't agree more," said Bridget.

They hugged and kissed each other.

"And of course that you—we—are going to have a baby. I cannot believe I'm going to be a father."

Bridget smiled softly, just enough that the edges of her mouth curled up a few millimeters. "I love the idea of our having a baby together and you being a daddy and me being a mommy."

"Maybe after seeing all the destruction and death, we could do something as a family where they won't be trying to kill each other."

Bridget looked a bit puzzled. "Ah, sure. Like what."

"I don't know. Hey, how about we go to the zoo?"

"The zoo! Why the zoo?"

"Why not? It's generally a mellow place where all the dangerous things are in cages. I was thinking it might be fun to look at all the other animals we live with on earth, and I was also thinking that it's amazing that we're the only ones on this planet that kill each other for reasons other than the need for food and survival, yet we think of ourselves as the most intelligent ones on the planet."

"I can think of many other places, but if that's what ... okay then, let's do it."

"Great. I often thought about someday having a family and going to the zoo."

Bridget snuggled up against Miller and whispered, "I like the part about the family very much."

"Hey, I have a crazy idea, Bridget," Jacob said with excitement in his voice.

She looked at him with a curious look. "What?"

"How about we make a commitment to being only with each other."

Bridget's face lit up like the fireworks light up the sky on the night of the Fourth of July. "Do you really mean it? What about your insecurity with that?"

"After all we've been through, babe, I think I'm over that."

Bridget looked into his eyes, and he looked into hers, and both smiled. "Then I- and our child-- would love to be a family with you," said Bridget. They hugged and kissed like it was their last kiss as the sailboat that they had noticed sailing toward them, now was sailing the other way, into the sunset, with the wind against its back.

Lightning Source UK Ltd.
Milton Keynes UK
UKOW02f0503231116
288248UK00001B/56/P